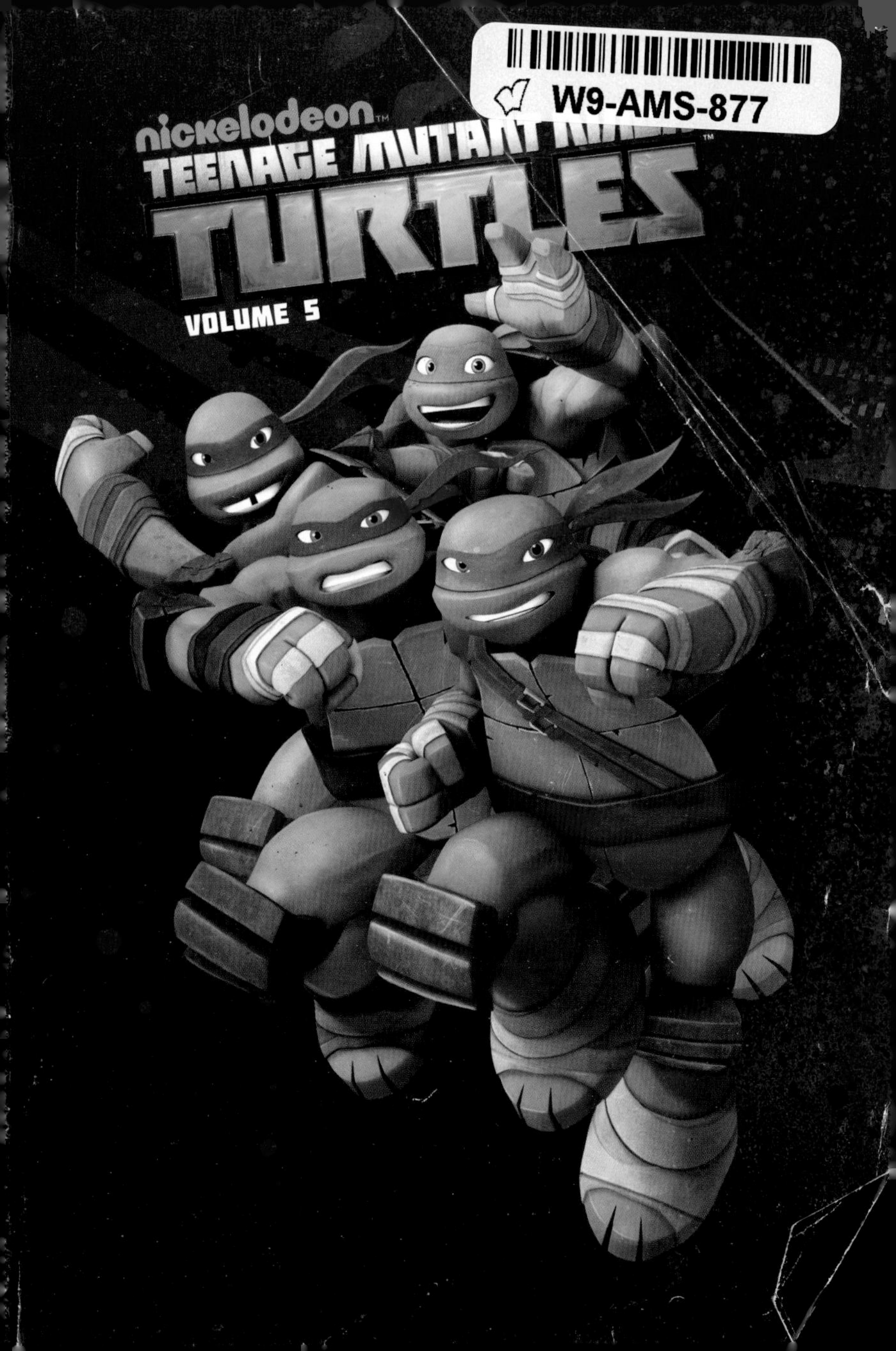
nickelodeon™
TEENAGE MUTANT
TURTLES™
VOLUME 5

nickelodeon™
TEENAGE MUTANT NINJA TURTLES™

THE GOOD, THE BAD, AND CASEY JONES

Written by
JOHNNY HARTMANN

THE LONELY MUTATION OF BAXTER STOCKMAN

Written by
BRANDON AUMAN

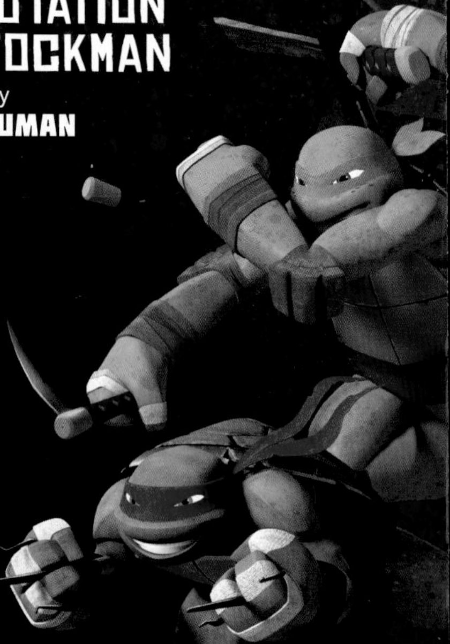

Adaptation by
JUSTIN EISINGER

Edits by
ALONZO SIMON

Lettering and Design by
TOM B. LONG

Special thanks to Joan Hilty,
Linda Lee, and Kat van Dam
for their invaluable assistance.

Based on characters created by Peter Laird and Kevin Eastman.

ISBN: 978-1-63140-180-0
17 16 15 14   1 2 3 4

www.IDWPUBLISHING.com

IDW®

Ted Adams, CEO & Publisher
Greg Goldstein, President & COO
Robbie Robbins, EVP/Sr. Graphic Artist
Chris Ryall, Chief Creative Officer/Editor-in-Chief
Matthew Ruzicka, CPA, Chief Financial Officer
Alan Payne, VP of Sales
Dirk Wood, VP of Marketing
Lorelei Bunjes, VP of Digital Services

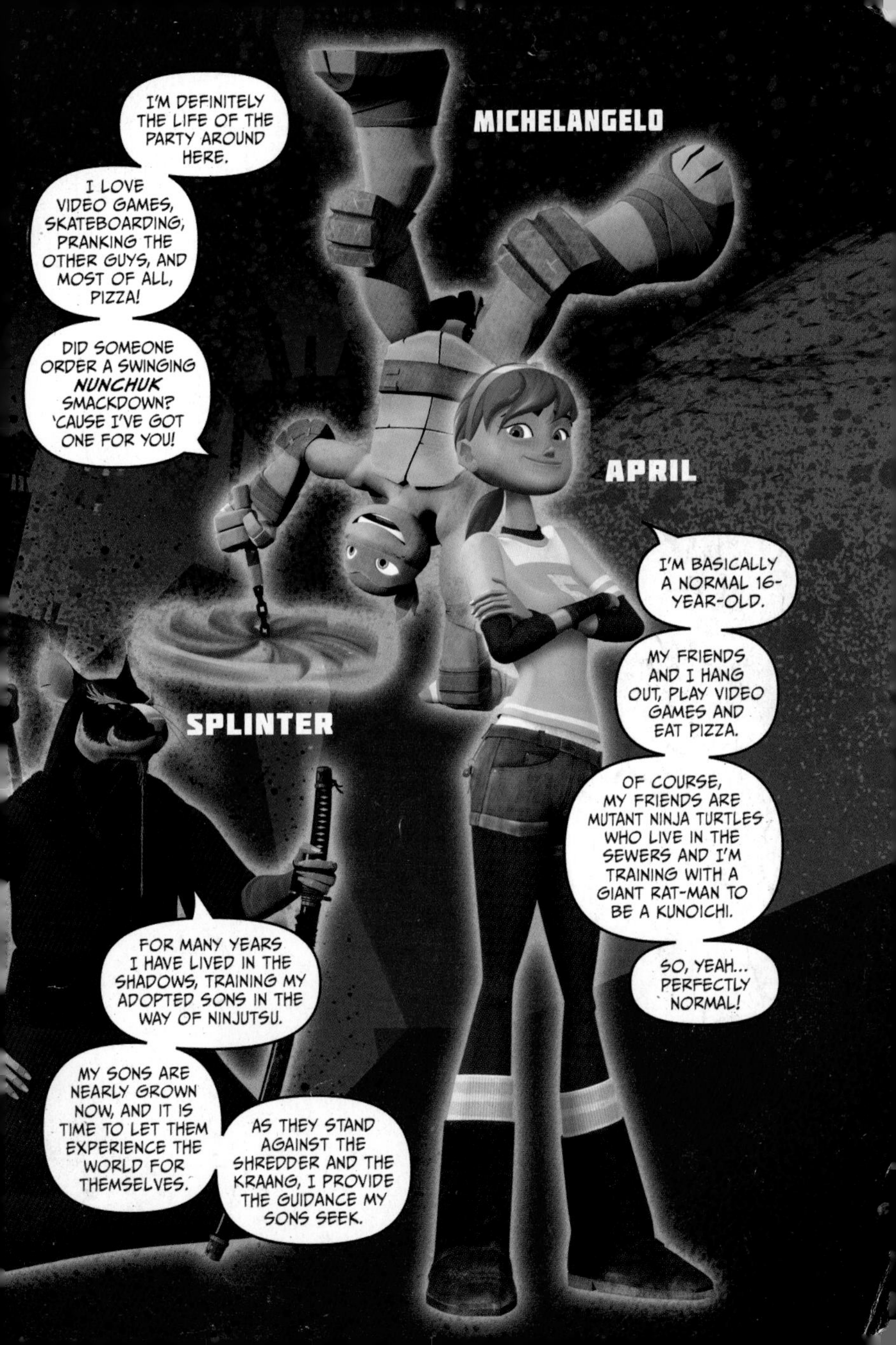

MICHELANGELO
I'M DEFINITELY THE LIFE OF THE PARTY AROUND HERE.
I LOVE VIDEO GAMES, SKATEBOARDING, PRANKING THE OTHER GUYS, AND MOST OF ALL, PIZZA!
DID SOMEONE ORDER A SWINGING NUNCHUK SMACKDOWN? 'CAUSE I'VE GOT ONE FOR YOU!
APRIL
I'M BASICALLY A NORMAL 16-YEAR-OLD.
MY FRIENDS AND I HANG OUT, PLAY VIDEO GAMES AND EAT PIZZA.
OF COURSE, MY FRIENDS ARE MUTANT NINJA TURTLES WHO LIVE IN THE SEWERS AND I'M TRAINING WITH A GIANT RAT-MAN TO BE A KUNOICHI.
SO, YEAH... PERFECTLY NORMAL!
SPLINTER
FOR MANY YEARS I HAVE LIVED IN THE SHADOWS, TRAINING MY ADOPTED SONS IN THE WAY OF NINJUTSU.
MY SONS ARE NEARLY GROWN NOW, AND IT IS TIME TO LET THEM EXPERIENCE THE WORLD FOR THEMSELVES.
AS THEY STAND AGAINST THE SHREDDER AND THE KRAANG, I PROVIDE THE GUIDANCE MY SONS SEEK.

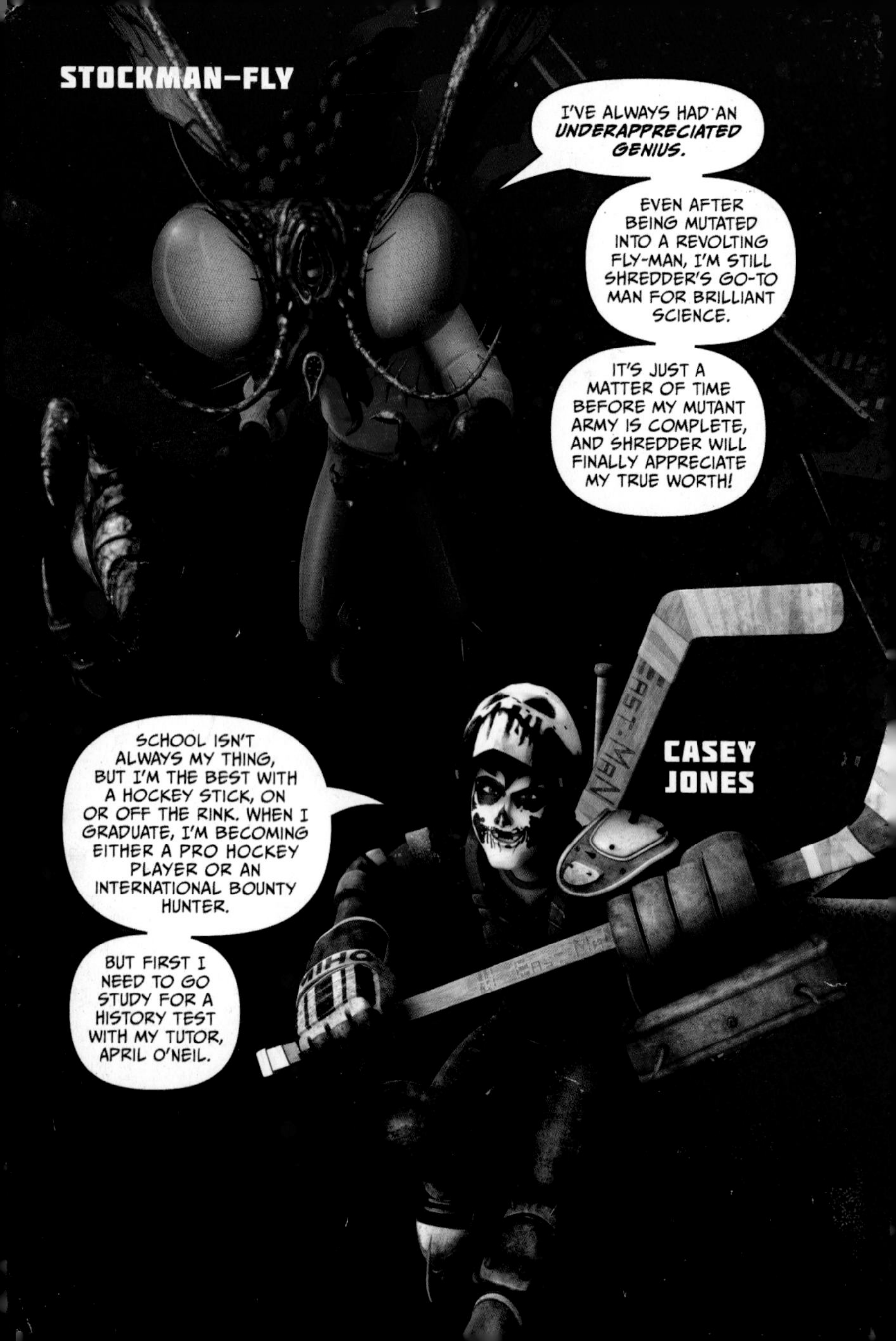
STOCKMAN-FLY
I'VE ALWAYS HAD AN UNDERAPPRECIATED GENIUS.
EVEN AFTER BEING MUTATED INTO A REVOLTING FLY-MAN, I'M STILL SHREDDER'S GO-TO MAN FOR BRILLIANT SCIENCE.
IT'S JUST A MATTER OF TIME BEFORE MY MUTANT ARMY IS COMPLETE, AND SHREDDER WILL FINALLY APPRECIATE MY TRUE WORTH!
CASEY JONES
SCHOOL ISN'T ALWAYS MY THING, BUT I'M THE BEST WITH A HOCKEY STICK, ON OR OFF THE RINK. WHEN I GRADUATE, I'M BECOMING EITHER A PRO HOCKEY PLAYER OR AN INTERNATIONAL BOUNTY HUNTER.
BUT FIRST I NEED TO GO STUDY FOR A HISTORY TEST WITH MY TUTOR, APRIL O'NEIL.

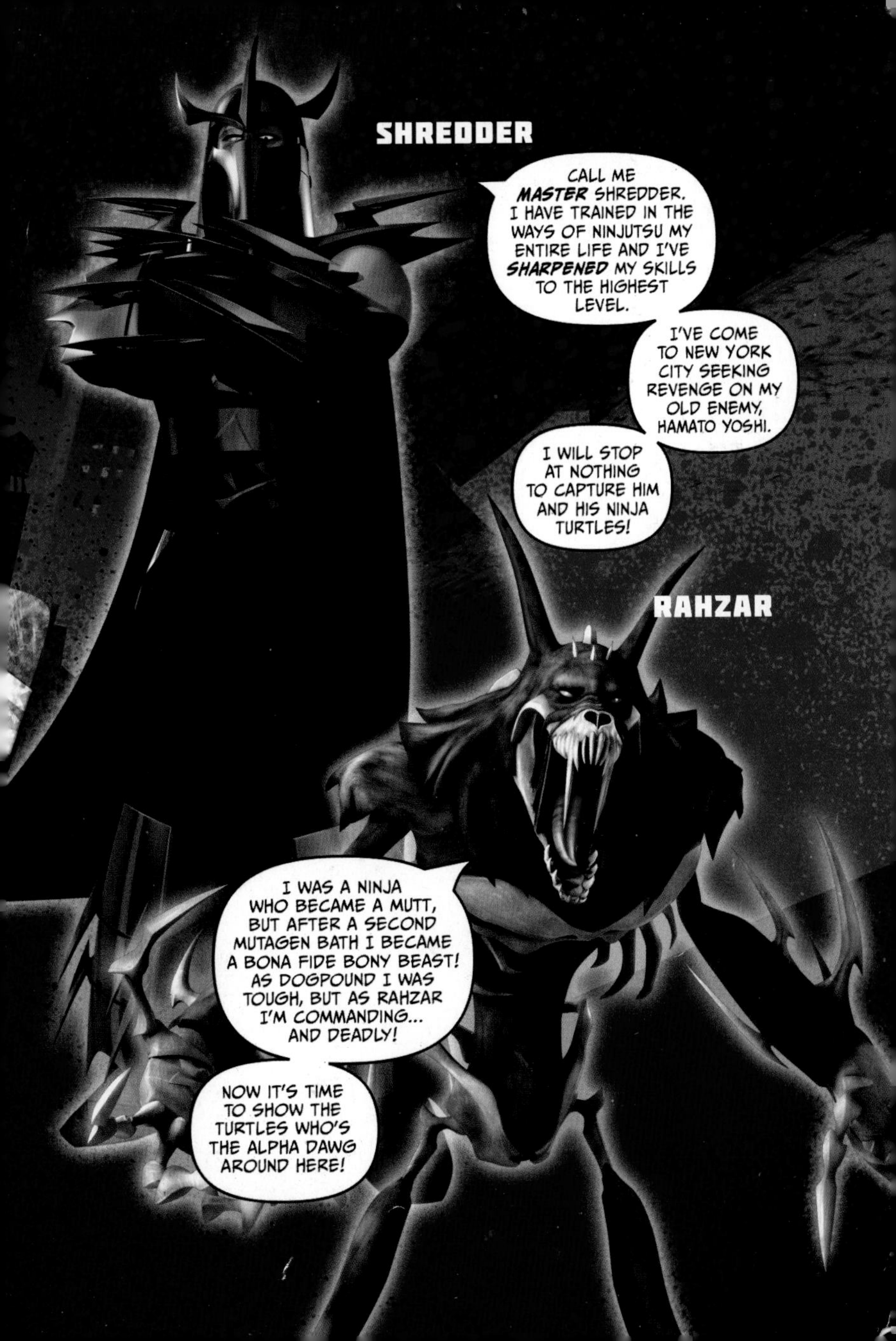
SHREDDER
CALL ME MASTER SHREDDER. I HAVE TRAINED IN THE WAYS OF NINJUTSU MY ENTIRE LIFE AND I'VE SHARPENED MY SKILLS TO THE HIGHEST LEVEL.
I'VE COME TO NEW YORK CITY SEEKING REVENGE ON MY OLD ENEMY, HAMATO YOSHI.
I WILL STOP AT NOTHING TO CAPTURE HIM AND HIS NINJA TURTLES!
RAHZAR
I WAS A NINJA WHO BECAME A MUTT, BUT AFTER A SECOND MUTAGEN BATH I BECAME A BONA FIDE BONY BEAST! AS DOGPOUND I WAS TOUGH, BUT AS RAHZAR I'M COMMANDING... AND DEADLY!
NOW IT'S TIME TO SHOW THE TURTLES WHO'S THE ALPHA DAWG AROUND HERE!

THE GOOD, THE BAD, AND CASEY JONES

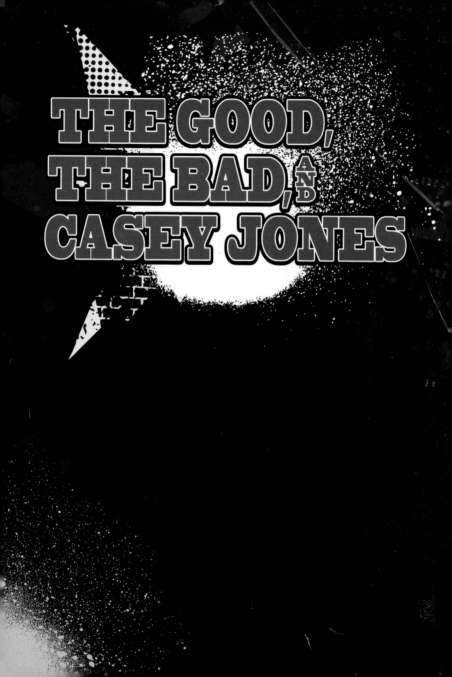

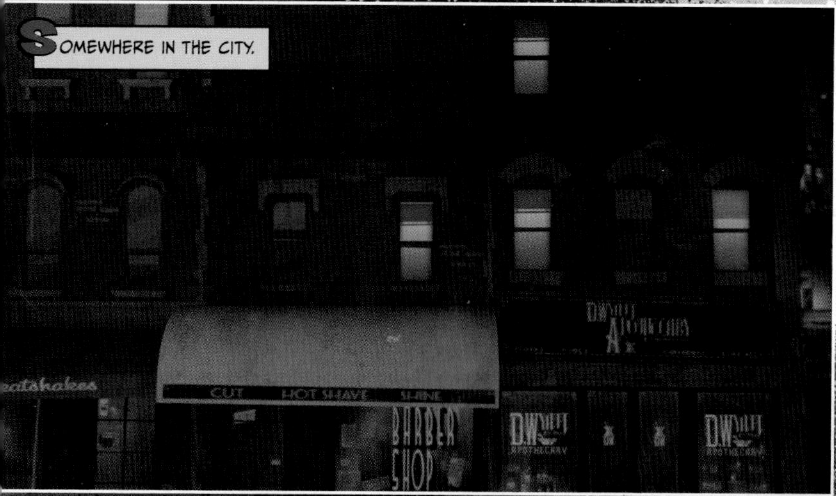
SOMEWHERE IN THE CITY.
CUT HOT SHAVE SHINE
BARBER SHOP

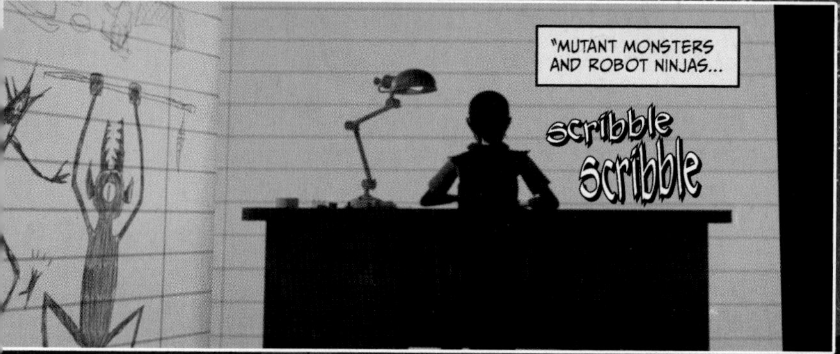
"MUTANT MONSTERS AND ROBOT NINJAS...
scribble
scribble

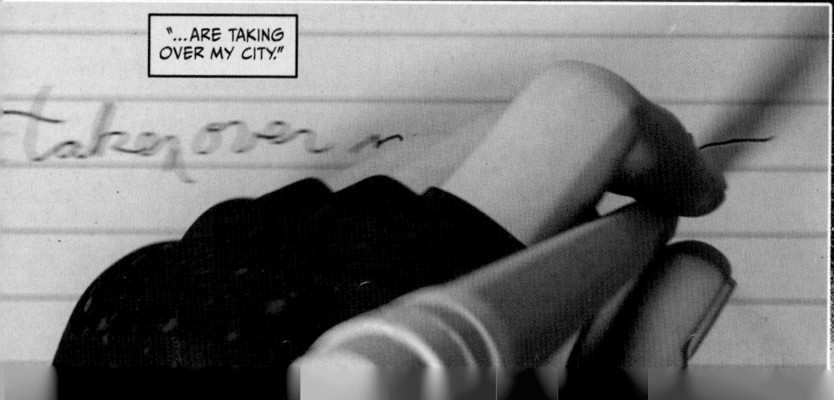
"...ARE TAKING OVER MY CITY."

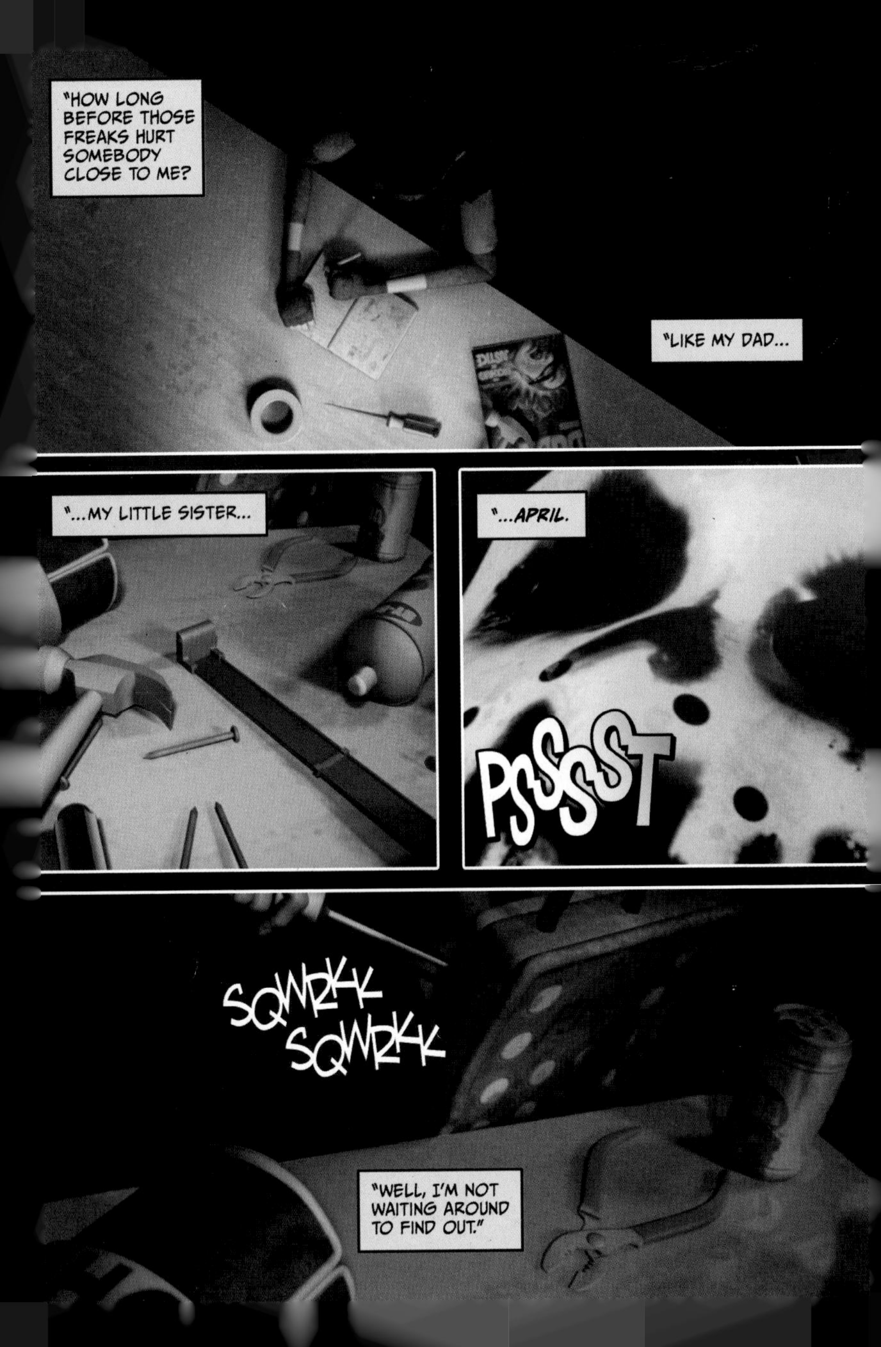
"HOW LONG BEFORE THOSE FREAKS HURT SOMEBODY CLOSE TO ME?
"LIKE MY DAD...
"...MY LITTLE SISTER...
"...APRIL.
PSSSST
SQWRKK SQWRKK
"WELL, I'M NOT WAITING AROUND TO FIND OUT."

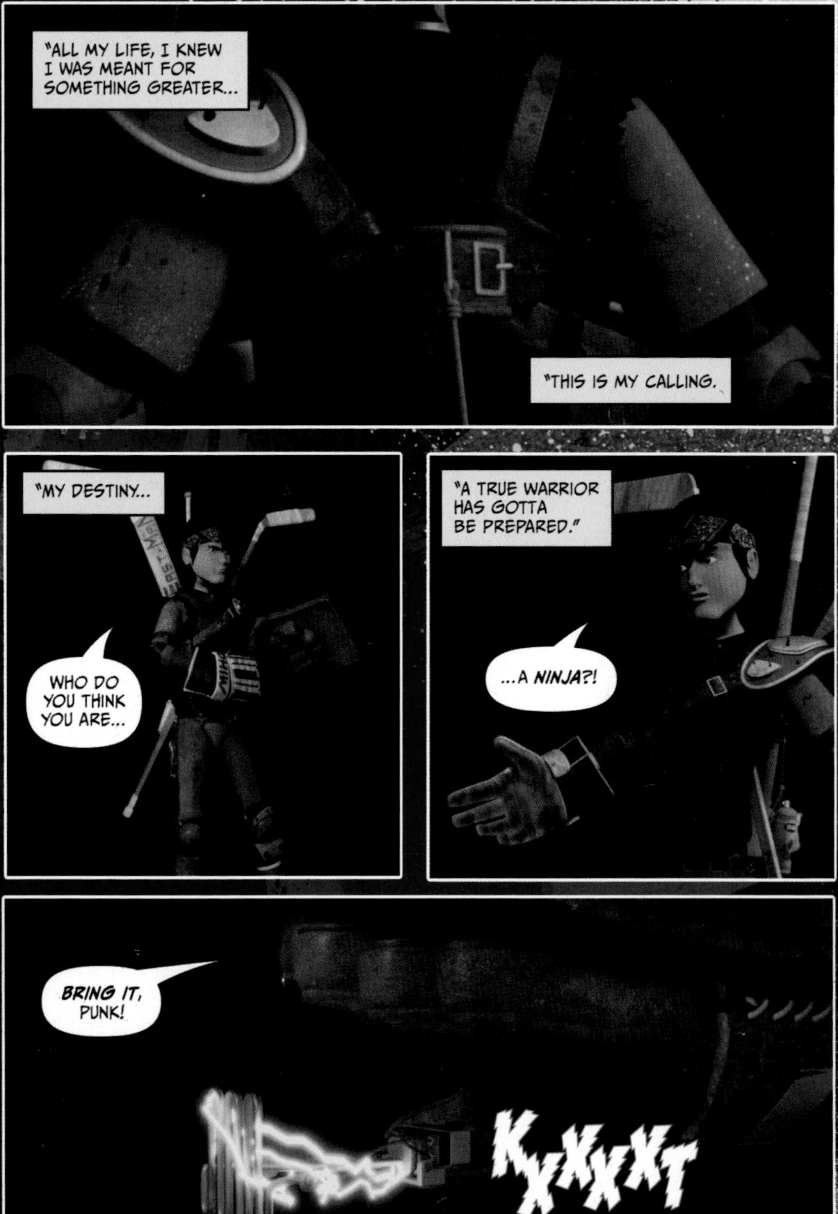
"ALL MY LIFE, I KNEW I WAS MEANT FOR SOMETHING GREATER...
"THIS IS MY CALLING.
"MY DESTINY...
WHO DO YOU THINK YOU ARE...
"A TRUE WARRIOR HAS GOTTA BE PREPARED."
...A NINJA?!
BRING IT, PUNK!
KXXXXT

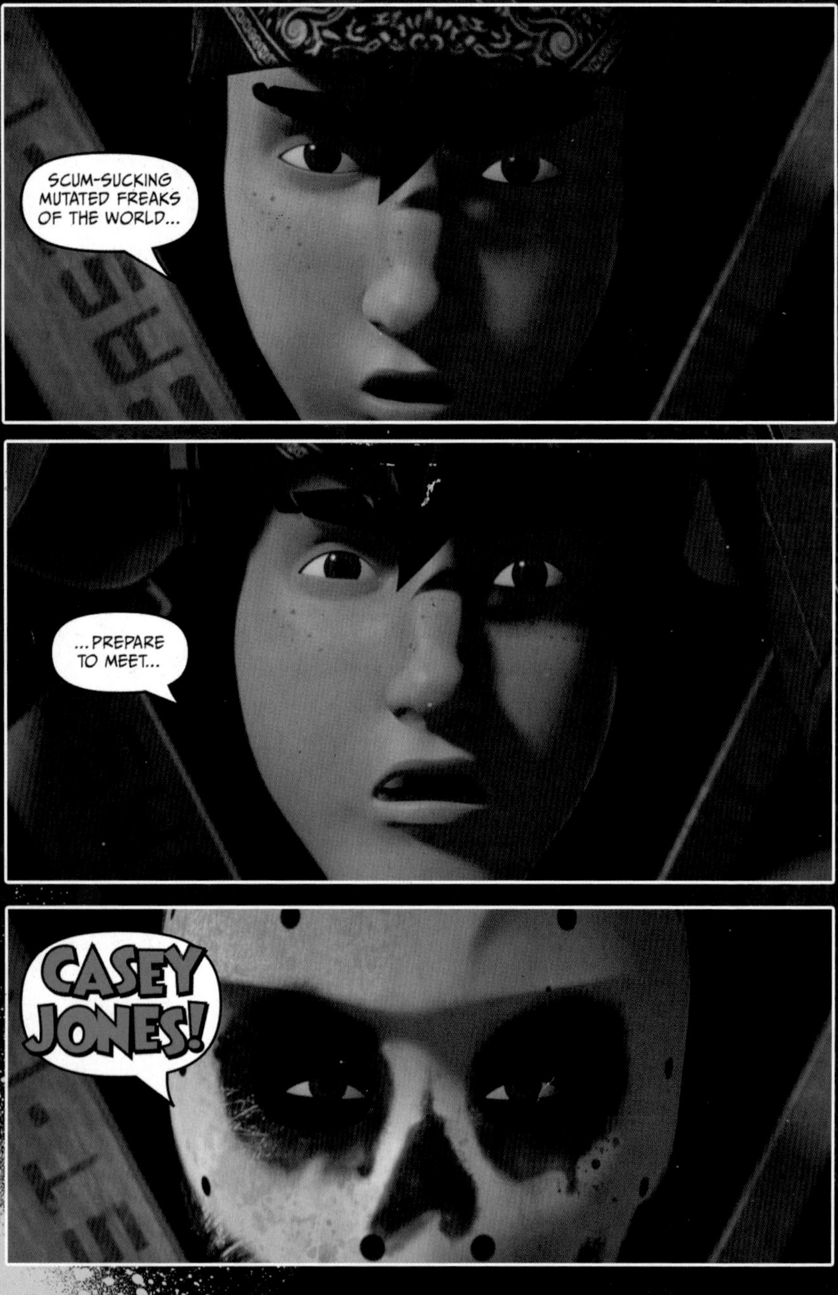
SCUM-SUCKING MUTATED FREAKS OF THE WORLD...
...PREPARE TO MEET...
CASEY JONES!

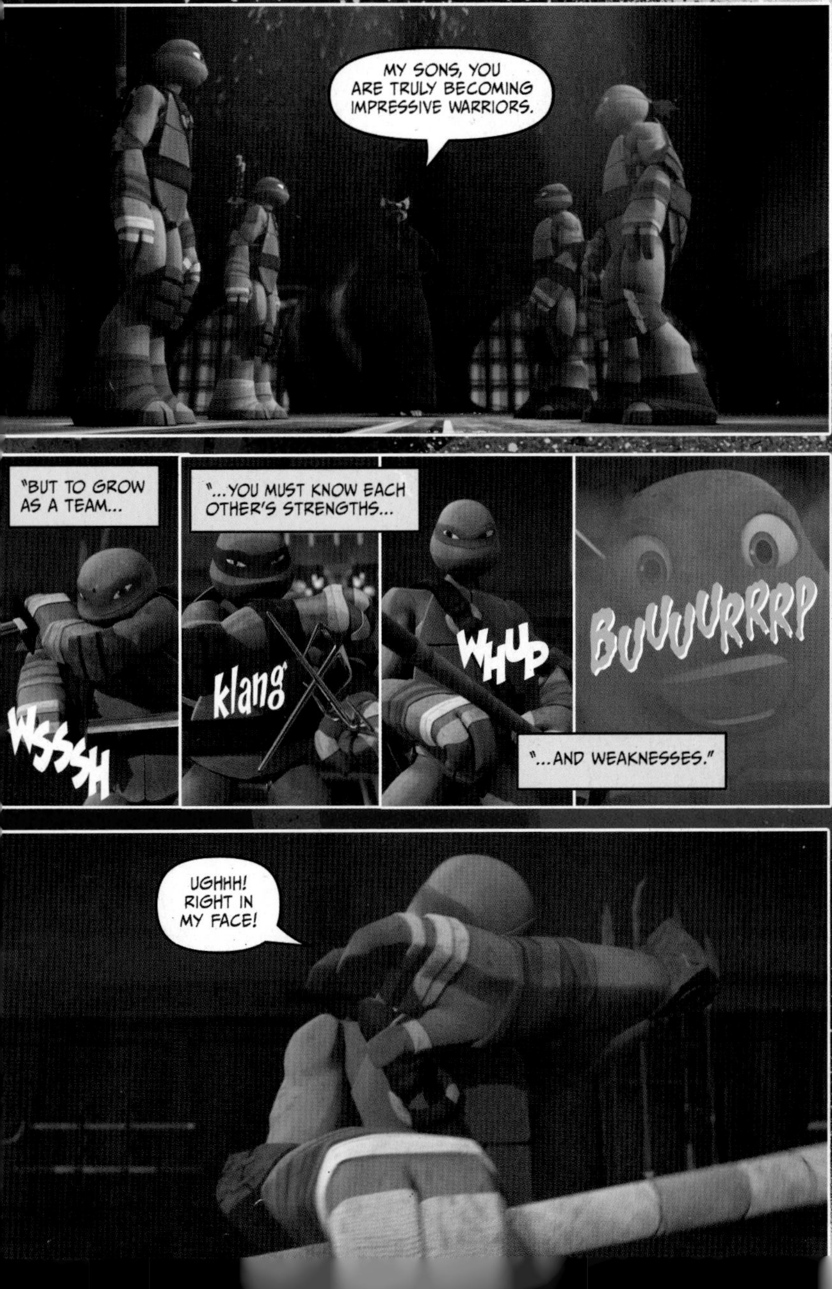
MY SONS, YOU ARE TRULY BECOMING IMPRESSIVE WARRIORS.
"BUT TO GROW AS A TEAM...
WSSSH
"...YOU MUST KNOW EACH OTHER'S STRENGTHS...
klang
WHUP
BUUUURRRP
"...AND WEAKNESSES."
UGHHH! RIGHT IN MY FACE!

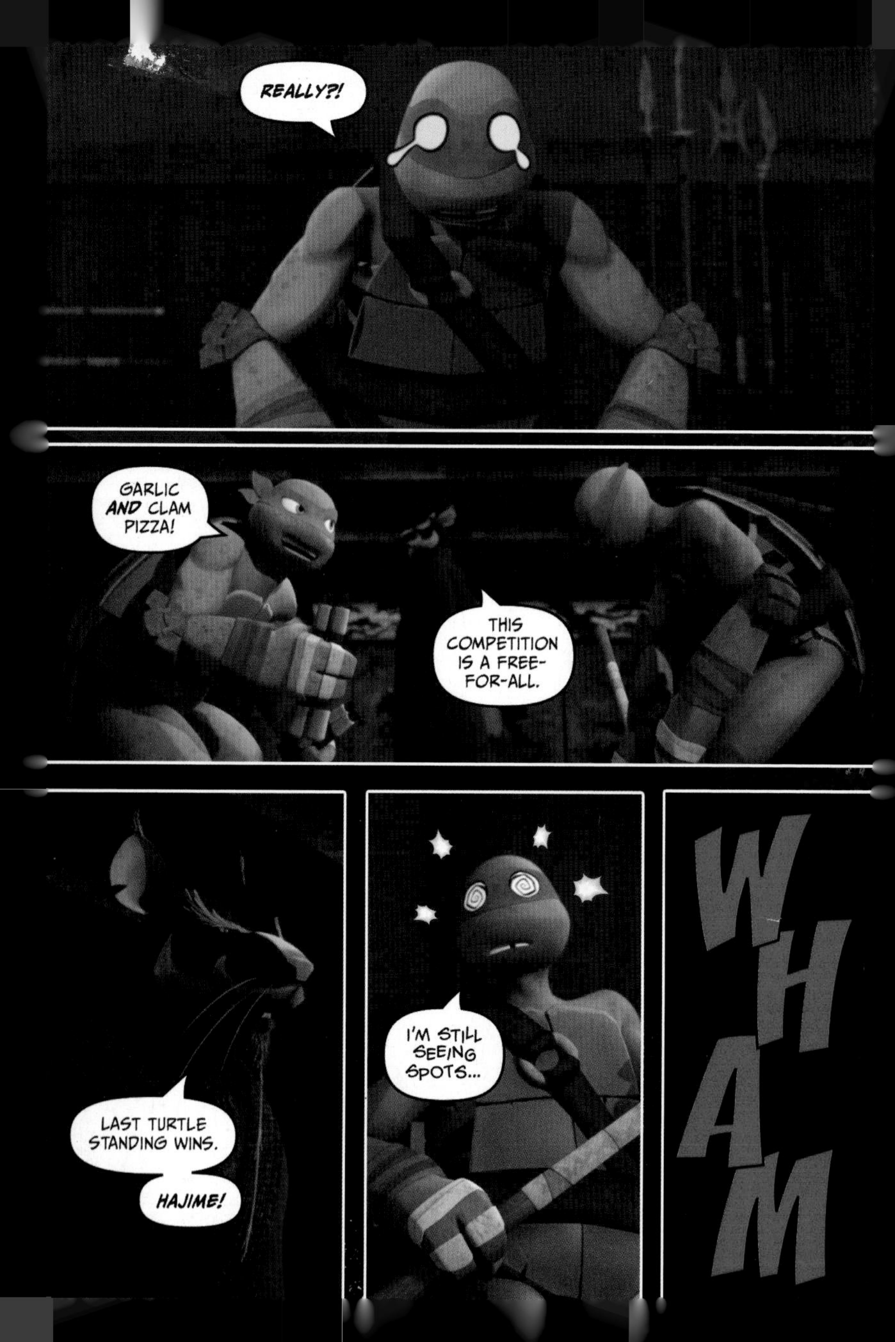
REALLY?!
GARLIC AND CLAM PIZZA!
THIS COMPETITION IS A FREE-FOR-ALL.
LAST TURTLE STANDING WINS.
HAJIME!
I'M STILL SEEING SPOTS...
WHAM

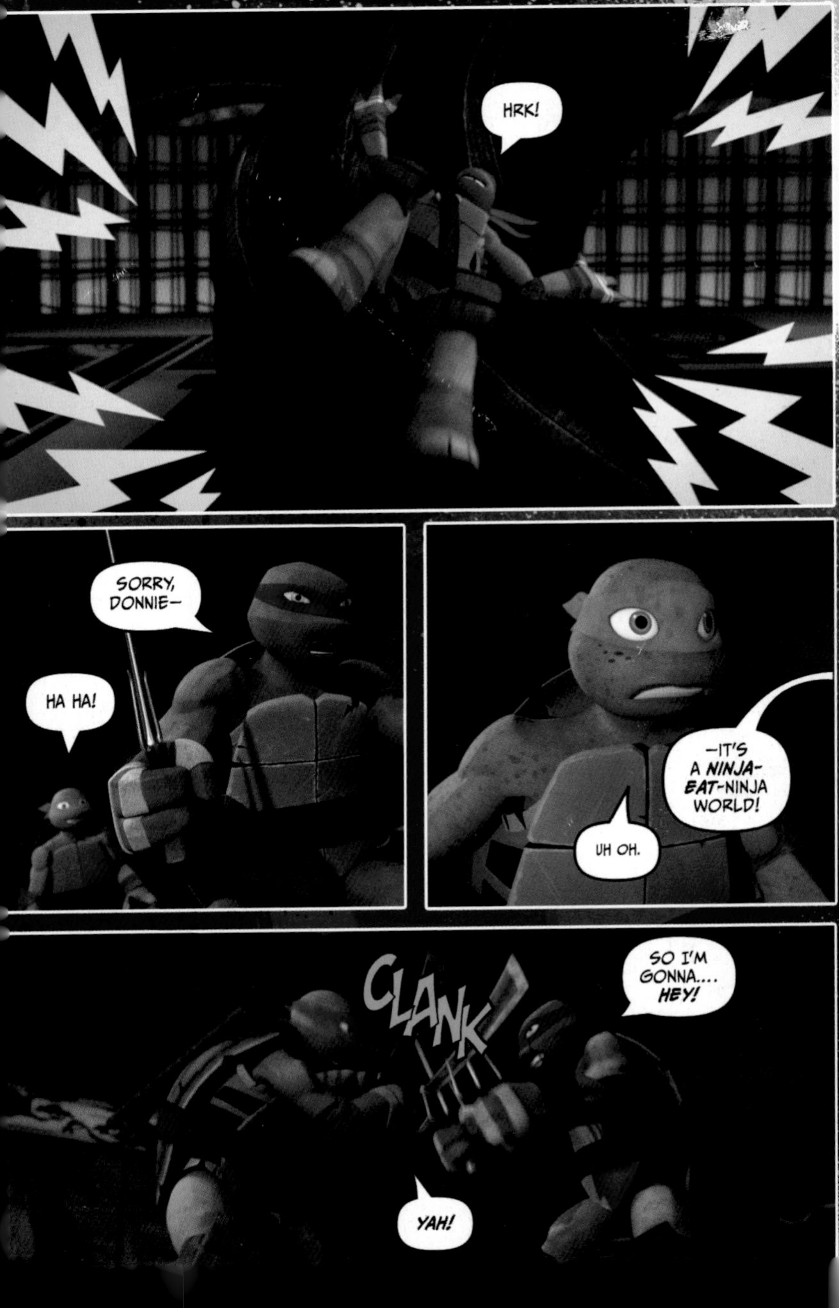
HRK!
SORRY, DONNIE—
HA HA!
—IT'S A NINJA-EAT-NINJA WORLD!
UH OH.
CLANK
SO I'M GONNA.... HEY!
YAH!

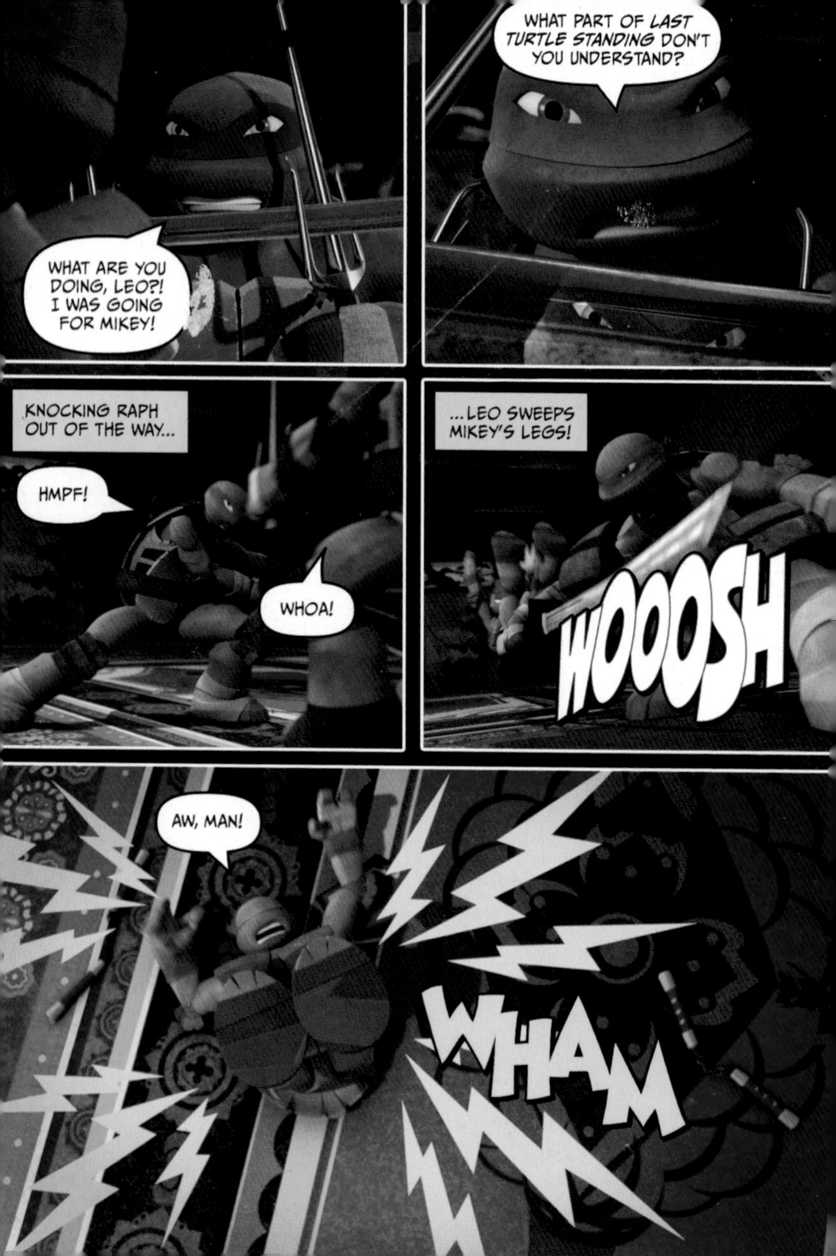
WHAT ARE YOU DOING, LEO?! I WAS GOING FOR MIKEY!
WHAT PART OF *LAST TURTLE STANDING* DON'T YOU UNDERSTAND?
KNOCKING RAPH OUT OF THE WAY...
HMPF!
WHOA!
...LEO SWEEPS MIKEY'S LEGS!
WOOOSH
AW, MAN!
WHAM

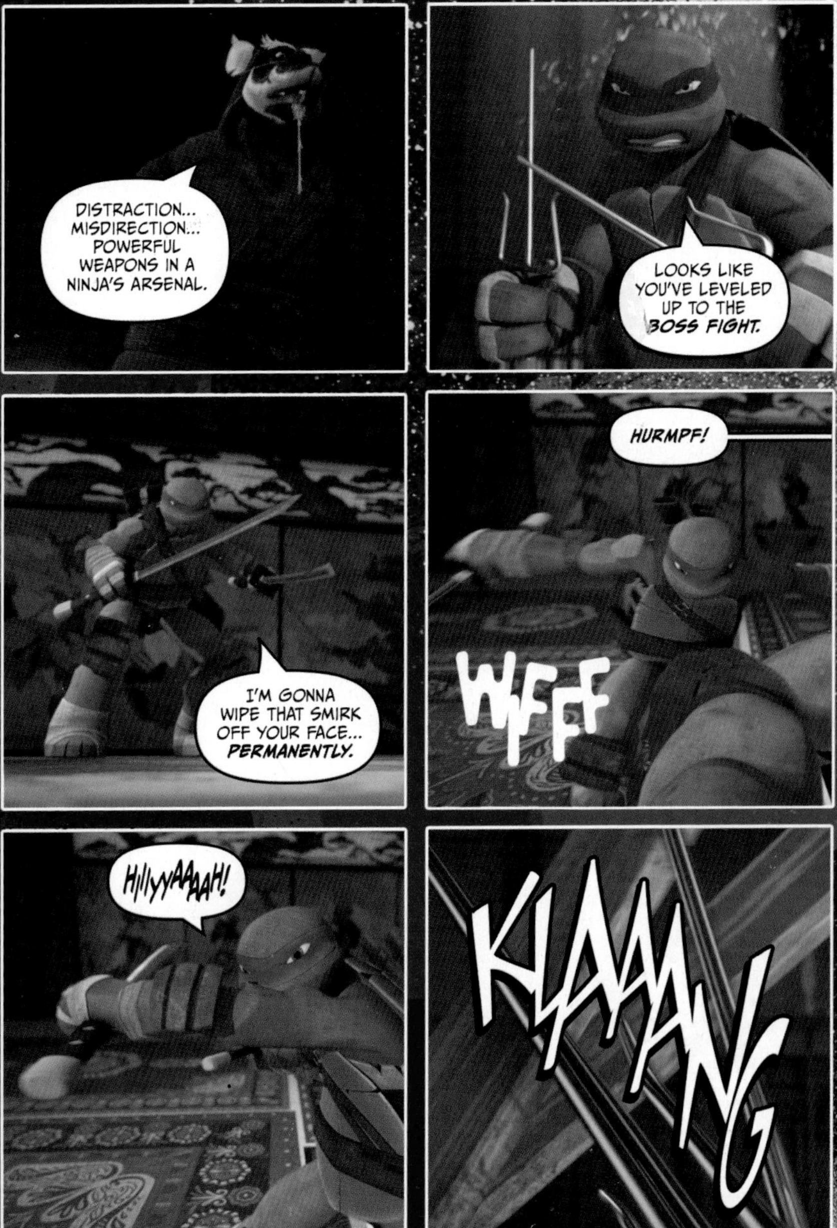
DISTRACTION... MISDIRECTION... POWERFUL WEAPONS IN A NINJA'S ARSENAL.
LOOKS LIKE YOU'VE LEVELED UP TO THE BOSS FIGHT.
I'M GONNA WIPE THAT SMIRK OFF YOUR FACE... PERMANENTLY.
HURMPF!
WFFF
HIIIYYAAAAAH!
KLAAAANG

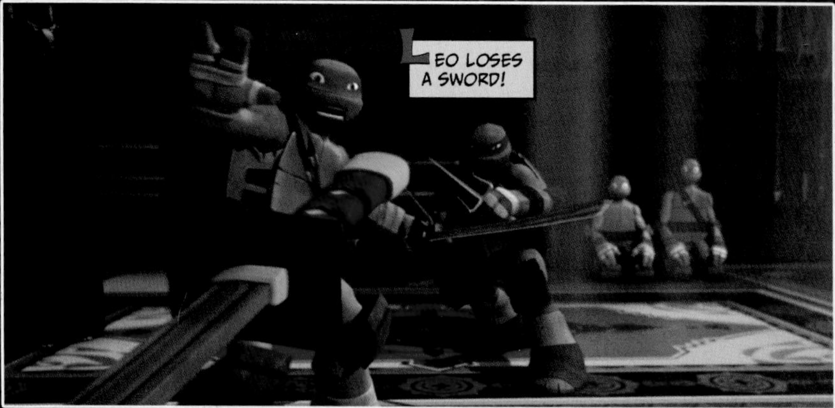
LEO LOSES A SWORD!

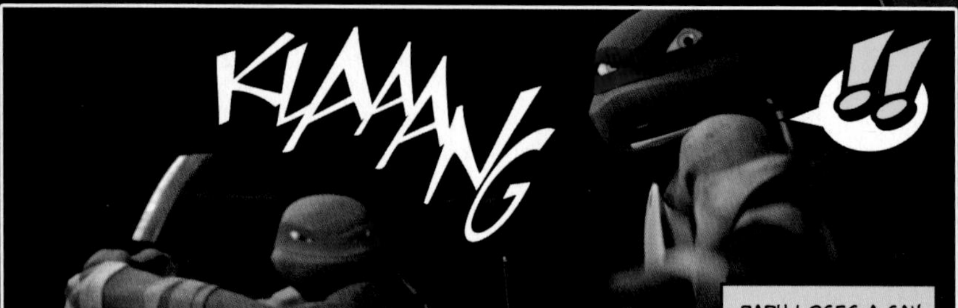
KLAAANG
!!
RAPH LOSES A SAI!

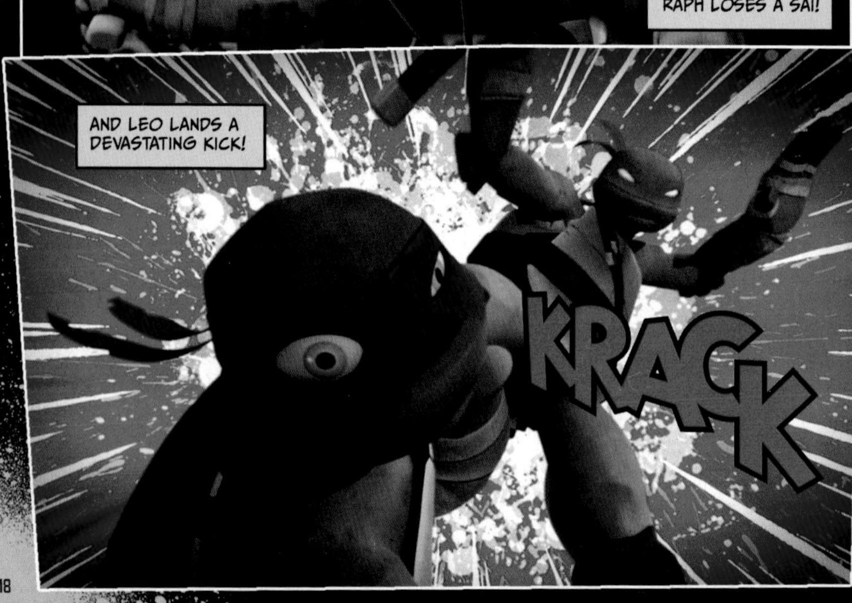
AND LEO LANDS A DEVASTATING KICK!
KRACK

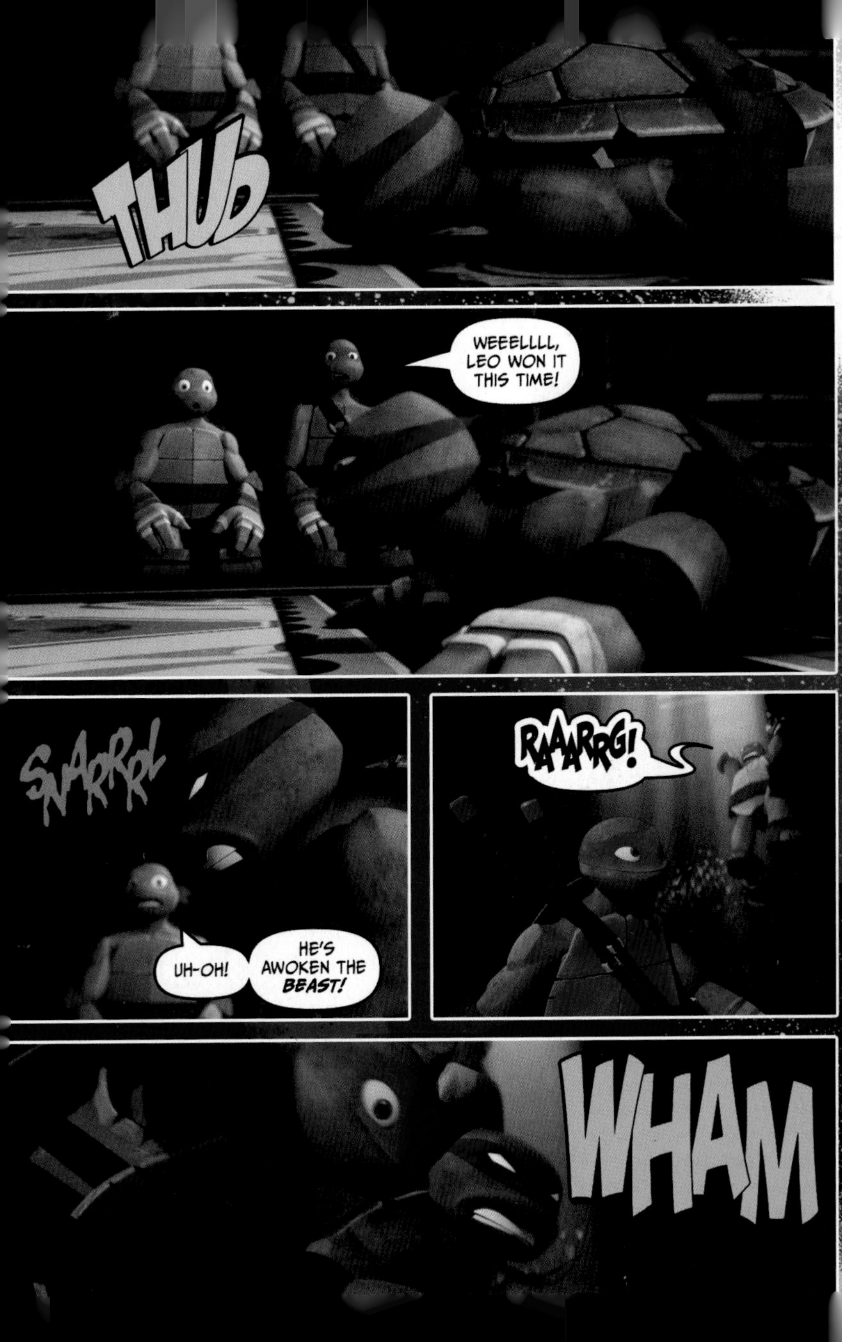
THUD
WEEELLLL, LEO WON IT THIS TIME!
SNARRL
UH-OH!
HE'S AWOKEN THE *BEAST!*
RAAARRG!
WHAM

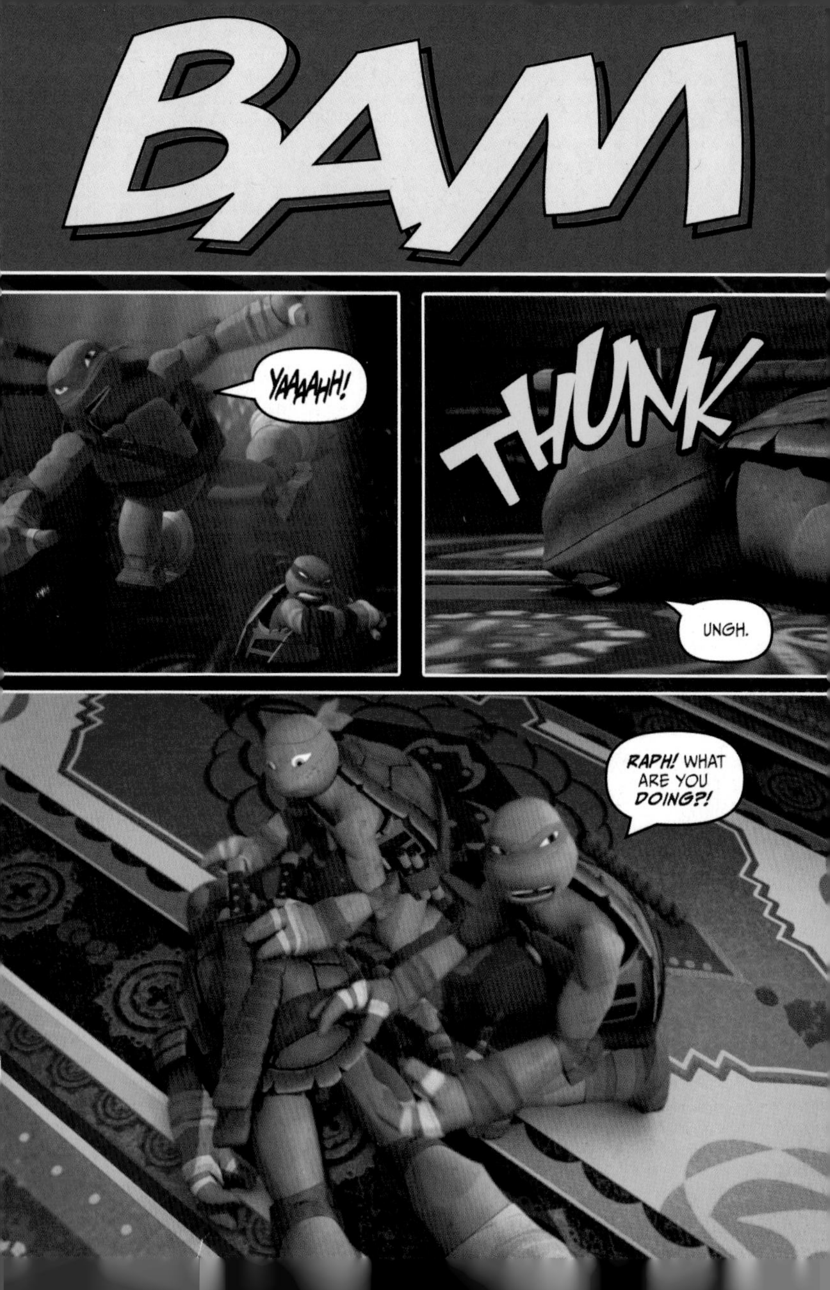
BAM
YAAAAHH!
THUNK
UNGH.
RAPH! WHAT ARE YOU DOING?!

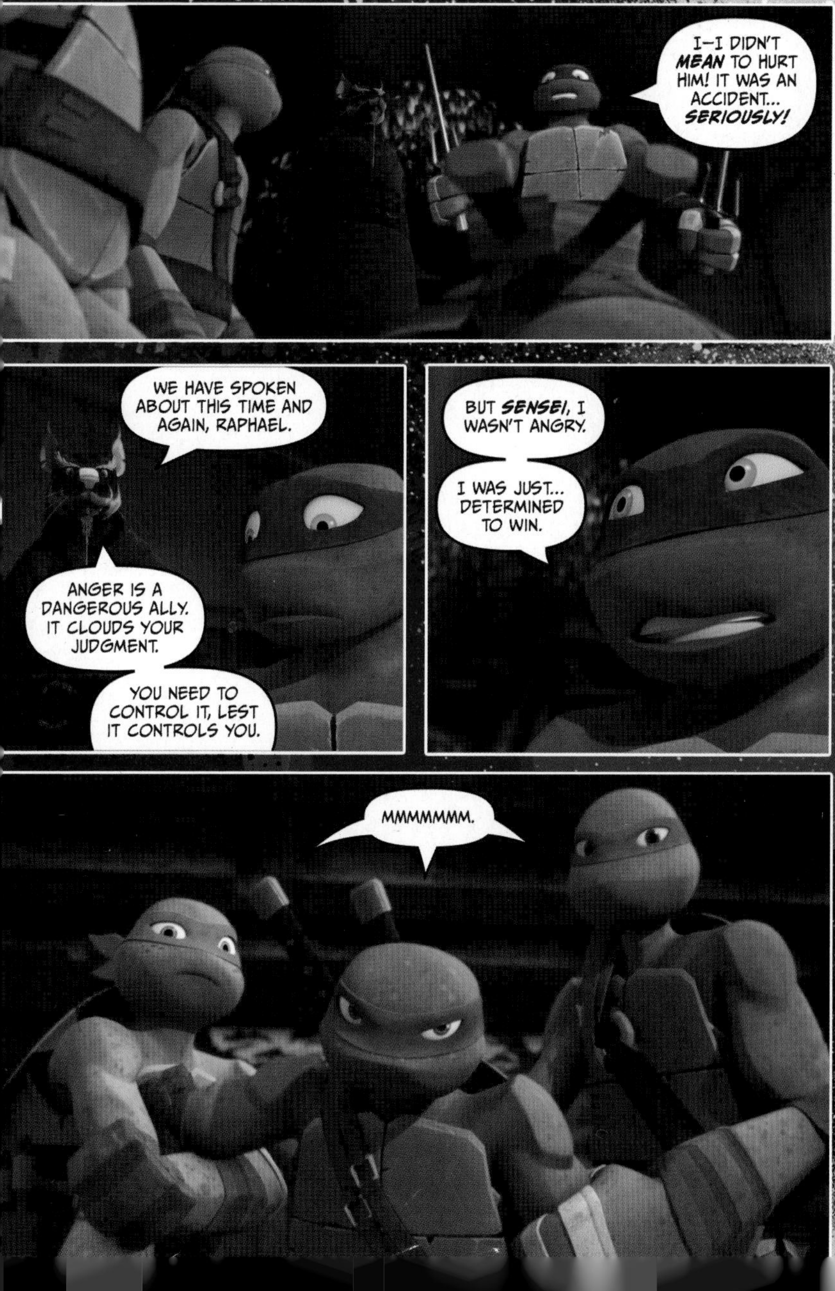
I—I DIDN'T *MEAN* TO HURT HIM! IT WAS AN ACCIDENT... *SERIOUSLY!*
WE HAVE SPOKEN ABOUT THIS TIME AND AGAIN, RAPHAEL.
ANGER IS A DANGEROUS ALLY. IT CLOUDS YOUR JUDGMENT.
YOU NEED TO CONTROL IT, LEST IT CONTROLS YOU.
BUT *SENSEI*, I WASN'T ANGRY.
I WAS JUST... DETERMINED TO WIN.
MMMMMMM.

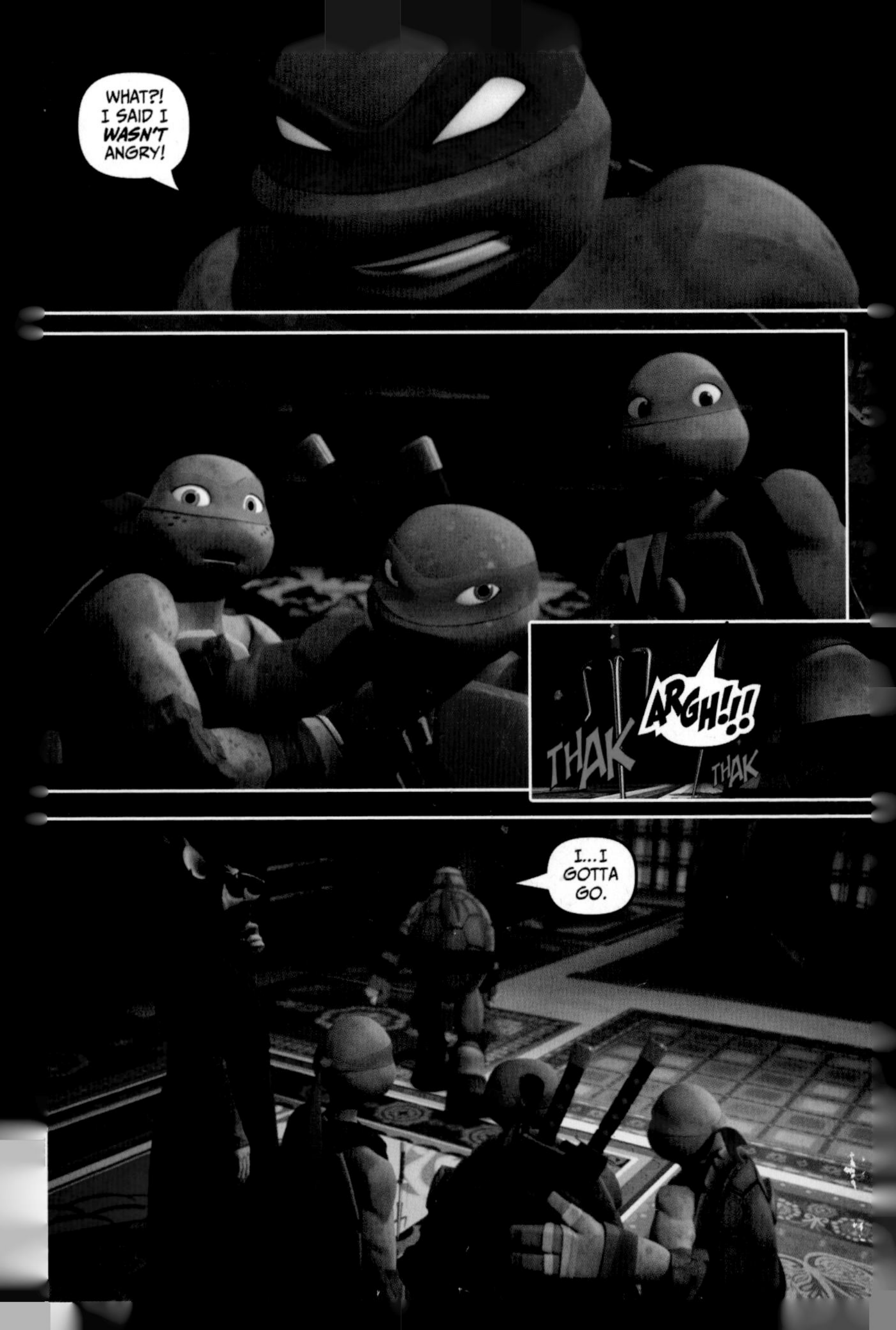
WHAT?! I SAID I WASN'T ANGRY!
THAK
ARGH!!!
THAK
I...I GOTTA GO.

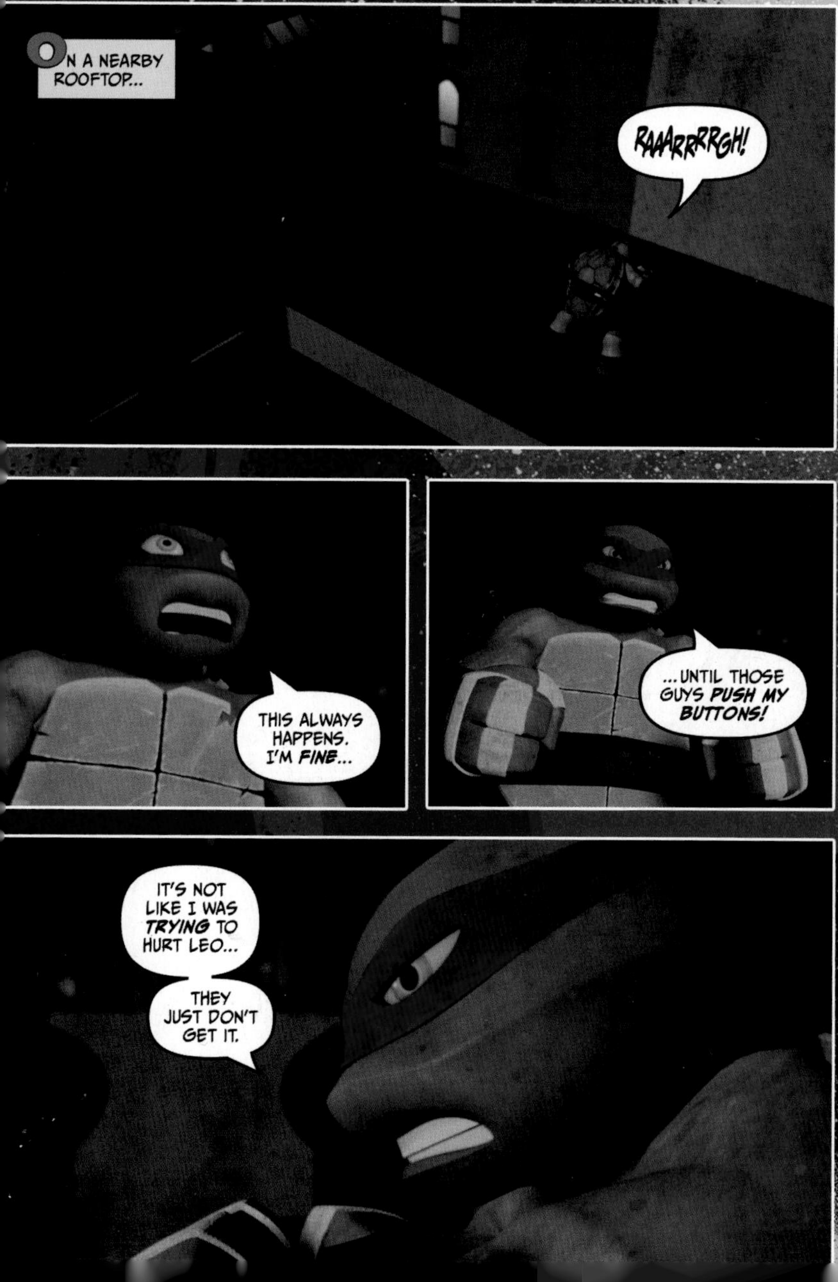
ON A NEARBY ROOFTOP...
RAAARRRRGH!
THIS ALWAYS HAPPENS. I'M *FINE*...
...UNTIL THOSE GUYS *PUSH MY BUTTONS!*
IT'S NOT LIKE I WAS *TRYING* TO HURT LEO...
THEY JUST DON'T GET IT.

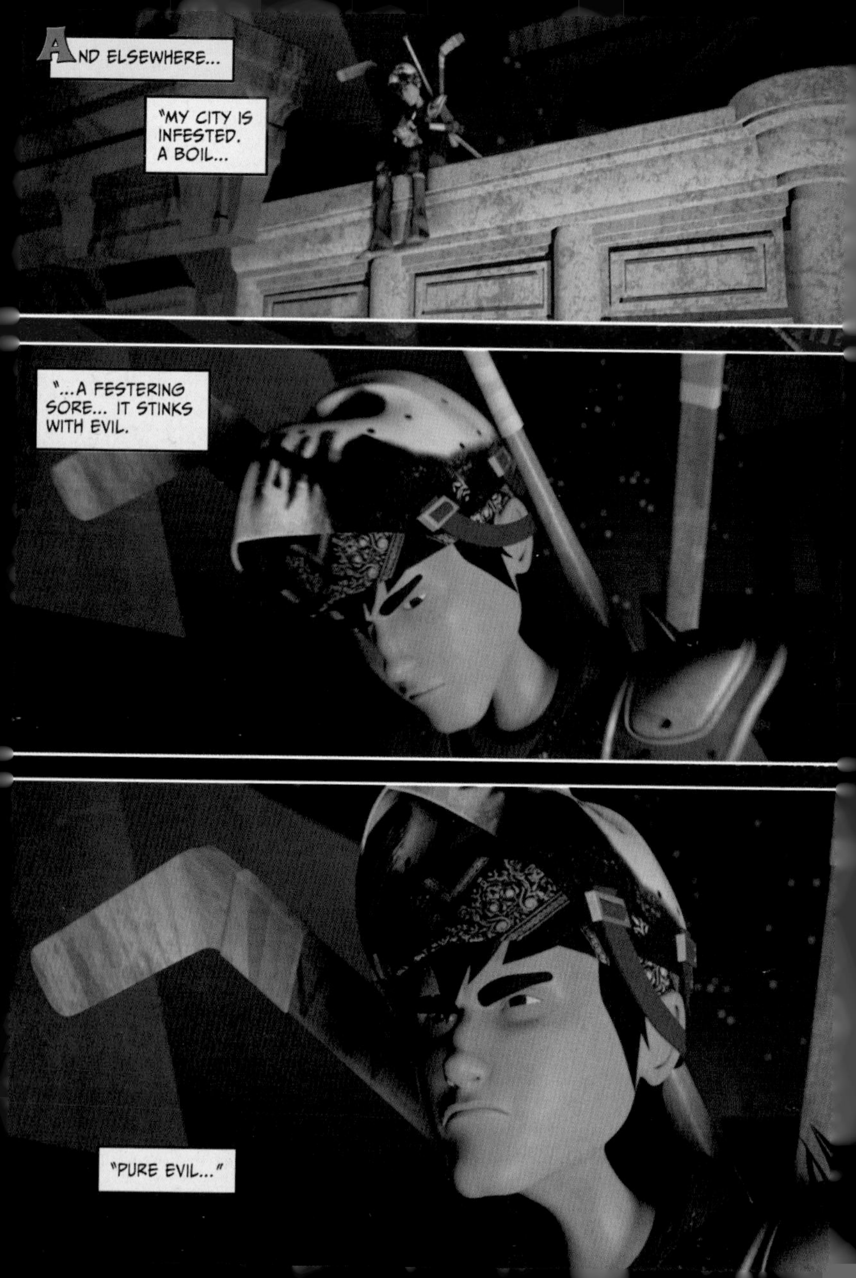
AND ELSEWHERE...
"MY CITY IS INFESTED. A BOIL...
"...A FESTERING SORE... IT STINKS WITH EVIL.
"PURE EVIL..."

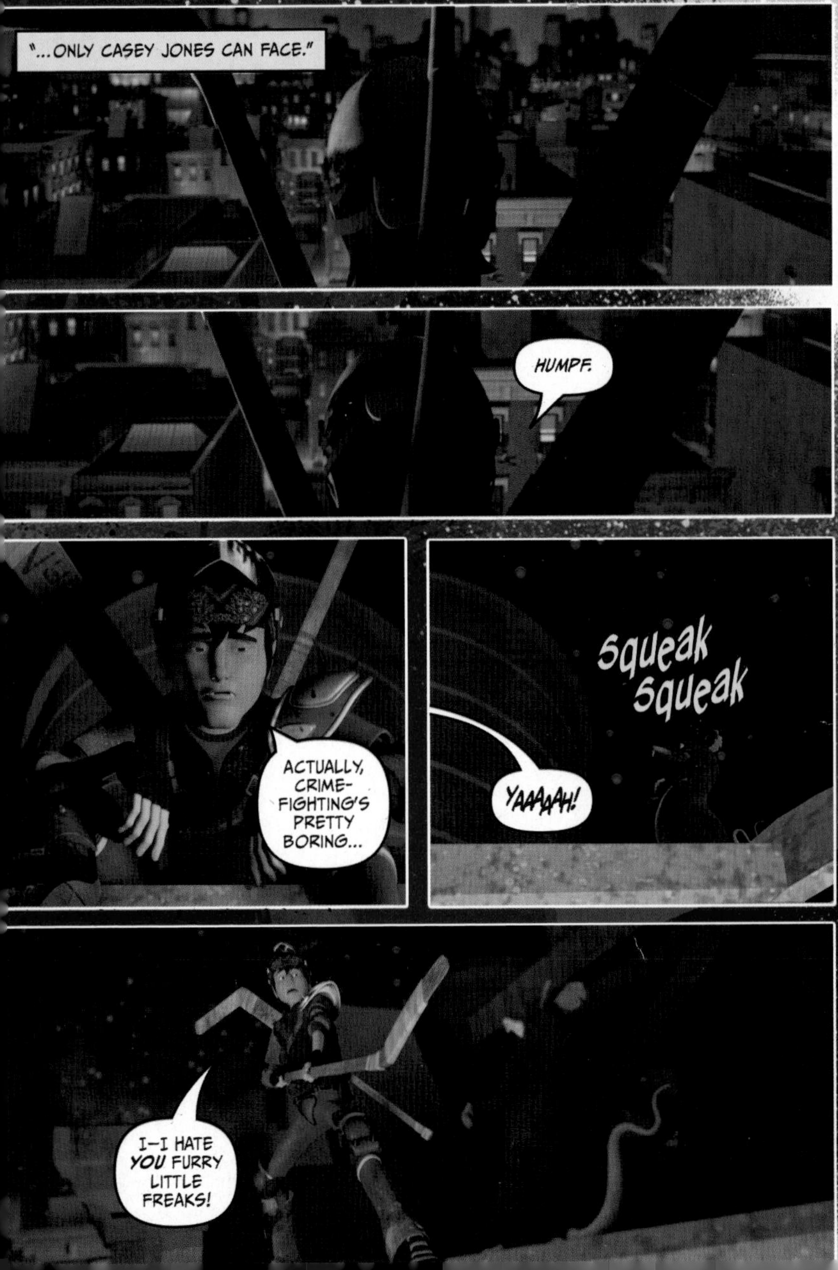
"...ONLY CASEY JONES CAN FACE."
HUMPF.
ACTUALLY, CRIME-FIGHTING'S PRETTY BORING...
Squeak Squeak
YAAAAAH!
I—I HATE YOU FURRY LITTLE FREAKS!

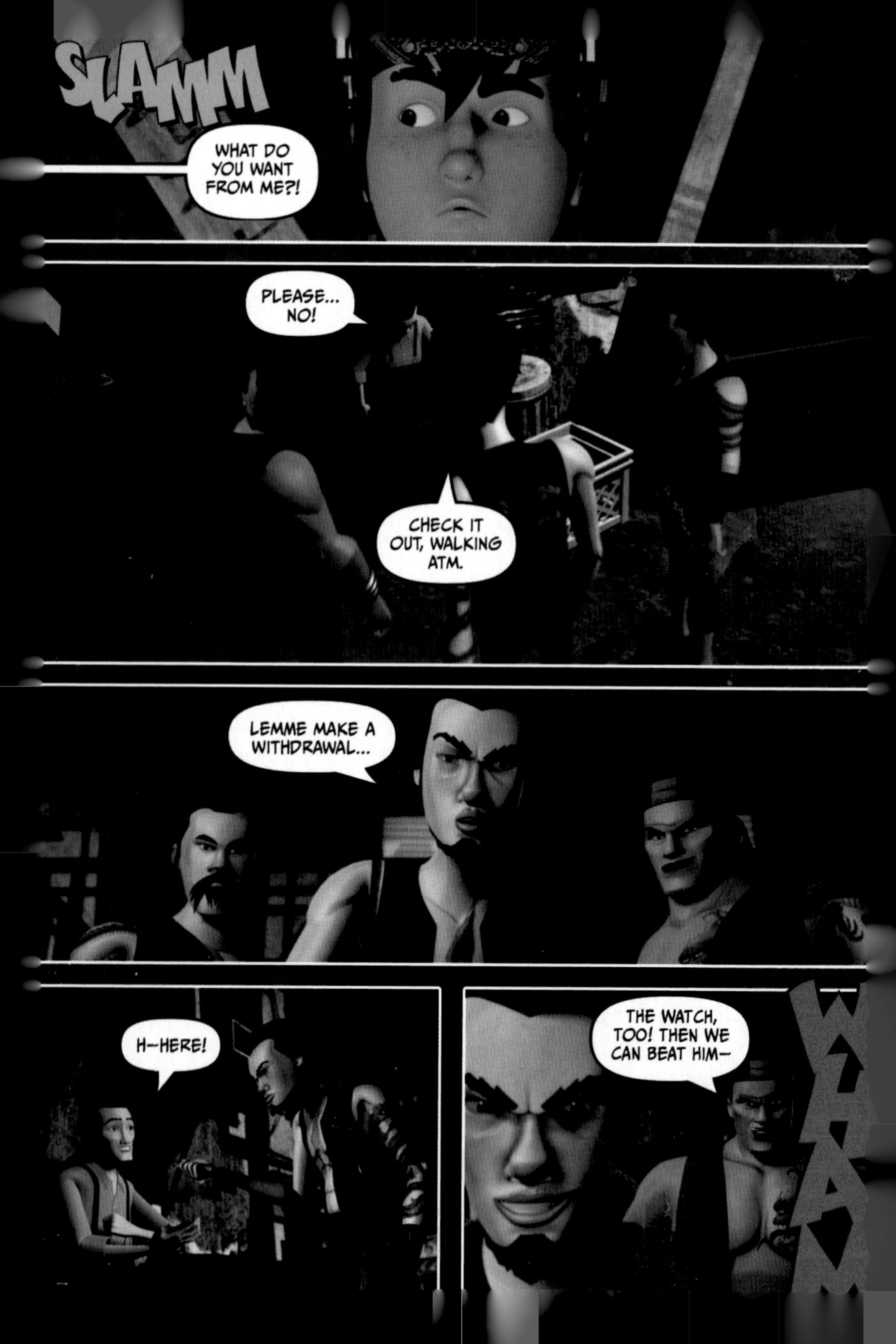
SLAMM
WHAT DO YOU WANT FROM ME?!
PLEASE... NO!
CHECK IT OUT, WALKING ATM.
LEMME MAKE A WITHDRAWAL...
H-HERE!
THE WATCH, TOO! THEN WE CAN BEAT HIM-

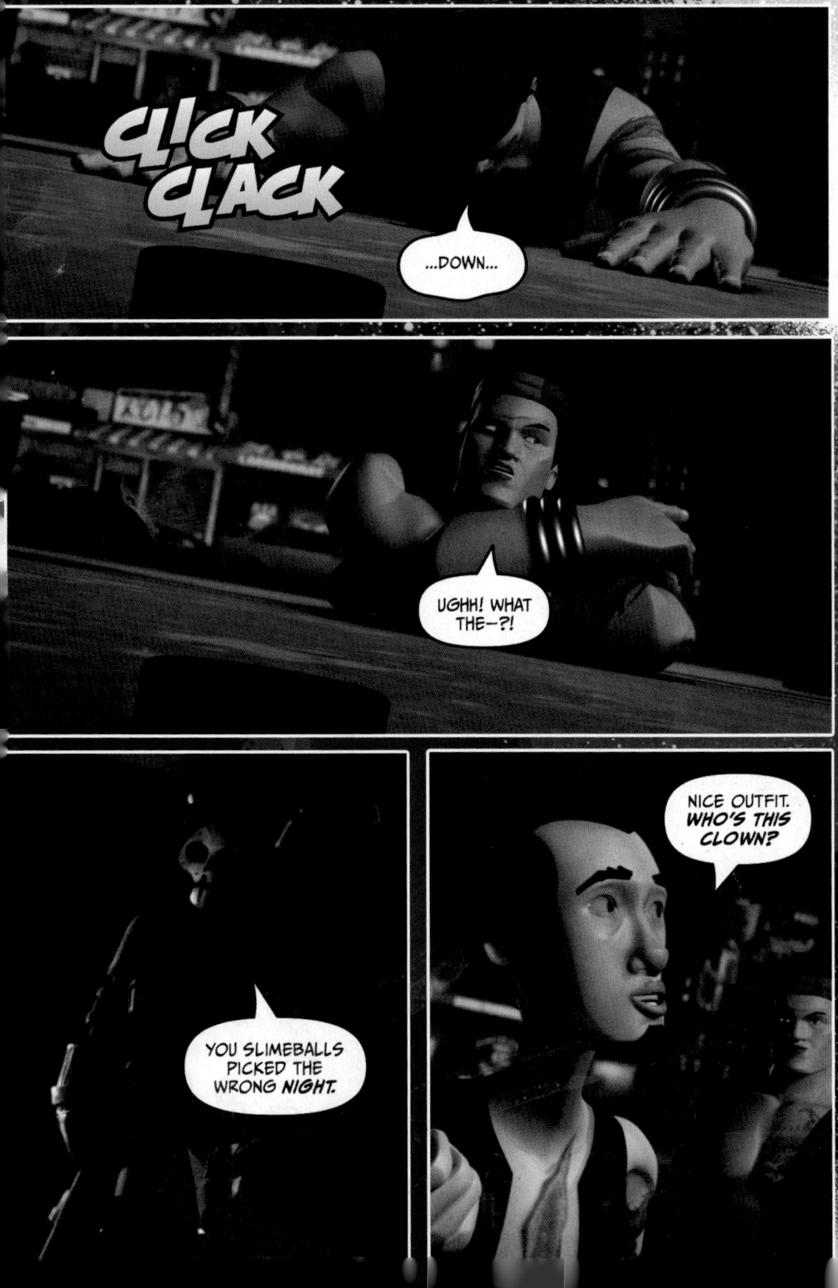
CLICK
CLACK
...DOWN...
UGHH! WHAT THE--?!
YOU SLIMEBALLS PICKED THE WRONG NIGHT.
NICE OUTFIT. WHO'S THIS CLOWN?

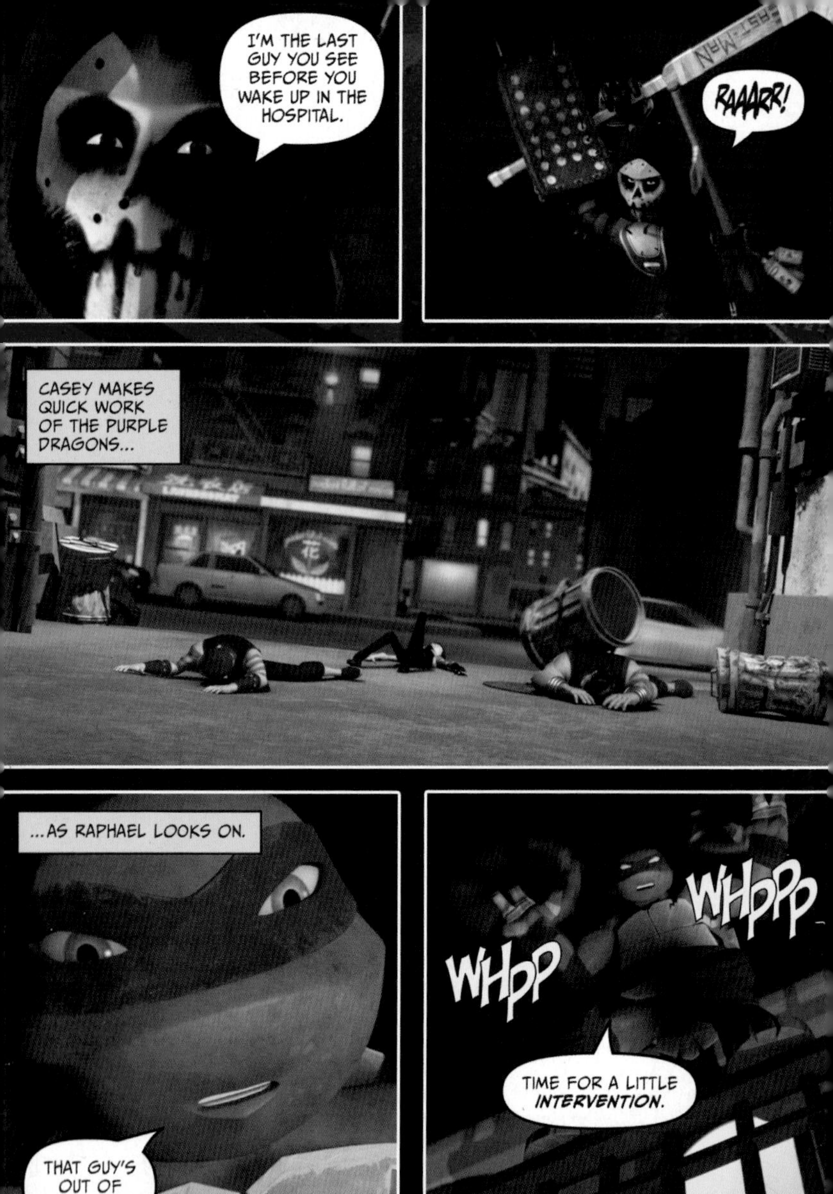
I'M THE LAST GUY YOU SEE BEFORE YOU WAKE UP IN THE HOSPITAL.
RAAARR!
CASEY MAKES QUICK WORK OF THE PURPLE DRAGONS...
...AS RAPHAEL LOOKS ON.
THAT GUY'S OUT OF CONTROL!
WHPP
WHPPP
TIME FOR A LITTLE *INTERVENTION*.

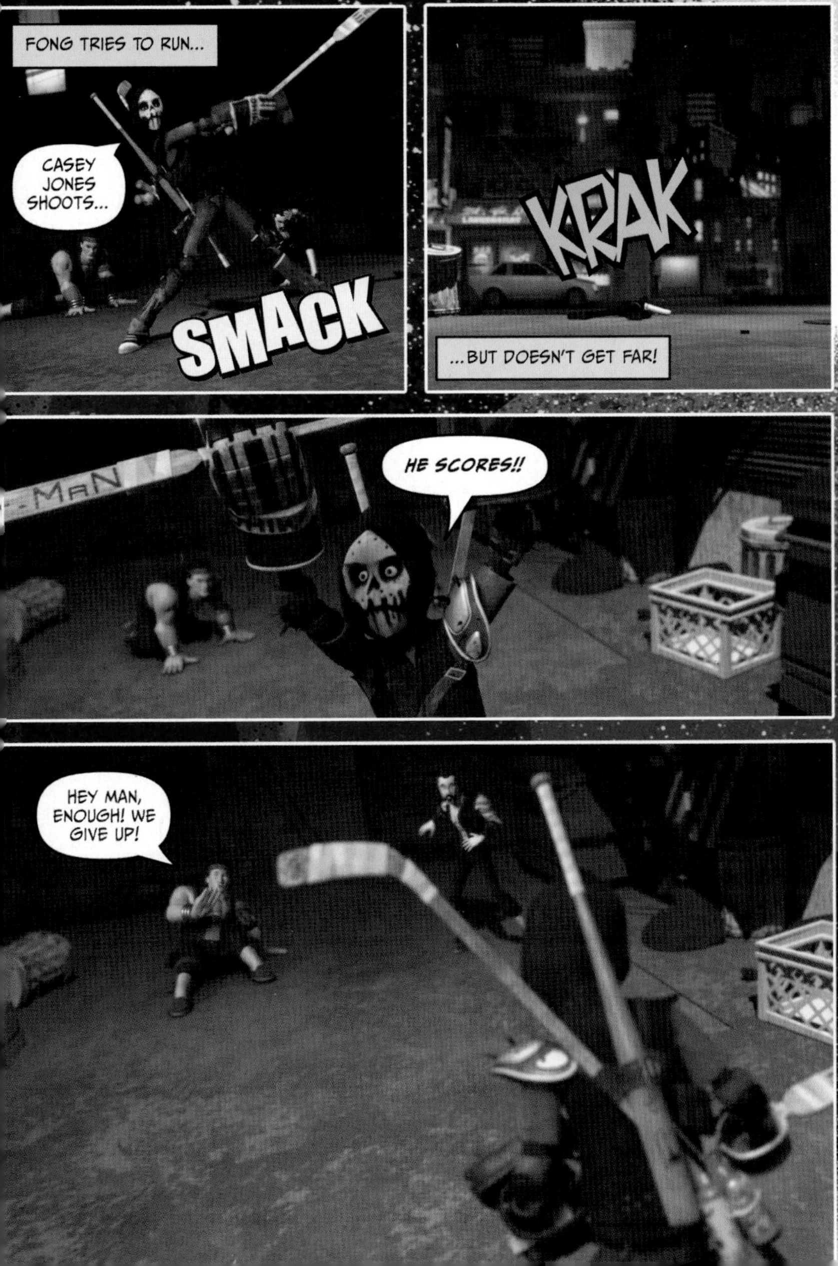
FONG TRIES TO RUN...
CASEY JONES SHOOTS...
SMACK
KRAK
...BUT DOESN'T GET FAR!
HE SCORES!!
HEY MAN, ENOUGH! WE GIVE UP!

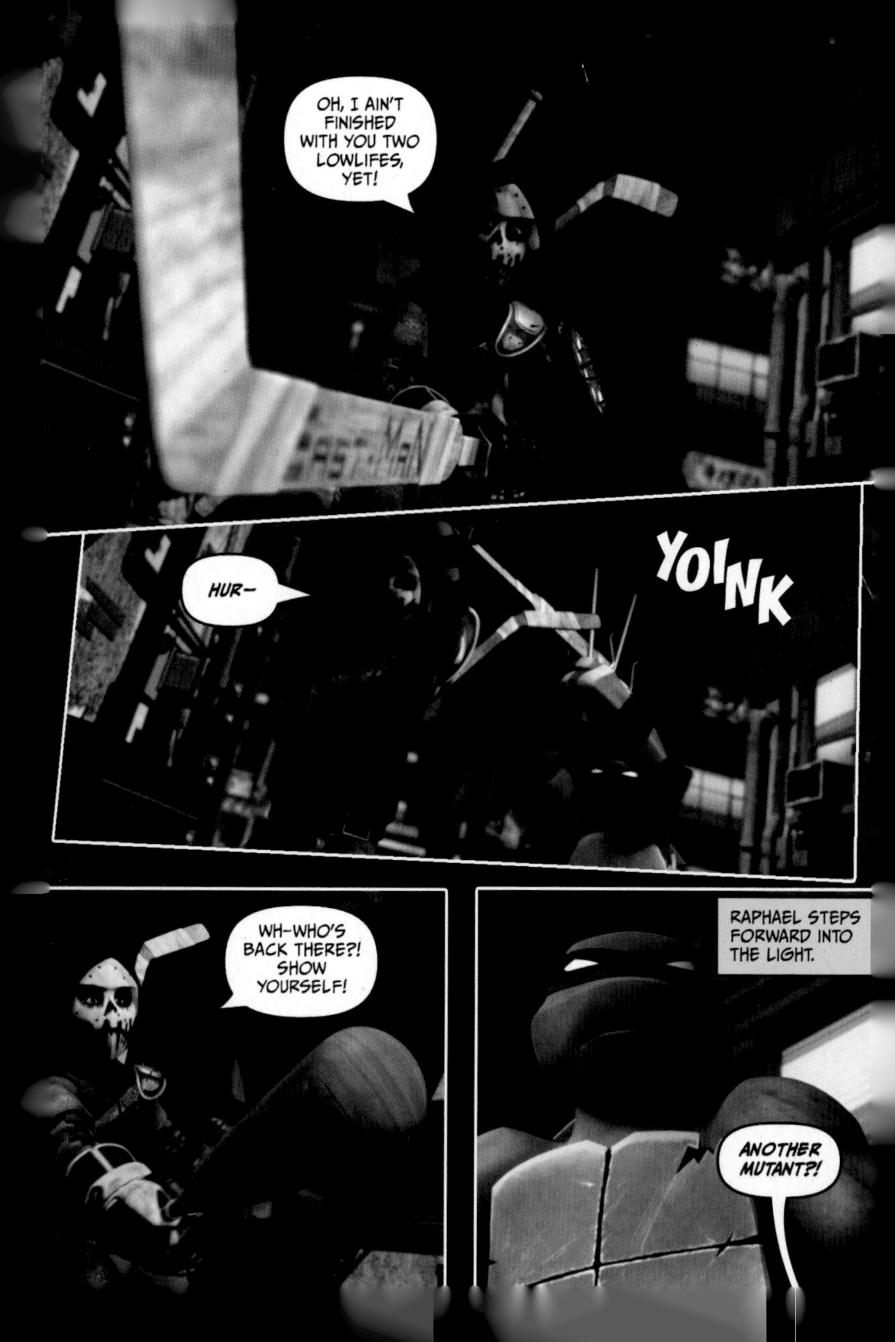
OH, I AIN'T FINISHED WITH YOU TWO LOWLIFES, YET!
HUR—
YOINK
WH-WHO'S BACK THERE?! SHOW YOURSELF!
RAPHAEL STEPS FORWARD INTO THE LIGHT.
ANOTHER MUTANT?!

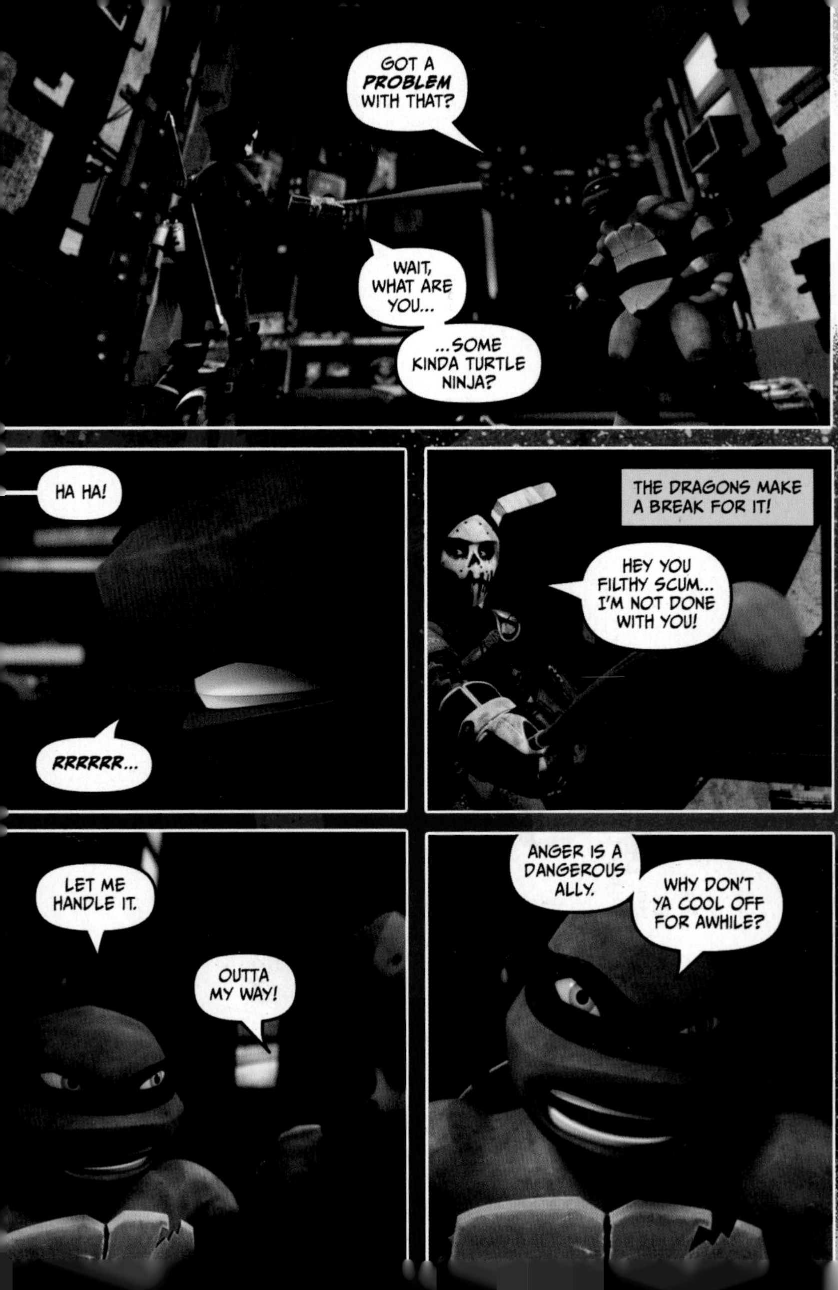

GOT A **PROBLEM** WITH THAT?
WAIT, WHAT ARE YOU...
...SOME KINDA TURTLE NINJA?
HA HA!
RRRRRR...
THE DRAGONS MAKE A BREAK FOR IT!
HEY YOU FILTHY SCUM... I'M NOT DONE WITH YOU!
LET ME HANDLE IT.
OUTTA MY WAY!
ANGER IS A DANGEROUS ALLY.
WHY DON'T YA COOL OFF FOR AWHILE?

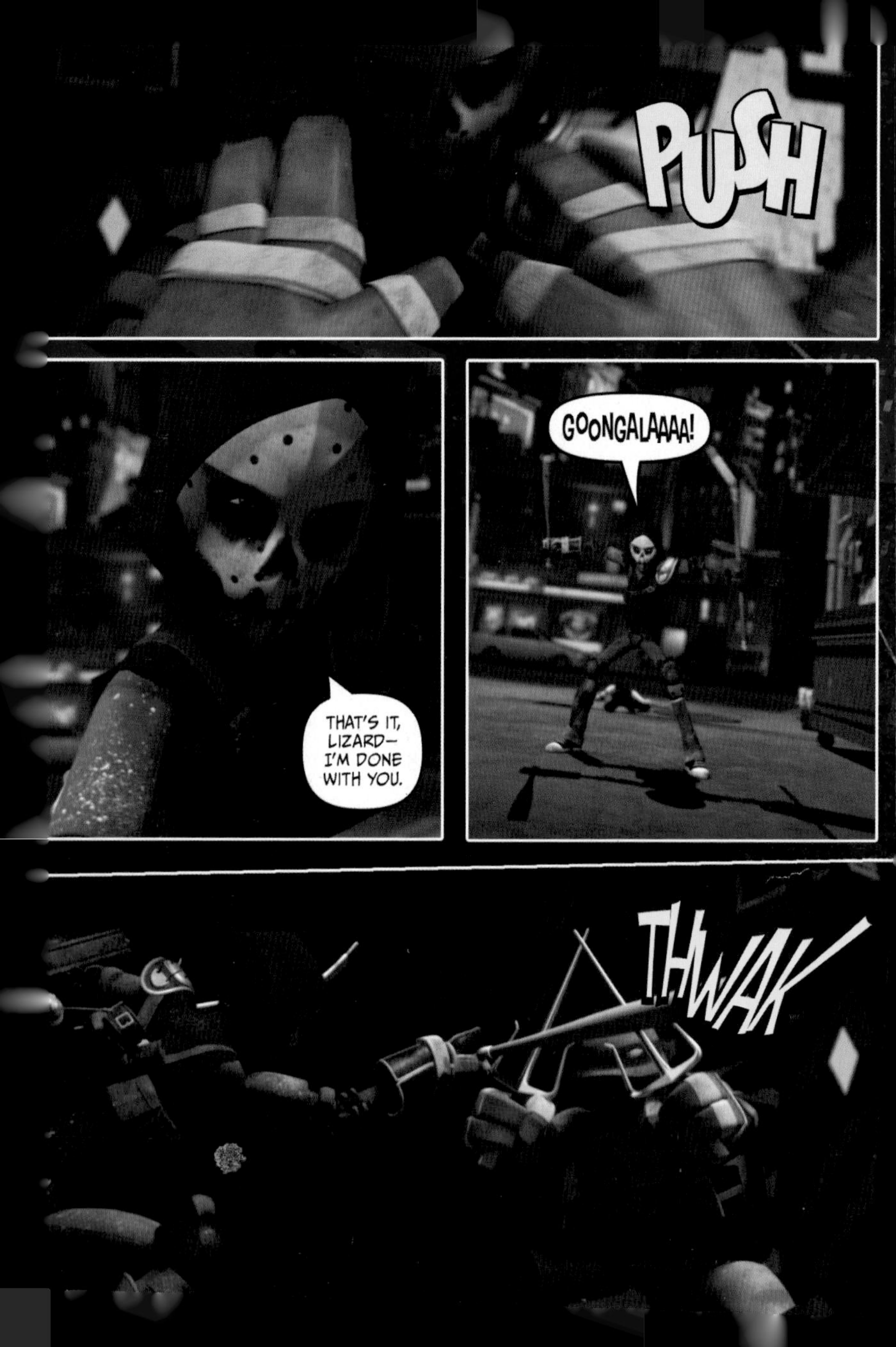
PUSH
THAT'S IT, LIZARD— I'M DONE WITH YOU.
GOONGALAAAA!
THWAK

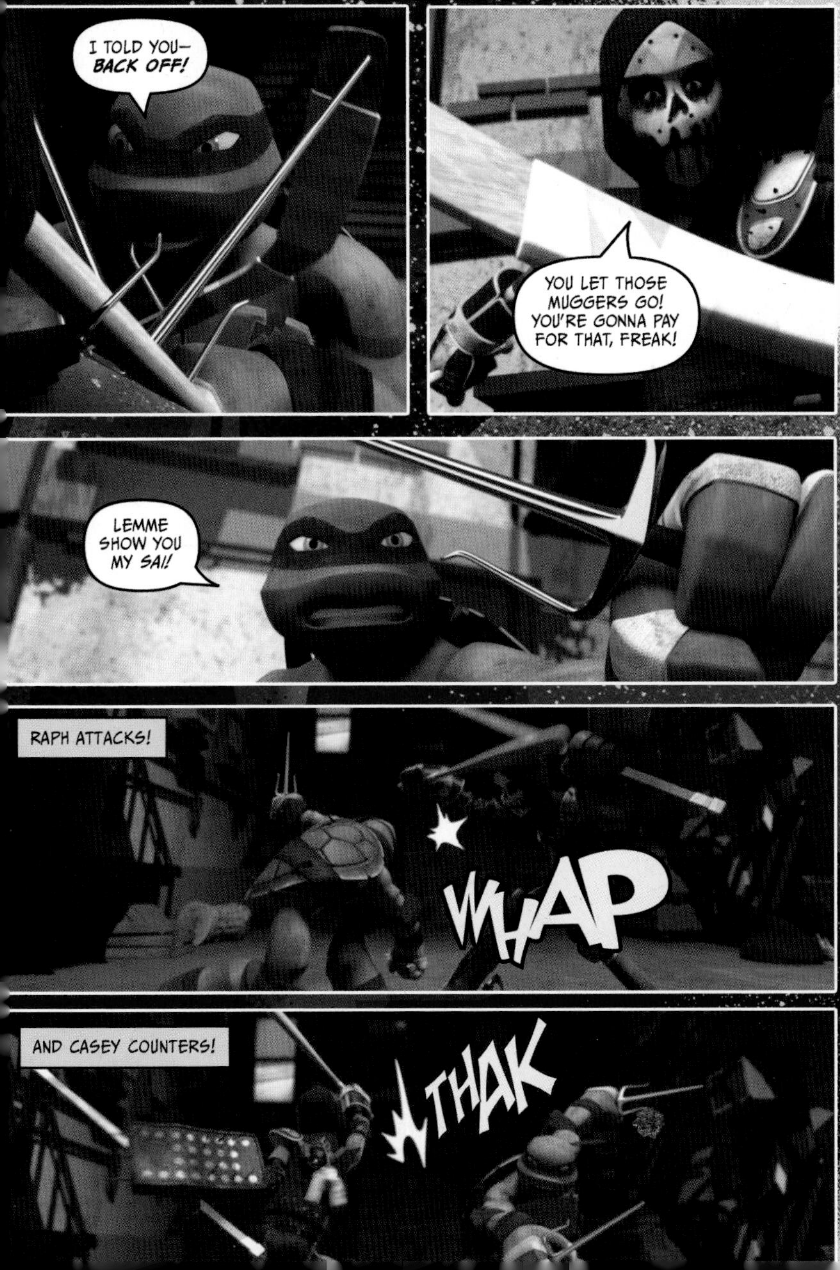
I TOLD YOU— BACK OFF!
YOU LET THOSE MUGGERS GO! YOU'RE GONNA PAY FOR THAT, FREAK!
LEMME SHOW YOU MY SAI!
RAPH ATTACKS!
WHAP
AND CASEY COUNTERS!
THAK

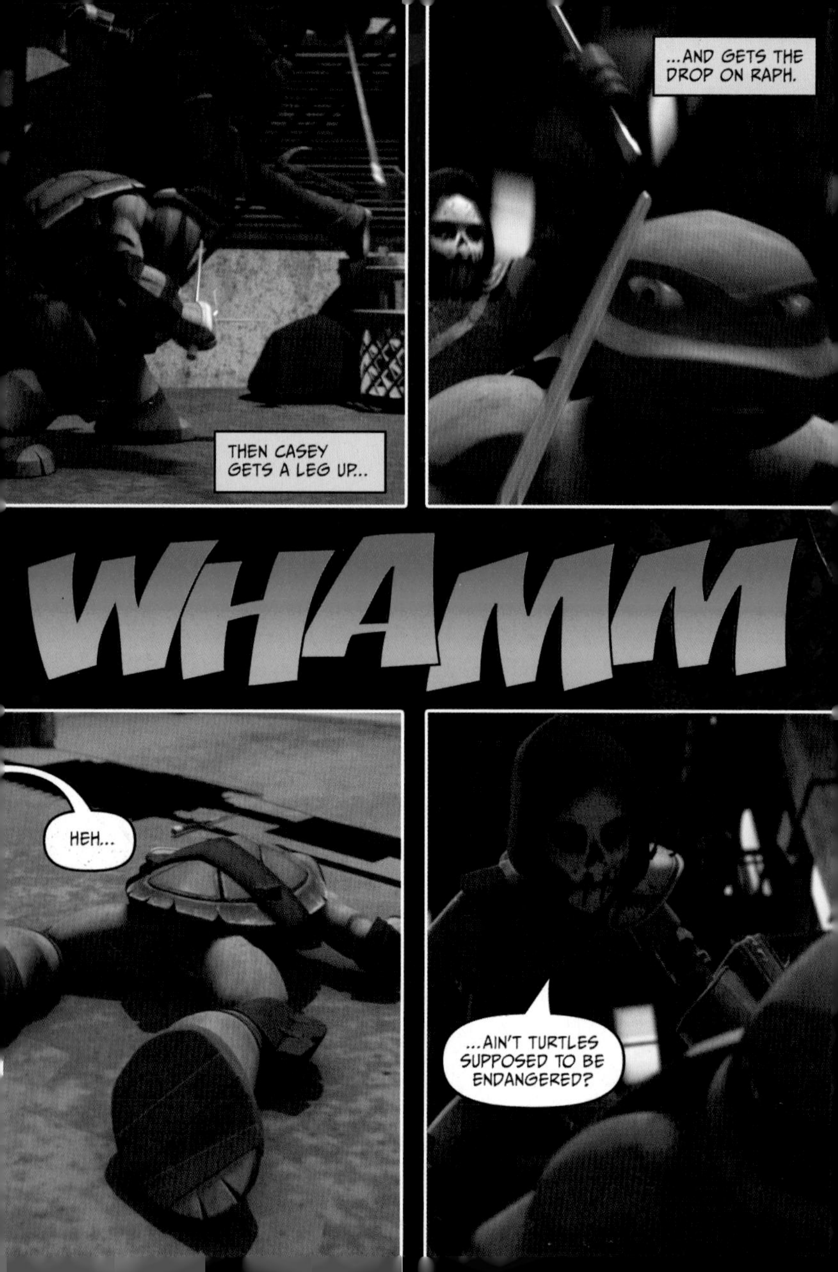
THEN CASEY GETS A LEG UP...
...AND GETS THE DROP ON RAPH.
WHAMM
HEH...
...AIN'T TURTLES SUPPOSED TO BE ENDANGERED?

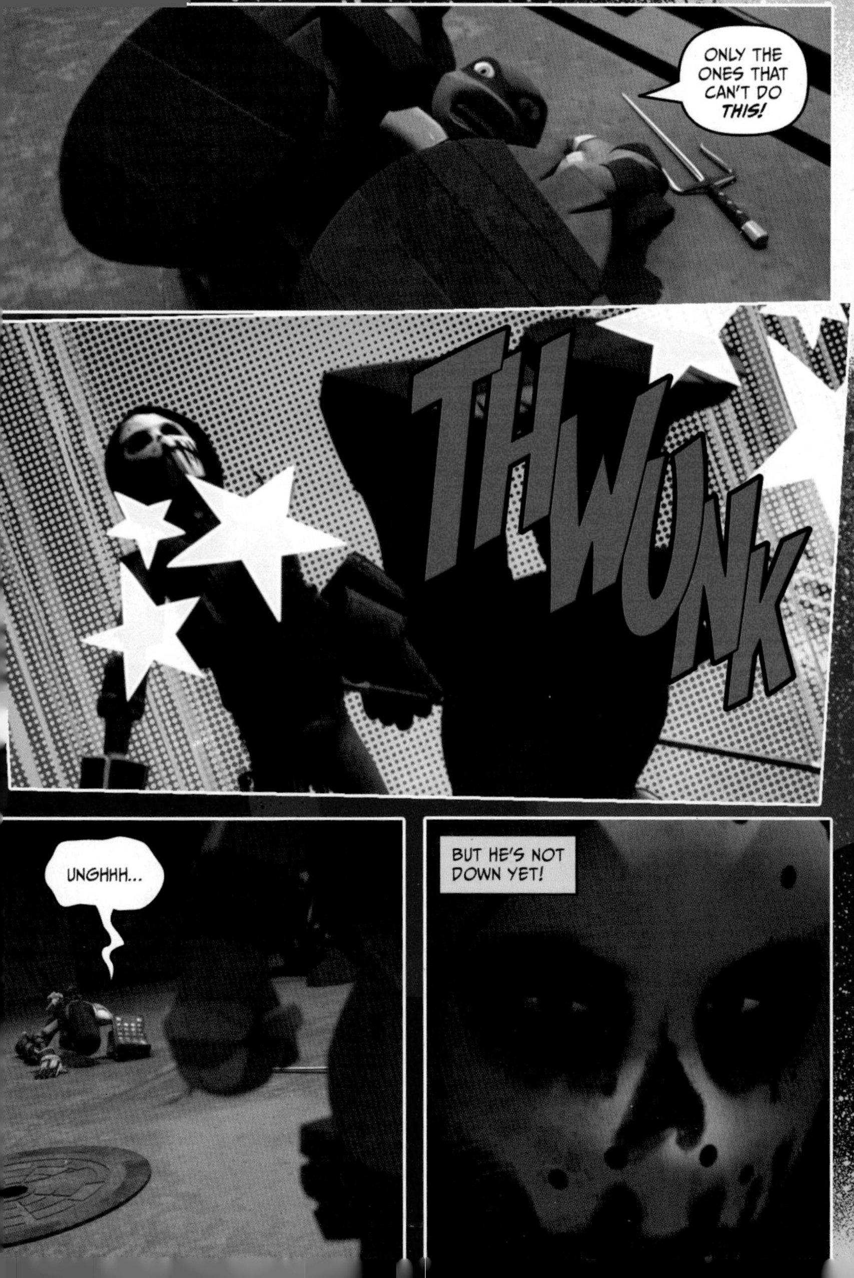
ONLY THE ONES THAT CAN'T DO THIS!
THWUNK
UNGHHH...
BUT HE'S NOT DOWN YET!

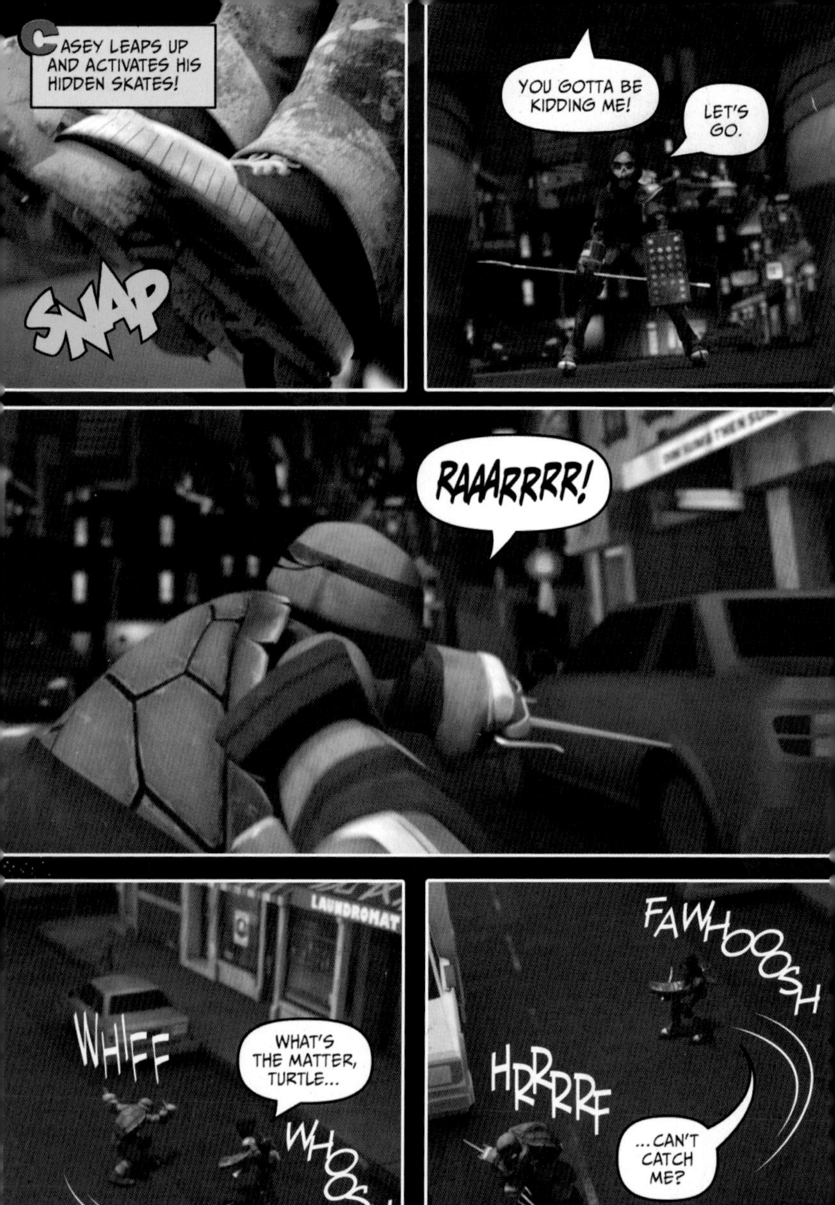

CASEY LEAPS UP AND ACTIVATES HIS HIDDEN SKATES!
SNAP
YOU GOTTA BE KIDDING ME!
LET'S GO.
RAAARRRR!
LAUNDROMAT
WHIFF
WHAT'S THE MATTER, TURTLE...
WHOOSH
FAWHOOOSH
HRRRRF
...CAN'T CATCH ME?

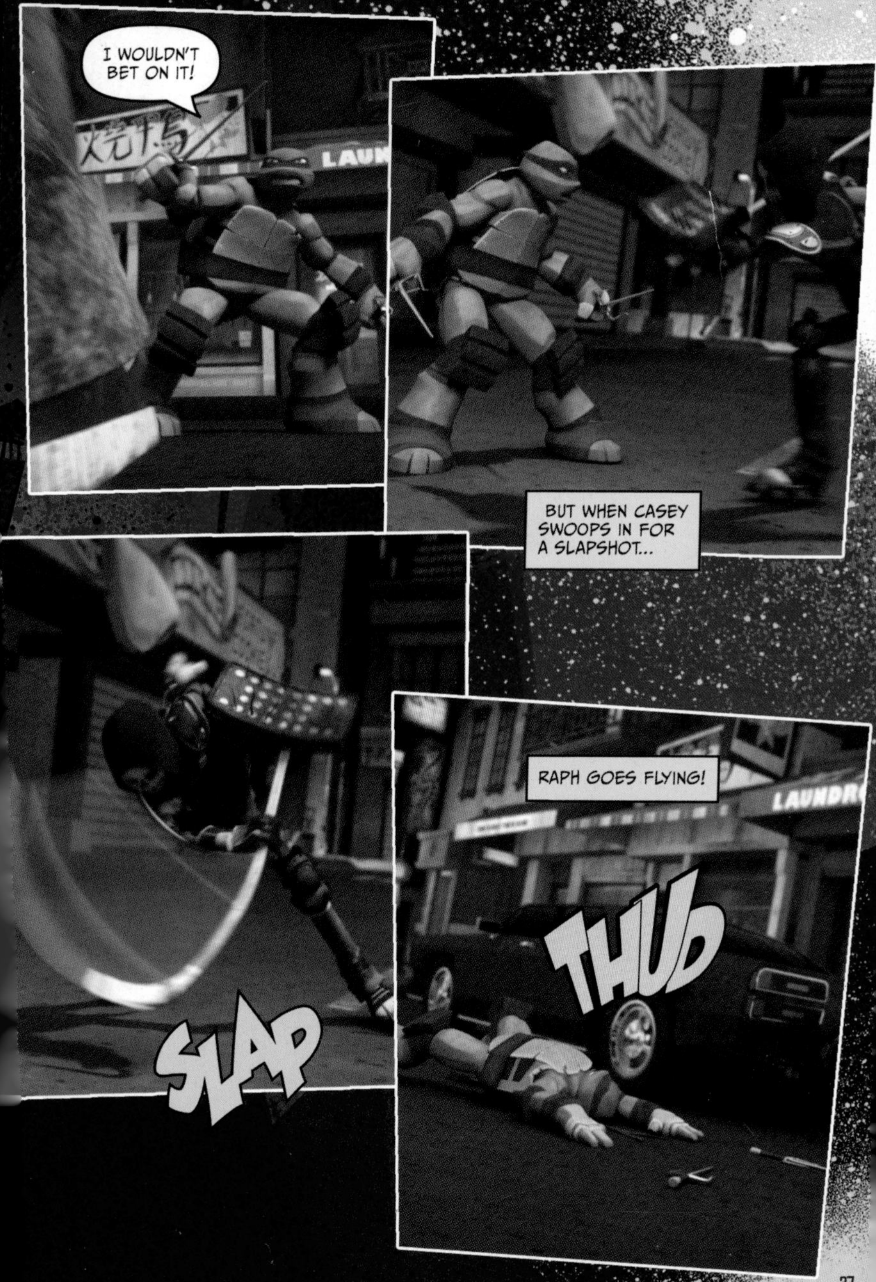
I WOULDN'T BET ON IT!
LAUN
BUT WHEN CASEY SWOOPS IN FOR A SLAPSHOT...
SLAP
RAPH GOES FLYING!
LAUNDRO
THUD

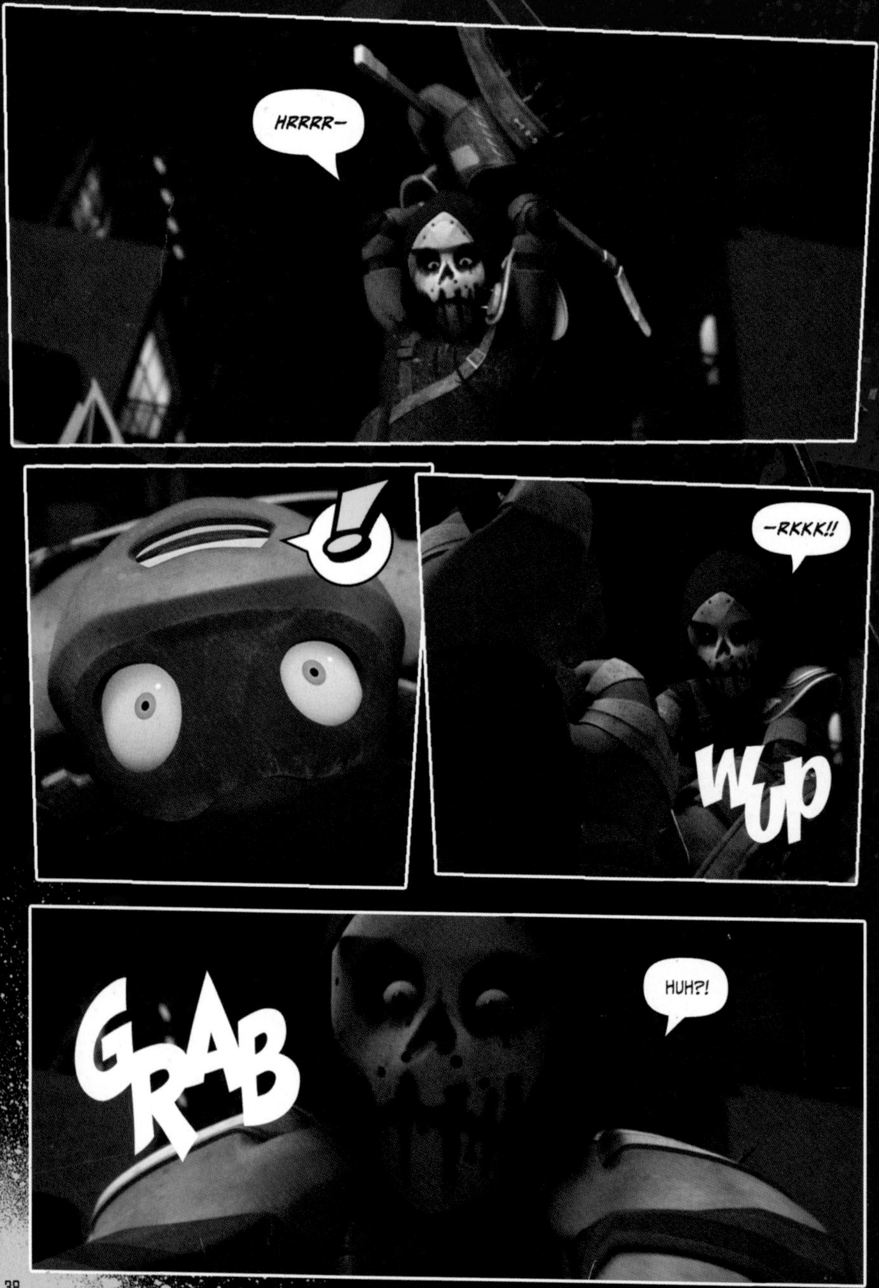
HRRRR-
!
-RKKK!!
WUP
GRAB
HUH?!

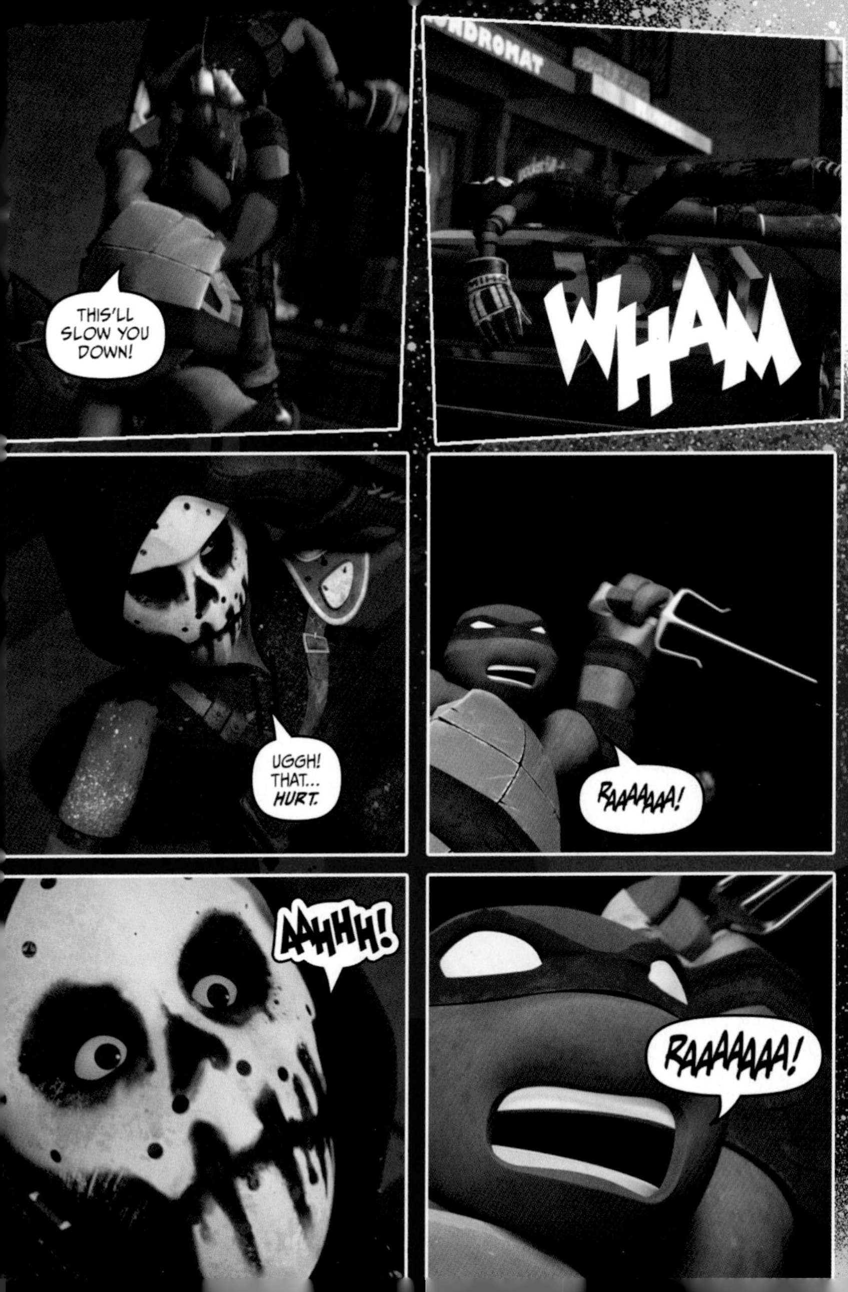
THIS'LL SLOW YOU DOWN!
WHAM
UGGH! THAT... HURT.
RAAAAAAA!
AAHHH!
RAAAAAAA!

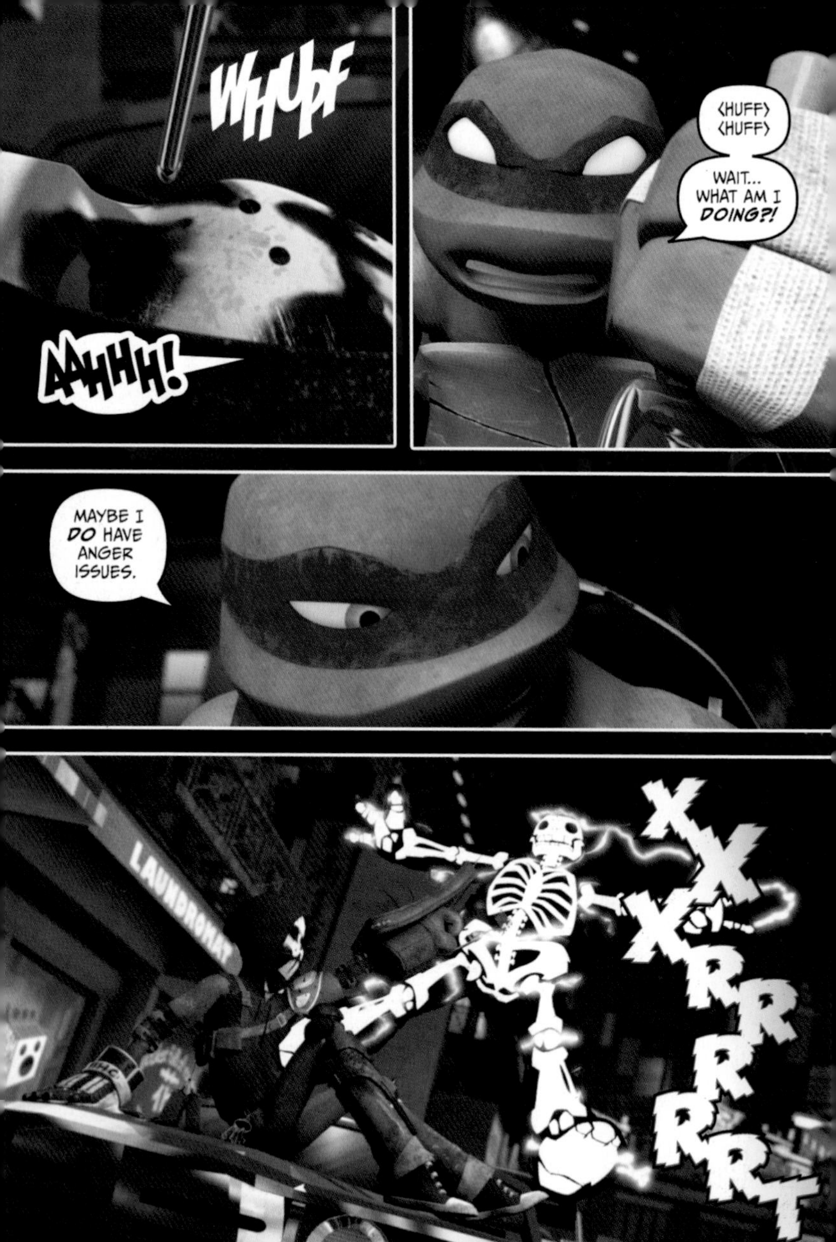
WHUDF
AAHHH!
‹HUFF› ‹HUFF›
WAIT... WHAT AM I DOING?!
MAYBE I DO HAVE ANGER ISSUES.
LAUNDROMAT
XXXRRRRRRT

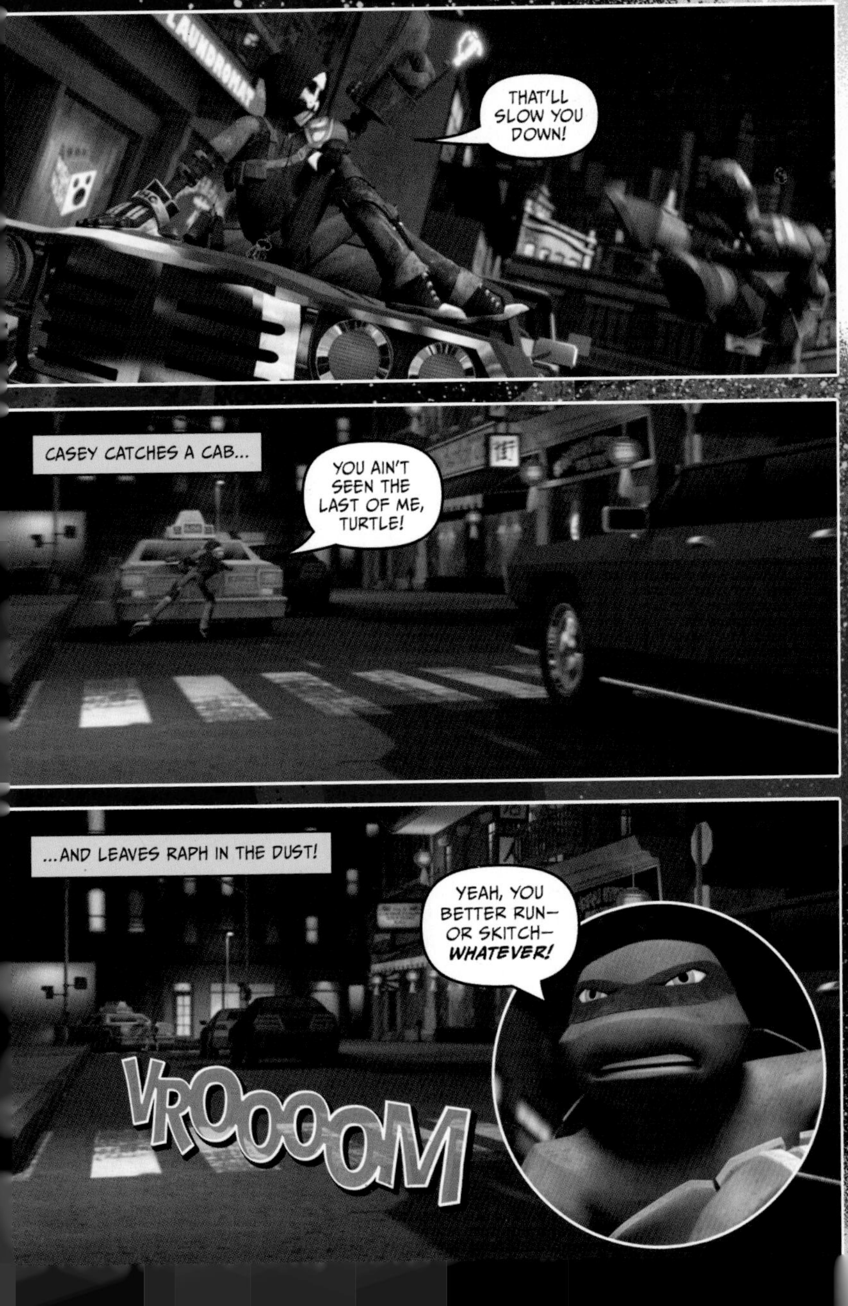
THAT'LL SLOW YOU DOWN!
CASEY CATCHES A CAB...
YOU AIN'T SEEN THE LAST OF ME, TURTLE!
...AND LEAVES RAPH IN THE DUST!
YEAH, YOU BETTER RUN— OR SKITCH— *WHATEVER!*
VROOOOM

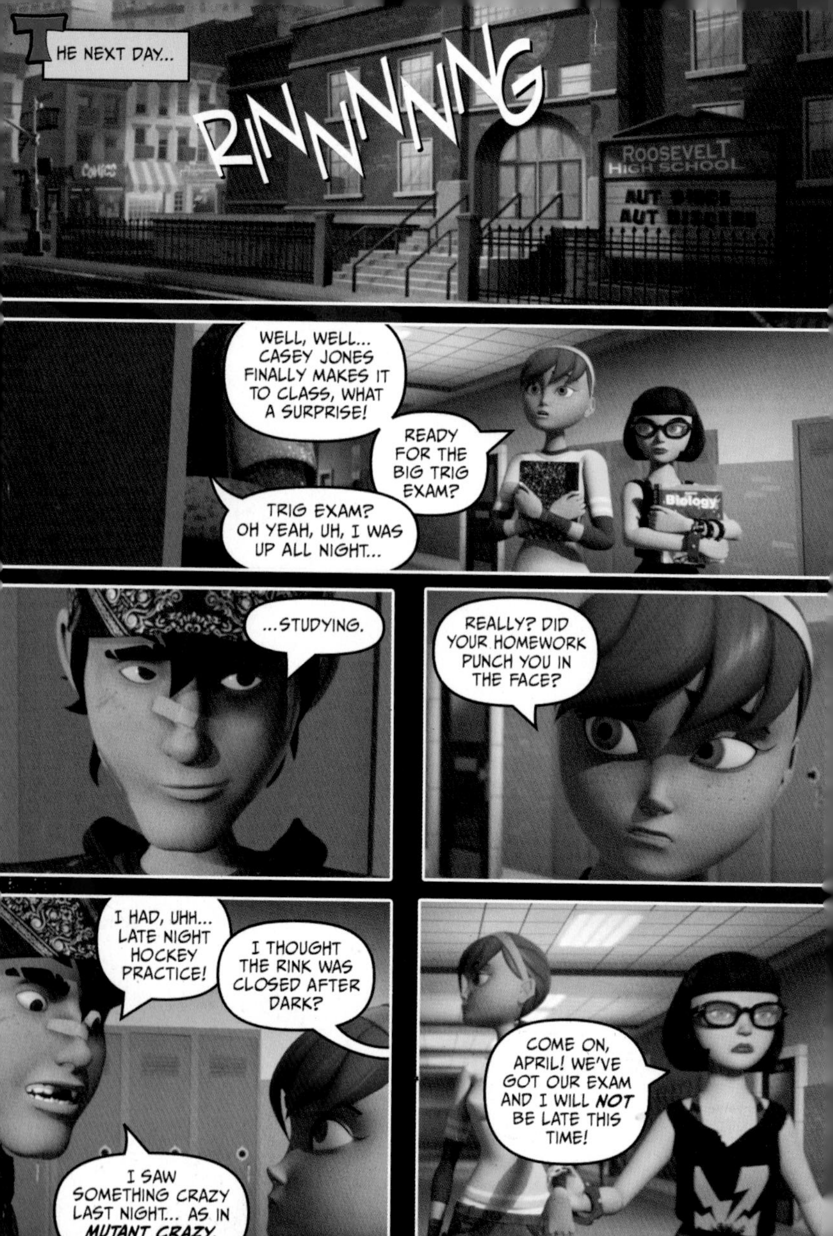
THE NEXT DAY...
RINNNNNG
ROOSEVELT HIGH SCHOOL
WELL, WELL... CASEY JONES FINALLY MAKES IT TO CLASS, WHAT A SURPRISE!
READY FOR THE BIG TRIG EXAM?
TRIG EXAM? OH YEAH, UH, I WAS UP ALL NIGHT...
Biology
...STUDYING.
REALLY? DID YOUR HOMEWORK PUNCH YOU IN THE FACE?
I HAD, UHH... LATE NIGHT HOCKEY PRACTICE!
I THOUGHT THE RINK WAS CLOSED AFTER DARK?
I SAW SOMETHING CRAZY LAST NIGHT... AS IN *MUTANT CRAZY.*
COME ON, APRIL! WE'VE GOT OUR EXAM AND I WILL *NOT* BE LATE THIS TIME!

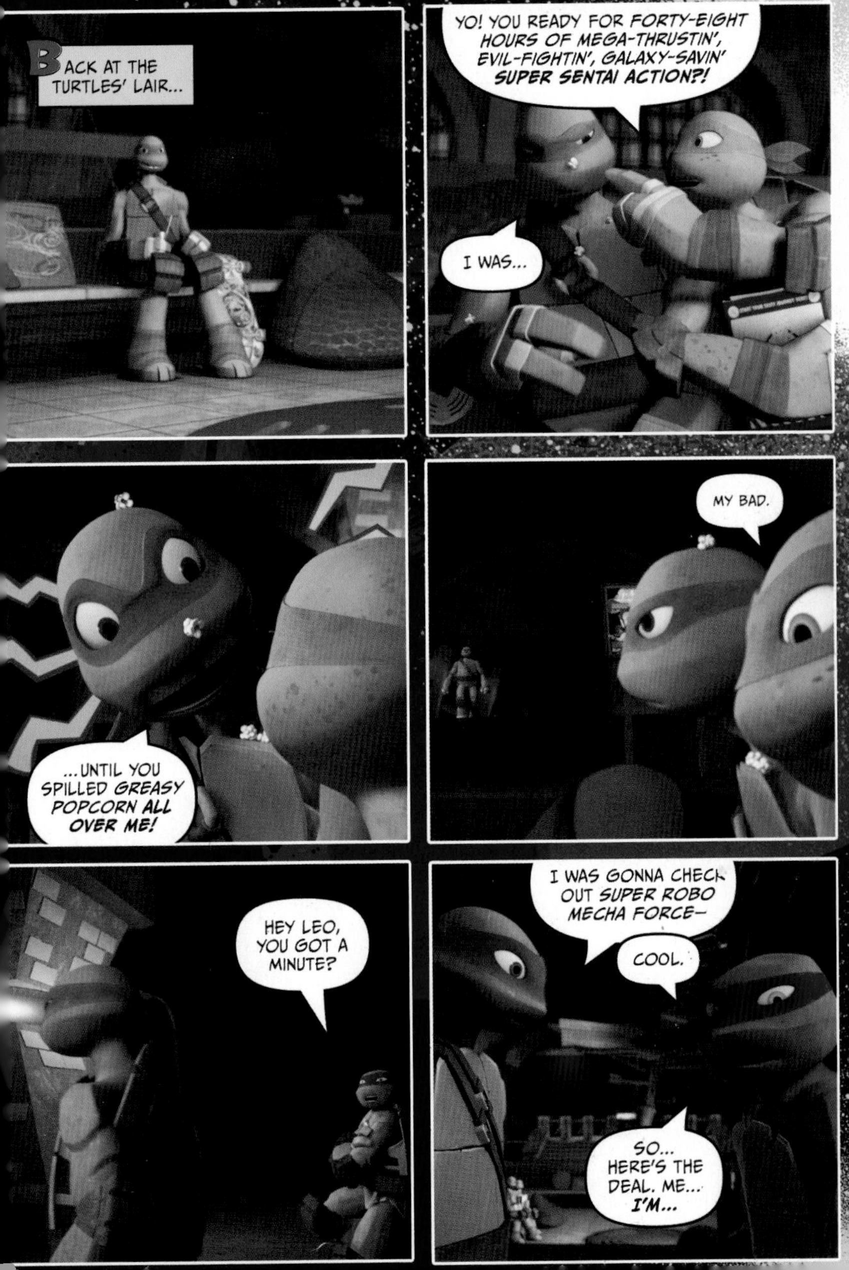
BACK AT THE TURTLES' LAIR...
YO! YOU READY FOR FORTY-EIGHT HOURS OF MEGA-THRUSTIN', EVIL-FIGHTIN', GALAXY-SAVIN' SUPER SENTAI ACTION?!
I WAS...
...UNTIL YOU SPILLED GREASY POPCORN ALL OVER ME!
MY BAD.
HEY LEO, YOU GOT A MINUTE?
I WAS GONNA CHECK OUT SUPER ROBO MECHA FORCE—
COOL.
SO... HERE'S THE DEAL. ME... I'M...

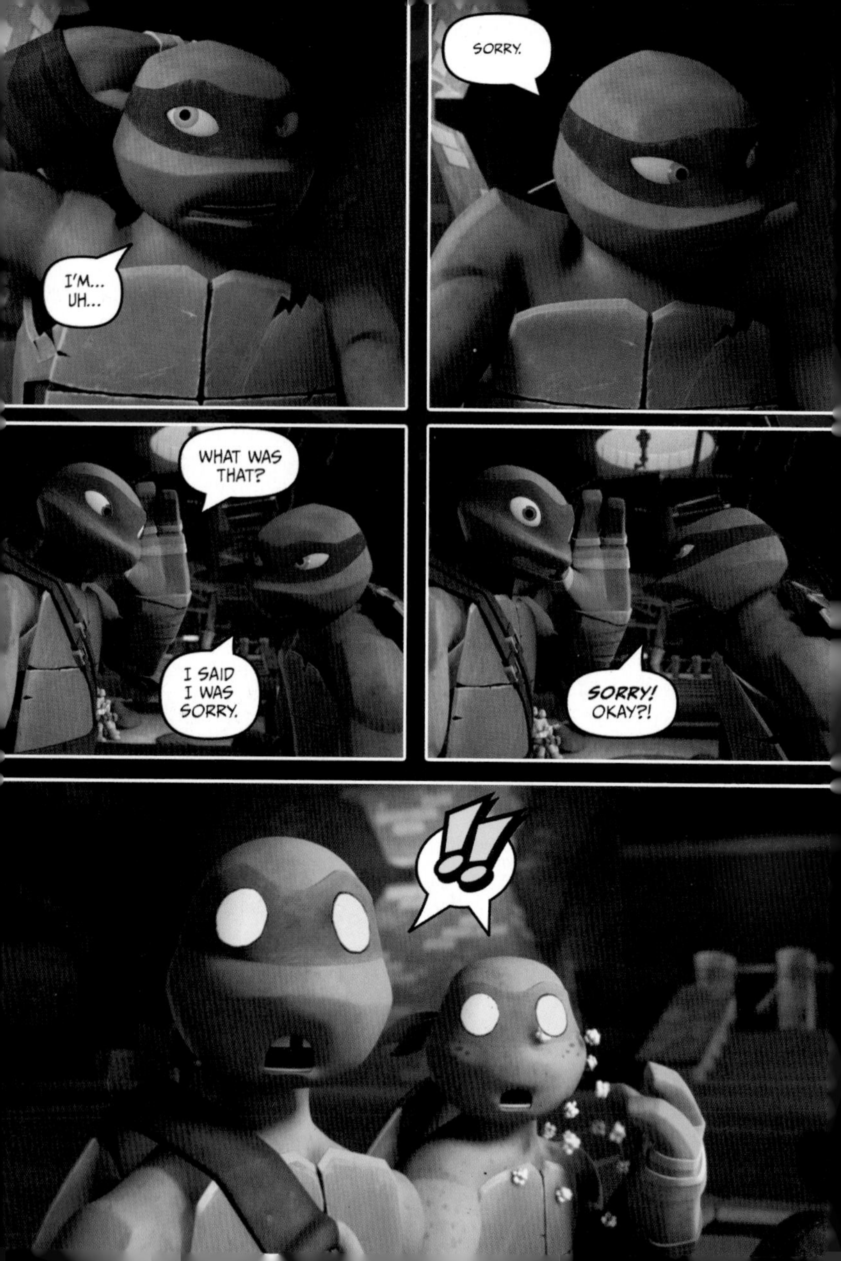
I'M... UH...
SORRY.
WHAT WAS THAT?
I SAID I WAS SORRY.
SORRY! OKAY?!
!!

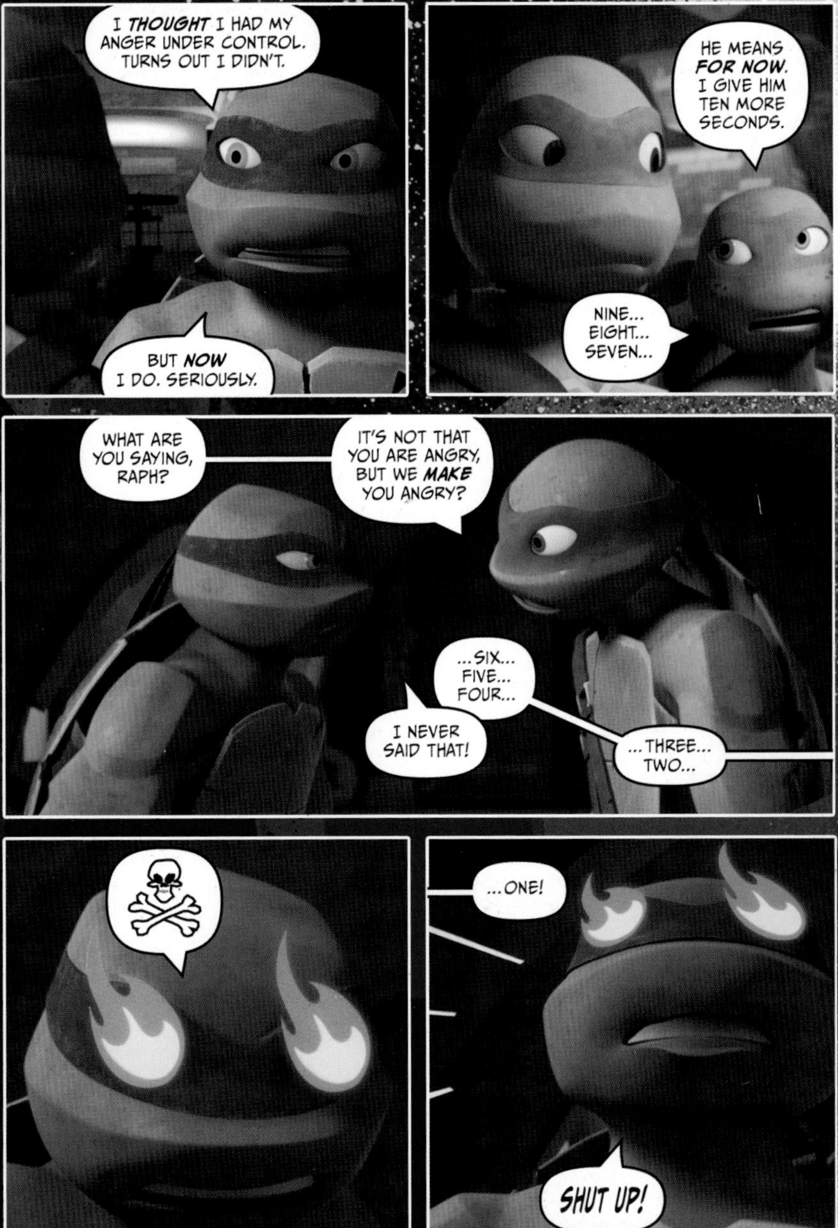
I THOUGHT I HAD MY ANGER UNDER CONTROL. TURNS OUT I DIDN'T.
BUT NOW I DO. SERIOUSLY.
HE MEANS FOR NOW. I GIVE HIM TEN MORE SECONDS.
NINE... EIGHT... SEVEN...
WHAT ARE YOU SAYING, RAPH?
IT'S NOT THAT YOU ARE ANGRY, BUT WE MAKE YOU ANGRY?
...SIX... FIVE... FOUR...
I NEVER SAID THAT!
...THREE... TWO...
...ONE!
SHUT UP!

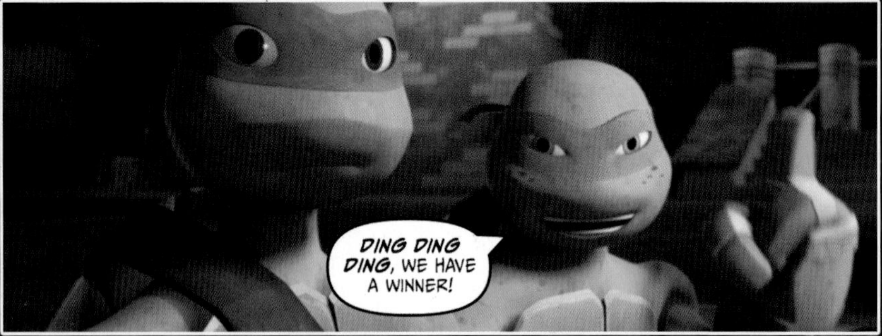
DING DING DING, WE HAVE A WINNER!
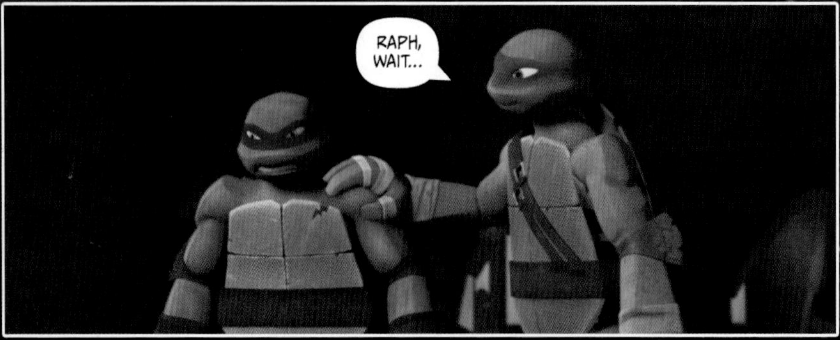
RAPH, WAIT...
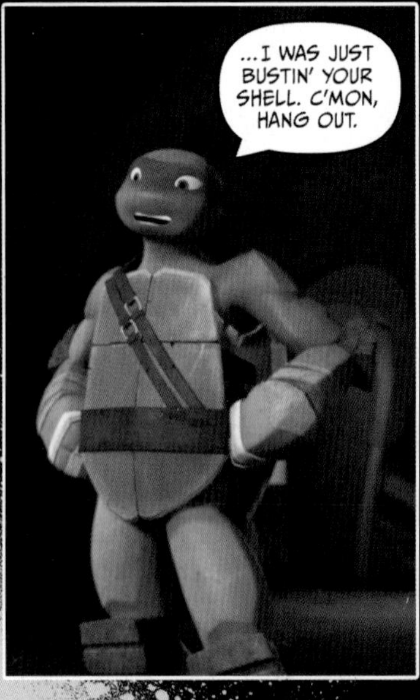
...I WAS JUST BUSTIN' YOUR SHELL. C'MON, HANG OUT.
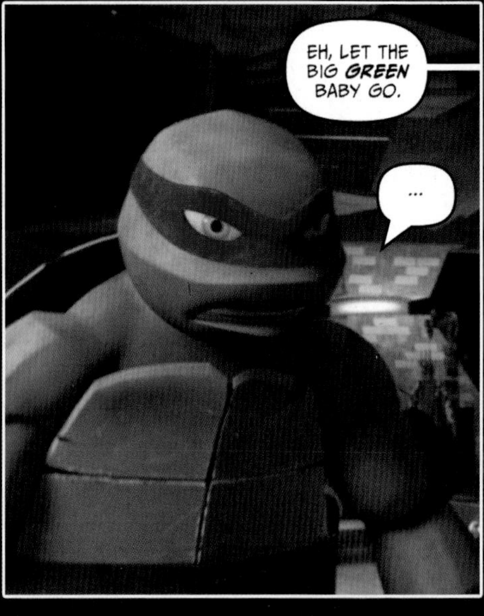
EH, LET THE BIG GREEN BABY GO.
...

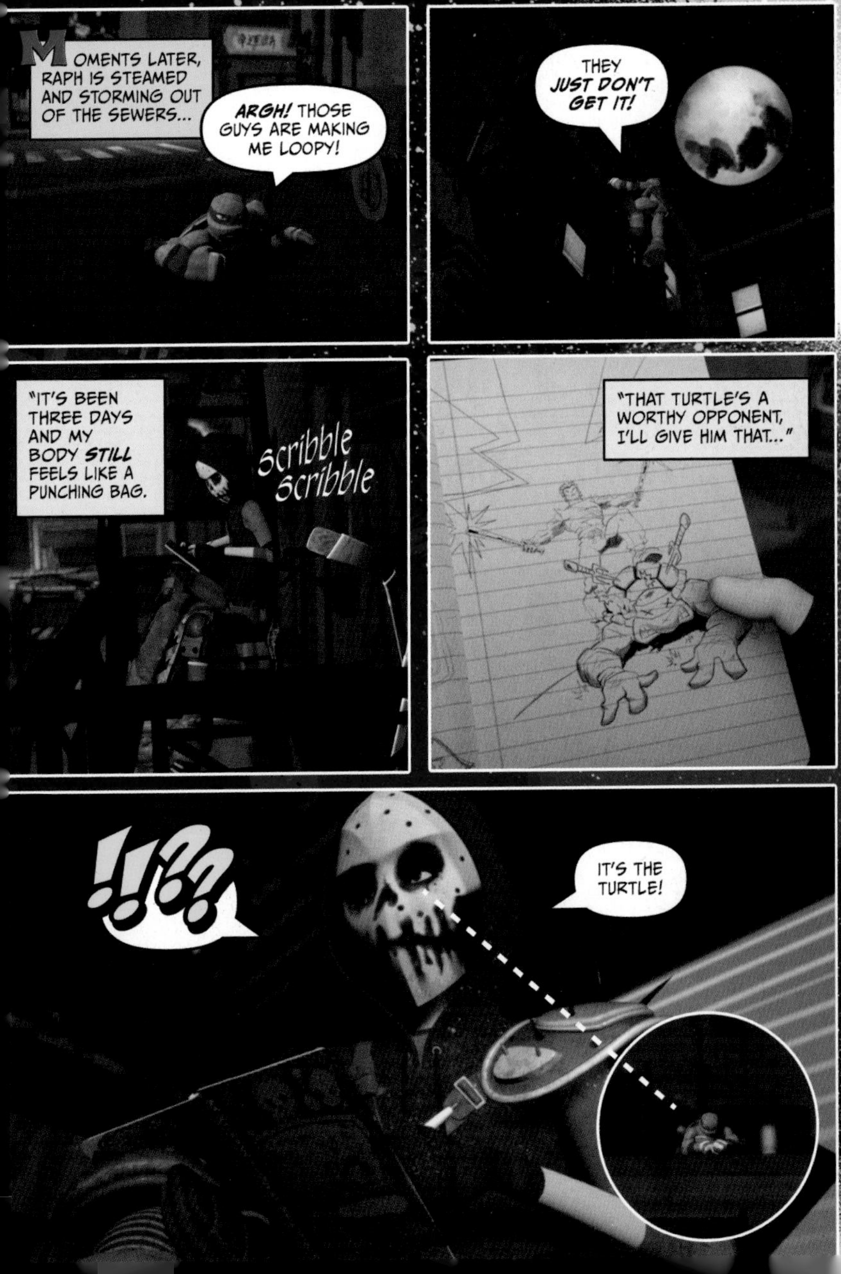
MOMENTS LATER, RAPH IS STEAMED AND STORMING OUT OF THE SEWERS...
ARGH! THOSE GUYS ARE MAKING ME LOOPY!
THEY JUST DON'T GET IT!
"IT'S BEEN THREE DAYS AND MY BODY STILL FEELS LIKE A PUNCHING BAG.
Scribble Scribble
"THAT TURTLE'S A WORTHY OPPONENT, I'LL GIVE HIM THAT..."
!!??
IT'S THE TURTLE!

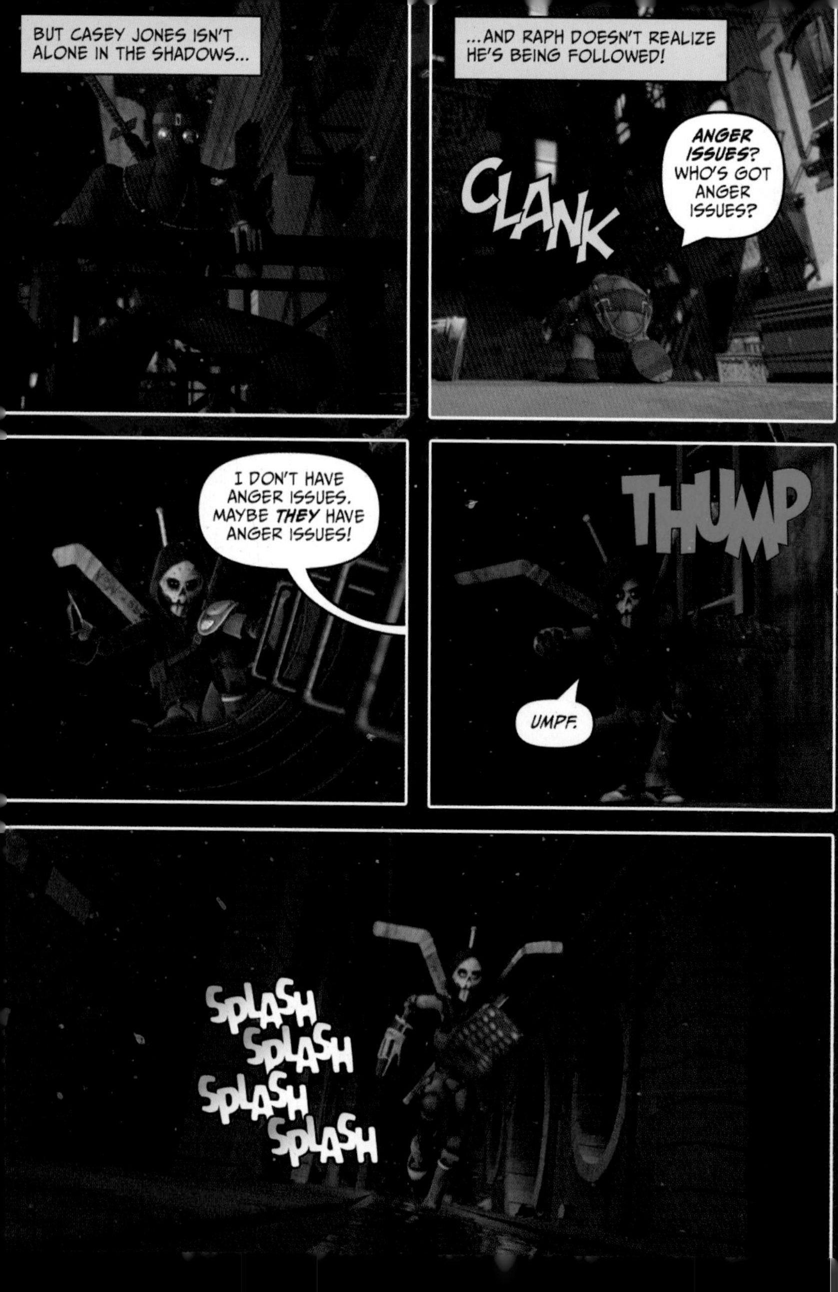
BUT CASEY JONES ISN'T ALONE IN THE SHADOWS...
...AND RAPH DOESN'T REALIZE HE'S BEING FOLLOWED!
CLANK
ANGER ISSUES? WHO'S GOT ANGER ISSUES?
I DON'T HAVE ANGER ISSUES. MAYBE THEY HAVE ANGER ISSUES!
THUMP
UMPF.
SPLASH
SPLASH
SPLASH
SPLASH

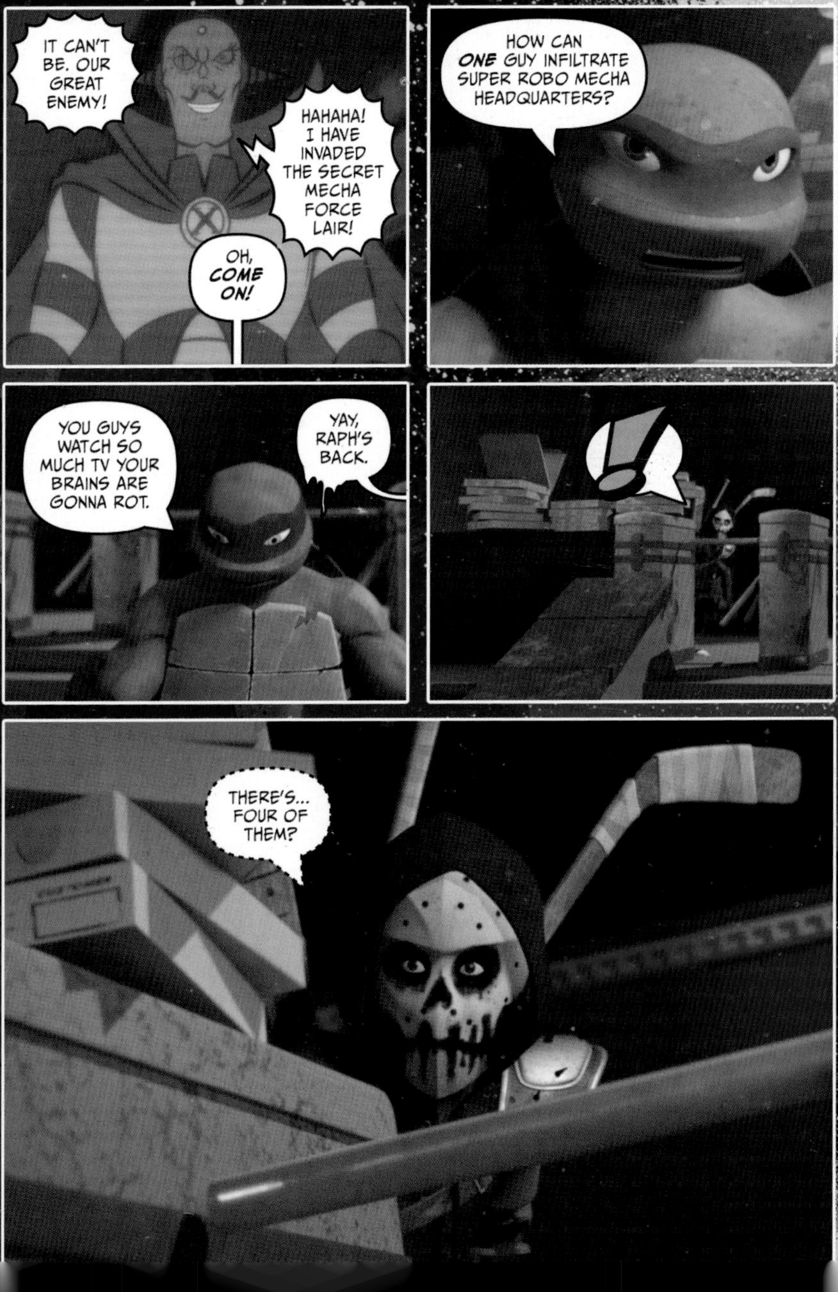

IT CAN'T BE. OUR GREAT ENEMY!
HAHAHA! I HAVE INVADED THE SECRET MECHA FORCE LAIR!
OH, *COME ON!*
HOW CAN *ONE* GUY INFILTRATE SUPER ROBO MECHA HEADQUARTERS?
YOU GUYS WATCH SO MUCH TV YOUR BRAINS ARE GONNA ROT.
YAY, RAPH'S BACK.
THERE'S... FOUR OF THEM?

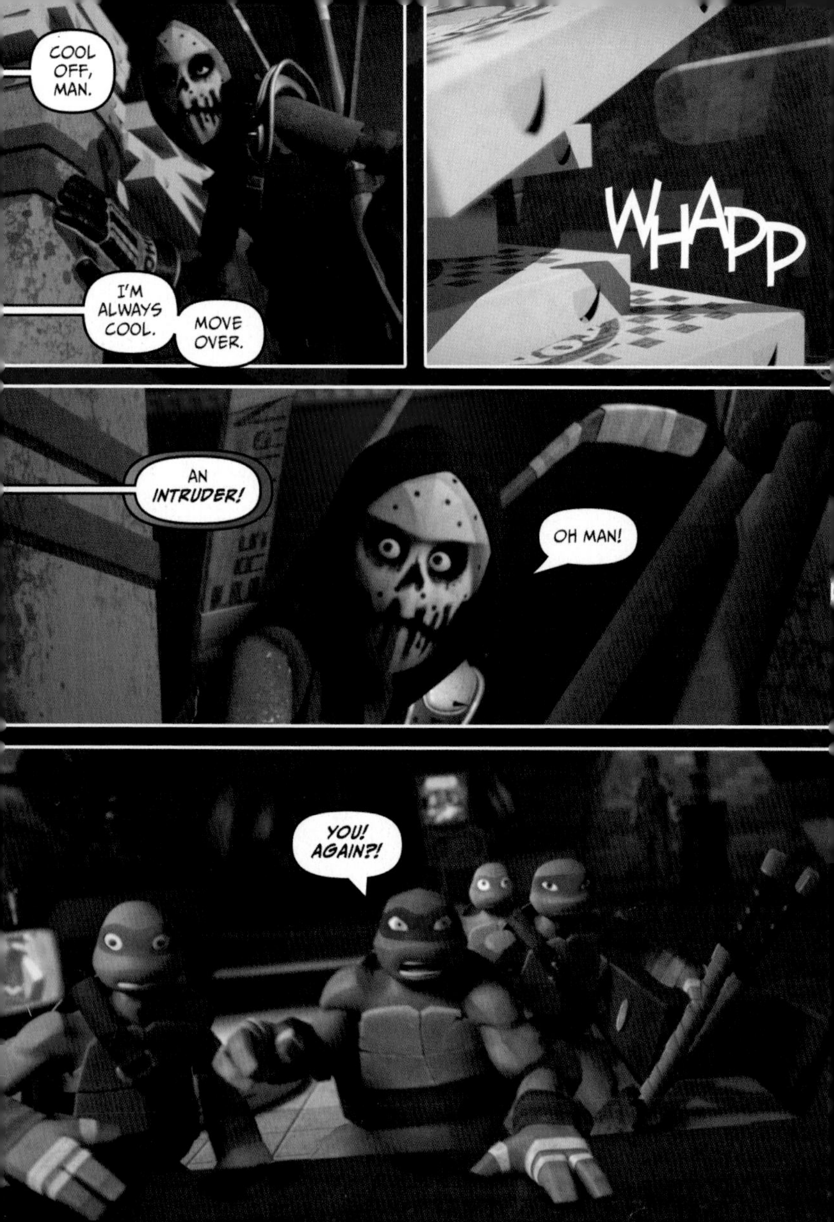

COOL OFF, MAN.
I'M ALWAYS COOL.
MOVE OVER.
WHAPP
AN INTRUDER!
OH MAN!
YOU! AGAIN?!

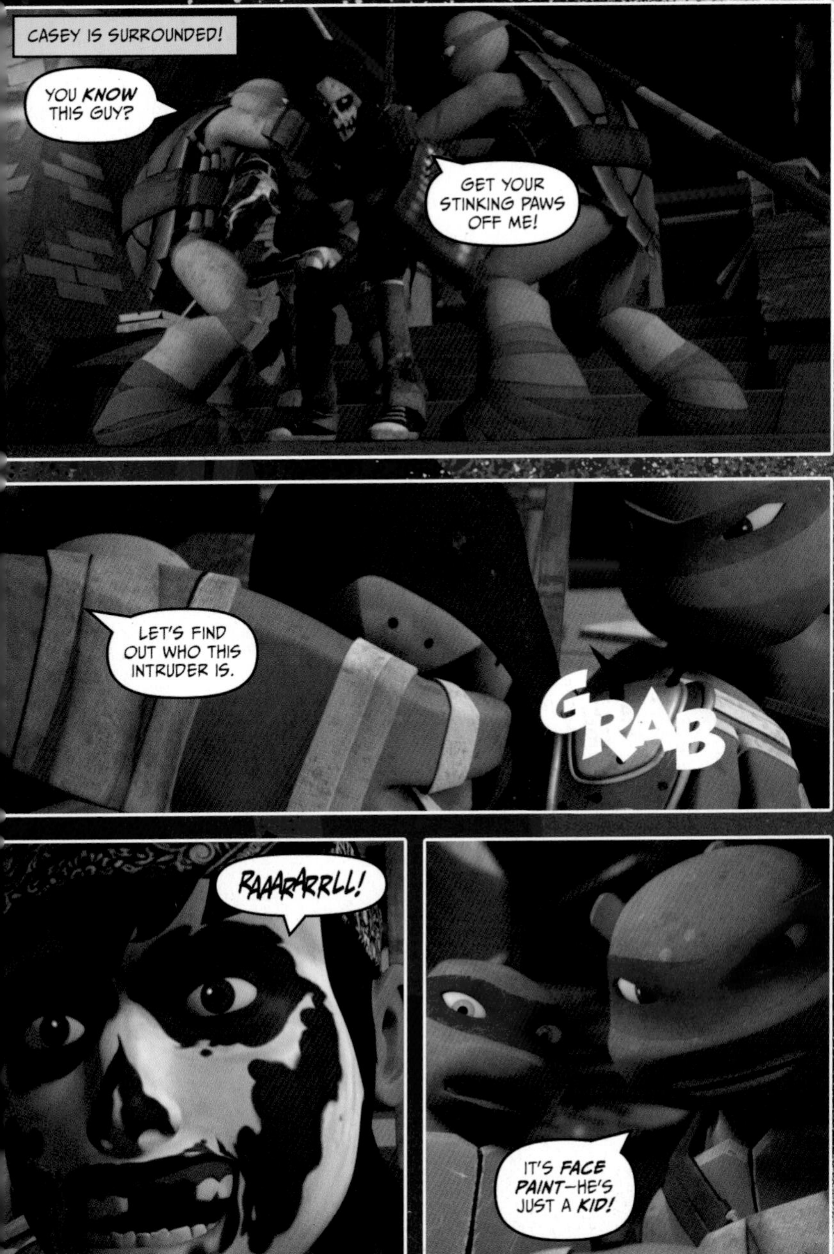
CASEY IS SURROUNDED!
YOU KNOW THIS GUY?
GET YOUR STINKING PAWS OFF ME!
LET'S FIND OUT WHO THIS INTRUDER IS.
GRAB
RAAARARRLL!
IT'S FACE PAINT—HE'S JUST A KID!

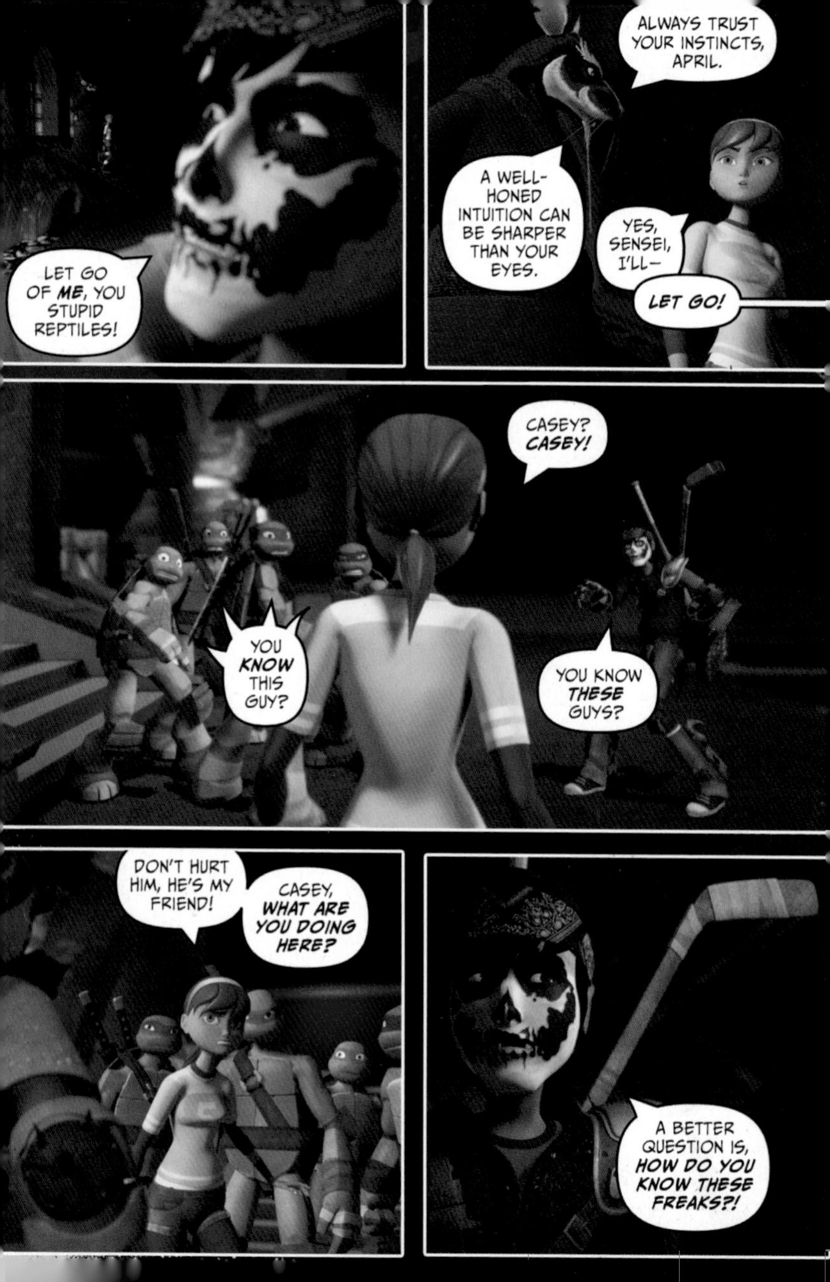
LET GO OF ME, YOU STUPID REPTILES!
ALWAYS TRUST YOUR INSTINCTS, APRIL.
A WELL-HONED INTUITION CAN BE SHARPER THAN YOUR EYES.
YES, SENSEI, I'LL—
LET GO!
CASEY? CASEY!
YOU KNOW THIS GUY?
YOU KNOW THESE GUYS?
DON'T HURT HIM, HE'S MY FRIEND!
CASEY, WHAT ARE YOU DOING HERE?
A BETTER QUESTION IS, HOW DO YOU KNOW THESE FREAKS?!

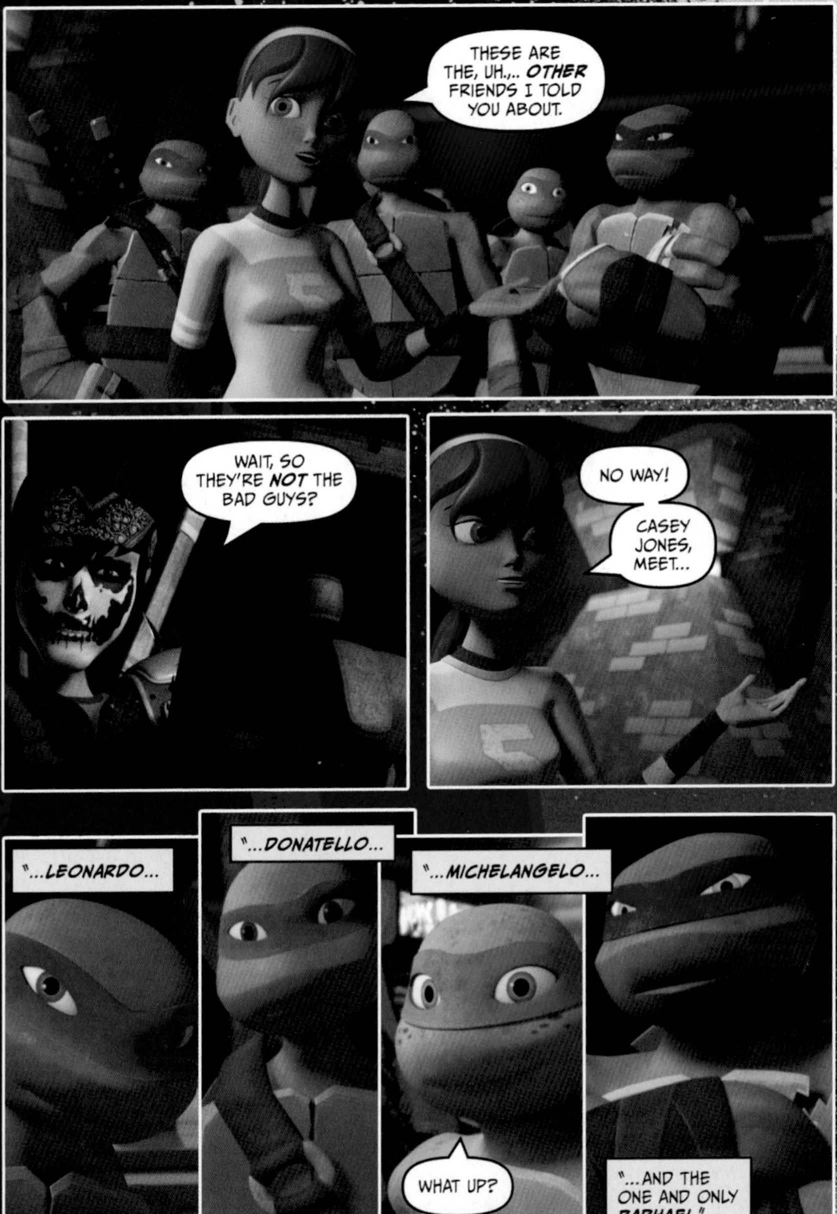
THESE ARE THE, UH.,.. OTHER FRIENDS I TOLD YOU ABOUT.
WAIT, SO THEY'RE NOT THE BAD GUYS?
NO WAY!
CASEY JONES, MEET...
"...LEONARDO...
"...DONATELLO...
"...MICHELANGELO...
WHAT UP?
"...AND THE ONE AND ONLY RAPHAEL."

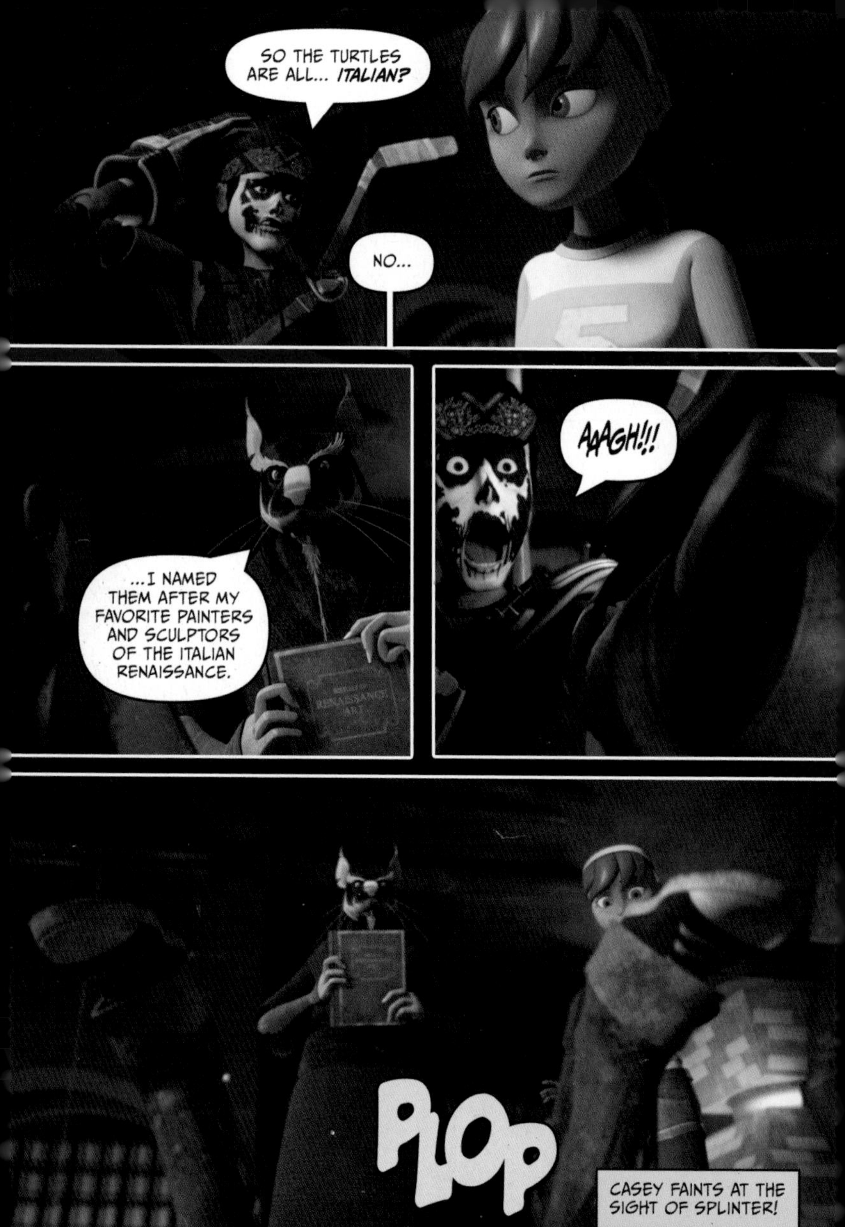
SO THE TURTLES ARE ALL... *ITALIAN?*
NO...
...I NAMED THEM AFTER MY FAVORITE PAINTERS AND SCULPTORS OF THE ITALIAN RENAISSANCE.
AAAGH!!!
PLOP
CASEY FAINTS AT THE SIGHT OF SPLINTER!

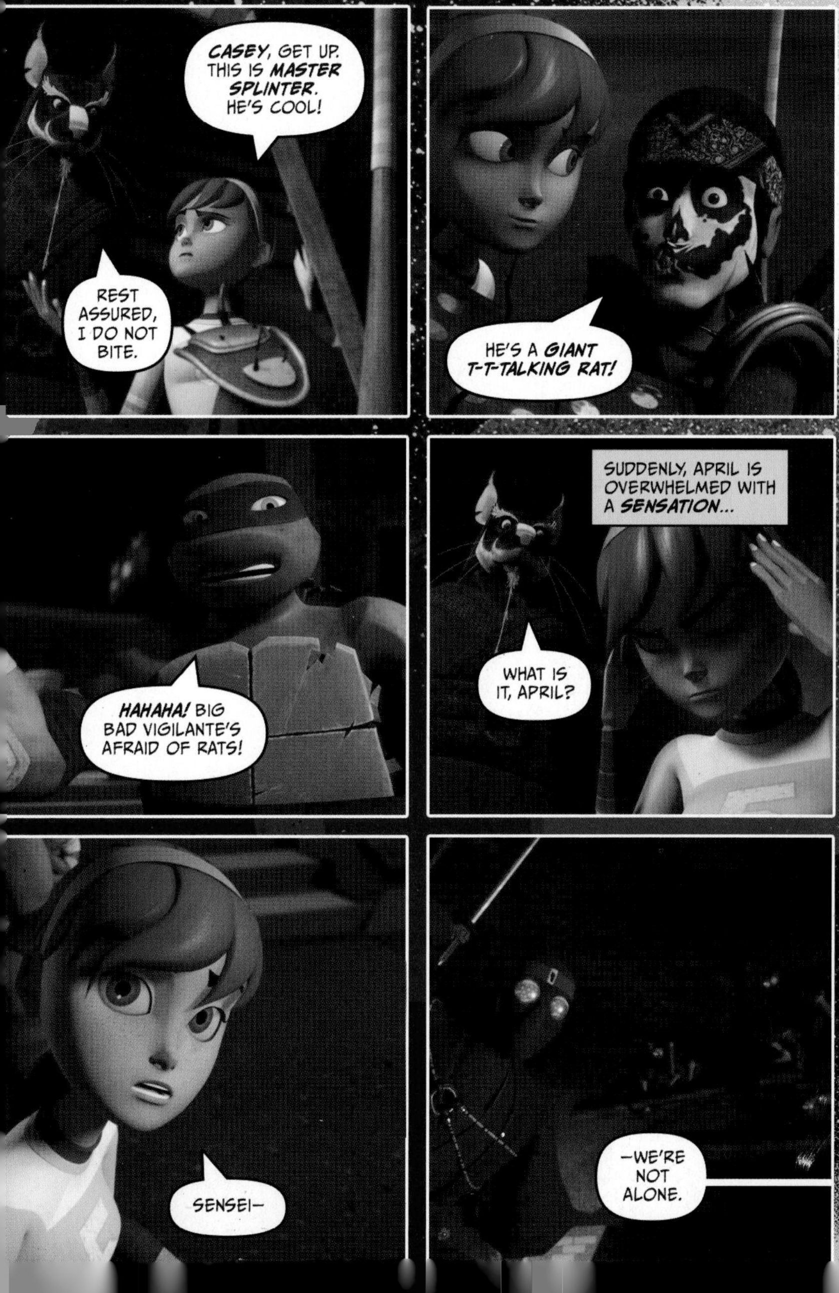
CASEY, GET UP. THIS IS MASTER SPLINTER. HE'S COOL!
REST ASSURED, I DO NOT BITE.
HE'S A GIANT T-T-TALKING RAT!
HAHAHA! BIG BAD VIGILANTE'S AFRAID OF RATS!
SUDDENLY, APRIL IS OVERWHELMED WITH A SENSATION...
WHAT IS IT, APRIL?
SENSEI—
—WE'RE NOT ALONE.

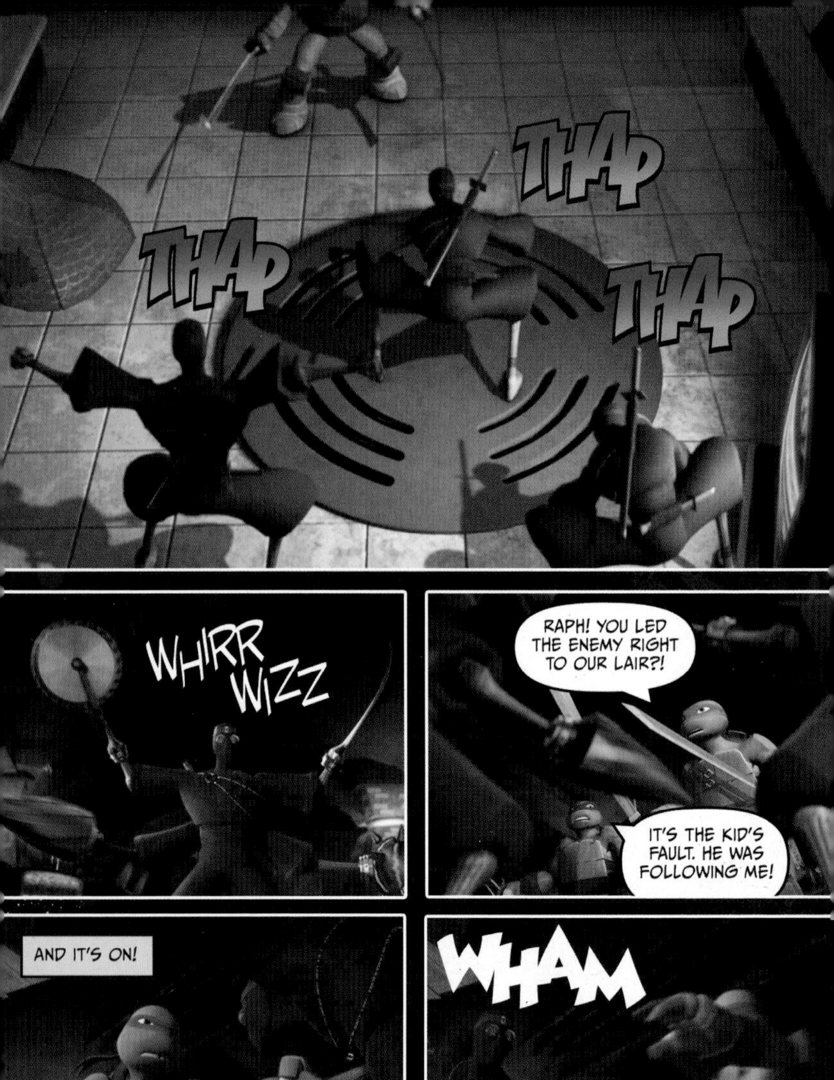
THAP
THAP
THAP
WHIRR
WIZZ
RAPH! YOU LED THE ENEMY RIGHT TO OUR LAIR?!
IT'S THE KID'S FAULT. HE WAS FOLLOWING ME!
AND IT'S ON!
SCHUKK
WHAM
DONNIE TAKES A BRUTAL BLOW!

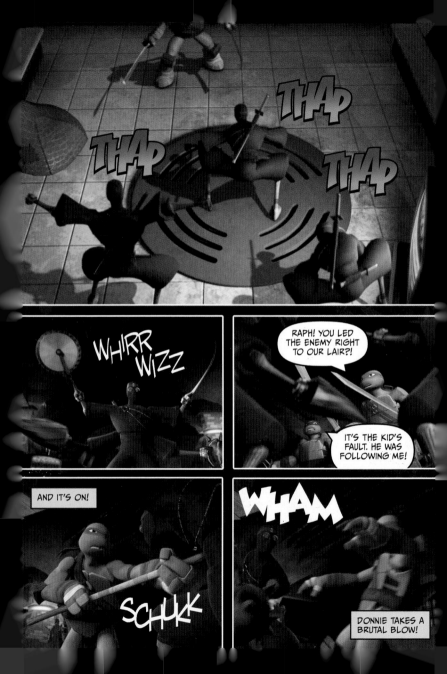

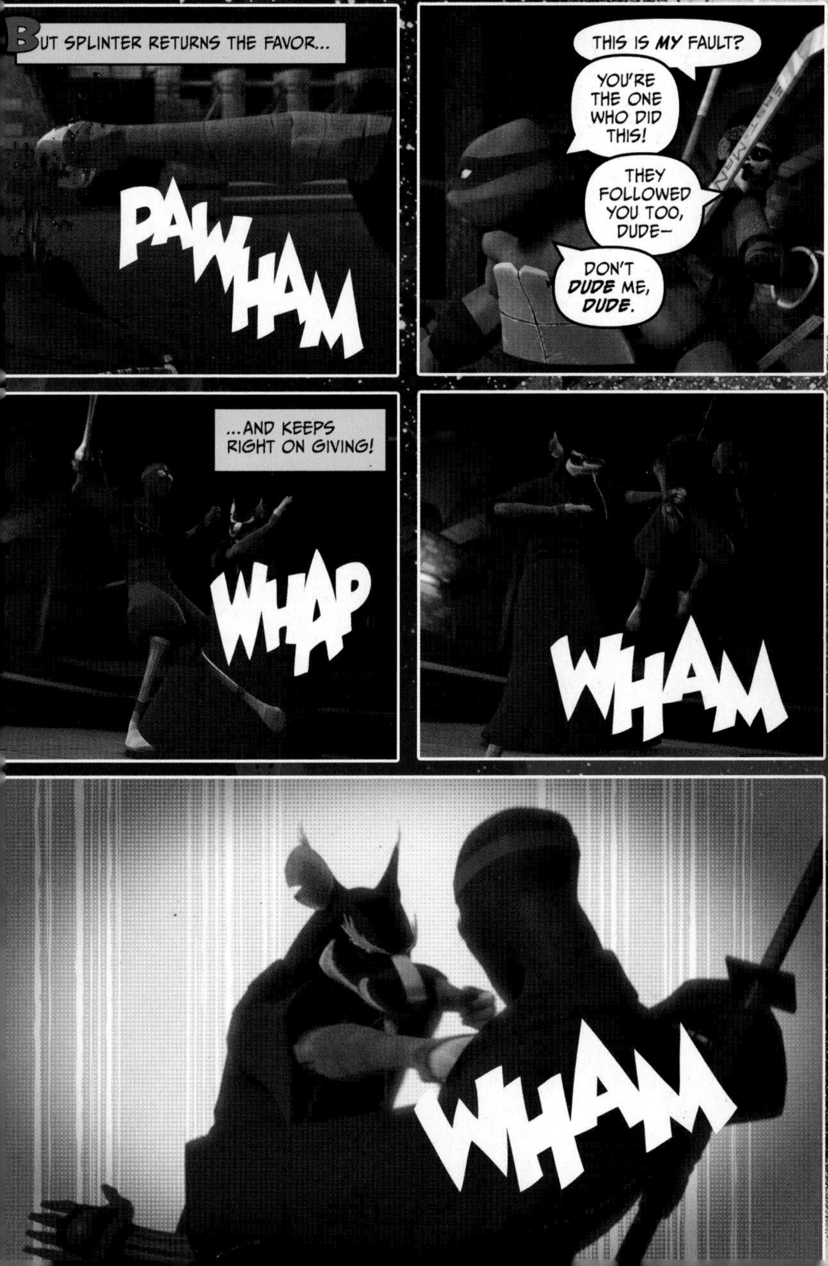
BUT SPLINTER RETURNS THE FAVOR...
PAWHAM
THIS IS *MY* FAULT?
YOU'RE THE ONE WHO DID THIS!
THEY FOLLOWED YOU TOO, DUDE–
DON'T *DUDE* ME, *DUDE*.
...AND KEEPS RIGHT ON GIVING!
WHAP
WHAM
WHAM

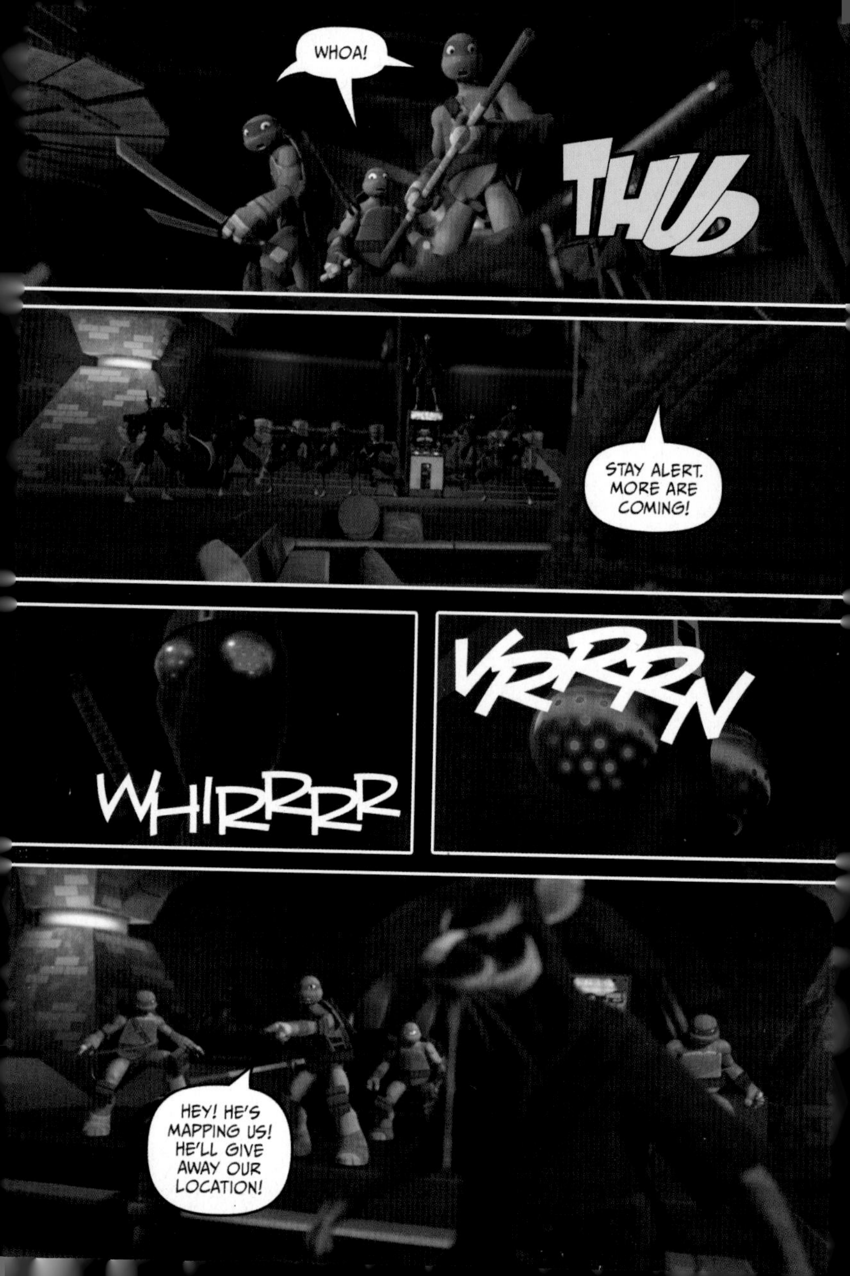
WHOA!
THUD
STAY ALERT. MORE ARE COMING!
WHIRRRR
VRRRN
HEY! HE'S MAPPING US! HE'LL GIVE AWAY OUR LOCATION!

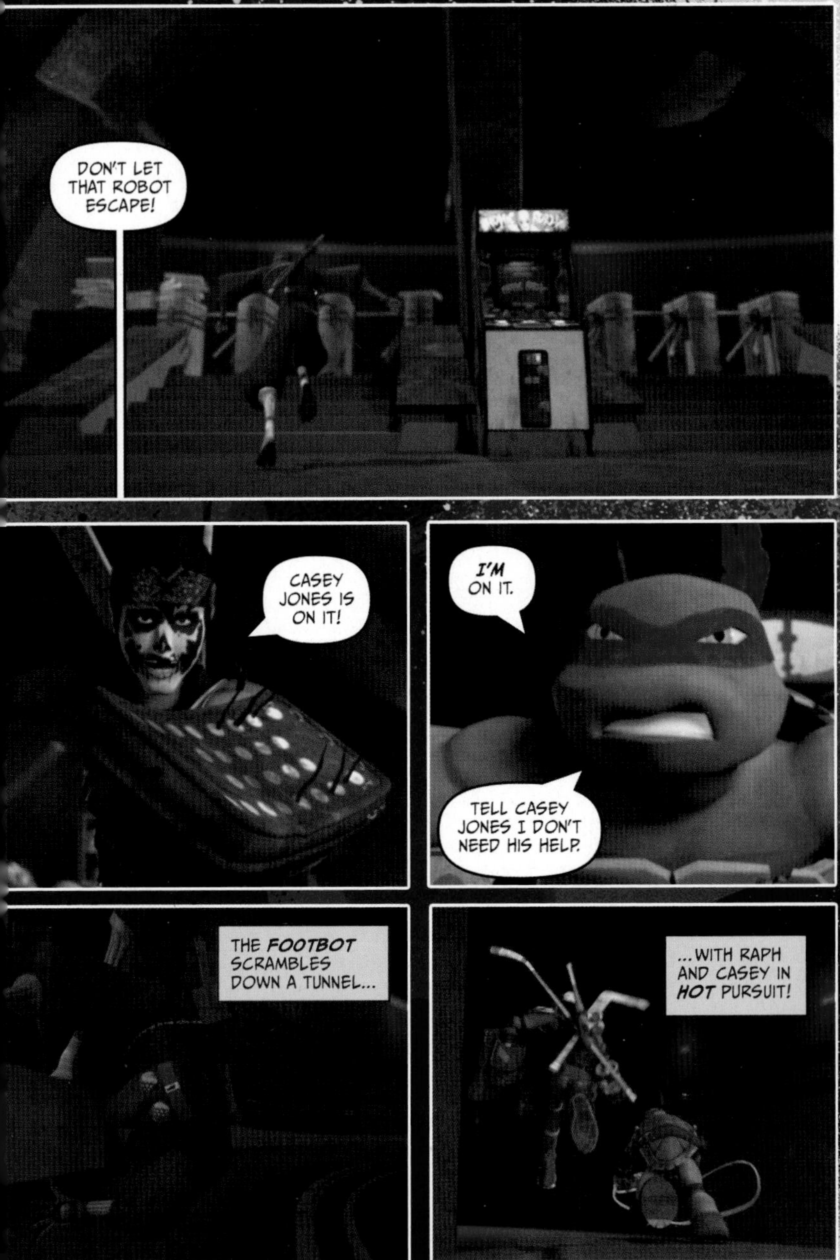
DON'T LET THAT ROBOT ESCAPE!
CASEY JONES IS ON IT!
I'M ON IT.
TELL CASEY JONES I DON'T NEED HIS HELP.
THE ***FOOTBOT*** SCRAMBLES DOWN A TUNNEL...
...WITH RAPH AND CASEY IN ***HOT*** PURSUIT!

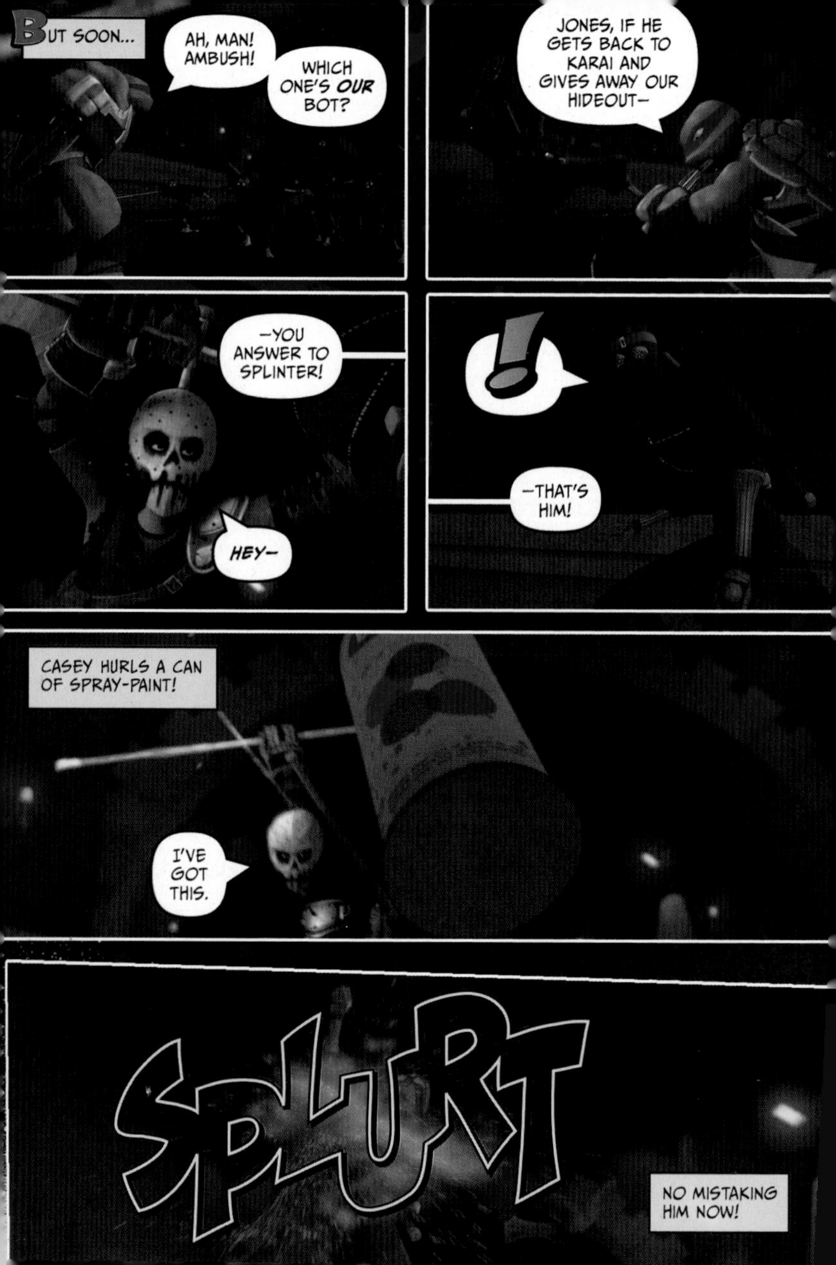

BUT SOON...
AH, MAN! AMBUSH!
WHICH ONE'S *OUR* BOT?
JONES, IF HE GETS BACK TO KARAI AND GIVES AWAY OUR HIDEOUT—
—YOU ANSWER TO SPLINTER!
HEY—
!
—THAT'S HIM!
CASEY HURLS A CAN OF SPRAY-PAINT!
I'VE GOT THIS.
SPLURT
NO MISTAKING HIM NOW!

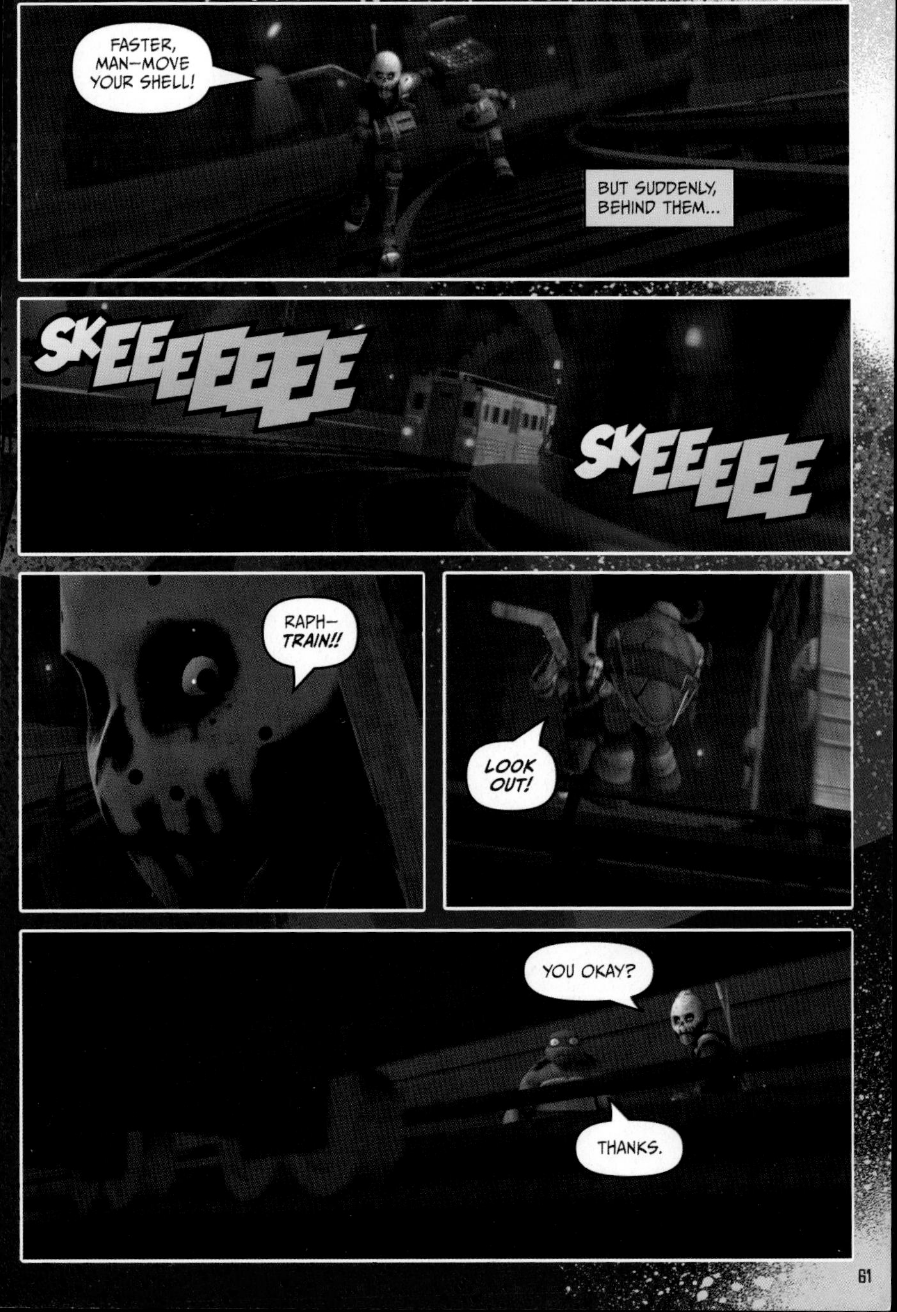
FASTER, MAN—MOVE YOUR SHELL!
BUT SUDDENLY, BEHIND THEM...
SKEEEEEEE
SKEEEEE
RAPH—TRAIN!!
LOOK OUT!
YOU OKAY?
THANKS.

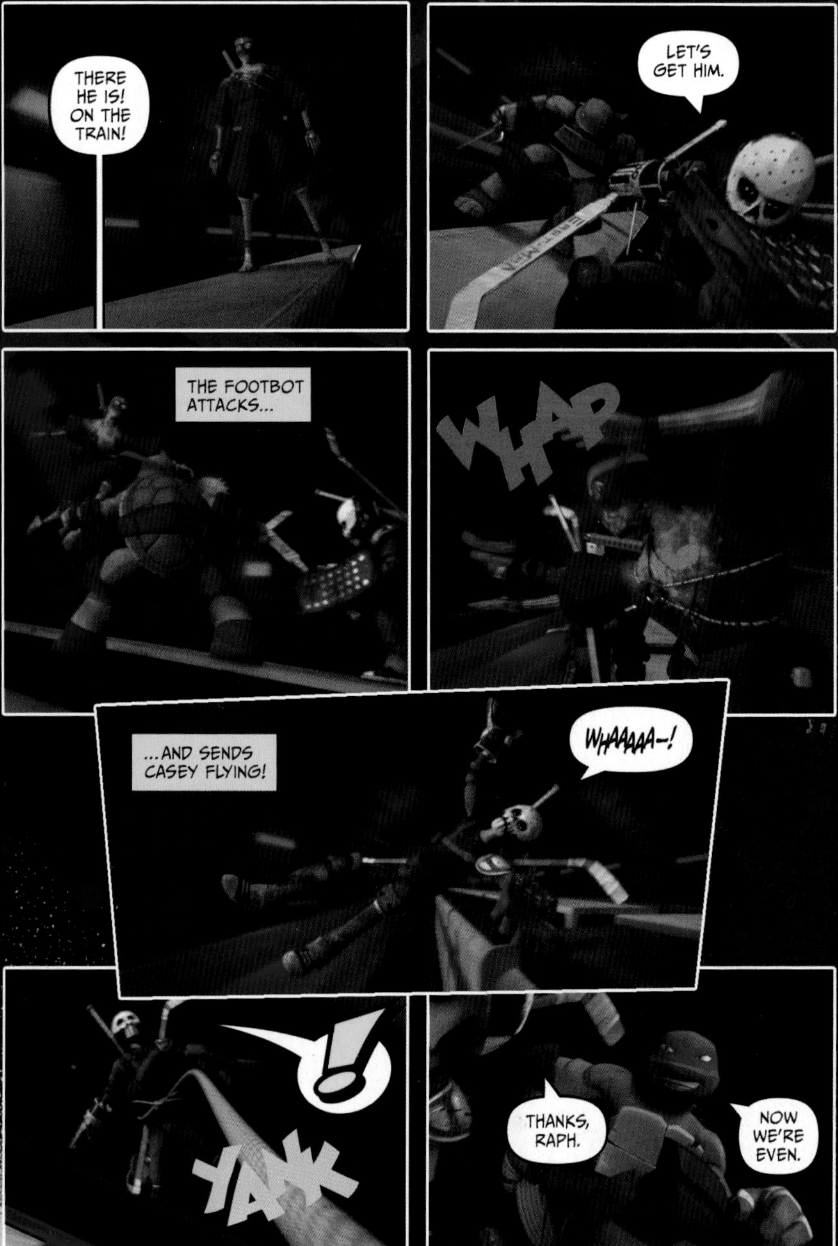
THERE HE IS! ON THE TRAIN!
LET'S GET HIM.
THE FOOTBOT ATTACKS...
WHAP
...AND SENDS CASEY FLYING!
WHAAAAA-!
!
YANK
THANKS, RAPH.
NOW WE'RE EVEN.

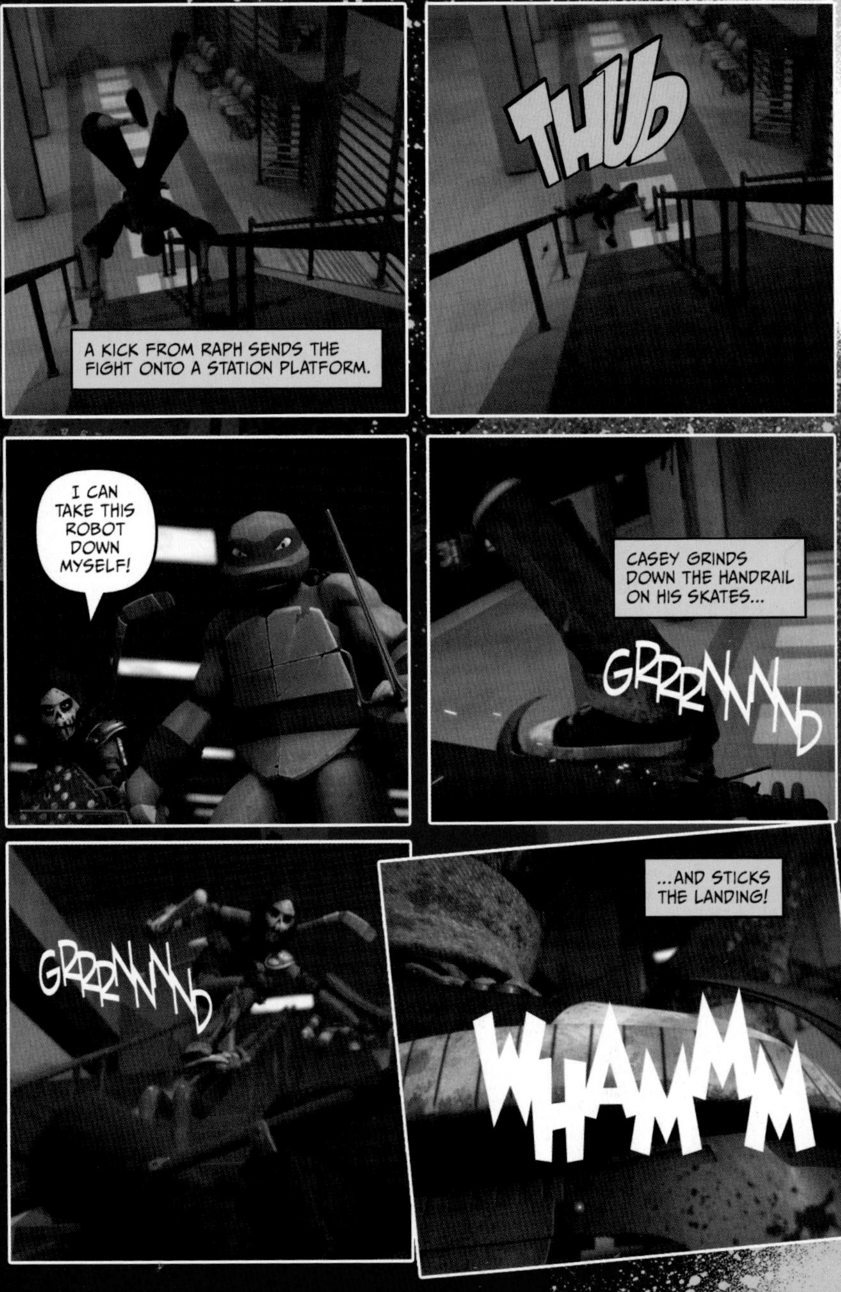
A KICK FROM RAPH SENDS THE FIGHT ONTO A STATION PLATFORM.
THUD
I CAN TAKE THIS ROBOT DOWN MYSELF!
CASEY GRINDS DOWN THE HANDRAIL ON HIS SKATES...
GRRRNNNND
GRRRNNNND
...AND STICKS THE LANDING!
WHAMMM

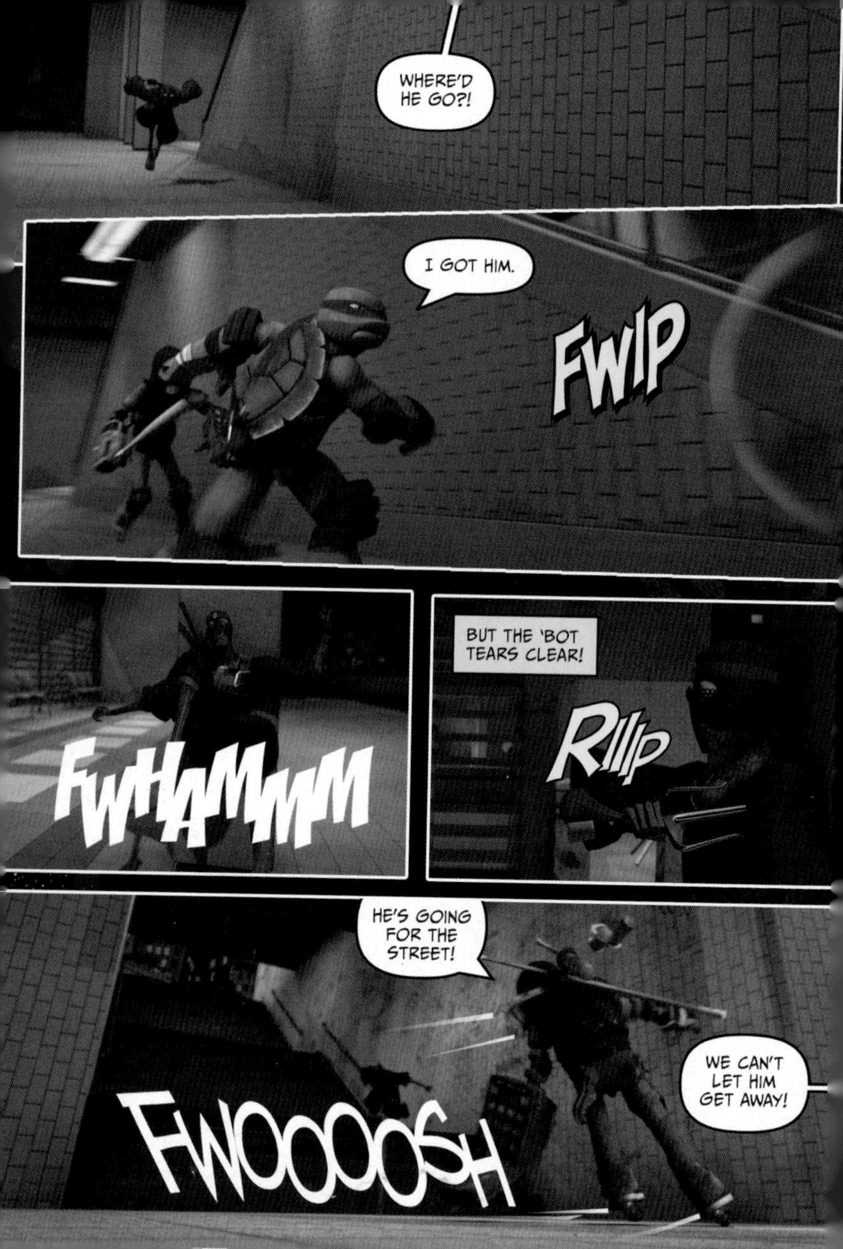
WHERE'D HE GO?!
I GOT HIM.
FWIP
FWHAMMM
BUT THE 'BOT TEARS CLEAR!
RIIP
HE'S GOING FOR THE STREET!
WE CAN'T LET HIM GET AWAY!
FWOOOSH

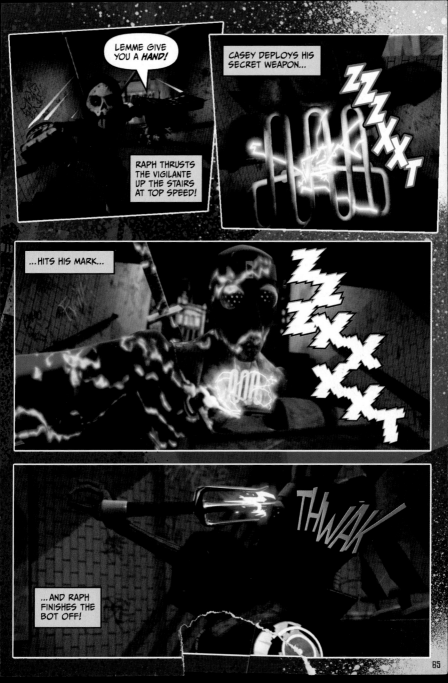

LEMME GIVE YOU A *HAND!*

CASEY DEPLOYS HIS SECRET WEAPON...

RAPH THRUSTS THE VIGILANTE UP THE STAIRS AT TOP SPEED!

ZZZXXT

...HITS HIS MARK...

ZZZXXXT

THWAK

...AND RAPH FINISHES THE BOT OFF!

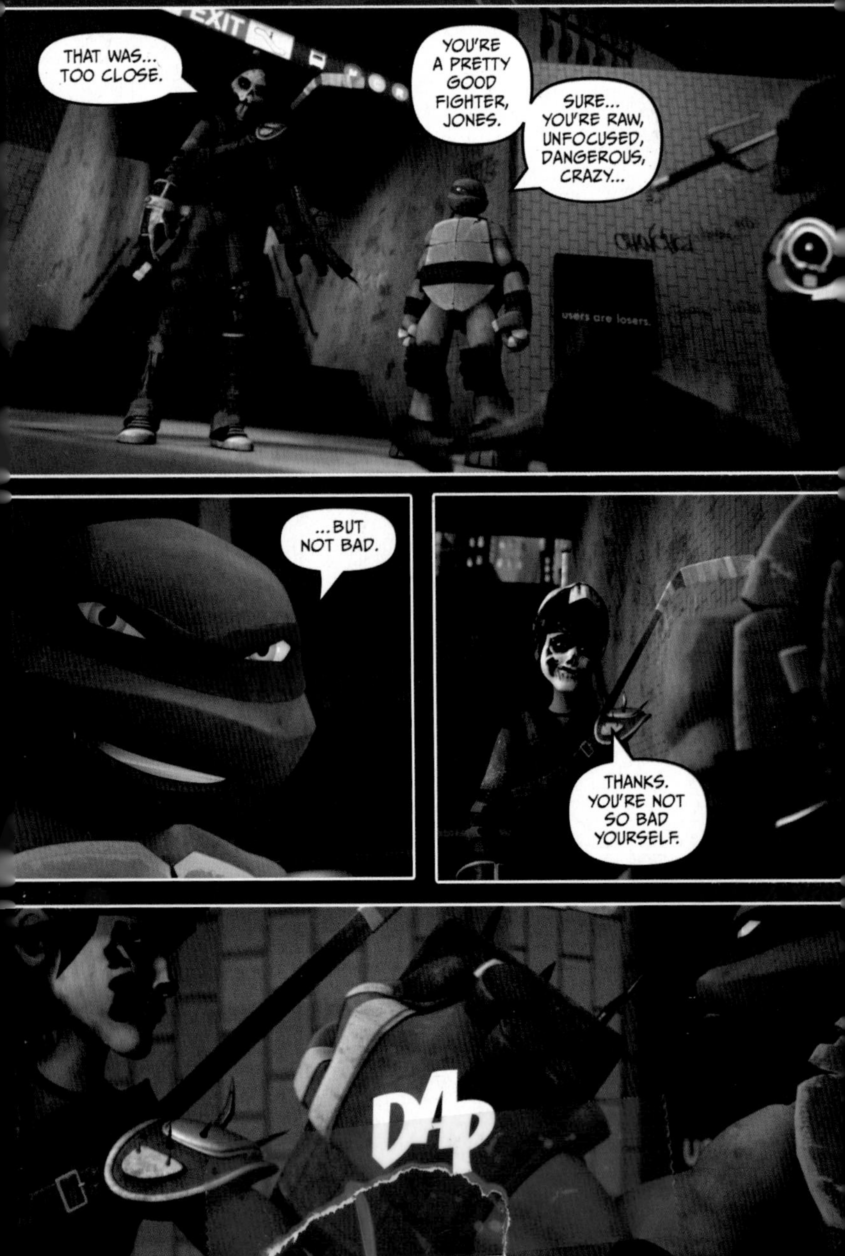

EXIT
THAT WAS... TOO CLOSE.
YOU'RE A PRETTY GOOD FIGHTER, JONES.
SURE... YOU'RE RAW, UNFOCUSED, DANGEROUS, CRAZY...
users are losers.
...BUT NOT BAD.
THANKS. YOU'RE NOT SO BAD YOURSELF.
DAP

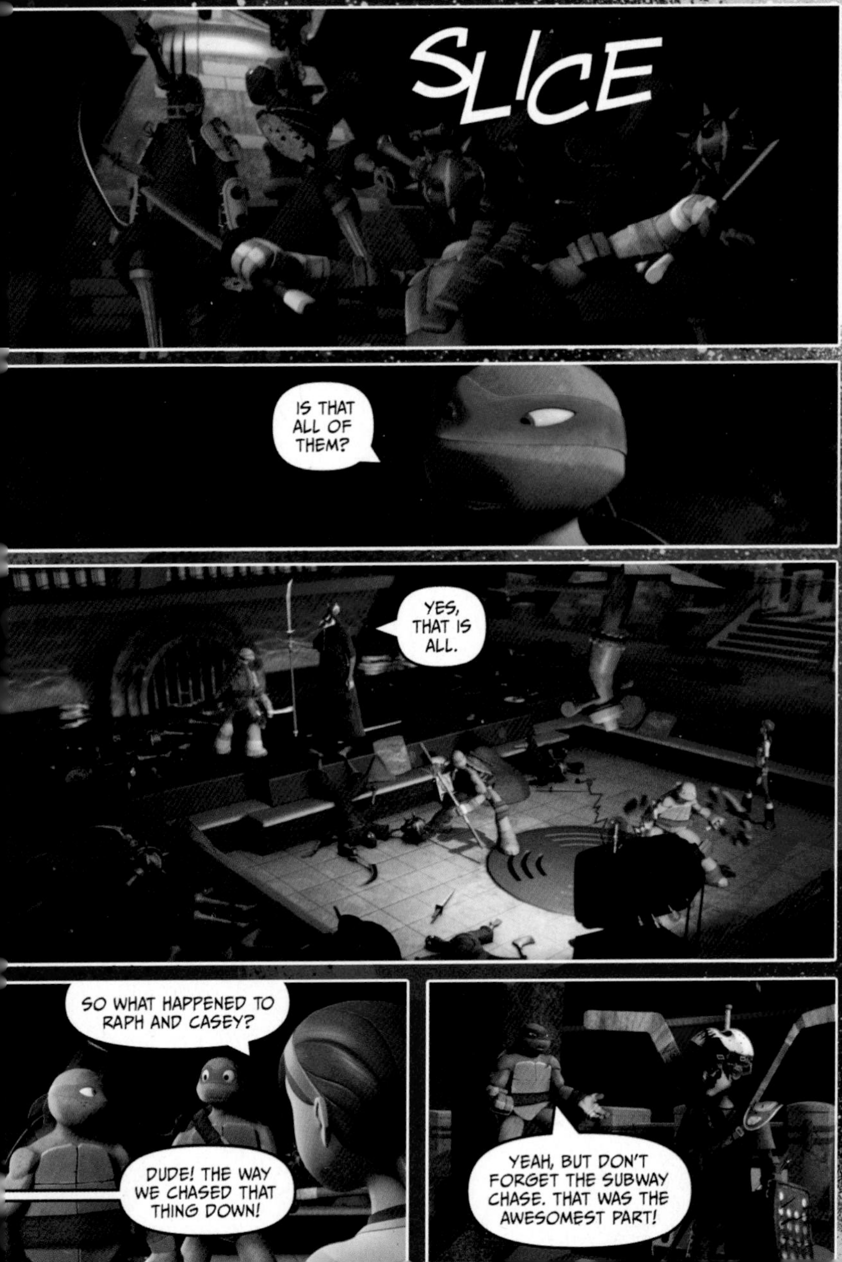
SLICE
IS THAT ALL OF THEM?
YES, THAT IS ALL.
SO WHAT HAPPENED TO RAPH AND CASEY?
DUDE! THE WAY WE CHASED THAT THING DOWN!
YEAH, BUT DON'T FORGET THE SUBWAY CHASE. THAT WAS THE AWESOMEST PART!

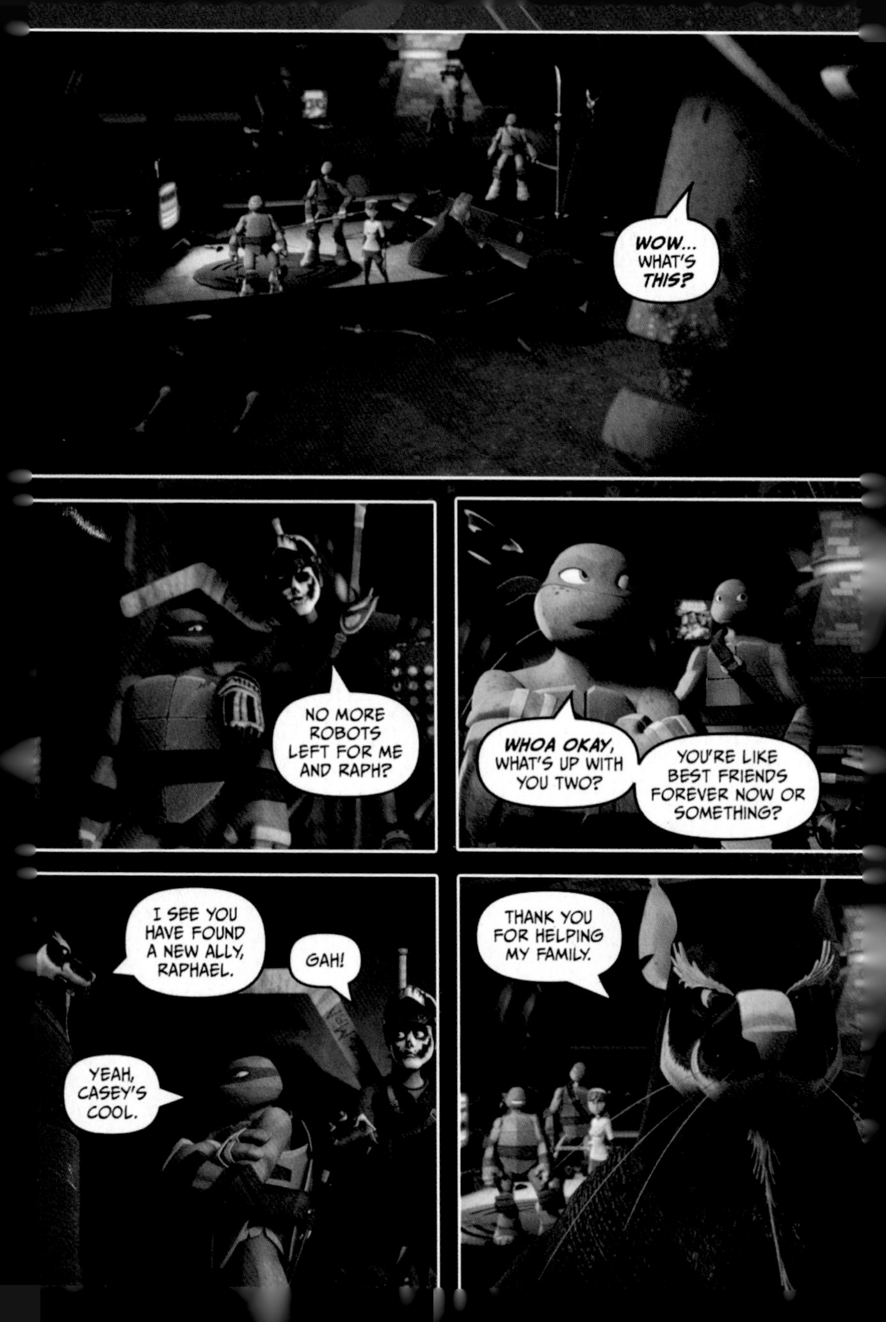
WOW... WHAT'S THIS?
NO MORE ROBOTS LEFT FOR ME AND RAPH?
WHOA OKAY, WHAT'S UP WITH YOU TWO?
YOU'RE LIKE BEST FRIENDS FOREVER NOW OR SOMETHING?
I SEE YOU HAVE FOUND A NEW ALLY, RAPHAEL.
GAH!
YEAH, CASEY'S COOL.
THANK YOU FOR HELPING MY FAMILY.

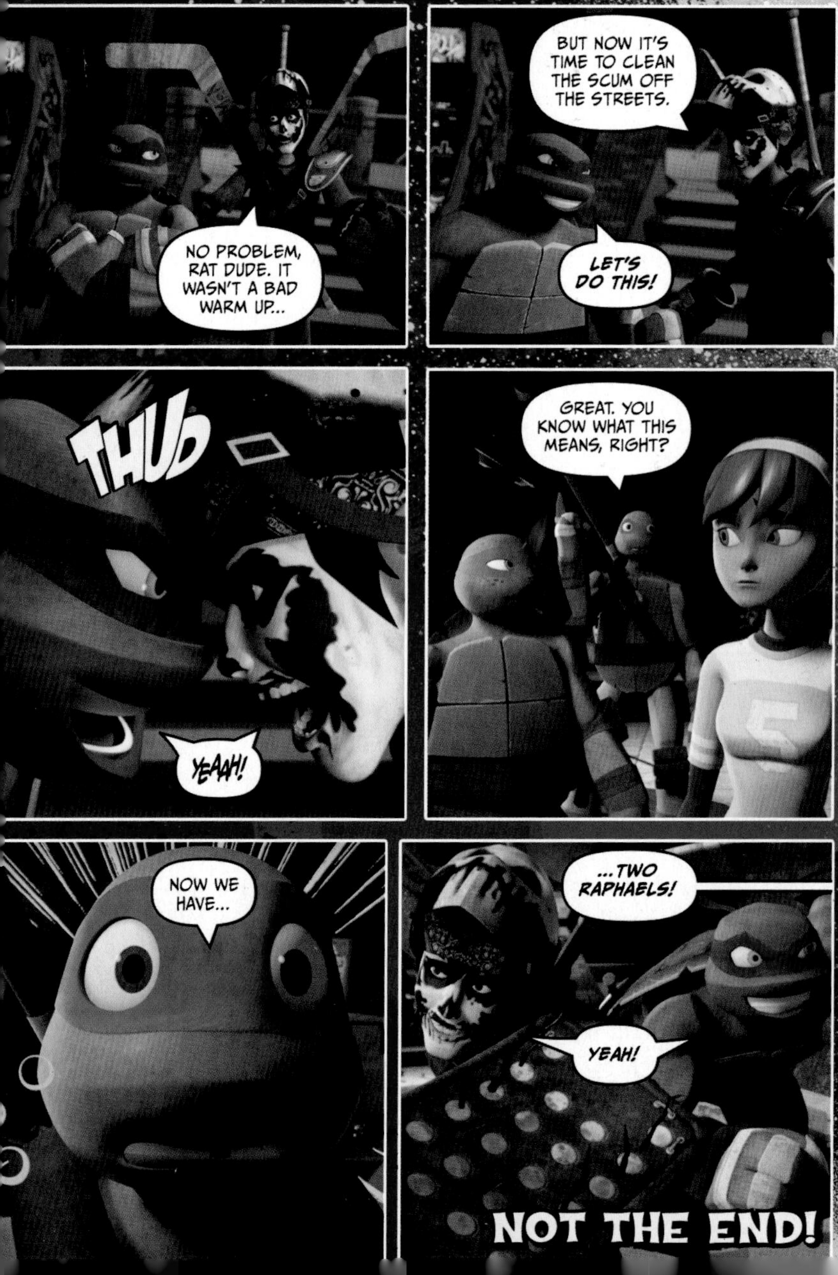
NO PROBLEM, RAT DUDE. IT WASN'T A BAD WARM UP...
BUT NOW IT'S TIME TO CLEAN THE SCUM OFF THE STREETS.
LET'S DO THIS!
THUD
YEAAH!
GREAT. YOU KNOW WHAT THIS MEANS, RIGHT?
NOW WE HAVE...
...TWO RAPHAELS!
YEAH!
NOT THE END!

THE LONELY MUTATION OF BAXTER STOCKMAN

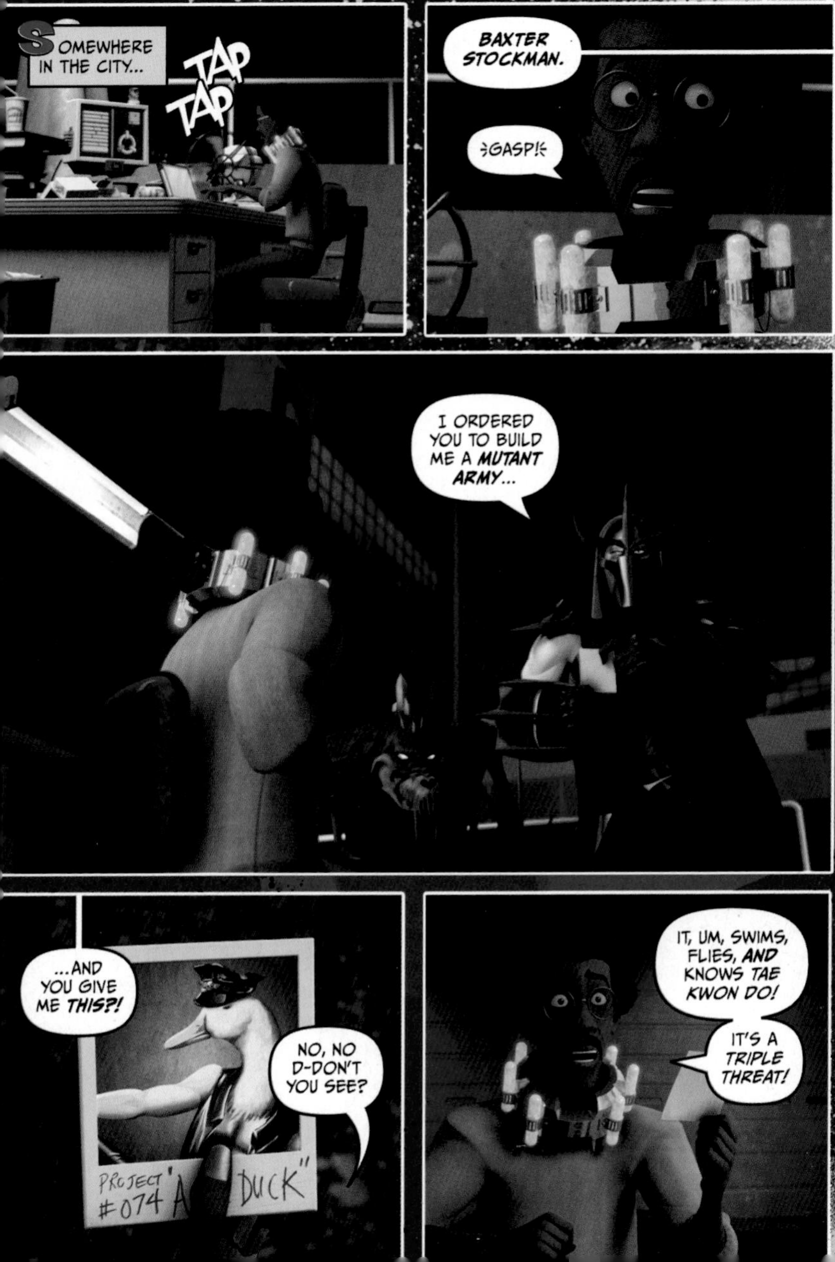
SOMEWHERE IN THE CITY...
TAP TAP
BAXTER STOCKMAN.
GASP!
I ORDERED YOU TO BUILD ME A MUTANT ARMY...
...AND YOU GIVE ME THIS?!
PROJECT #074 "A
DUCK"
NO, NO D-DON'T YOU SEE?
IT, UM, SWIMS, FLIES, AND KNOWS TAE KWON DO!
IT'S A TRIPLE THREAT!

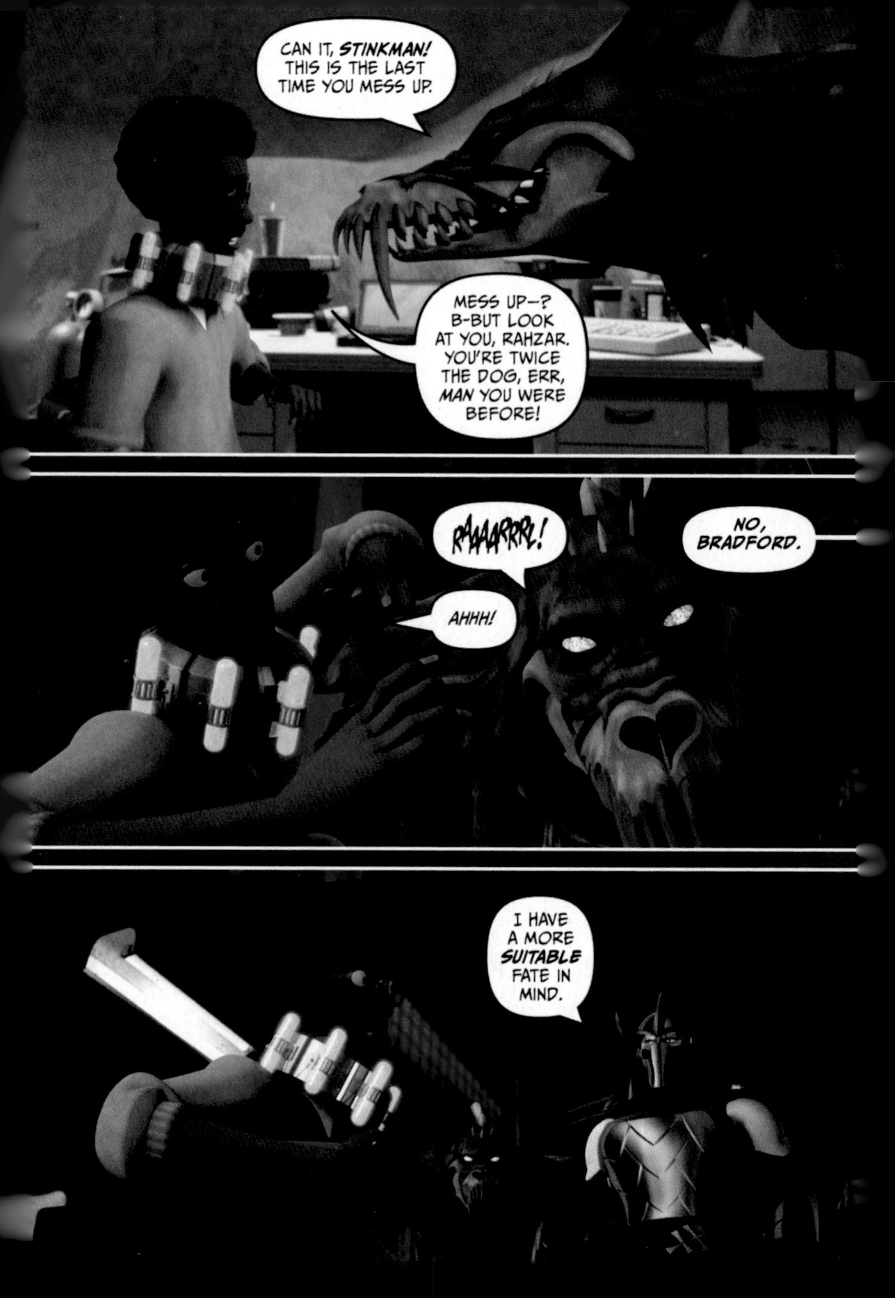
CAN IT, STINKMAN! THIS IS THE LAST TIME YOU MESS UP.
MESS UP—? B-BUT LOOK AT YOU, RAHZAR. YOU'RE TWICE THE DOG, ERR, MAN YOU WERE BEFORE!
RAAAARRRL!
NO, BRADFORD.
AHHH!
I HAVE A MORE SUITABLE FATE IN MIND.

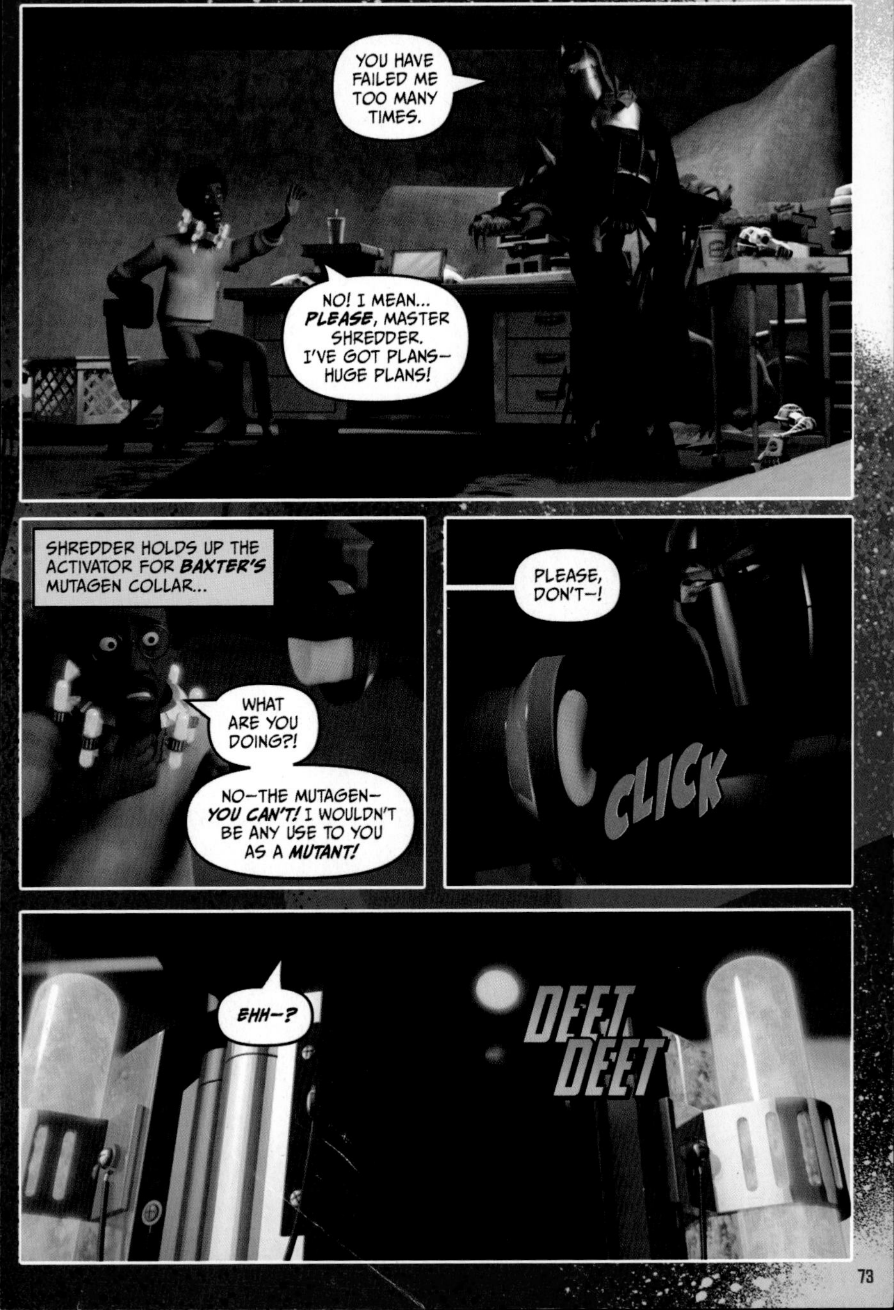
YOU HAVE FAILED ME TOO MANY TIMES.
NO! I MEAN... PLEASE, MASTER SHREDDER. I'VE GOT PLANS—HUGE PLANS!
SHREDDER HOLDS UP THE ACTIVATOR FOR BAXTER'S MUTAGEN COLLAR...
WHAT ARE YOU DOING?!
NO—THE MUTAGEN—YOU CAN'T! I WOULDN'T BE ANY USE TO YOU AS A MUTANT!
PLEASE, DON'T—!
CLICK
EHH—?
DEET DEET

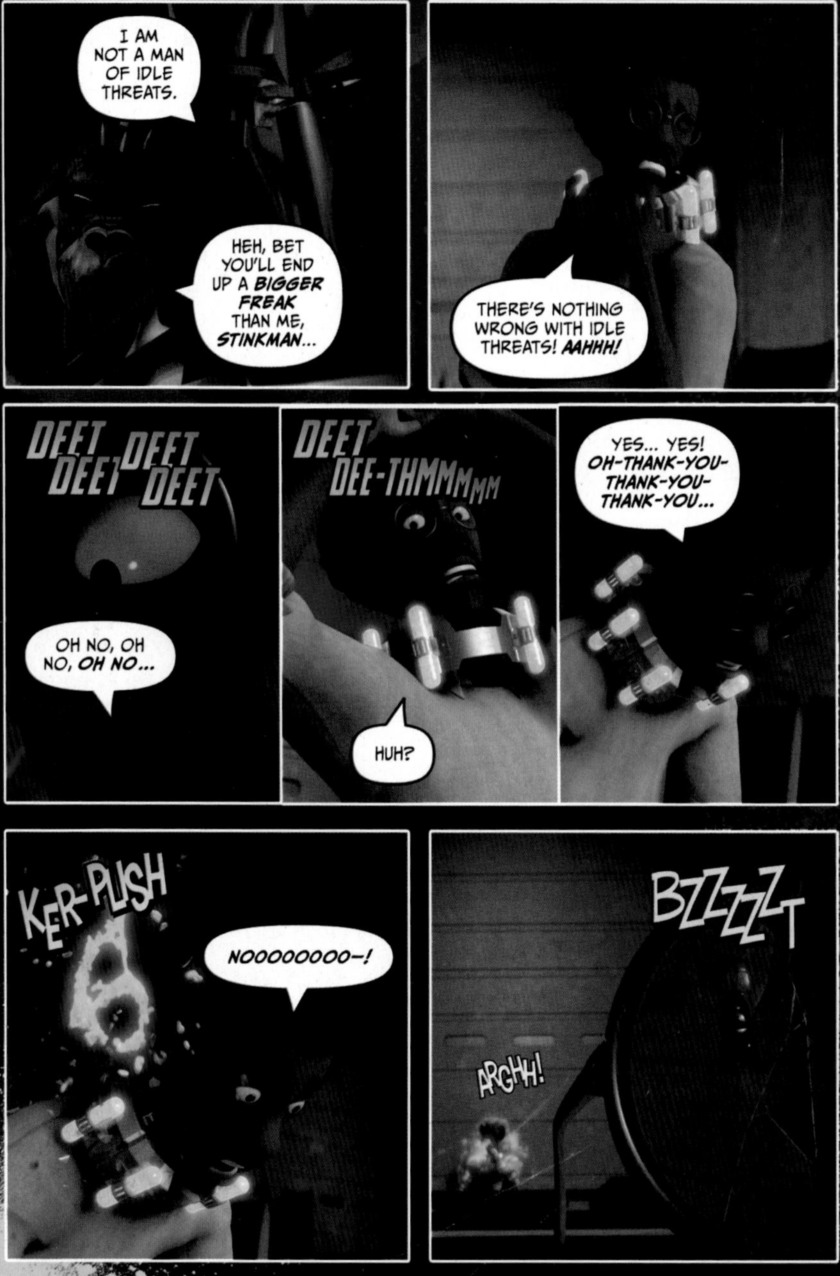
I AM NOT A MAN OF IDLE THREATS.
HEH, BET YOU'LL END UP A ***BIGGER FREAK*** THAN ME, ***STINKMAN***...
THERE'S NOTHING WRONG WITH IDLE THREATS! ***AAHHH!***
DEET DEET DEET DEET
OH NO, OH NO, ***OH NO...***
DEET DEE-THMMMMM
HUH?
YES... YES! ***OH-THANK-YOU-THANK-YOU-THANK-YOU...***
KER-PLUSH
NOOOOOOOO-!
BZZZZZT
ARGHH!

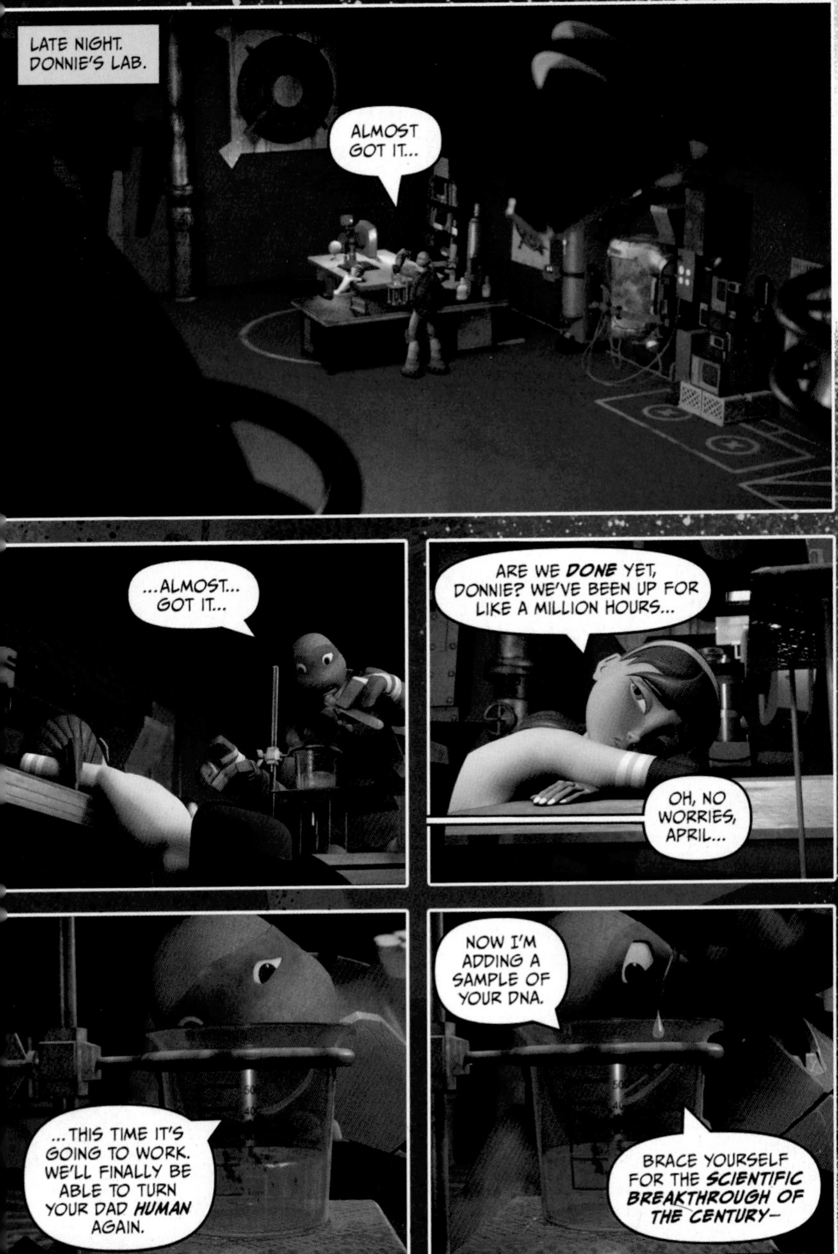
LATE NIGHT. DONNIE'S LAB.
ALMOST GOT IT...
...ALMOST... GOT IT...
ARE WE DONE YET, DONNIE? WE'VE BEEN UP FOR LIKE A MILLION HOURS...
OH, NO WORRIES, APRIL...
...THIS TIME IT'S GOING TO WORK. WE'LL FINALLY BE ABLE TO TURN YOUR DAD HUMAN AGAIN.
NOW I'M ADDING A SAMPLE OF YOUR DNA.
BRACE YOURSELF FOR THE SCIENTIFIC BREAKTHROUGH OF THE CENTURY—

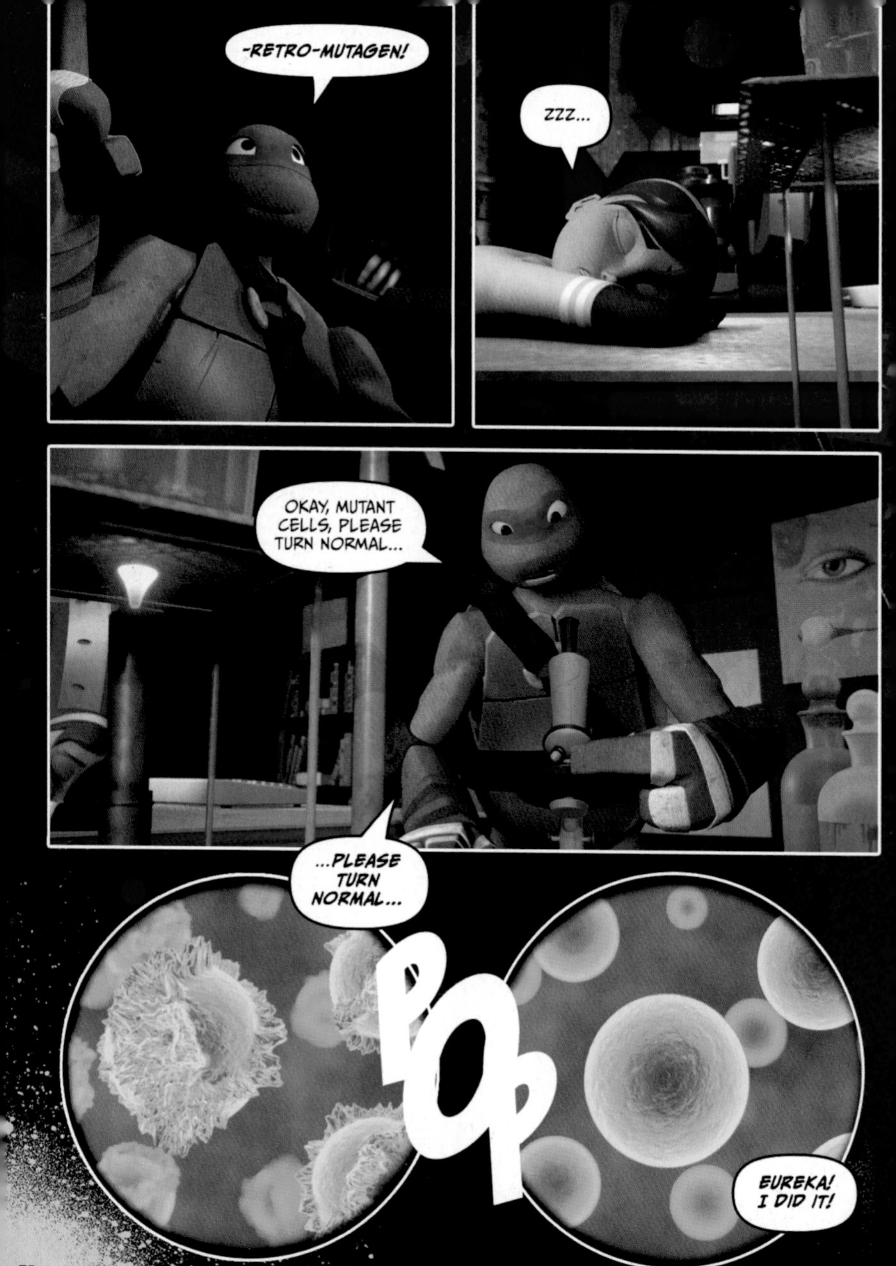
-RETRO-MUTAGEN!
ZZZ...
OKAY, MUTANT CELLS, PLEASE TURN NORMAL...
...PLEASE TURN NORMAL...
POP
EUREKA! I DID IT!

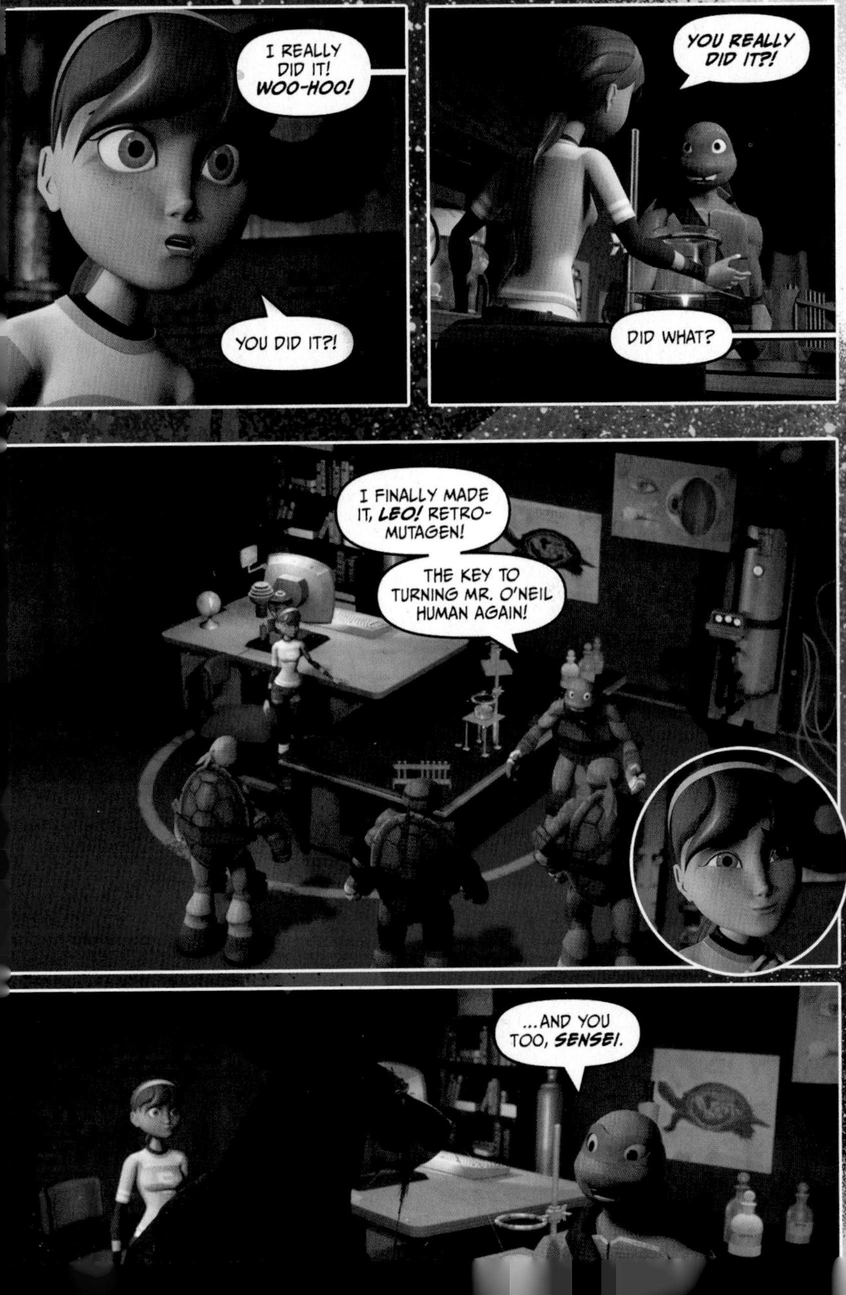
I REALLY DID IT! WOO-HOO!
YOU DID IT?!
YOU REALLY DID IT?!
DID WHAT?
I FINALLY MADE IT, LEO! RETRO-MUTAGEN!
THE KEY TO TURNING MR. O'NEIL HUMAN AGAIN!
...AND YOU TOO, SENSEI.

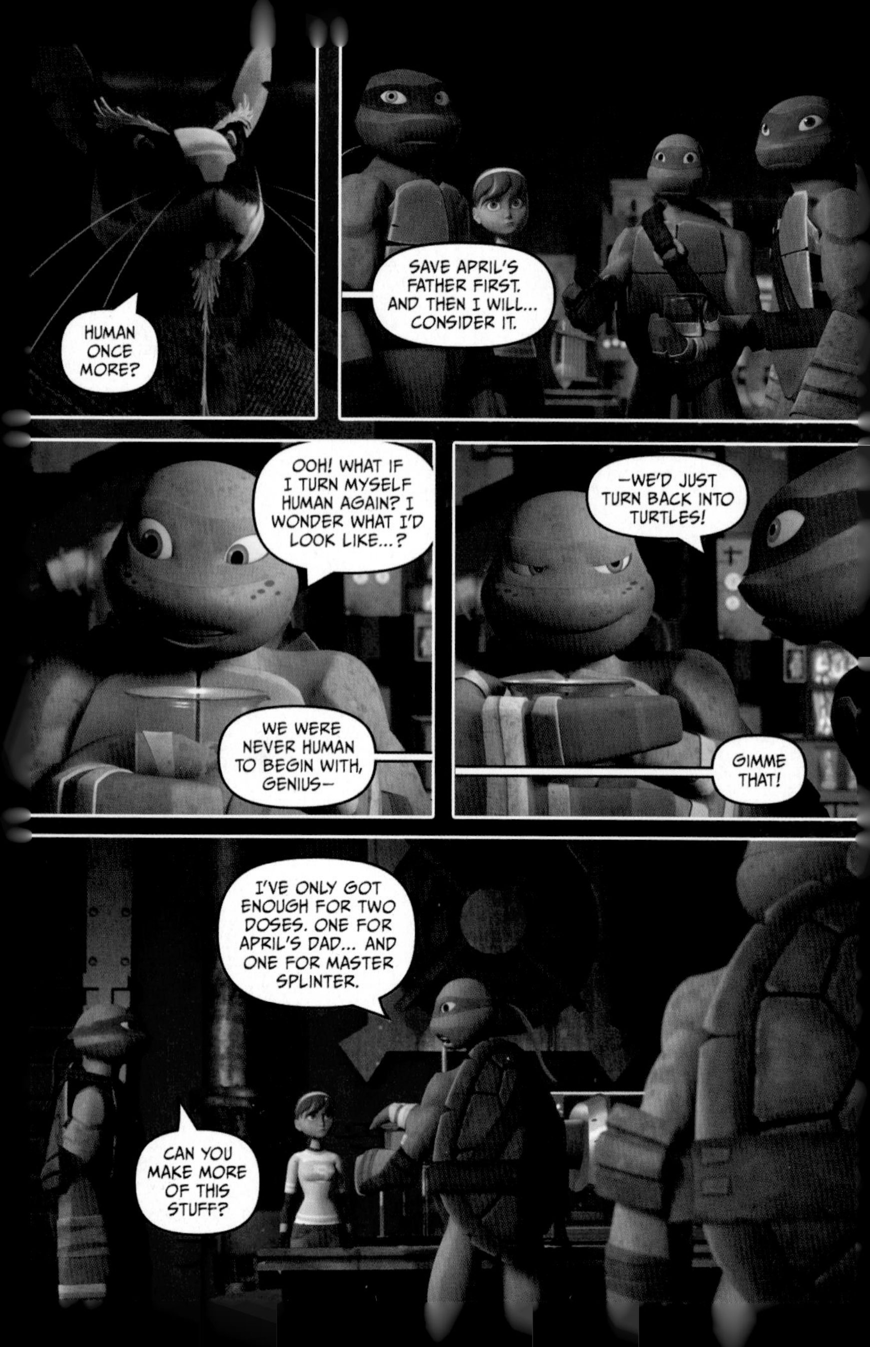
HUMAN ONCE MORE?
SAVE APRIL'S FATHER FIRST. AND THEN I WILL... CONSIDER IT.
OOH! WHAT IF I TURN MYSELF HUMAN AGAIN? I WONDER WHAT I'D LOOK LIKE...?
WE WERE NEVER HUMAN TO BEGIN WITH, GENIUS—
—WE'D JUST TURN BACK INTO TURTLES!
GIMME THAT!
I'VE ONLY GOT ENOUGH FOR TWO DOSES. ONE FOR APRIL'S DAD... AND ONE FOR MASTER SPLINTER.
CAN YOU MAKE MORE OF THIS STUFF?

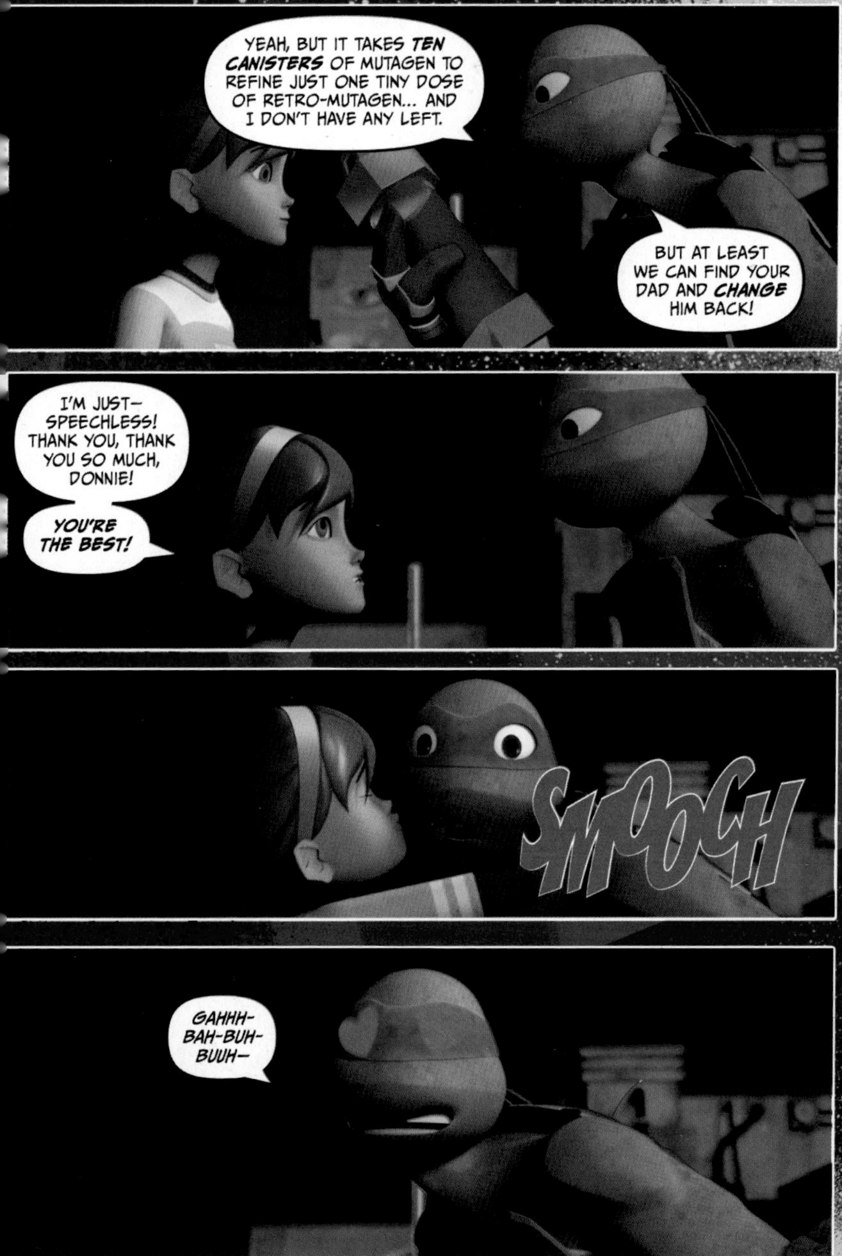
YEAH, BUT IT TAKES TEN CANISTERS OF MUTAGEN TO REFINE JUST ONE TINY DOSE OF RETRO-MUTAGEN... AND I DON'T HAVE ANY LEFT.
BUT AT LEAST WE CAN FIND YOUR DAD AND CHANGE HIM BACK!
I'M JUST— SPEECHLESS! THANK YOU, THANK YOU SO MUCH, DONNIE!
YOU'RE THE BEST!
SMOOCH
GAHHH-BAH-BUH-BUUH—

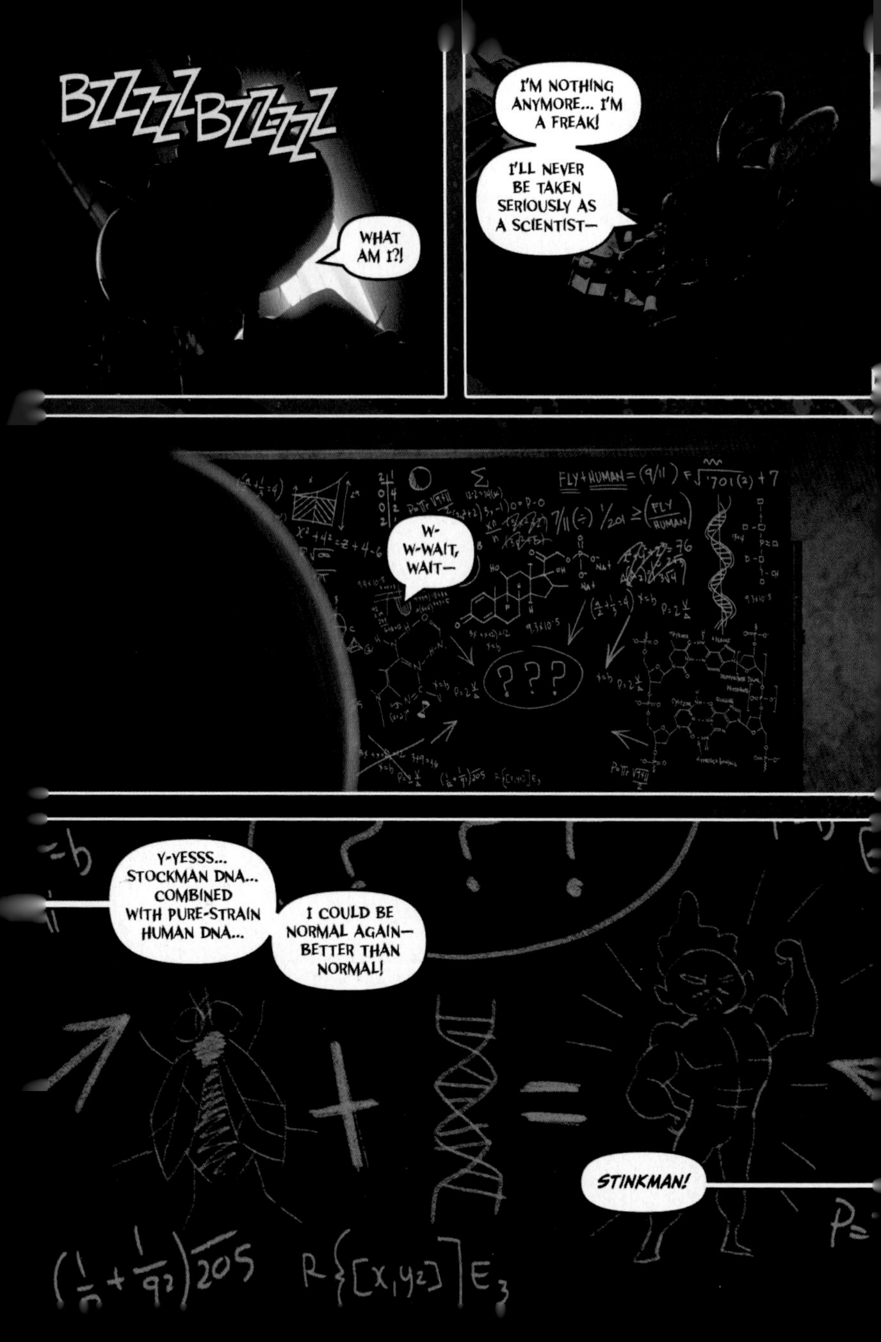
BZZZZ BZZZZ
WHAT AM I?!
I'M NOTHING ANYMORE... I'M A FREAK!
I'LL NEVER BE TAKEN SERIOUSLY AS A SCIENTIST—
W- W-WAIT, WAIT—
Y-YESSS... STOCKMAN DNA... COMBINED WITH PURE-STRAIN HUMAN DNA...
I COULD BE NORMAL AGAIN—BETTER THAN NORMAL!
STINKMAN!

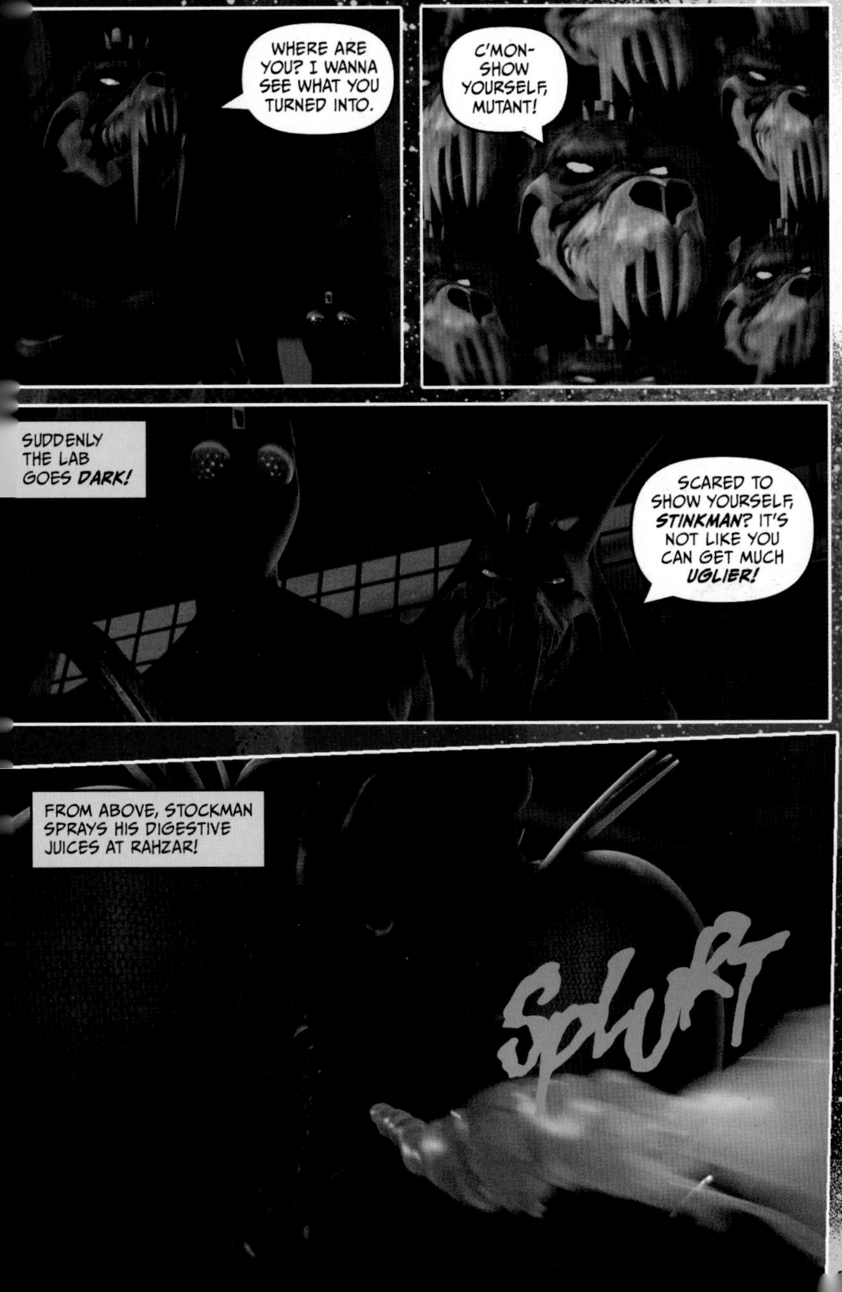
WHERE ARE YOU? I WANNA SEE WHAT YOU TURNED INTO.
C'MON- SHOW YOURSELF, MUTANT!
SUDDENLY THE LAB GOES DARK!
SCARED TO SHOW YOURSELF, STINKMAN? IT'S NOT LIKE YOU CAN GET MUCH UGLIER!
FROM ABOVE, STOCKMAN SPRAYS HIS DIGESTIVE JUICES AT RAHZAR!
SPLURT

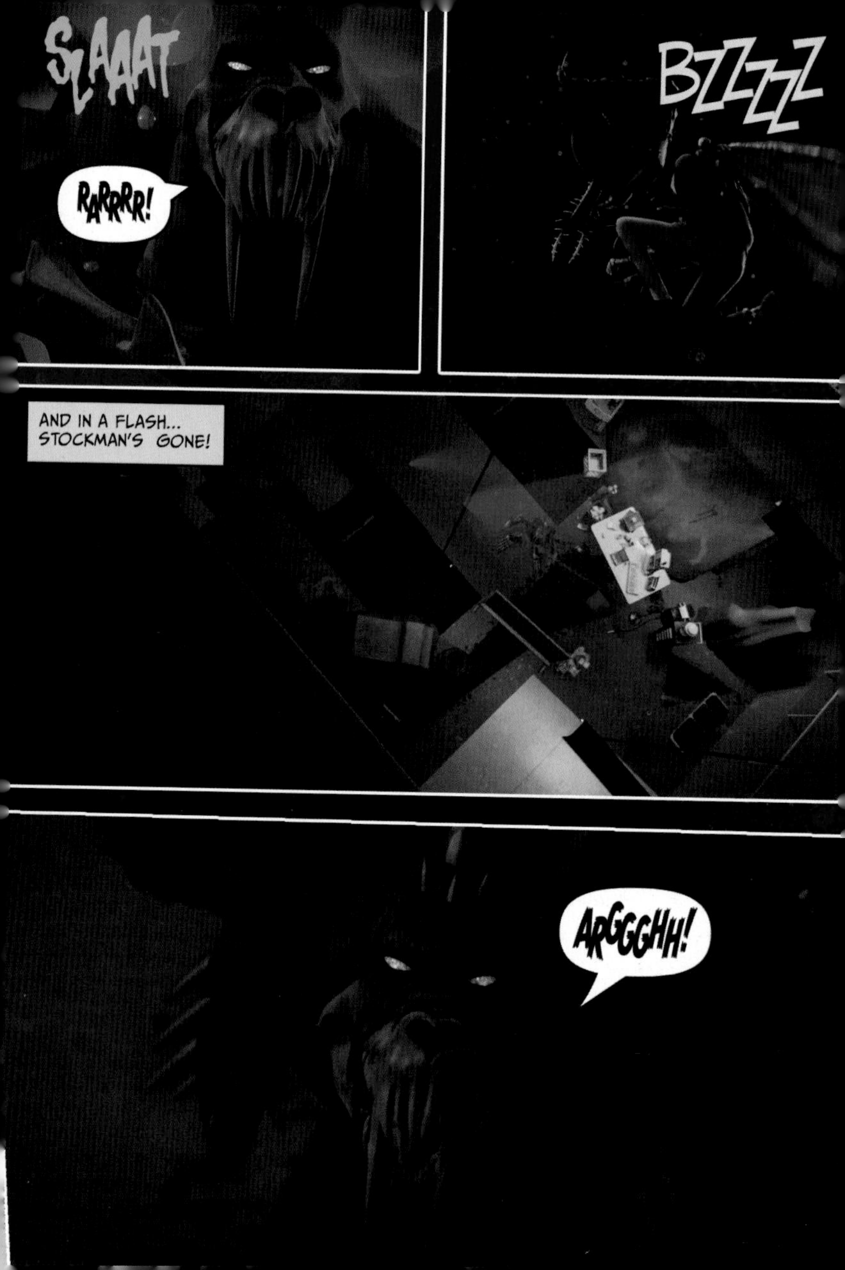
SLAAAT
RARRRR!
BZZZZZ
AND IN A FLASH... STOCKMAN'S GONE!
ARGGGHH!

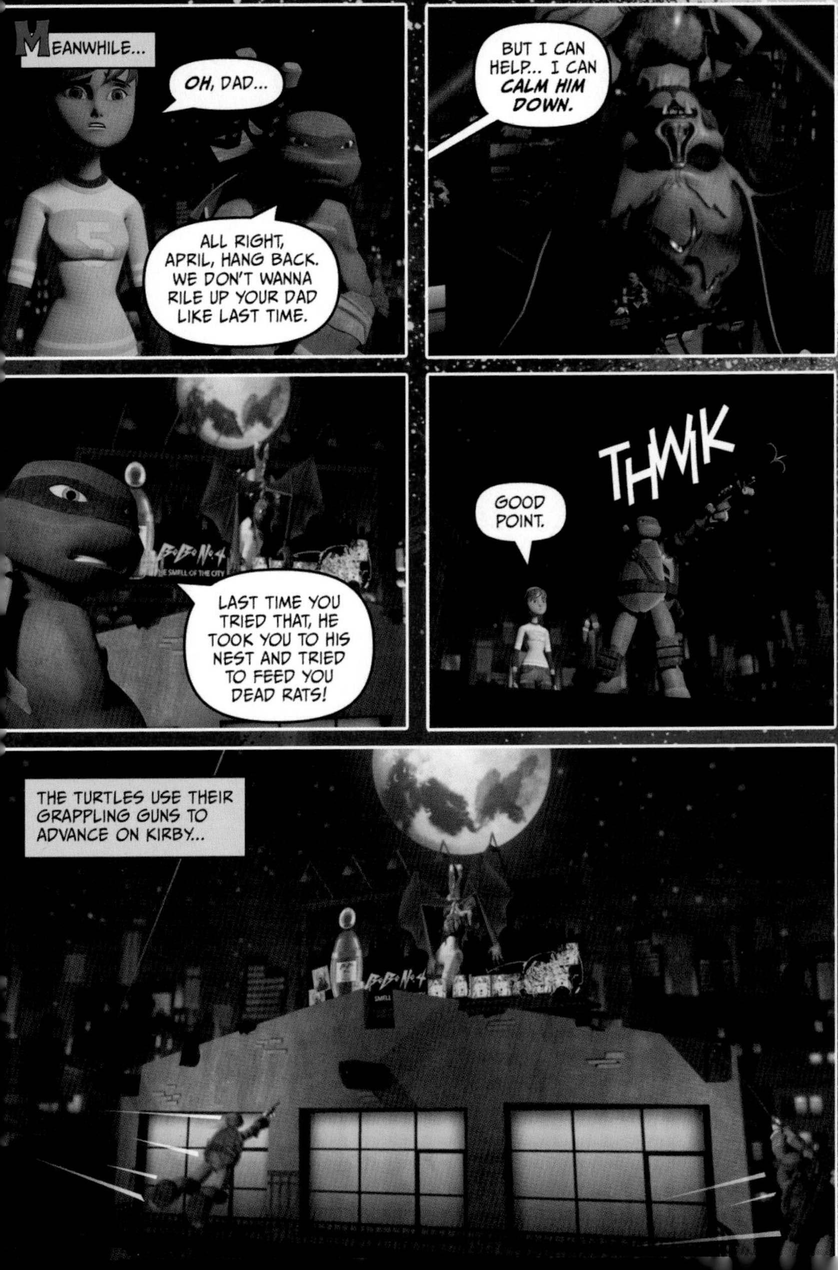
MEANWHILE...
OH, DAD...
ALL RIGHT, APRIL, HANG BACK. WE DON'T WANNA RILE UP YOUR DAD LIKE LAST TIME.
BUT I CAN HELP... I CAN CALM HIM DOWN.
LAST TIME YOU TRIED THAT, HE TOOK YOU TO HIS NEST AND TRIED TO FEED YOU DEAD RATS!
GOOD POINT.
THWIK
THE TURTLES USE THEIR GRAPPLING GUNS TO ADVANCE ON KIRBY...

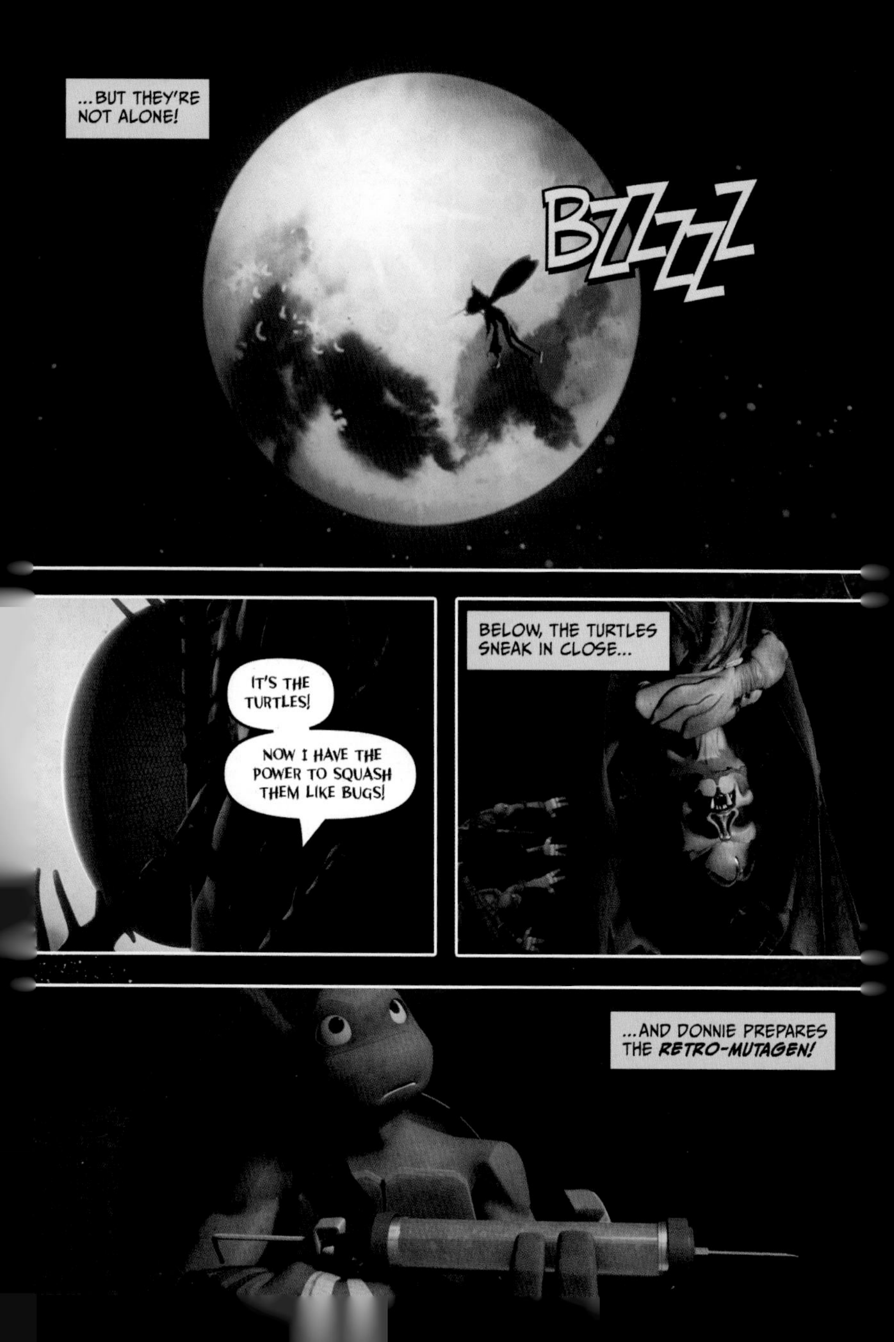
...BUT THEY'RE NOT ALONE!
BZZZZ
IT'S THE TURTLES!
NOW I HAVE THE POWER TO SQUASH THEM LIKE BUGS!
BELOW, THE TURTLES SNEAK IN CLOSE...
...AND DONNIE PREPARES THE RETRO-MUTAGEN!

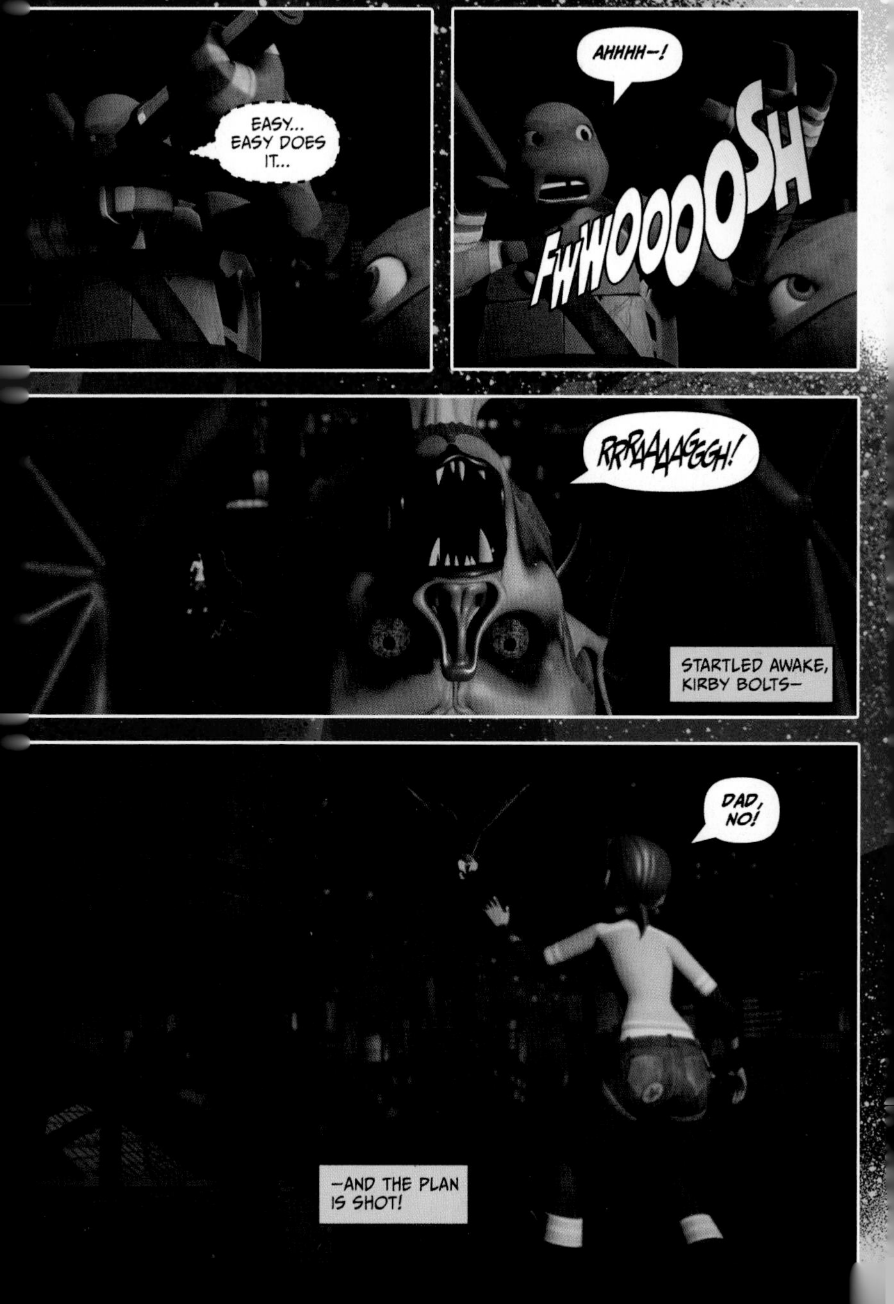
EASY... EASY DOES IT...
AHHHH–!
FWWOOOOOSH
RRRRAAAAGGGH!
STARTLED AWAKE, KIRBY BOLTS—
DAD, NO!
—AND THE PLAN IS SHOT!

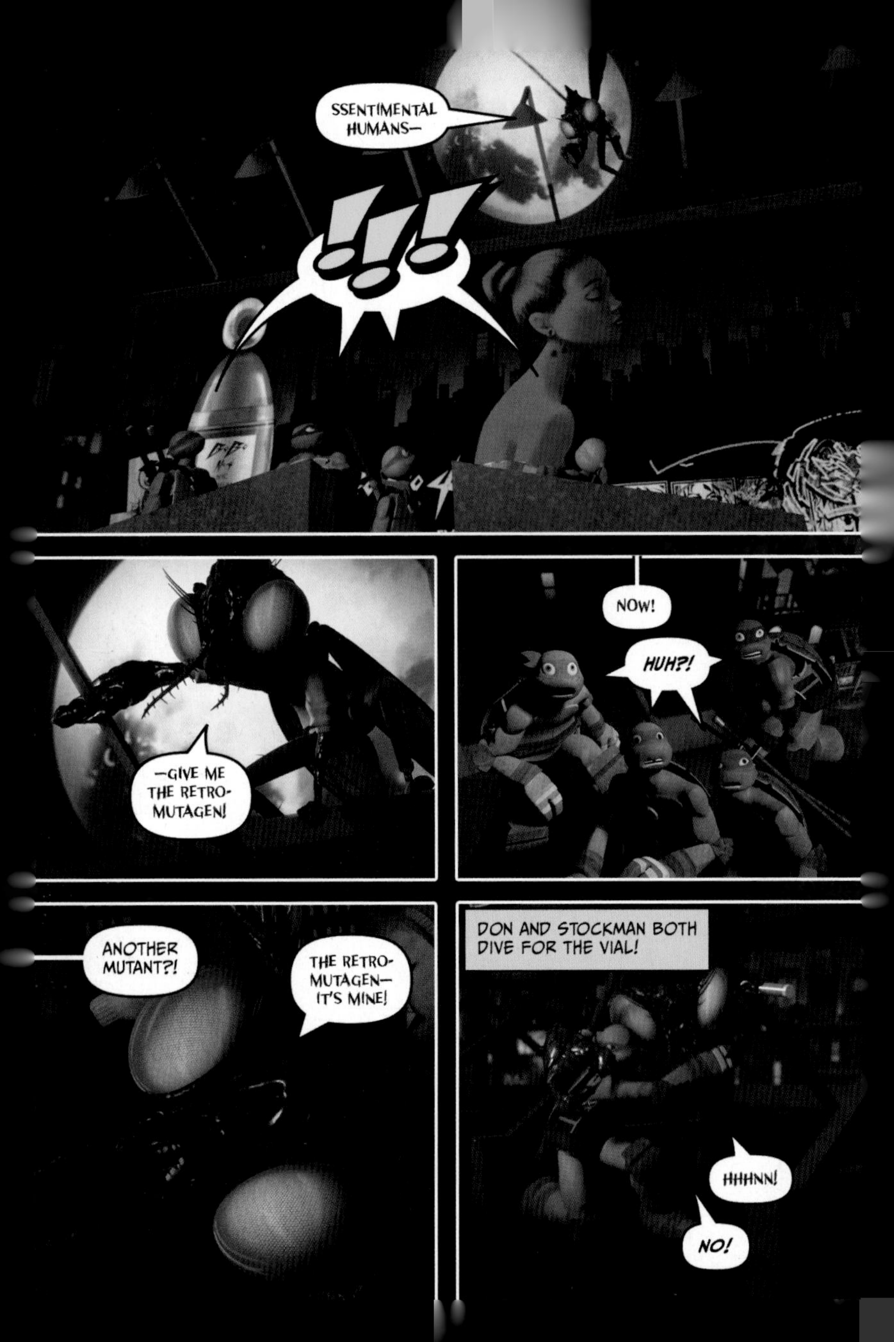
SSENTIMENTAL HUMANS—
!!!
—GIVE ME THE RETRO-MUTAGEN!
NOW!
HUH?!
ANOTHER MUTANT?!
THE RETRO-MUTAGEN—IT'S MINE!
DON AND STOCKMAN BOTH DIVE FOR THE VIAL!
HHHNN!
NO!

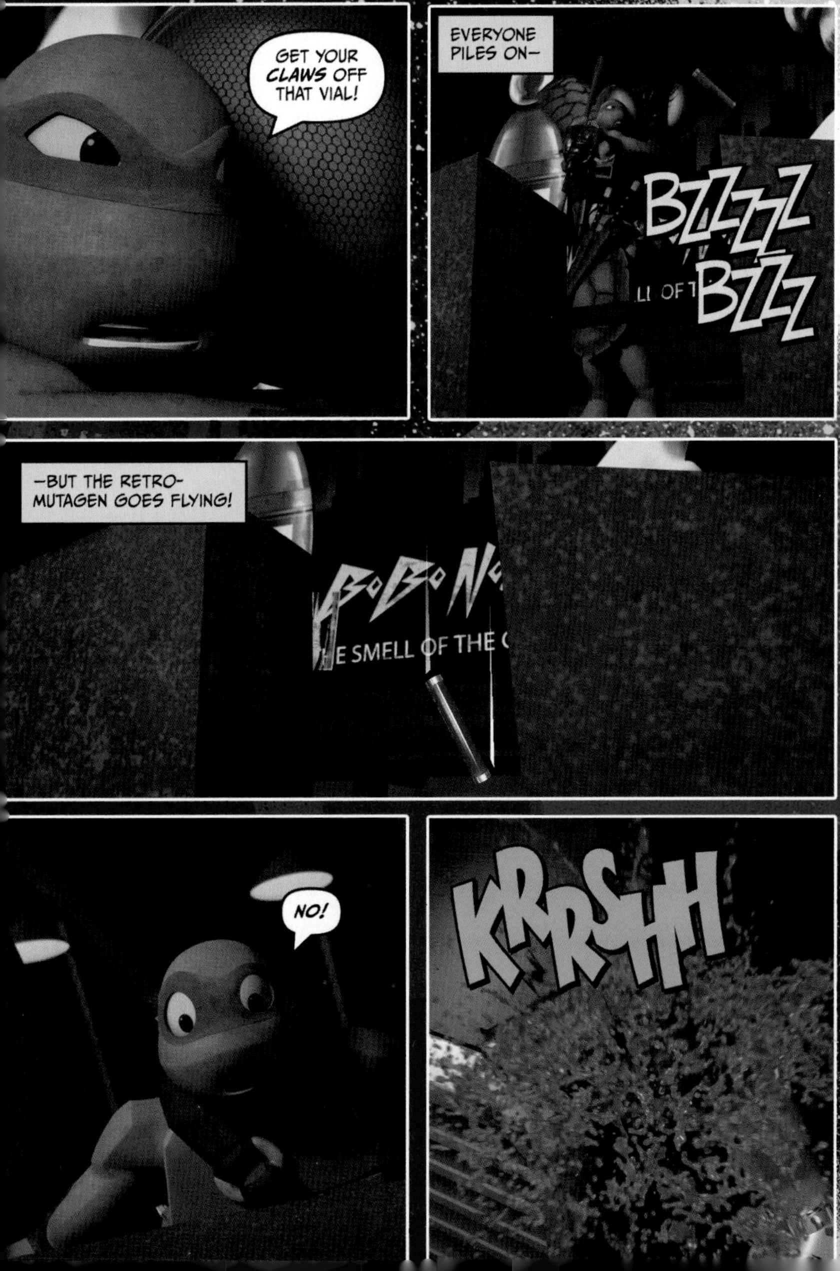
GET YOUR *CLAWS* OFF THAT VIAL!
EVERYONE PILES ON—
BZZZZZ BZZZ
—BUT THE RETRO-MUTAGEN GOES FLYING!
E SMELL OF THE
NO!
KRRSHH

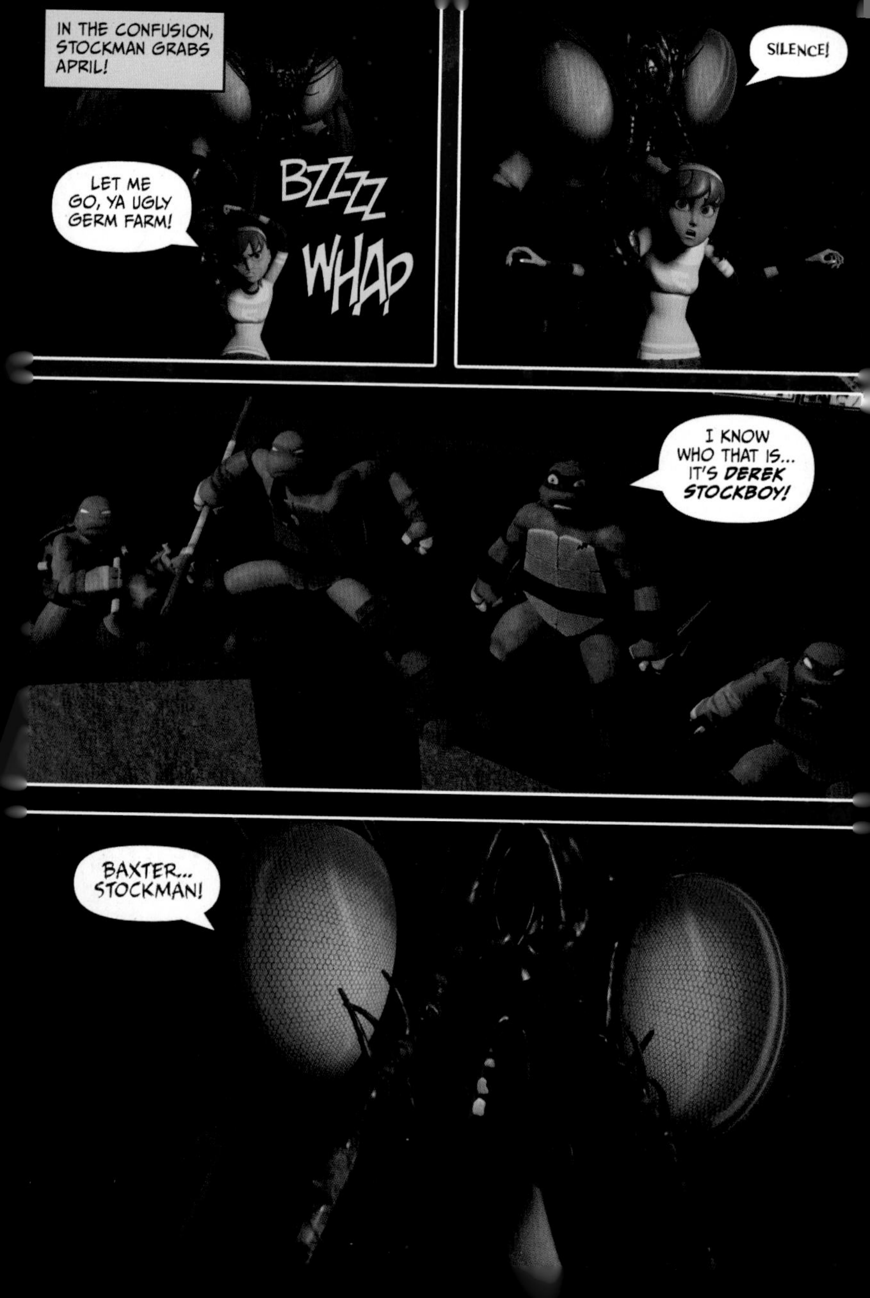
IN THE CONFUSION, STOCKMAN GRABS APRIL!
LET ME GO, YA UGLY GERM FARM!
BZZZZ
WHAP
SILENCE!
I KNOW WHO THAT IS... IT'S DEREK STOCKBOY!
BAXTER... STOCKMAN!

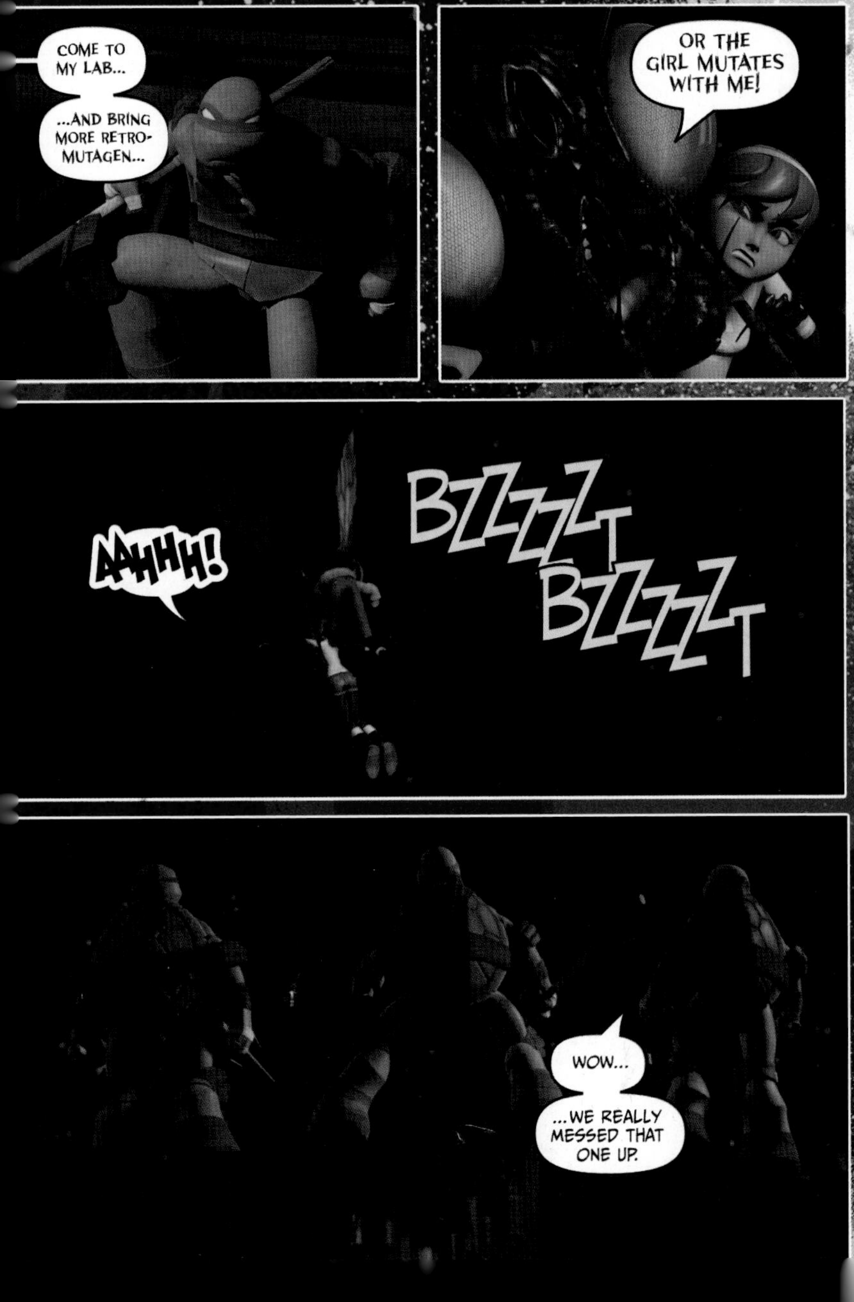
COME TO MY LAB...
...AND BRING MORE RETRO-MUTAGEN...
OR THE GIRL MUTATES WITH ME!
AAHHH!
BZZZZZT BZZZZZT
WOW...
...WE REALLY MESSED THAT ONE UP.

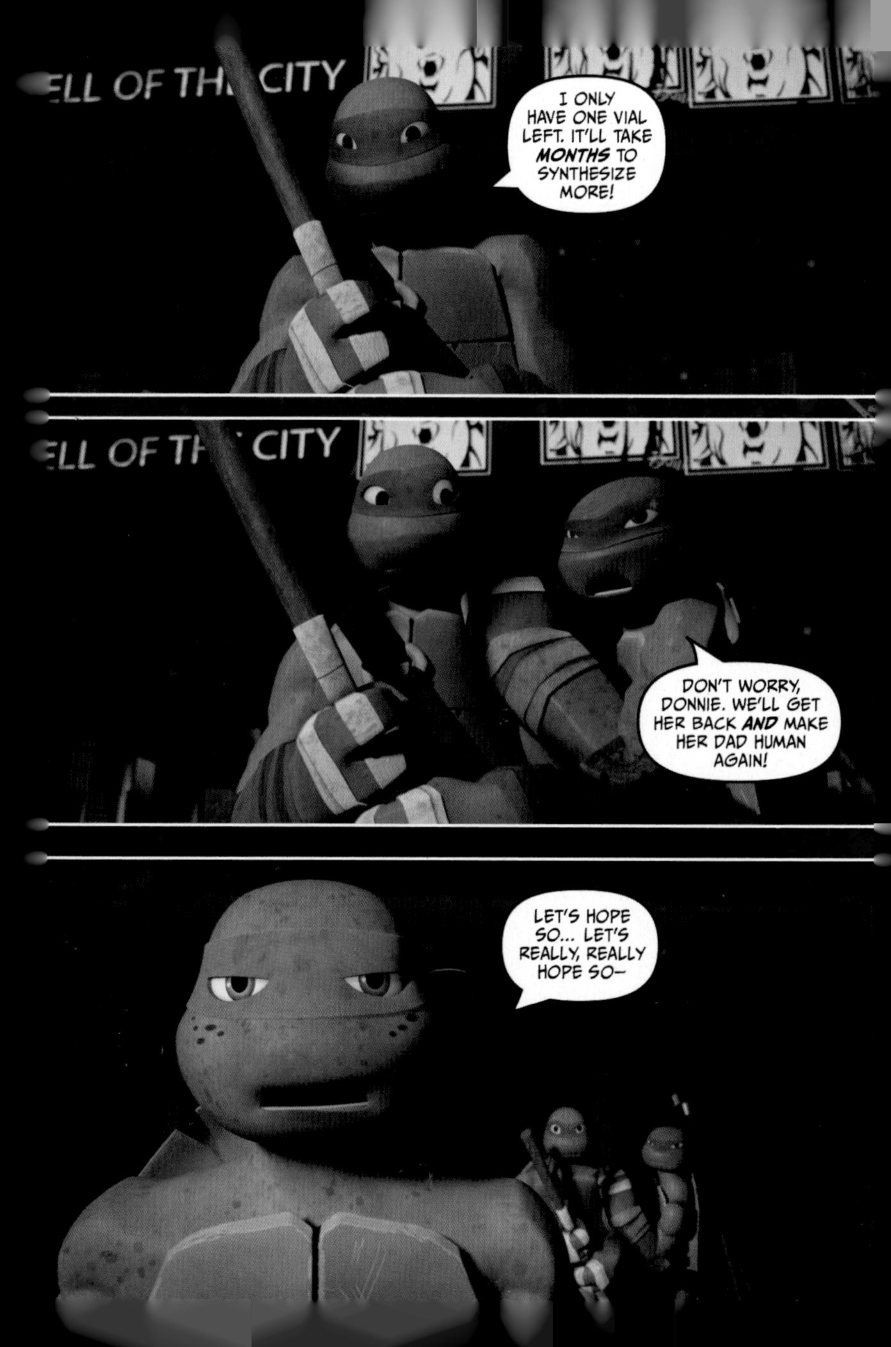
ELL OF TH CITY
I ONLY HAVE ONE VIAL LEFT. IT'LL TAKE ***MONTHS*** TO SYNTHESIZE MORE!
ELL OF TH CITY
DON'T WORRY, DONNIE. WE'LL GET HER BACK ***AND*** MAKE HER DAD HUMAN AGAIN!
LET'S HOPE SO... LET'S REALLY, REALLY HOPE SO—

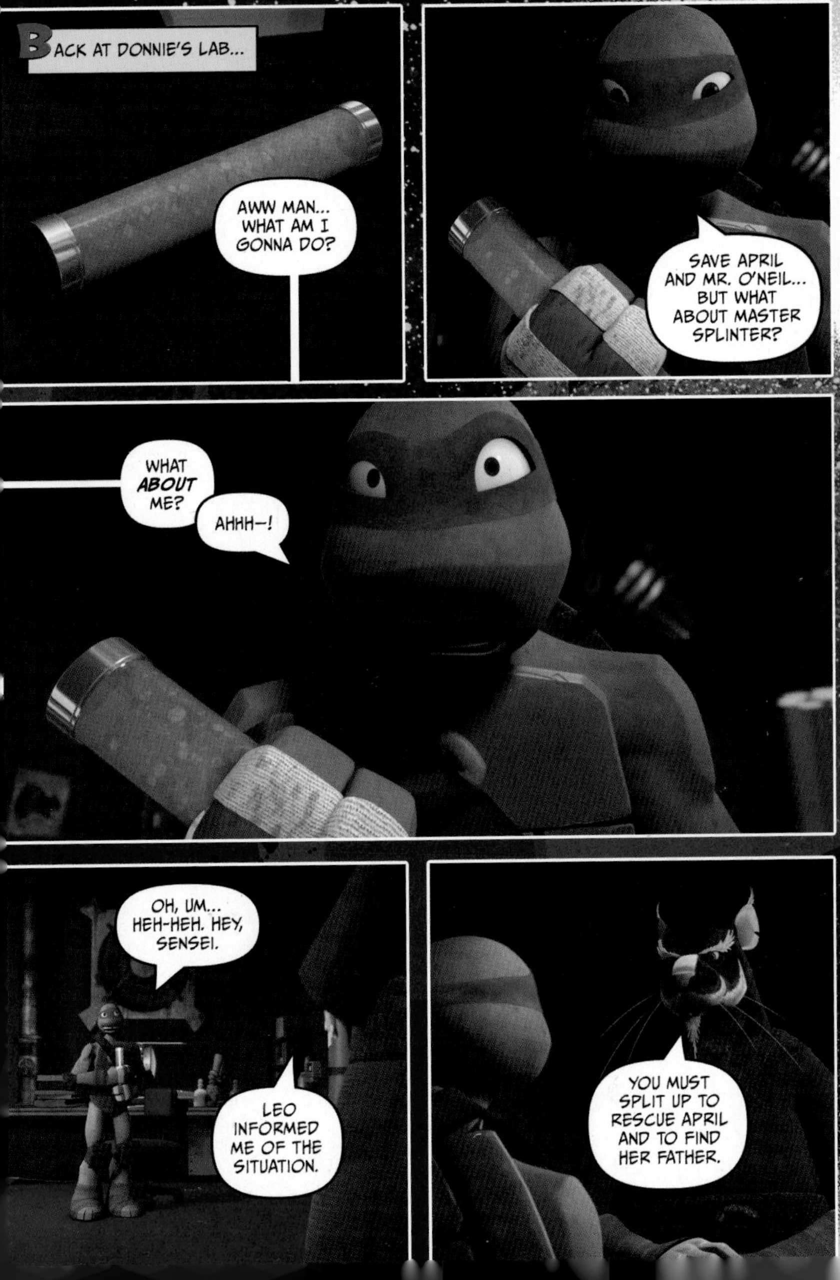
BACK AT DONNIE'S LAB...
AWW MAN... WHAT AM I GONNA DO?
SAVE APRIL AND MR. O'NEIL... BUT WHAT ABOUT MASTER SPLINTER?
WHAT ABOUT ME?
AHHH—!
OH, UM... HEH-HEH. HEY, SENSEI.
LEO INFORMED ME OF THE SITUATION.
YOU MUST SPLIT UP TO RESCUE APRIL AND TO FIND HER FATHER.

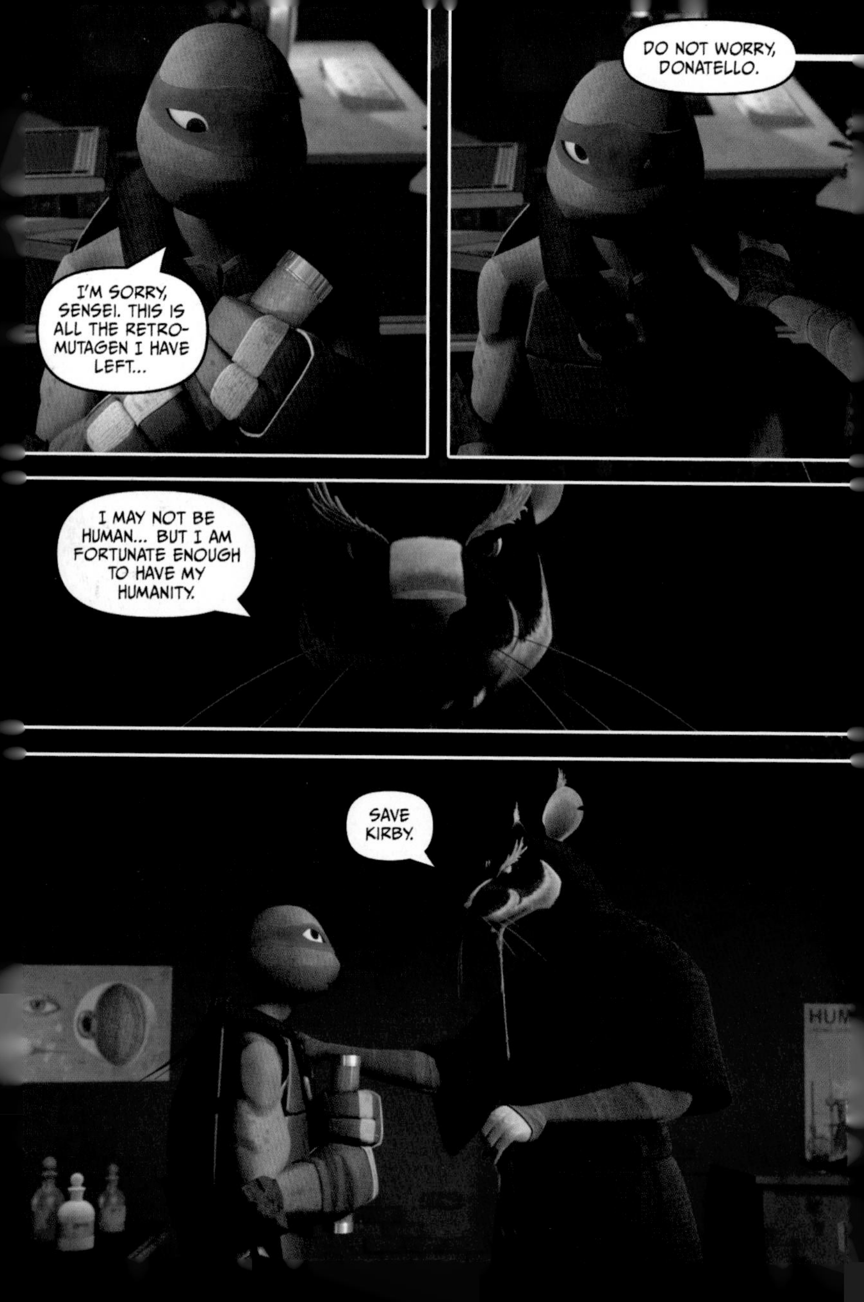
I'M SORRY, SENSEI. THIS IS ALL THE RETRO-MUTAGEN I HAVE LEFT...
DO NOT WORRY, DONATELLO.
I MAY NOT BE HUMAN... BUT I AM FORTUNATE ENOUGH TO HAVE MY HUMANITY.
SAVE KIRBY.

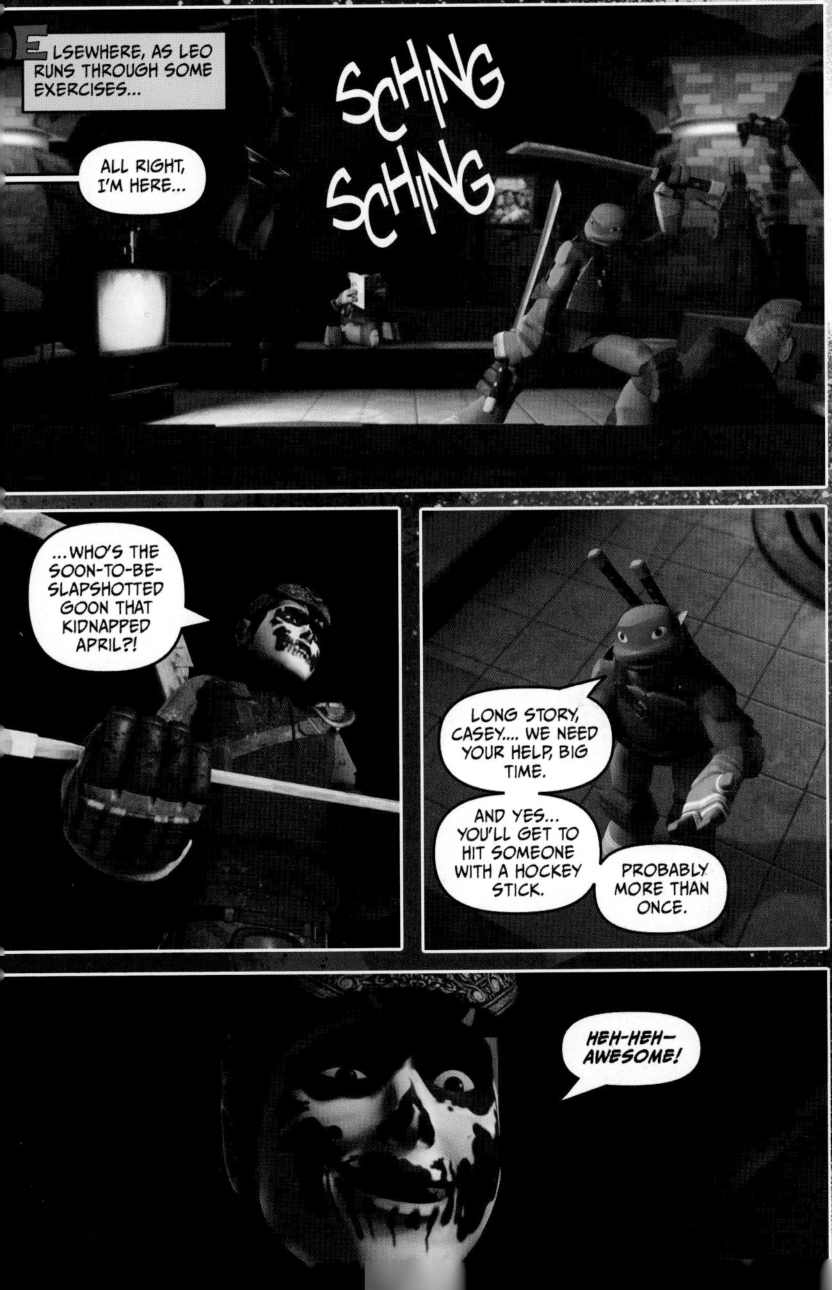
ELSEWHERE, AS LEO RUNS THROUGH SOME EXERCISES...
SCHING SCHING
ALL RIGHT, I'M HERE...
...WHO'S THE SOON-TO-BE-SLAPSHOTTED GOON THAT KIDNAPPED APRIL?!
LONG STORY, CASEY.... WE NEED YOUR HELP, BIG TIME.
AND YES... YOU'LL GET TO HIT SOMEONE WITH A HOCKEY STICK.
PROBABLY MORE THAN ONCE.
HEH-HEH— AWESOME!

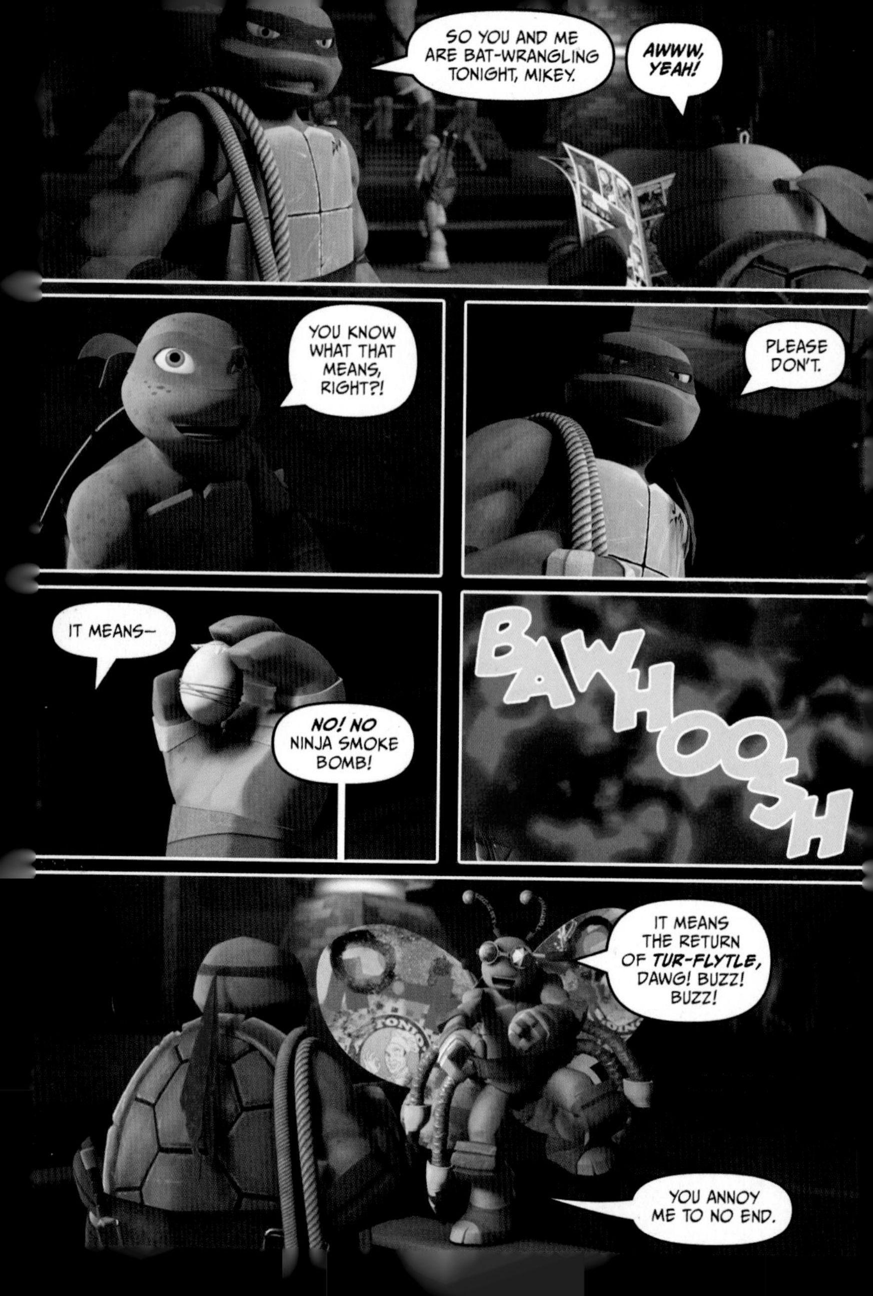
SO YOU AND ME ARE BAT-WRANGLING TONIGHT, MIKEY.
AWWW, YEAH!
YOU KNOW WHAT THAT MEANS, RIGHT?!
PLEASE DON'T.
IT MEANS—
NO! NO NINJA SMOKE BOMB!
BAWHOOOSH
IT MEANS THE RETURN OF TUR-FLYTLE, DAWG! BUZZ! BUZZ!
YOU ANNOY ME TO NO END.

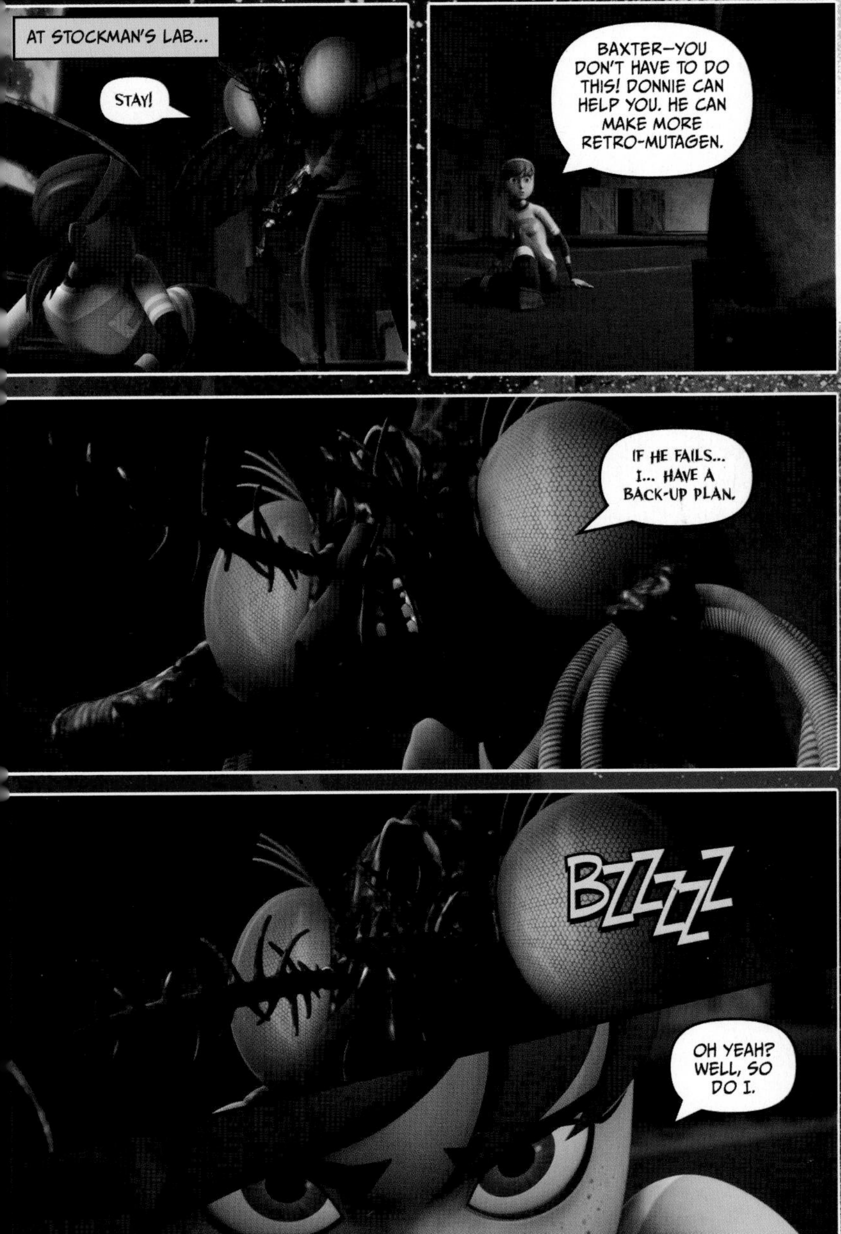
AT STOCKMAN'S LAB...
STAY!
BAXTER—YOU DON'T HAVE TO DO THIS! DONNIE CAN HELP YOU. HE CAN MAKE MORE RETRO-MUTAGEN.
IF HE FAILS... I... HAVE A BACK-UP PLAN.
BZZZZ
OH YEAH? WELL, SO DO I.

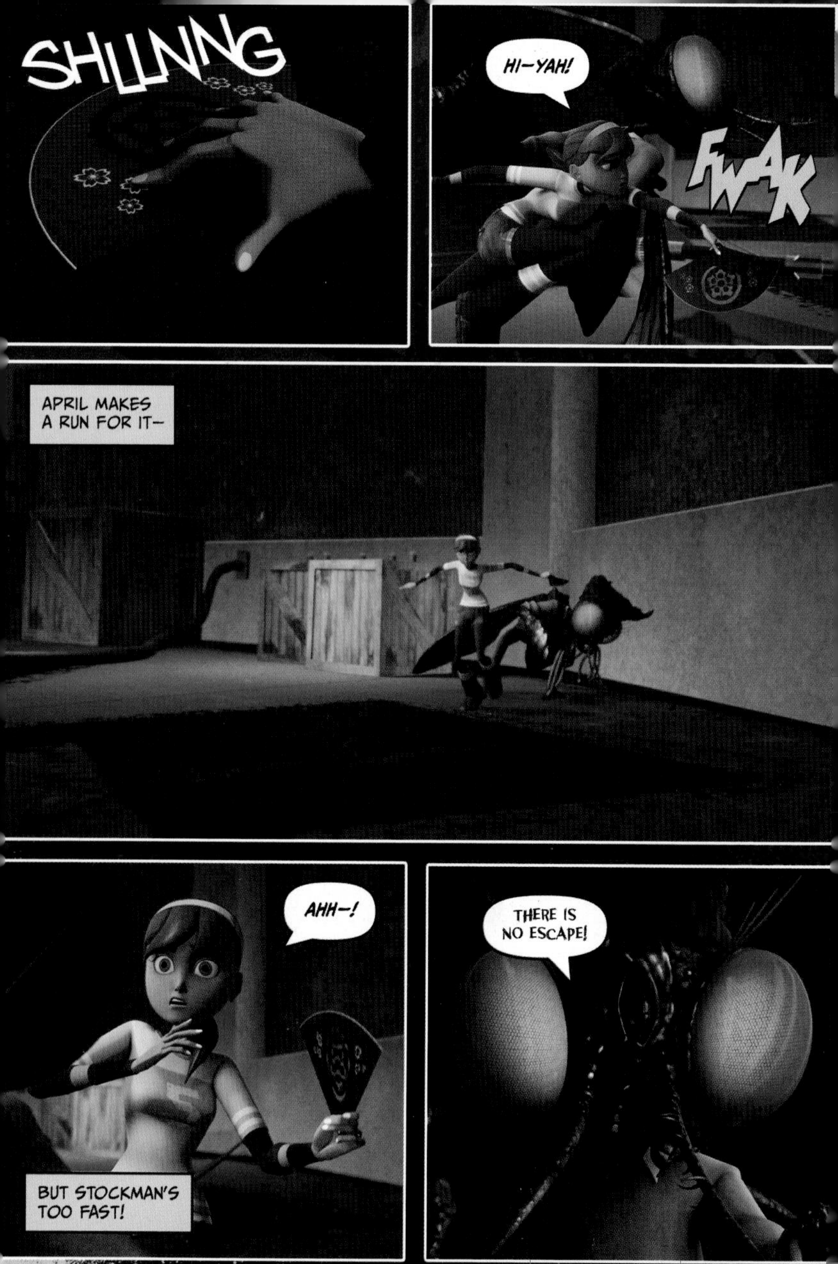

SHLLNNG
HI-YAH!
FWAK
APRIL MAKES A RUN FOR IT—
AHH—!
BUT STOCKMAN'S TOO FAST!
THERE IS NO ESCAPE!

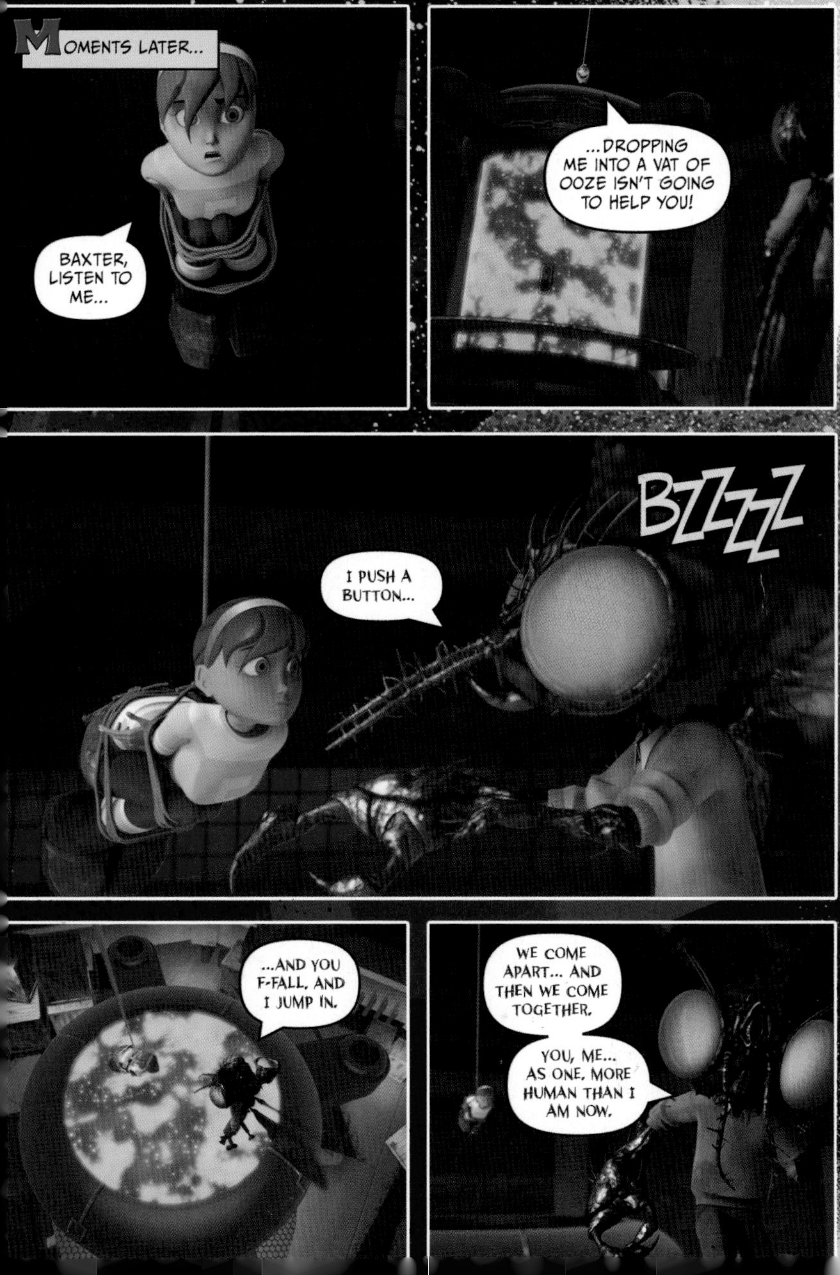
MOMENTS LATER...
BAXTER, LISTEN TO ME...
...DROPPING ME INTO A VAT OF OOZE ISN'T GOING TO HELP YOU!
BZZZZ
I PUSH A BUTTON...
...AND YOU F-FALL, AND I JUMP IN.
WE COME APART... AND THEN WE COME TOGETHER.
YOU, ME... AS ONE, MORE HUMAN THAN I AM NOW.

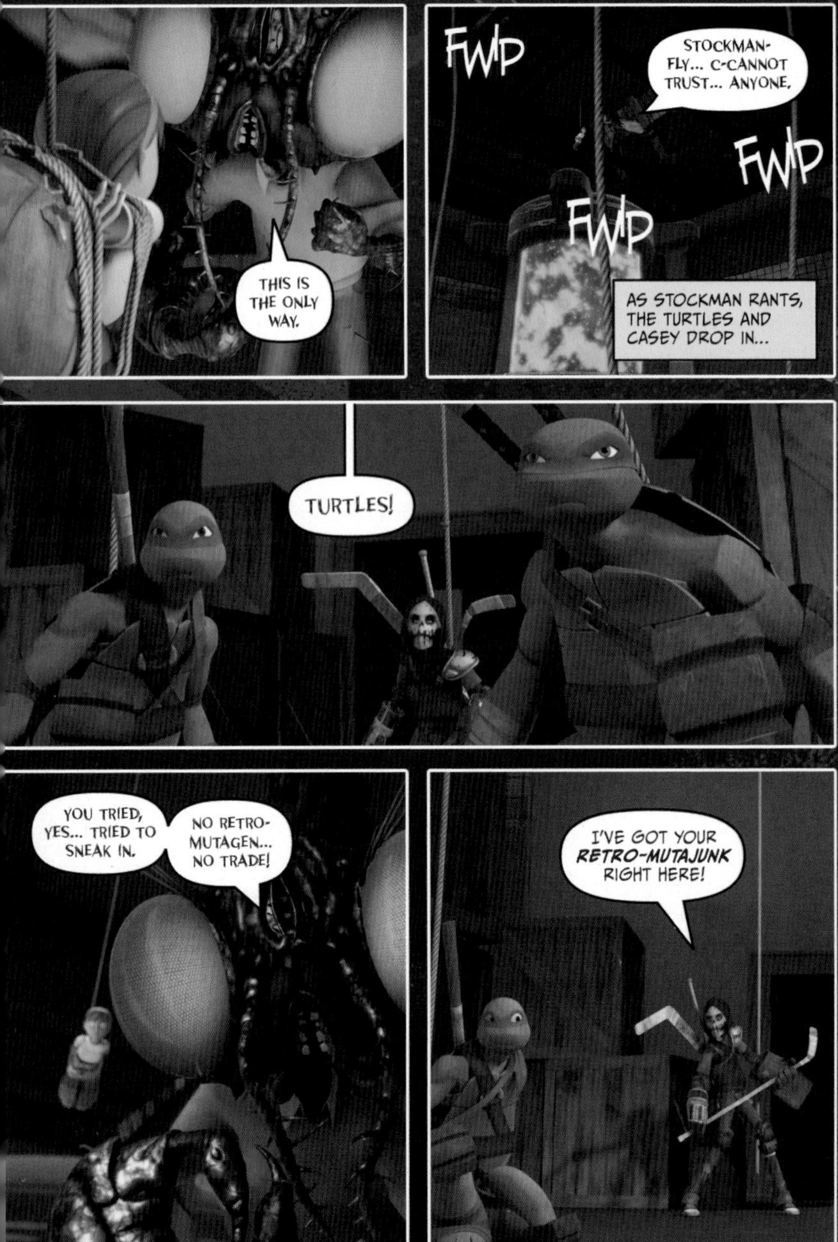
THIS IS THE ONLY WAY.
FWIP
STOCKMAN-FLY... C-CANNOT TRUST... ANYONE.
FWIP
FWIP
AS STOCKMAN RANTS, THE TURTLES AND CASEY DROP IN...
TURTLES!
YOU TRIED, YES... TRIED TO SNEAK IN.
NO RETRO-MUTAGEN... NO TRADE!
I'VE GOT YOUR RETRO-MUTAJUNK RIGHT HERE!

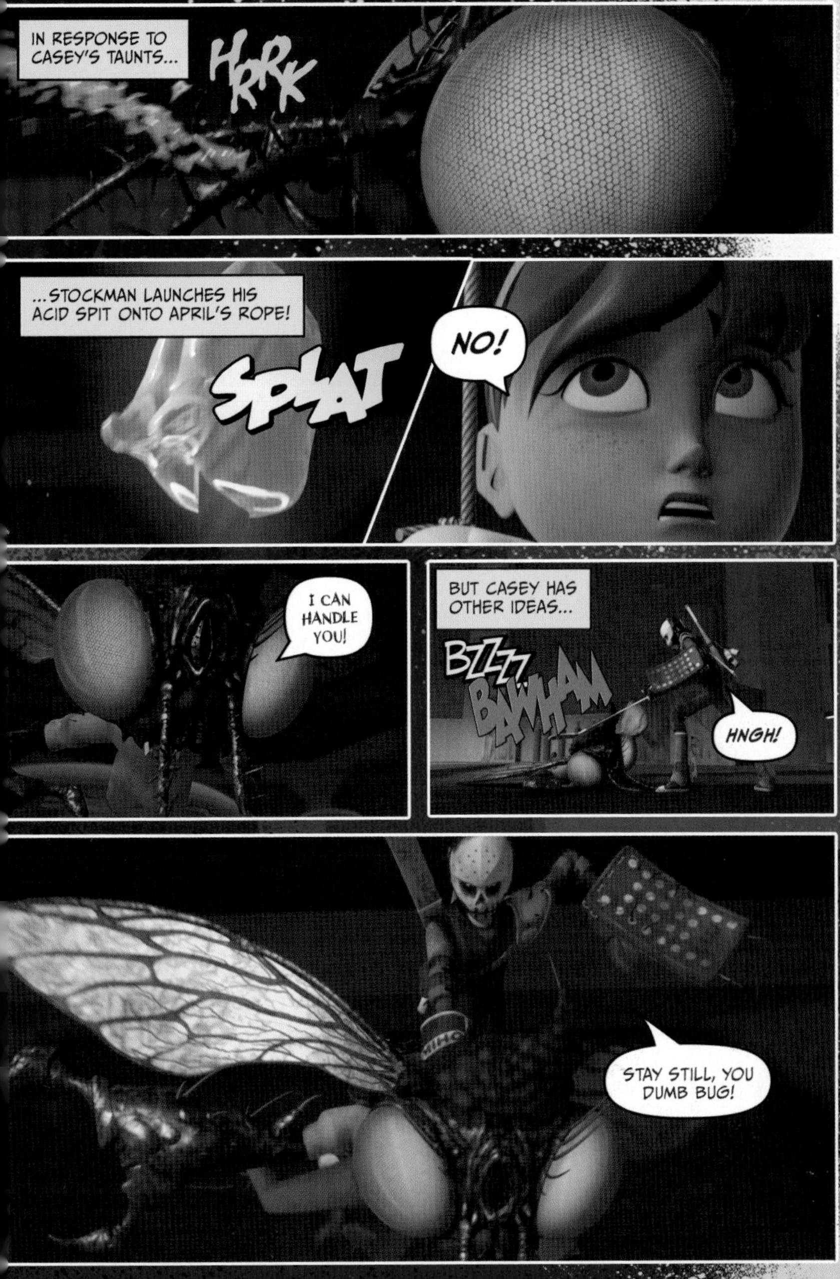
IN RESPONSE TO CASEY'S TAUNTS...
HRRK
...STOCKMAN LAUNCHES HIS ACID SPIT ONTO APRIL'S ROPE!
SPLAT
NO!
I CAN HANDLE YOU!
BUT CASEY HAS OTHER IDEAS...
BZZZ
BAWHAM
HNGH!
STAY STILL, YOU DUMB BUG!

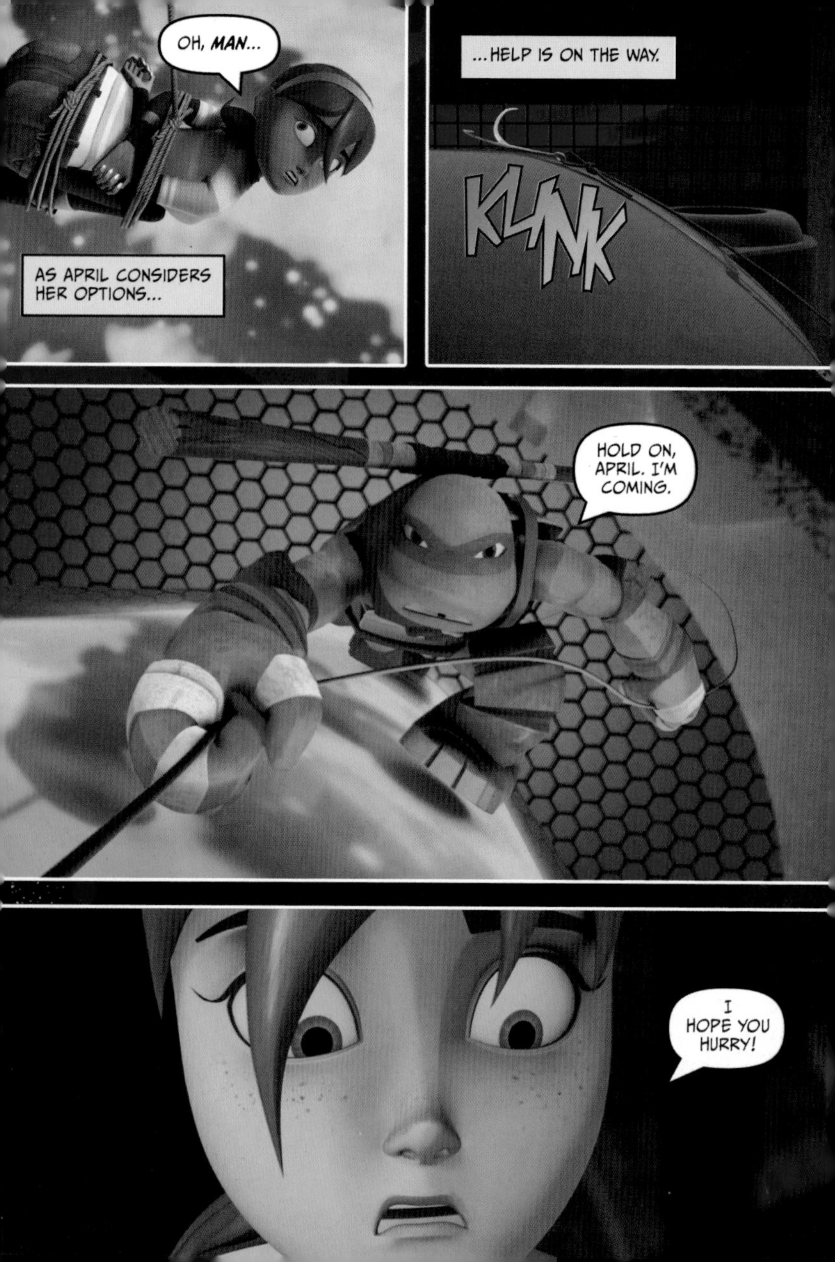
OH, MAN...
AS APRIL CONSIDERS HER OPTIONS...
...HELP IS ON THE WAY.
KLUNK
HOLD ON, APRIL. I'M COMING.
I HOPE YOU HURRY!

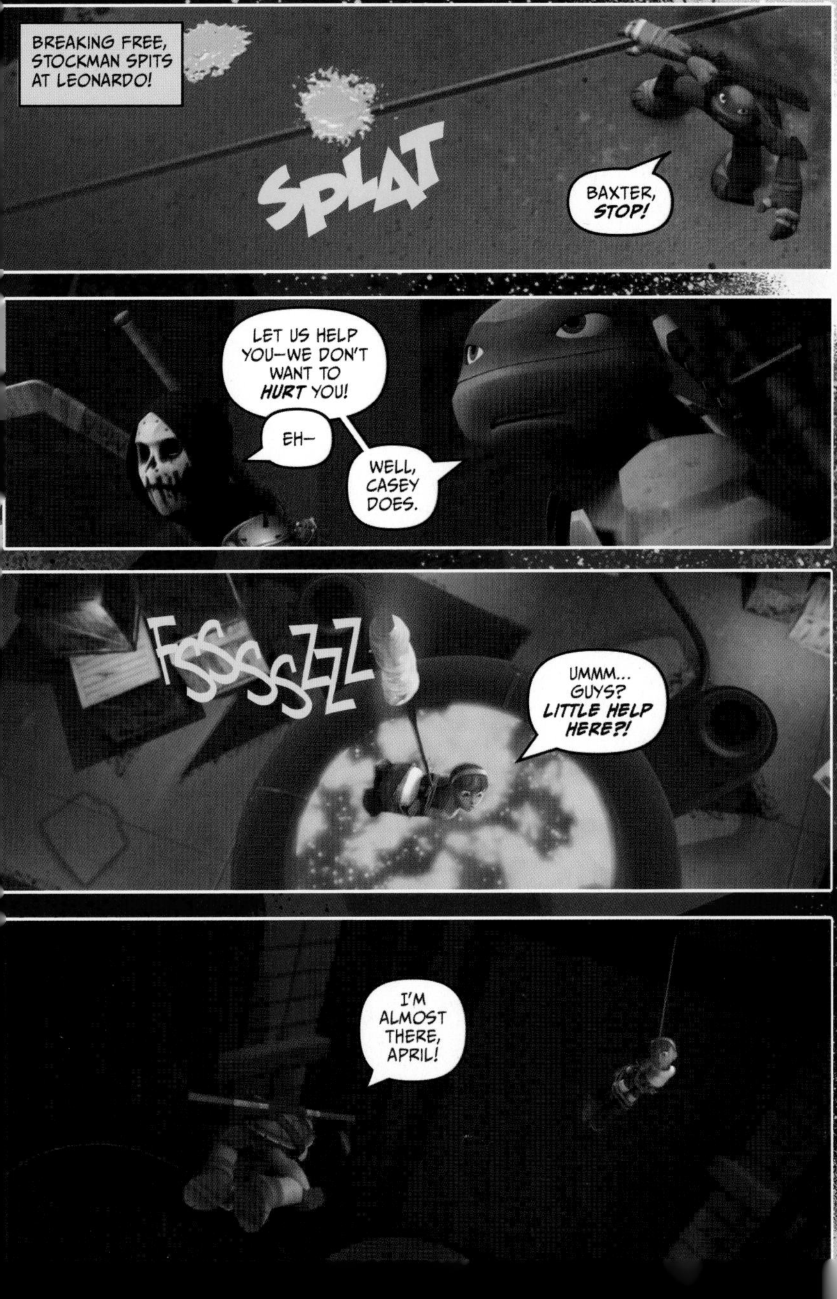
BREAKING FREE, STOCKMAN SPITS AT LEONARDO!
SPLAT
BAXTER, STOP!
LET US HELP YOU—WE DON'T WANT TO HURT YOU!
EH—
WELL, CASEY DOES.
FSSSSZZZ
UMMM... GUYS? LITTLE HELP HERE?!
I'M ALMOST THERE, APRIL!

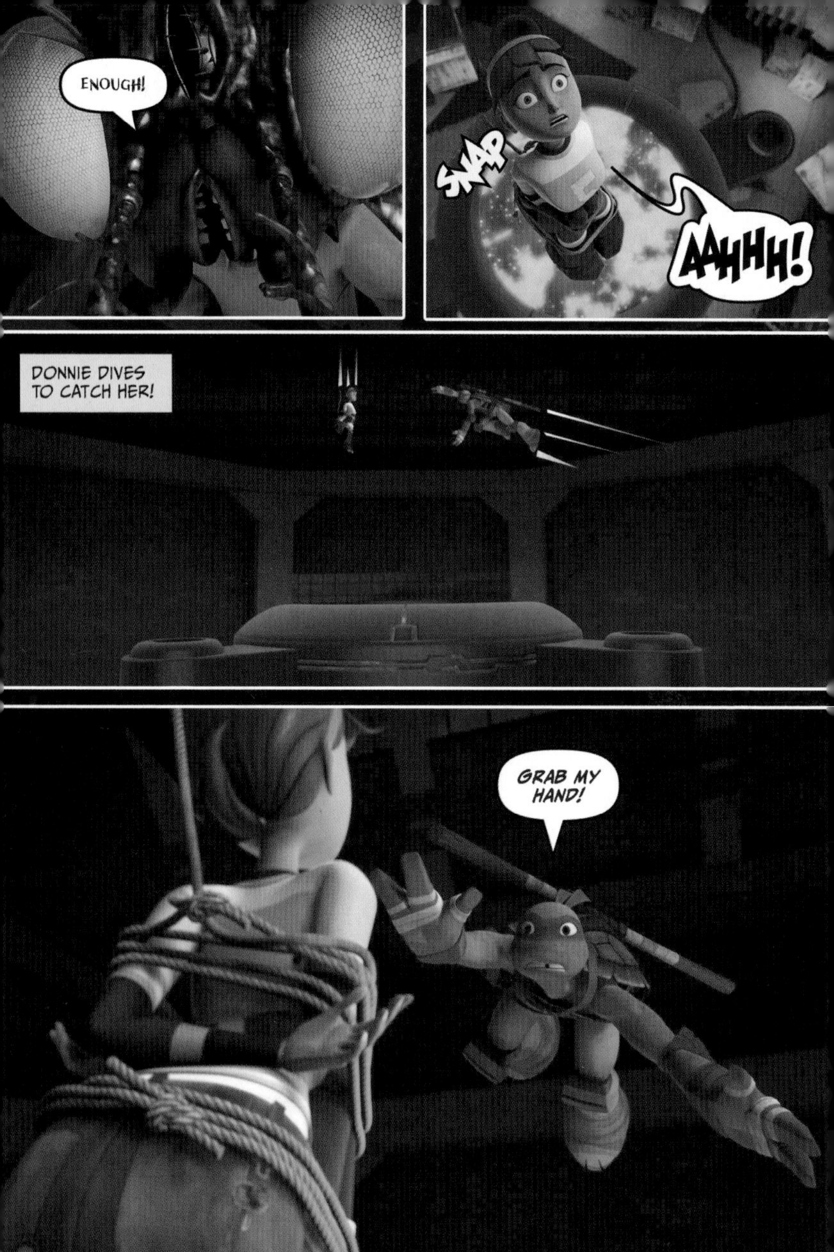
ENOUGH!
SNAP
AAHHH!
DONNIE DIVES TO CATCH HER!
GRAB MY HAND!

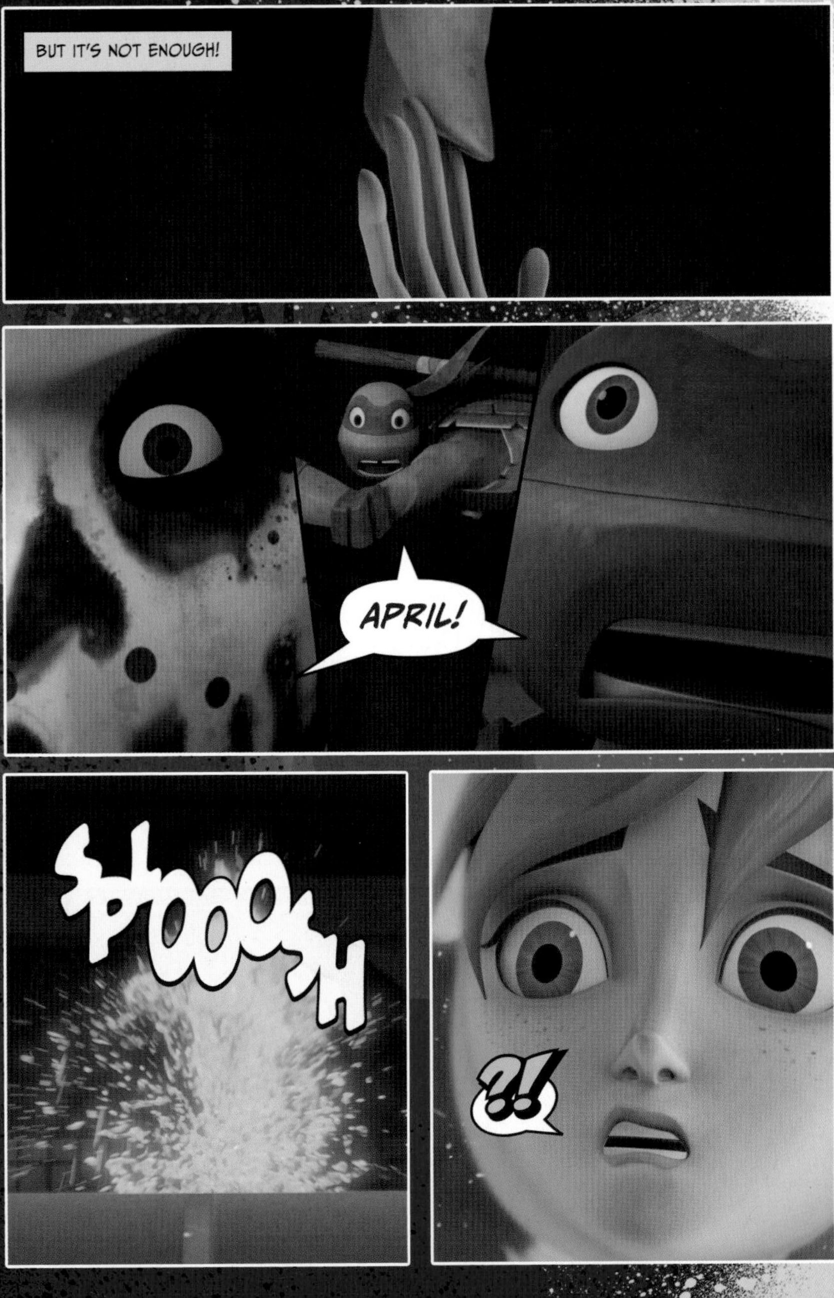
BUT IT'S NOT ENOUGH!
APRIL!
SPLOOOSH
?!

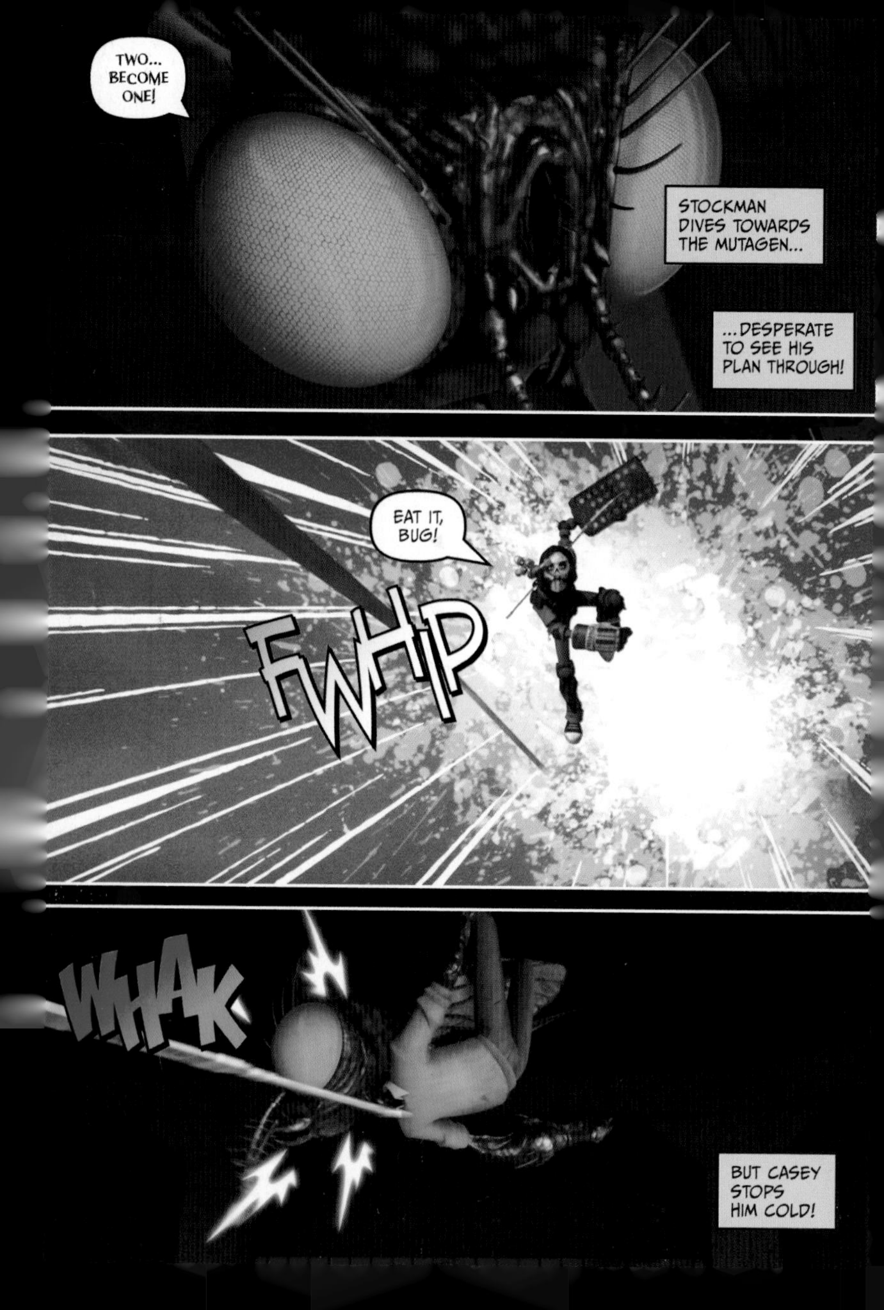
TWO... BECOME ONE!
STOCKMAN DIVES TOWARDS THE MUTAGEN...
...DESPERATE TO SEE HIS PLAN THROUGH!
EAT IT, BUG!
FWHIP
WHAK
BUT CASEY STOPS HIM COLD!

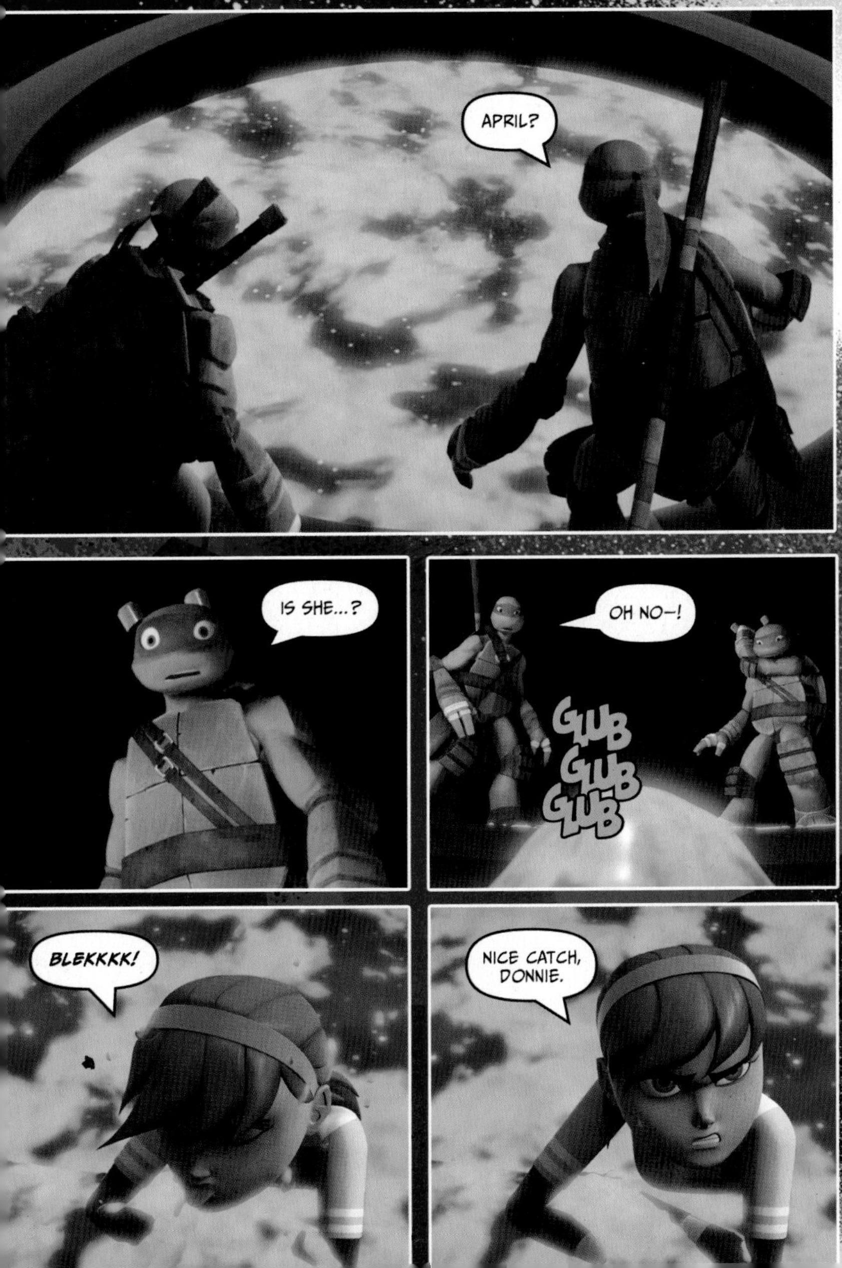
APRIL?
IS SHE...?
OH NO--!
GLUB GLUB GLUB
BLEKKKK!
NICE CATCH, DONNIE.

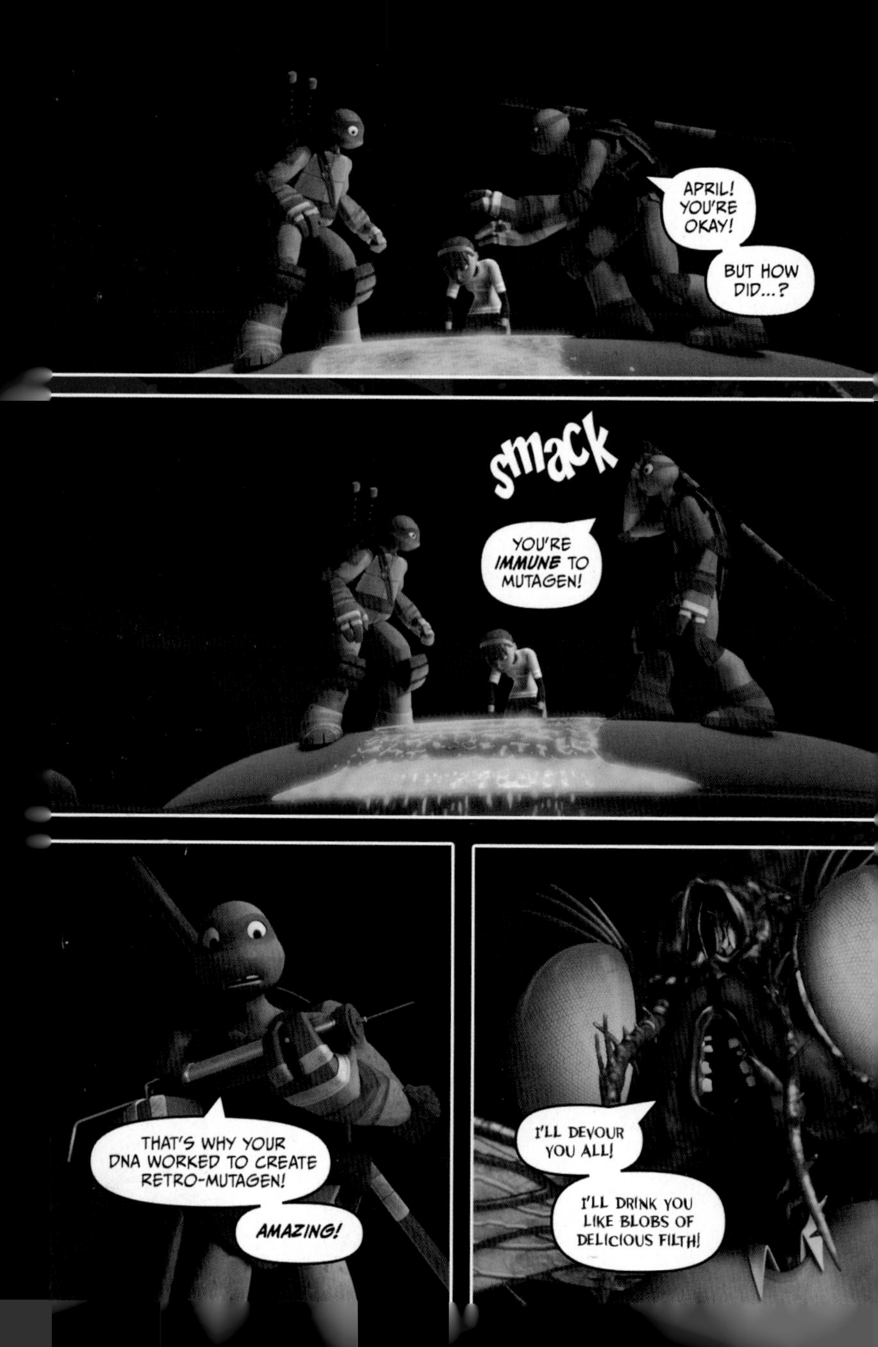
APRIL! YOU'RE OKAY!
BUT HOW DID...?
SMACK
YOU'RE IMMUNE TO MUTAGEN!
THAT'S WHY YOUR DNA WORKED TO CREATE RETRO-MUTAGEN!
AMAZING!
I'LL DEVOUR YOU ALL!
I'LL DRINK YOU LIKE BLOBS OF DELICIOUS FILTH!

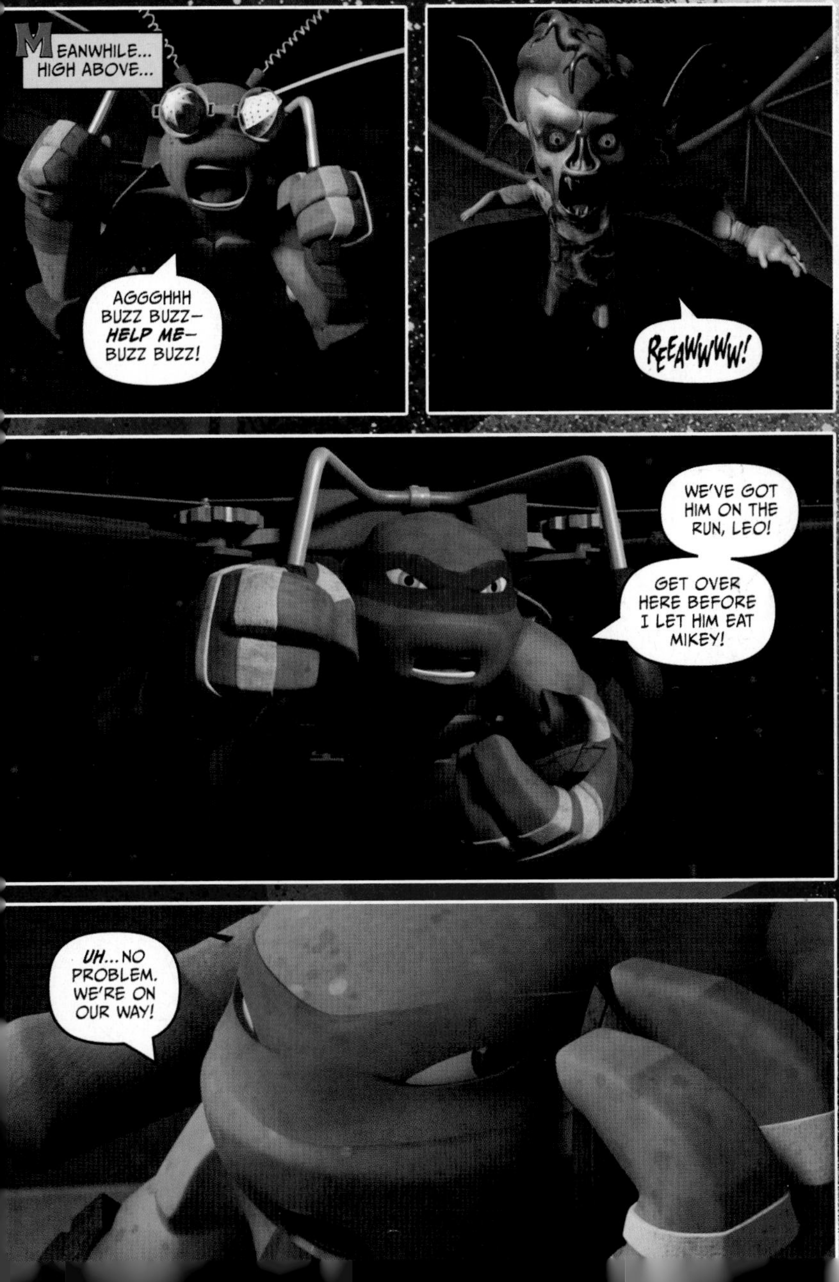
MEANWHILE... HIGH ABOVE...
AGGGHHH BUZZ BUZZ—**HELP ME**—BUZZ BUZZ!
REEAWWWW!
WE'VE GOT HIM ON THE RUN, LEO!
GET OVER HERE BEFORE I LET HIM EAT MIKEY!
UH...NO PROBLEM. WE'RE ON OUR WAY!

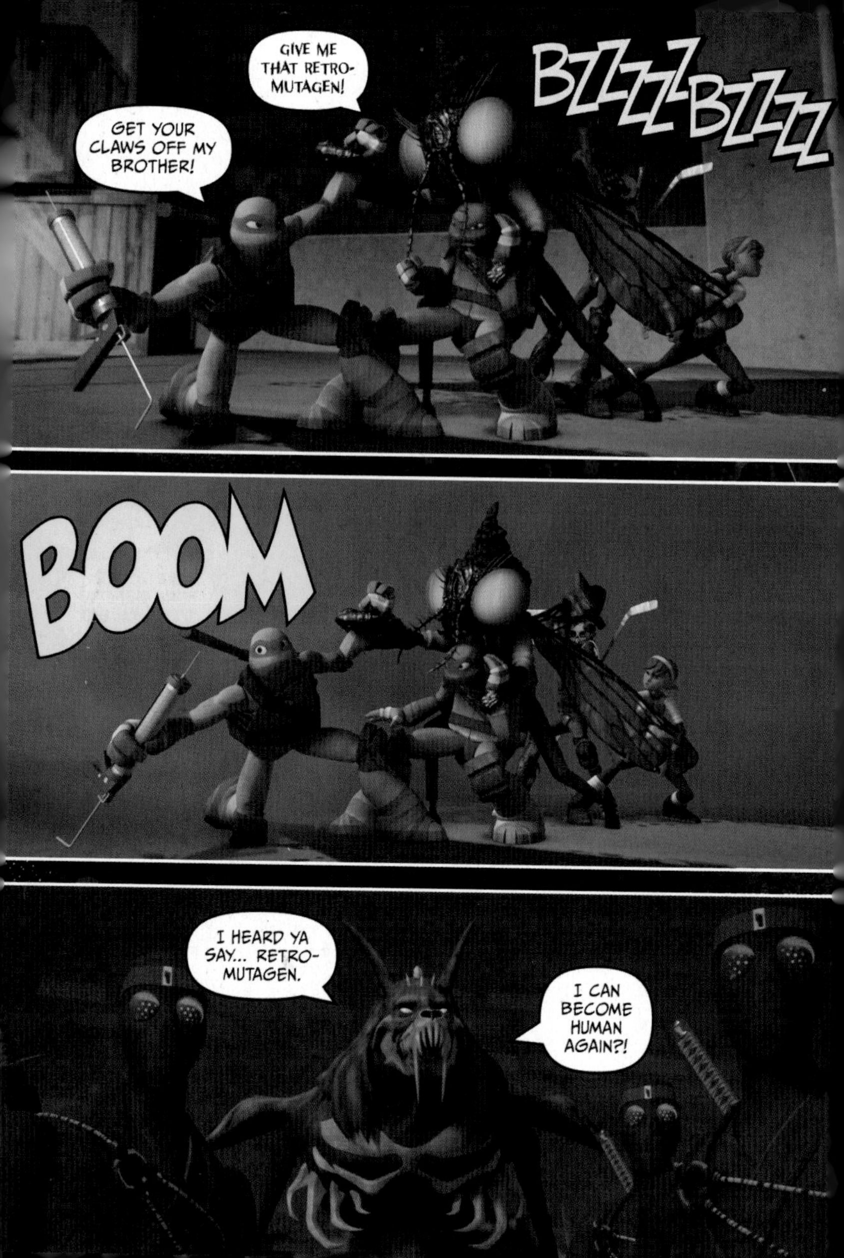
GIVE ME THAT RETRO-MUTAGEN!
GET YOUR CLAWS OFF MY BROTHER!
BZZZZ BZZZ
BOOM
I HEARD YA SAY... RETRO-MUTAGEN.
I CAN BECOME HUMAN AGAIN?!

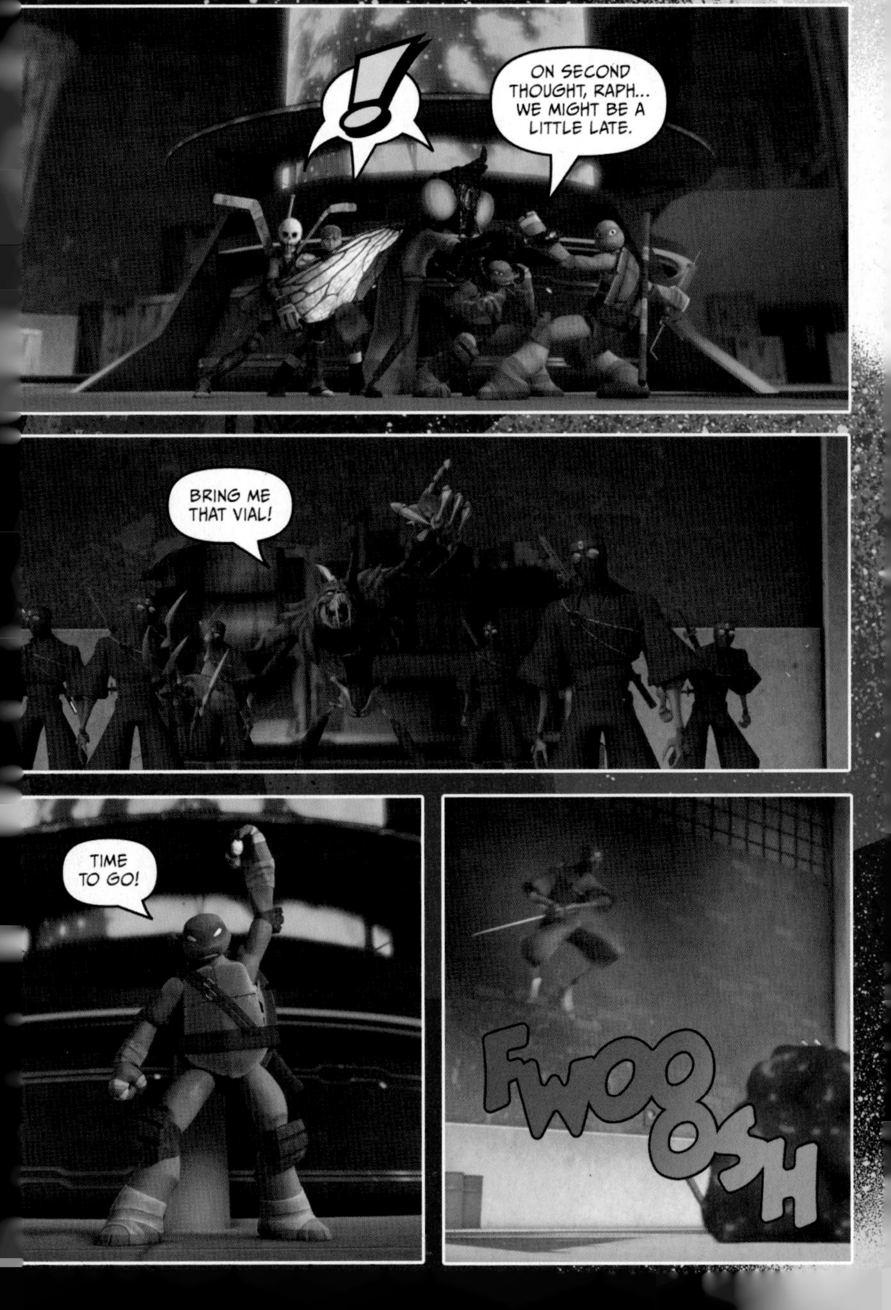
!
ON SECOND THOUGHT, RAPH... WE MIGHT BE A LITTLE LATE.
BRING ME THAT VIAL!
TIME TO GO!
FWOOOSH

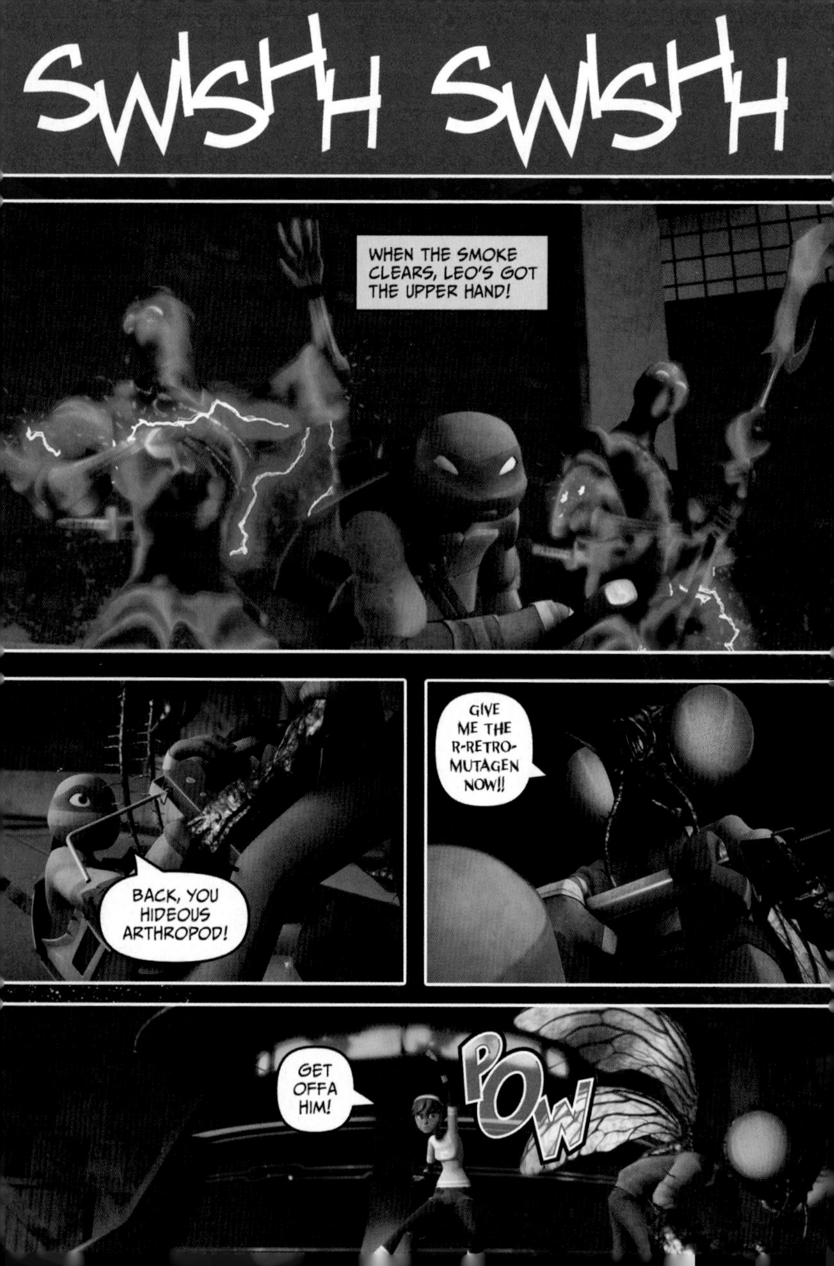
SWISHH SWISHH
WHEN THE SMOKE CLEARS, LEO'S GOT THE UPPER HAND!
BACK, YOU HIDEOUS ARTHROPOD!
GIVE ME THE R-RETRO-MUTAGEN NOW!!
GET OFFA HIM!
POW

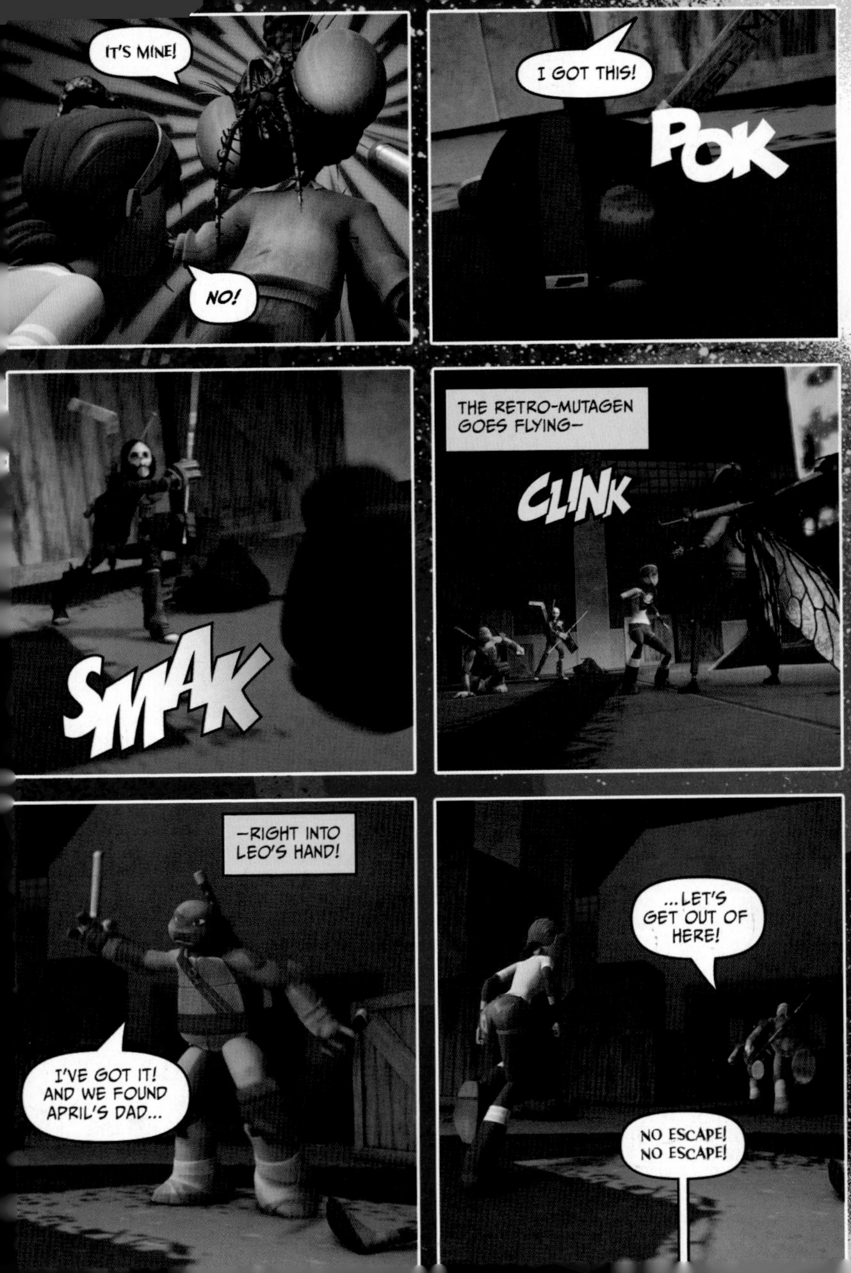
IT'S MINE!
NO!
I GOT THIS!
POK
SMAK
THE RETRO-MUTAGEN GOES FLYING—
CLINK
—RIGHT INTO LEO'S HAND!
I'VE GOT IT! AND WE FOUND APRIL'S DAD...
...LET'S GET OUT OF HERE!
NO ESCAPE! NO ESCAPE!

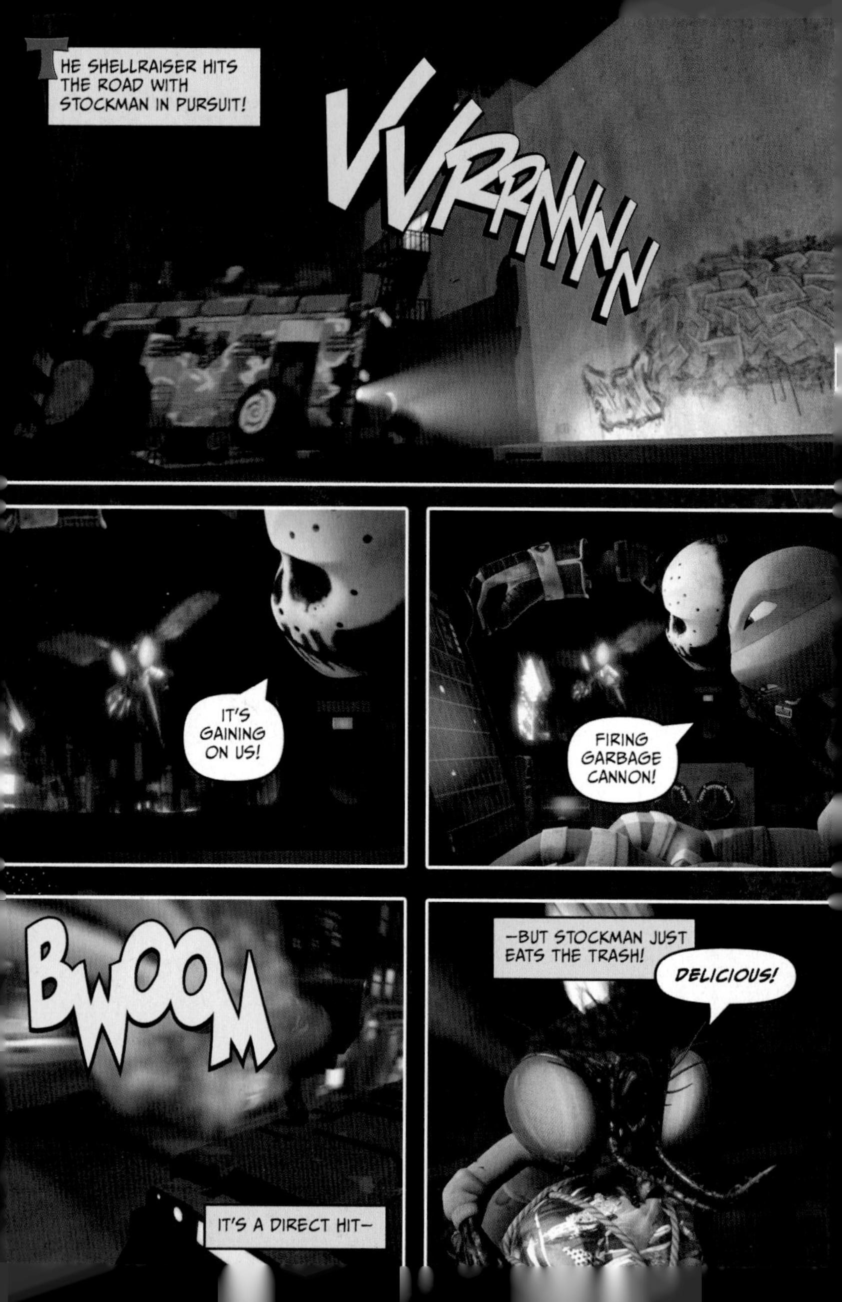
THE SHELLRAISER HITS THE ROAD WITH STOCKMAN IN PURSUIT!
VVRRNNNN
IT'S GAINING ON US!
FIRING GARBAGE CANNON!
BWOOM
IT'S A DIRECT HIT—
—BUT STOCKMAN JUST EATS THE TRASH!
DELICIOUS!

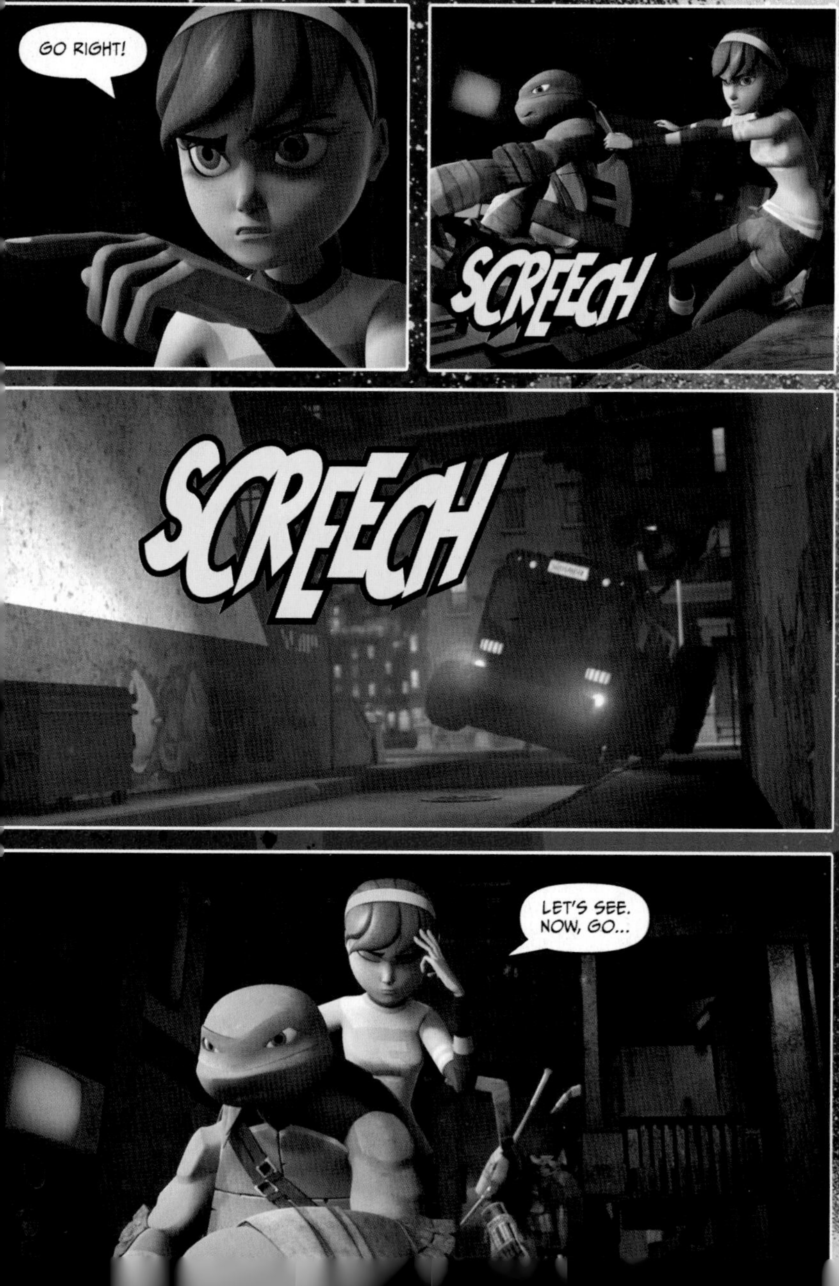
GO RIGHT!
SCREECH
SCREECH
LET'S SEE.
NOW, GO...

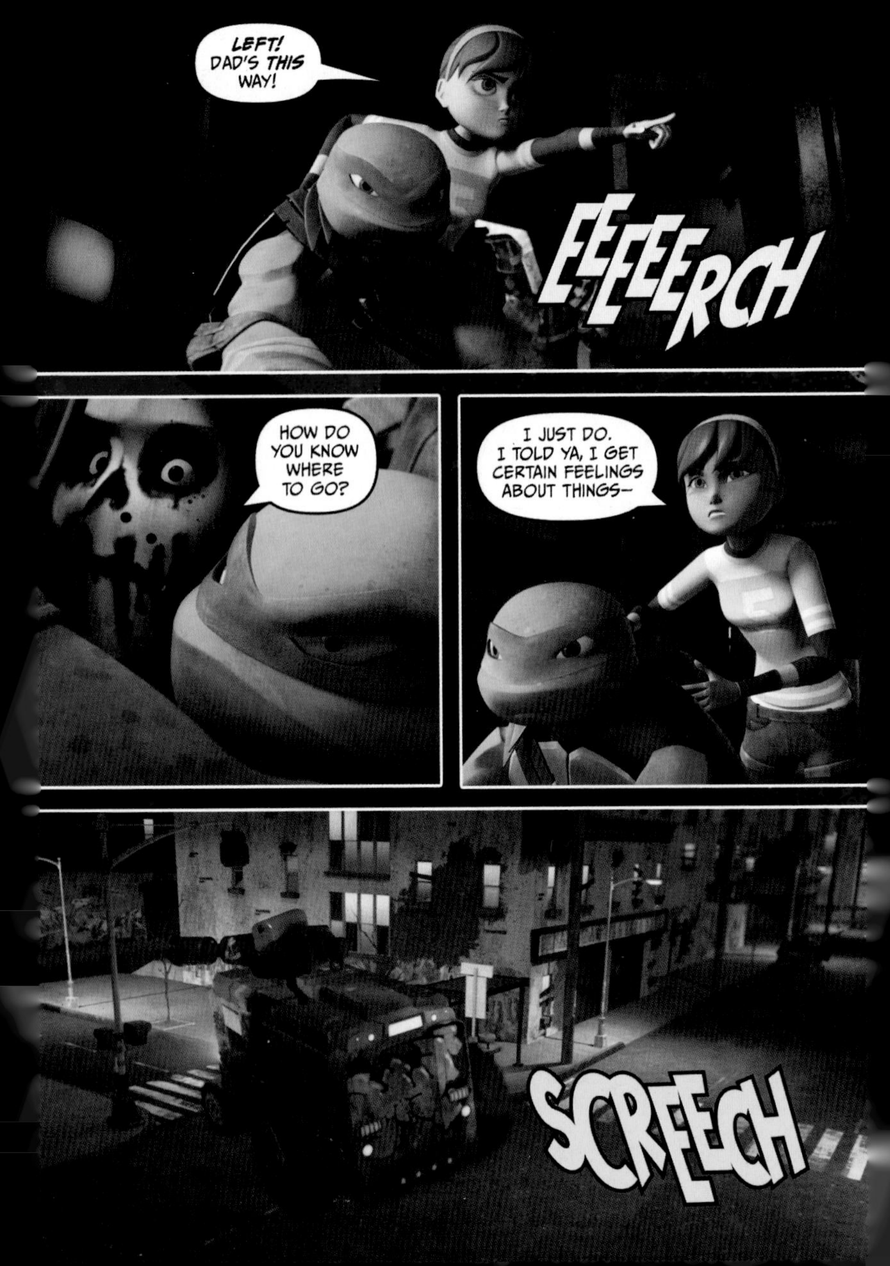
LEFT! DAD'S THIS WAY!
EEEEEERCH
HOW DO YOU KNOW WHERE TO GO?
I JUST DO. I TOLD YA, I GET CERTAIN FEELINGS ABOUT THINGS—
SCREECH

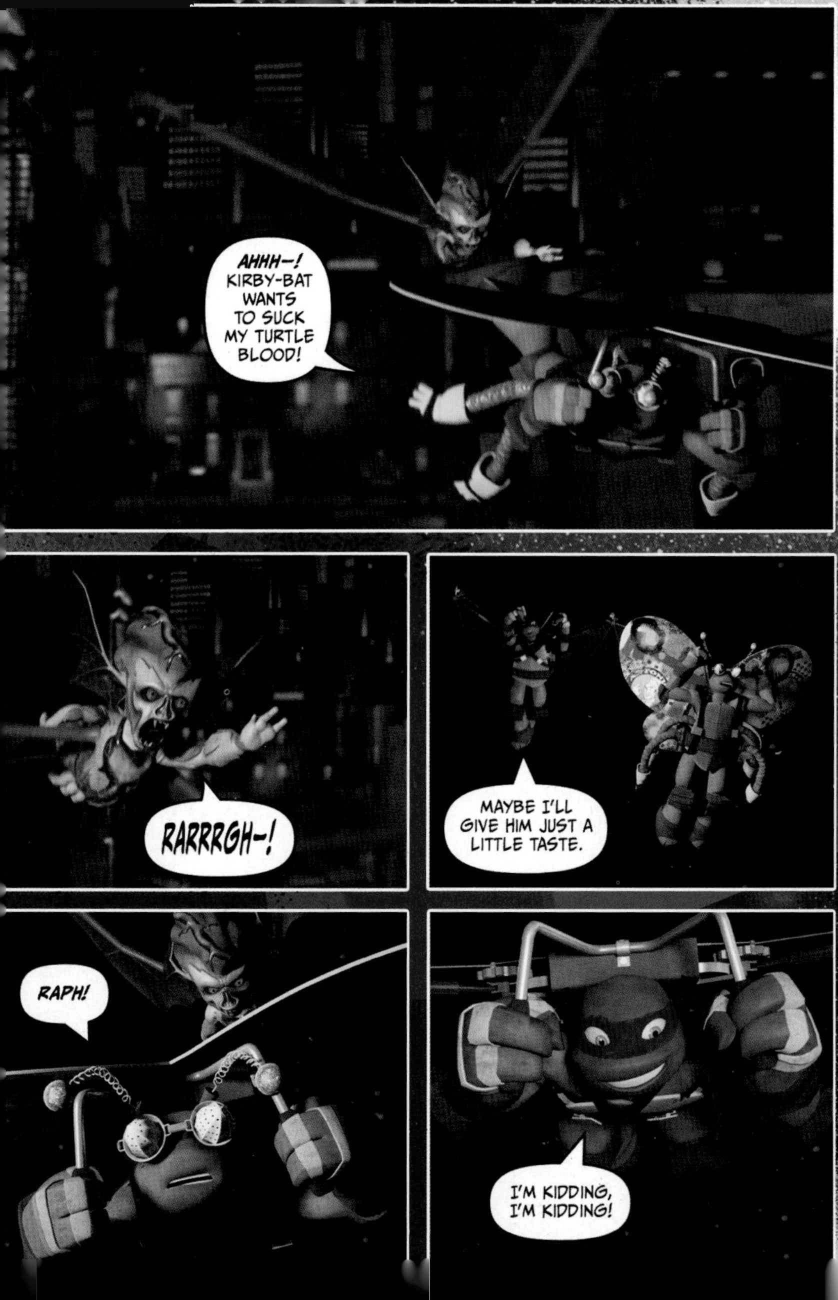
AHHH—! KIRBY-BAT WANTS TO SUCK MY TURTLE BLOOD!
RARRRGH—!
MAYBE I'LL GIVE HIM JUST A LITTLE TASTE.
RAPH!
I'M KIDDING, I'M KIDDING!

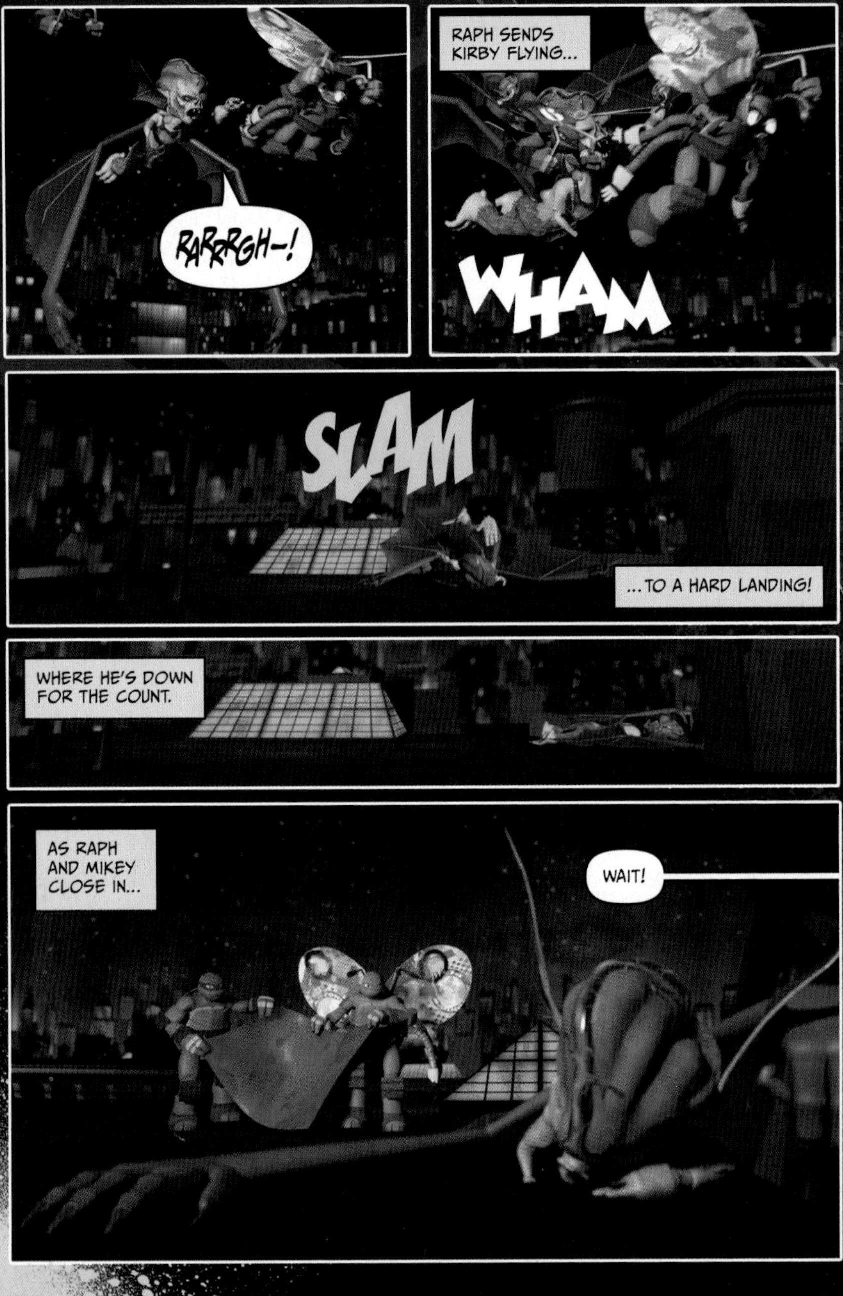
RARRRGH--!
RAPH SENDS KIRBY FLYING...
WHAM
SLAM
...TO A HARD LANDING!
WHERE HE'S DOWN FOR THE COUNT.
AS RAPH AND MIKEY CLOSE IN...
WAIT!

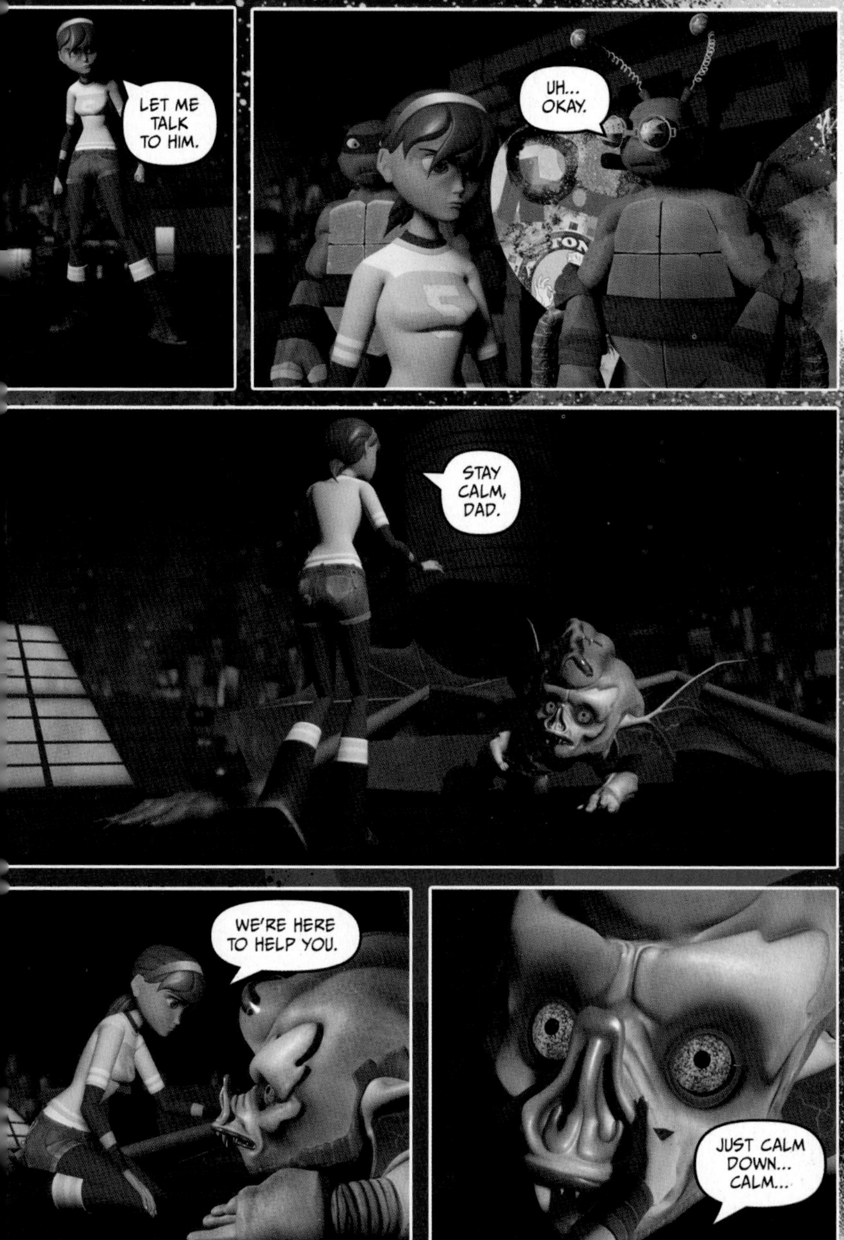
LET ME TALK TO HIM.
UH... OKAY.
STAY CALM, DAD.
WE'RE HERE TO HELP YOU.
JUST CALM DOWN... CALM...

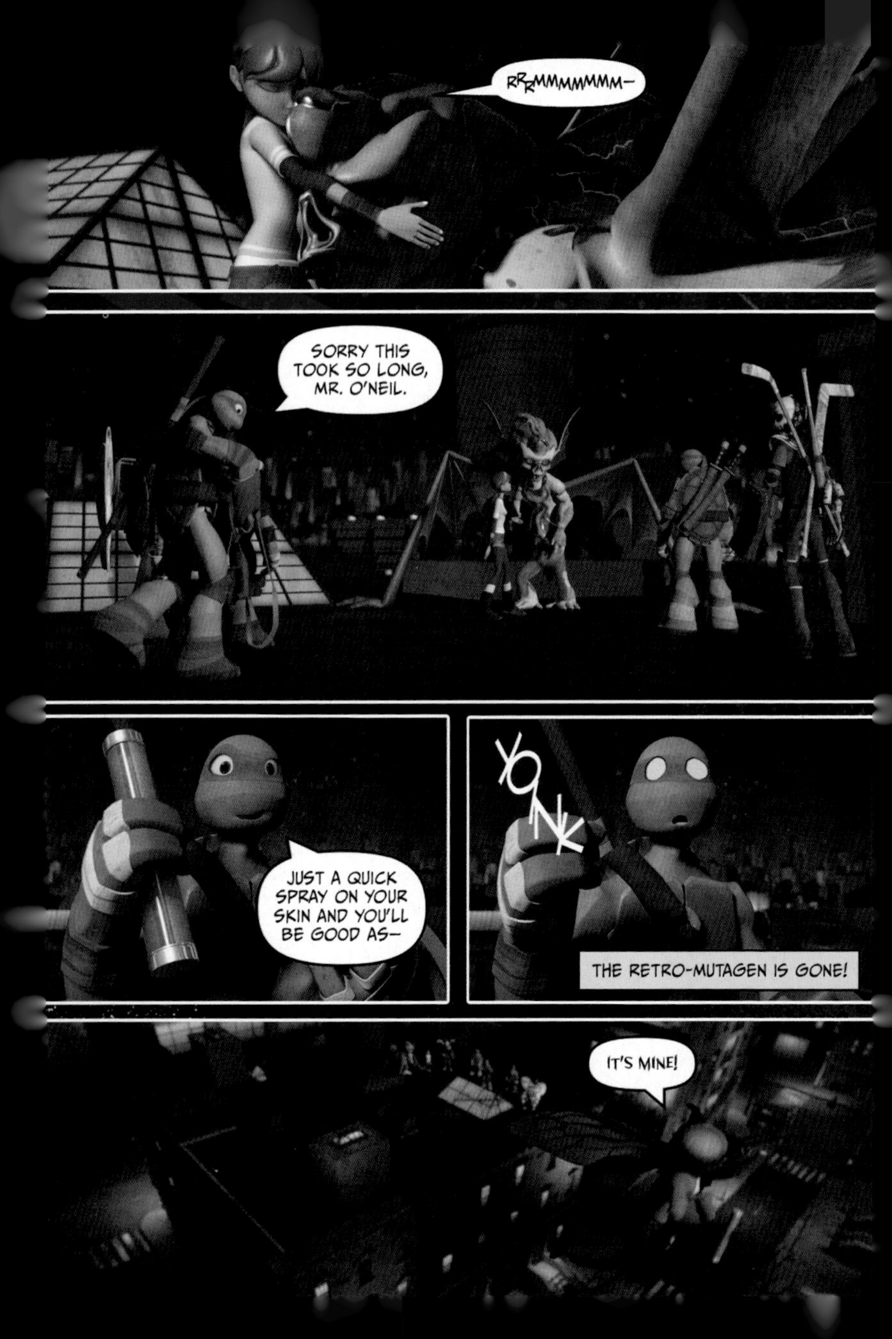
RRRMMMMMMM–
SORRY THIS TOOK SO LONG, MR. O'NEIL.
JUST A QUICK SPRAY ON YOUR SKIN AND YOU'LL BE GOOD AS–
YOINK
THE RETRO-MUTAGEN IS GONE!
IT'S MINE!

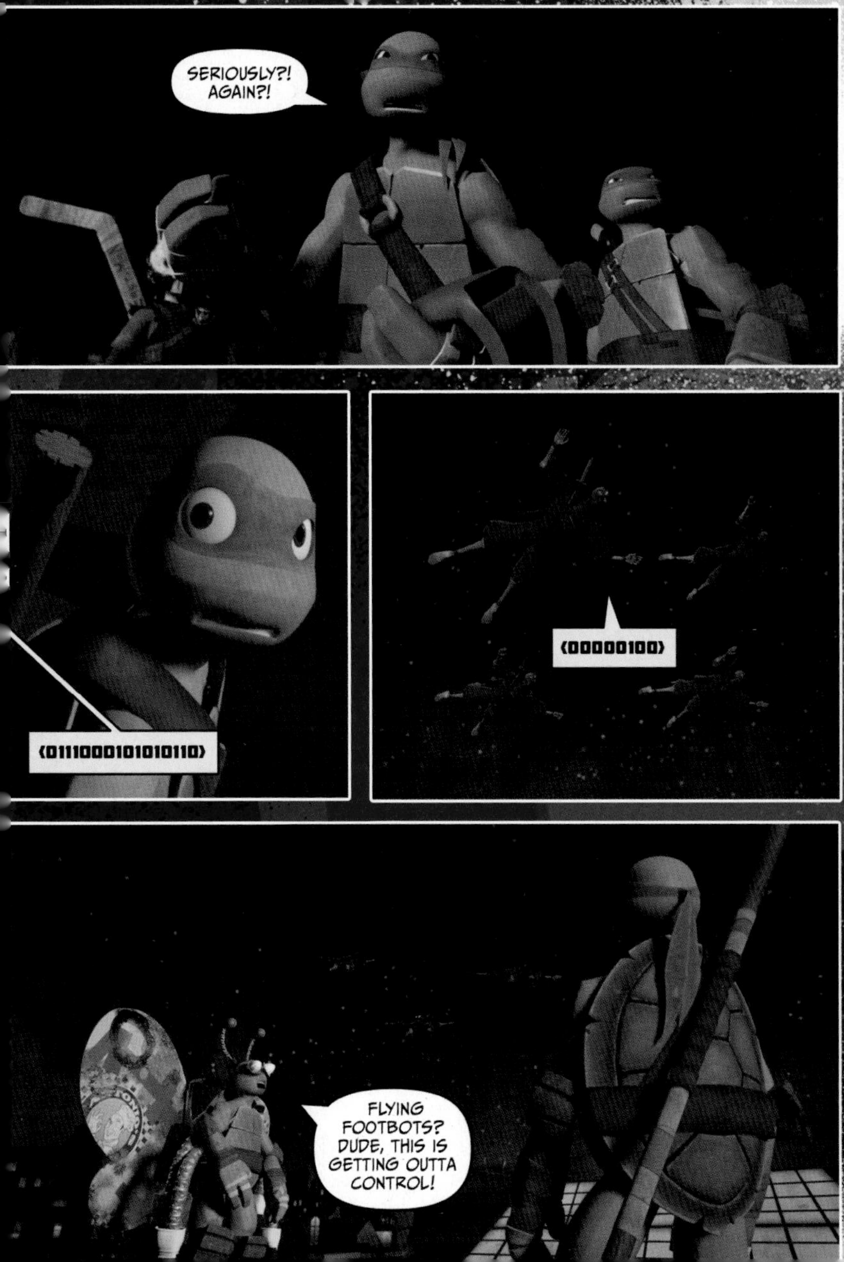
SERIOUSLY?! AGAIN?!
‹0111000101010110›
‹00000100›
FLYING FOOTBOTS? DUDE, THIS IS GETTING OUTTA CONTROL!

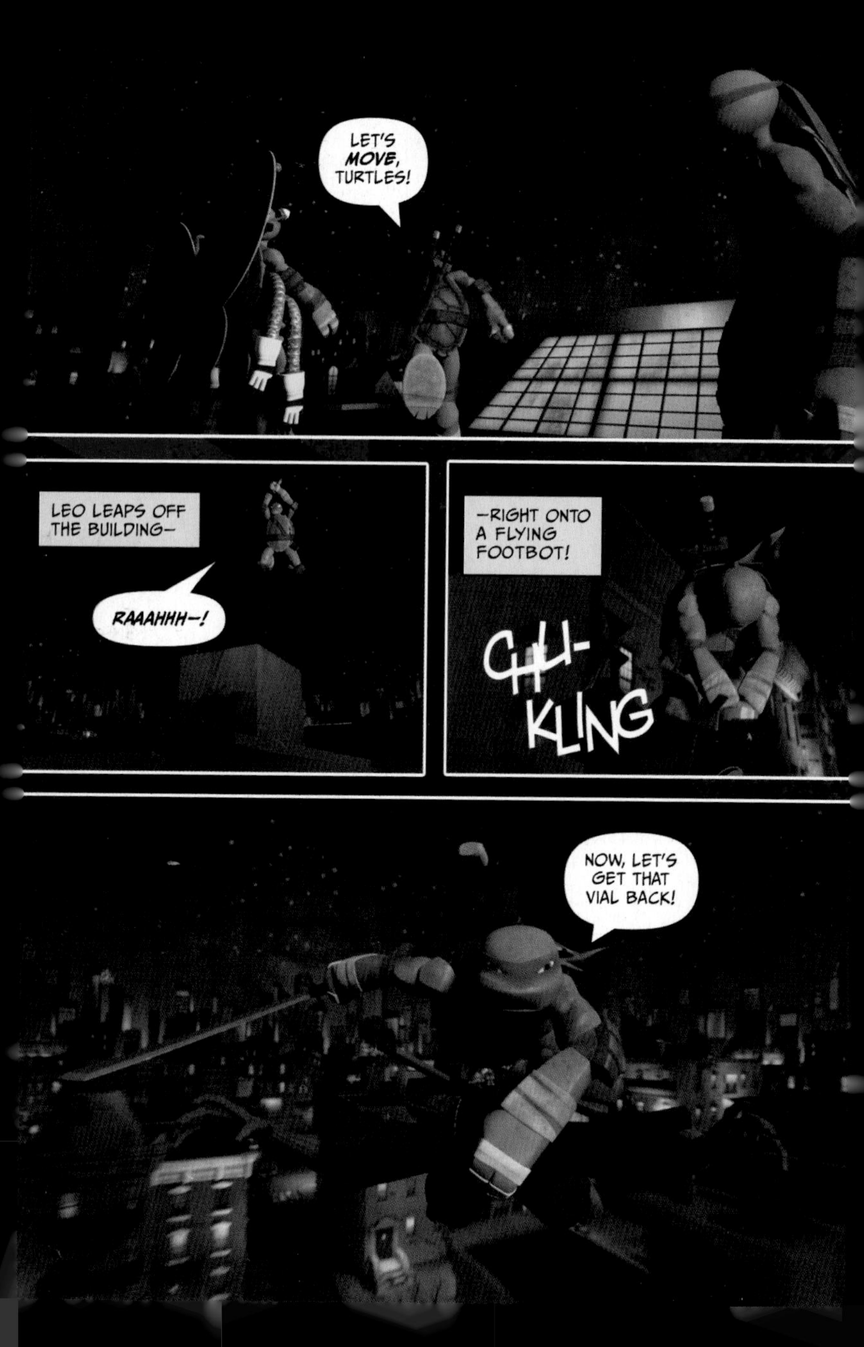
LET'S *MOVE*, TURTLES!
LEO LEAPS OFF THE BUILDING—
RAAAHHH—!
—RIGHT ONTO A FLYING FOOTBOT!
CHU-KLING
NOW, LET'S GET THAT VIAL BACK!

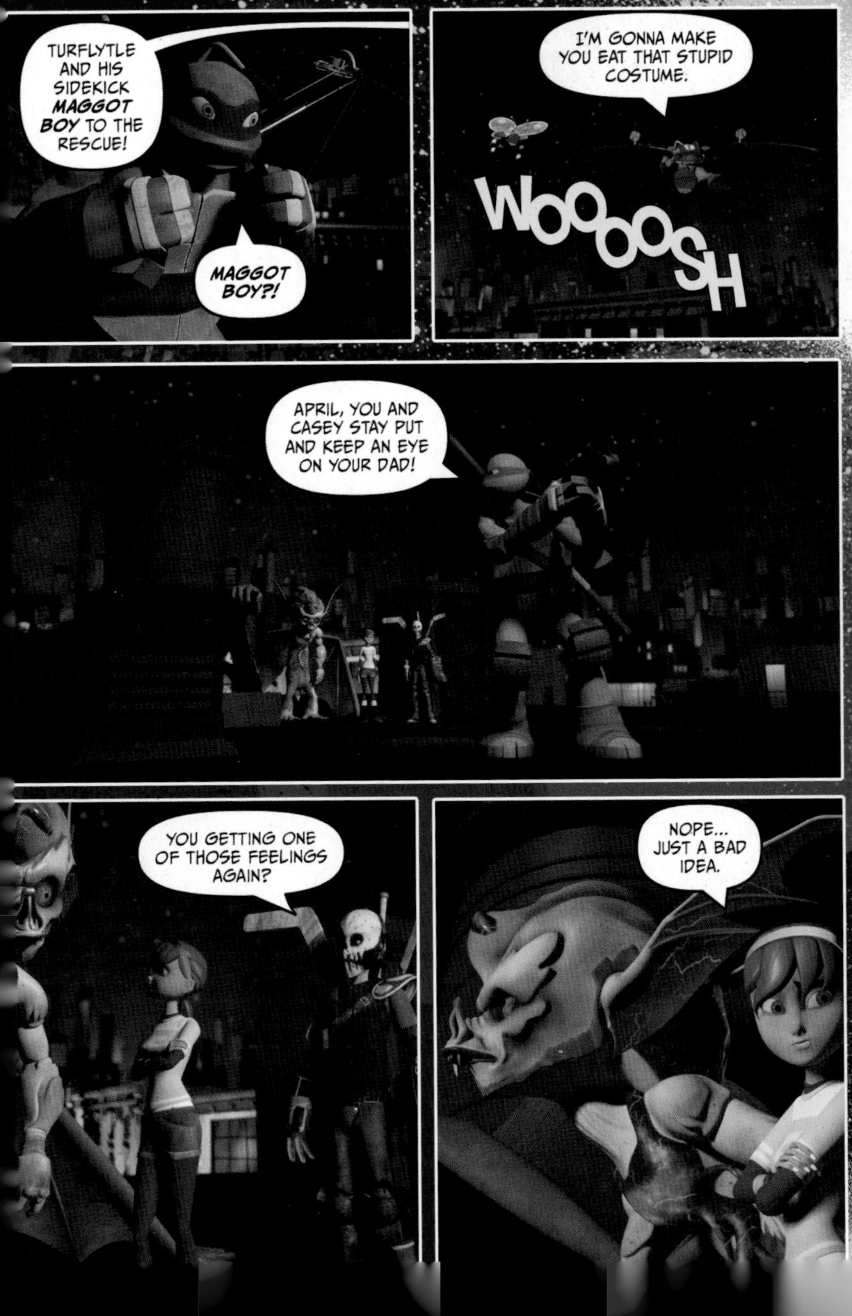
TURFLYTLE AND HIS SIDEKICK MAGGOT BOY TO THE RESCUE!
MAGGOT BOY?!
I'M GONNA MAKE YOU EAT THAT STUPID COSTUME.
WOOOOSH
APRIL, YOU AND CASEY STAY PUT AND KEEP AN EYE ON YOUR DAD!
YOU GETTING ONE OF THOSE FEELINGS AGAIN?
NOPE... JUST A BAD IDEA.

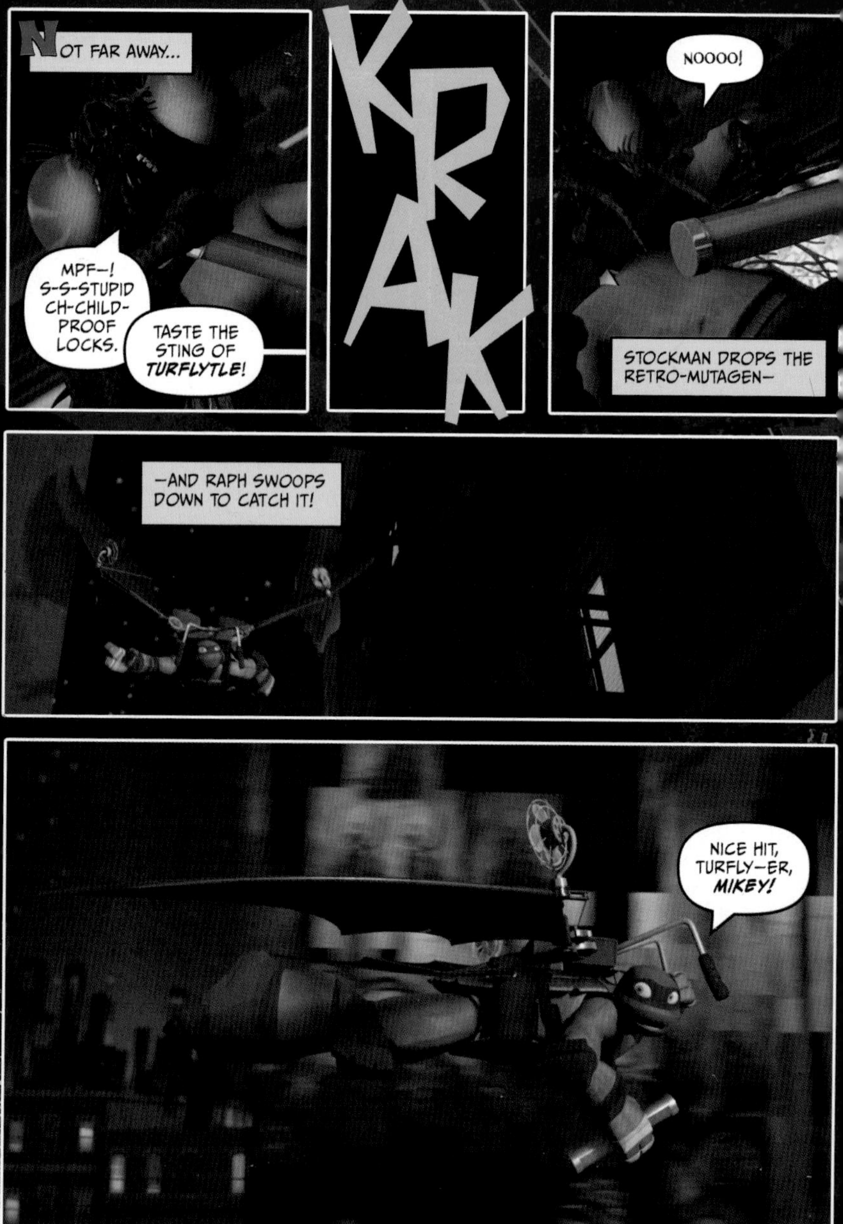
NOT FAR AWAY...
MPF—! S-S-STUPID CH-CHILD-PROOF LOCKS.
TASTE THE STING OF *TURFLYTLE*!
KRAK
NOOOO!
STOCKMAN DROPS THE RETRO-MUTAGEN—
—AND RAPH SWOOPS DOWN TO CATCH IT!
NICE HIT, TURFLY—ER, *MIKEY!*

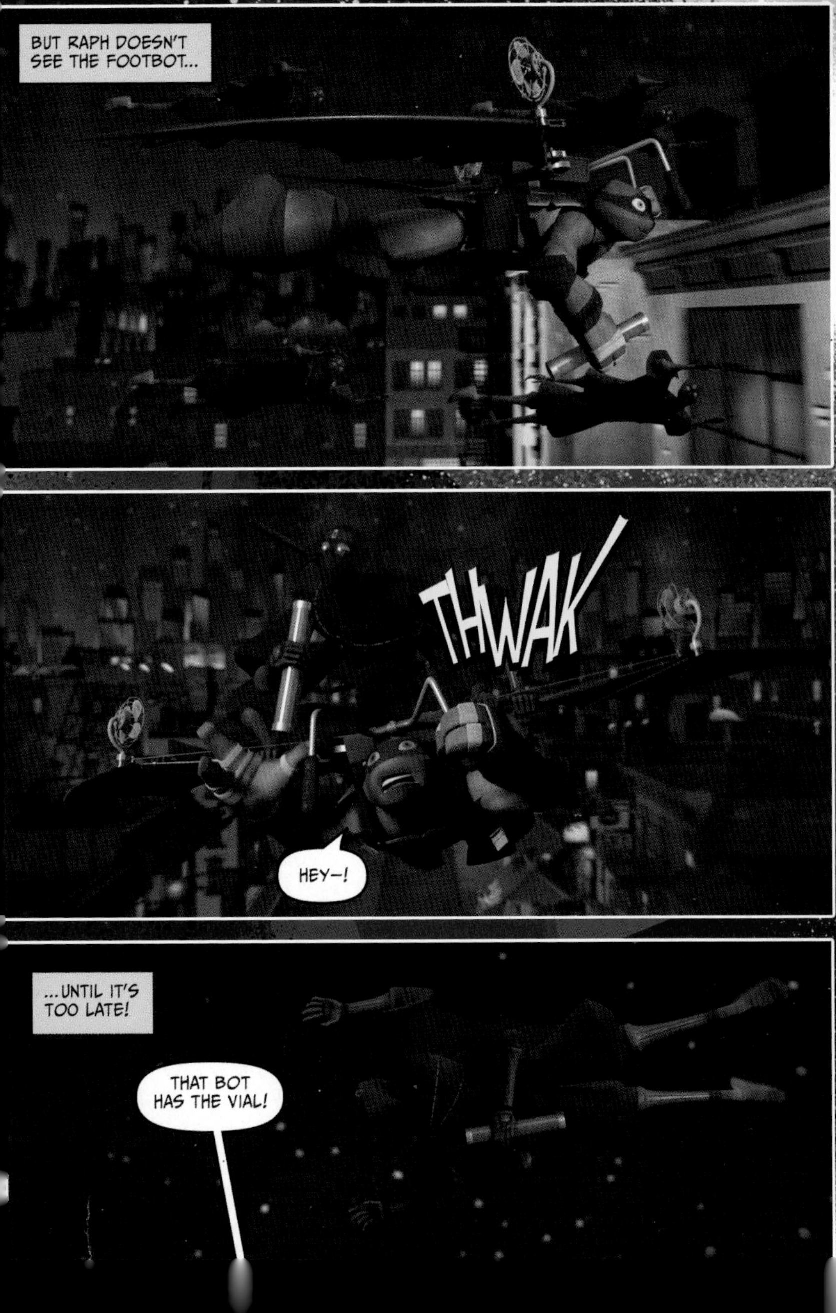
BUT RAPH DOESN'T SEE THE FOOTBOT...
THWAK
HEY–!
...UNTIL IT'S TOO LATE!
THAT BOT HAS THE VIAL!

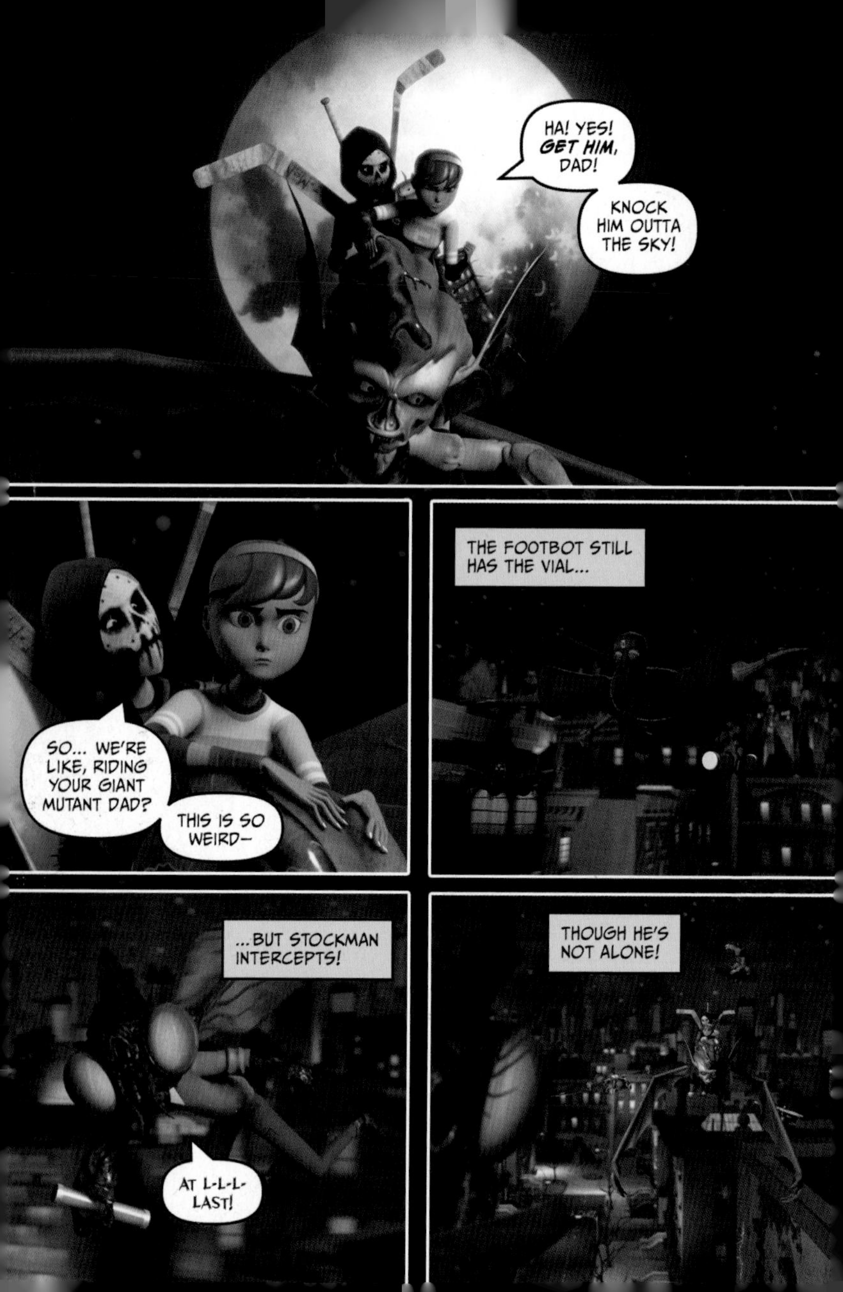
HA! YES! GET HIM, DAD!
KNOCK HIM OUTTA THE SKY!
SO... WE'RE LIKE, RIDING YOUR GIANT MUTANT DAD?
THIS IS SO WEIRD–
THE FOOTBOT STILL HAS THE VIAL...
...BUT STOCKMAN INTERCEPTS!
AT L-L-L-LAST!
THOUGH HE'S NOT ALONE!

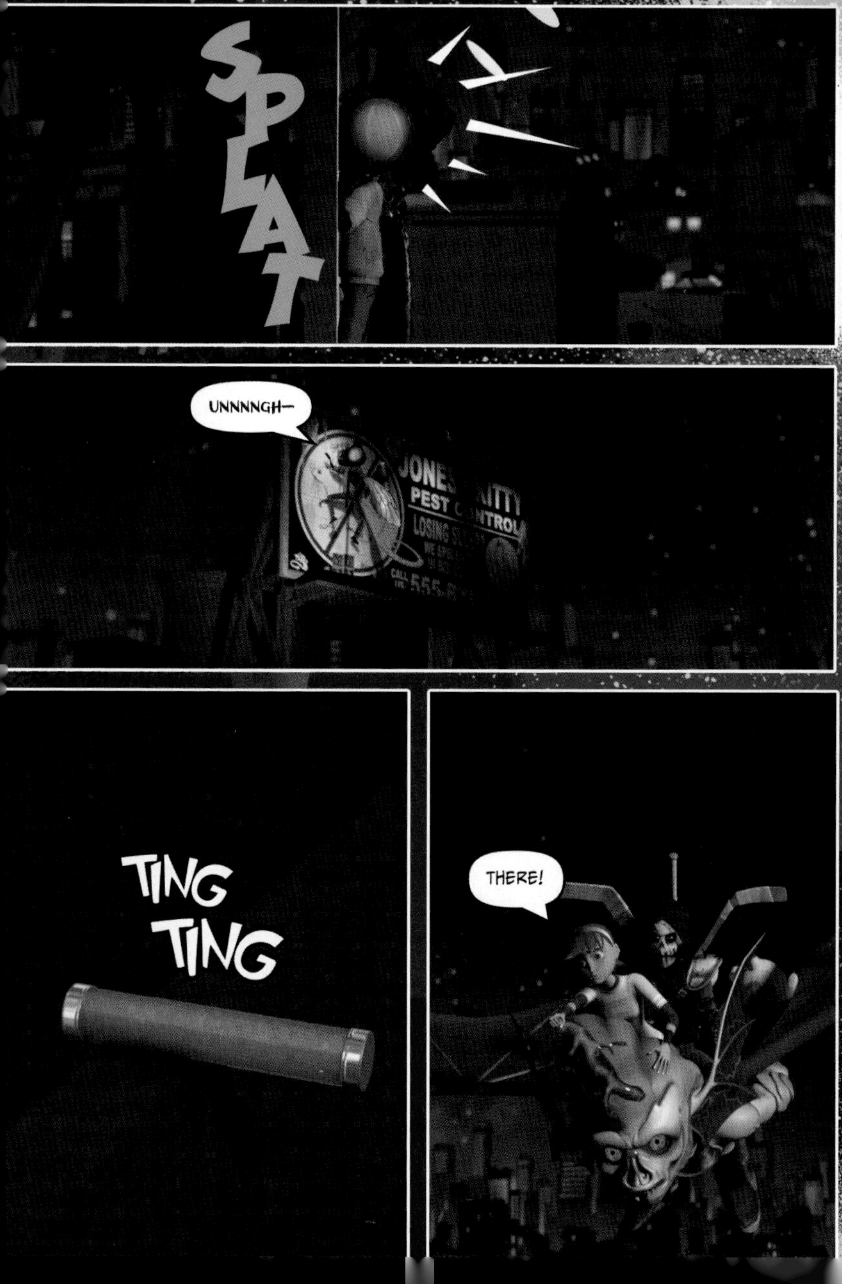
SPLAT
UNNNNGH—
TING
TING
THERE!

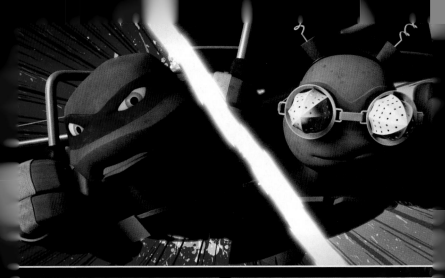

ALL FORCES CONVERGE ON THE VIAL!

BUT IT'S SLIPPING!

KRRRRRR

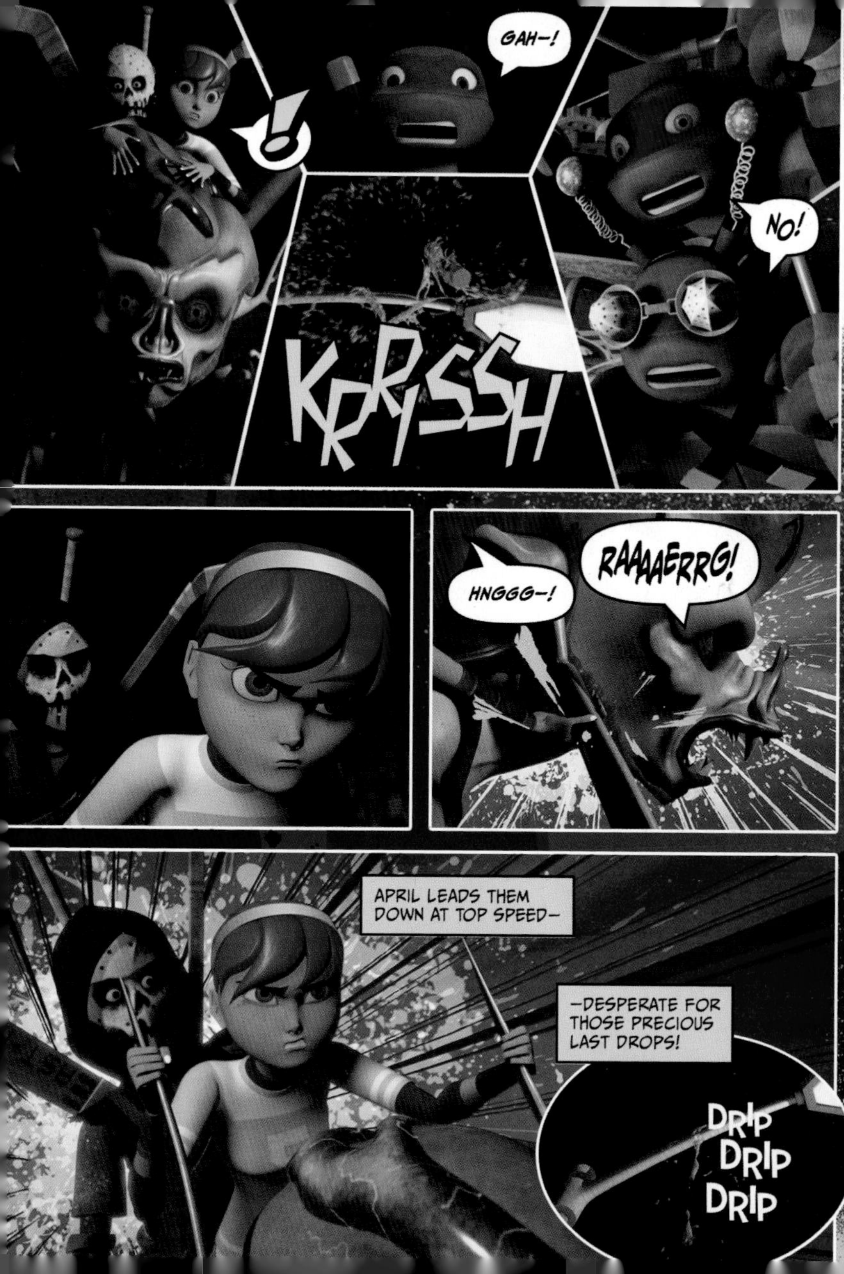
!
GAH–!
NO!
KRRYSSSH
HNGGG–!
RAAAAERRG!
APRIL LEADS THEM DOWN AT TOP SPEED–
–DESPERATE FOR THOSE PRECIOUS LAST DROPS!
DRIP
DRIP
DRIP

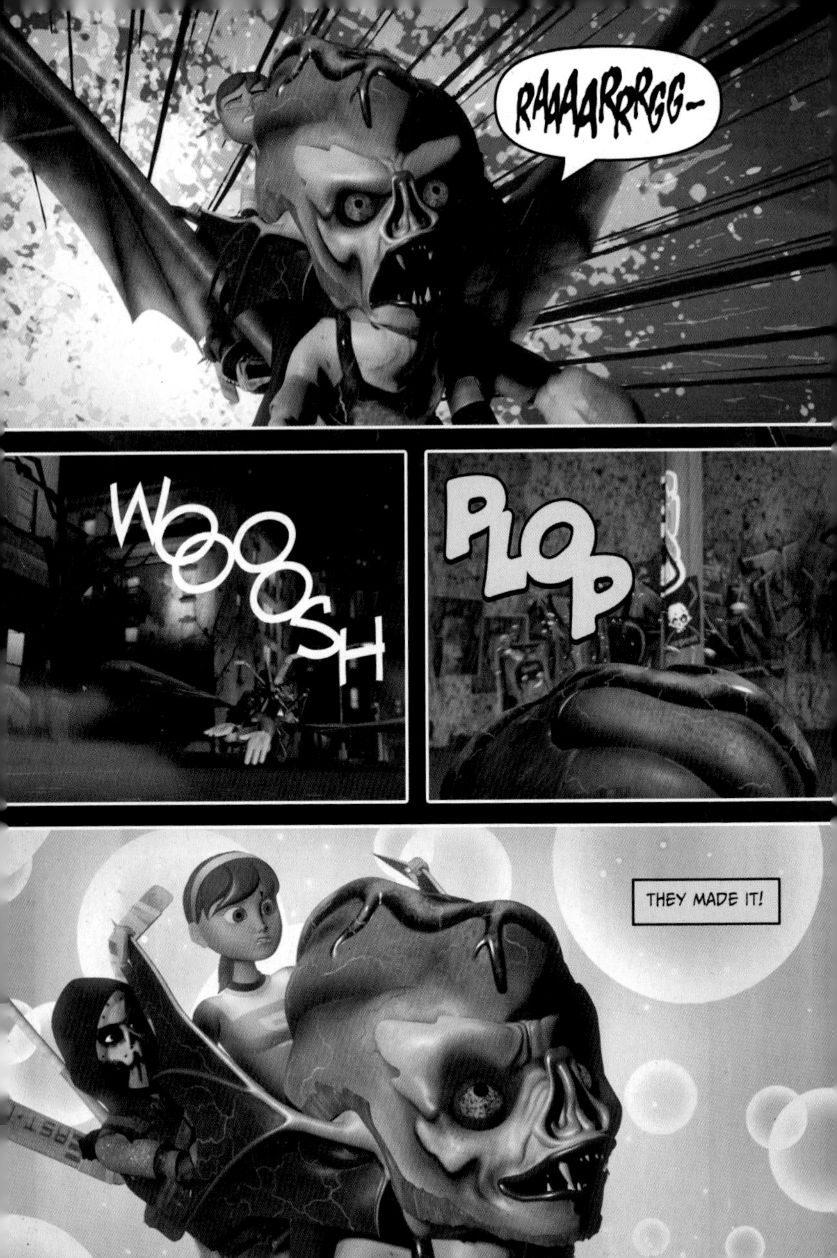
RAAAARRRGG-
WOOOOSH
PLOP
THEY MADE IT!

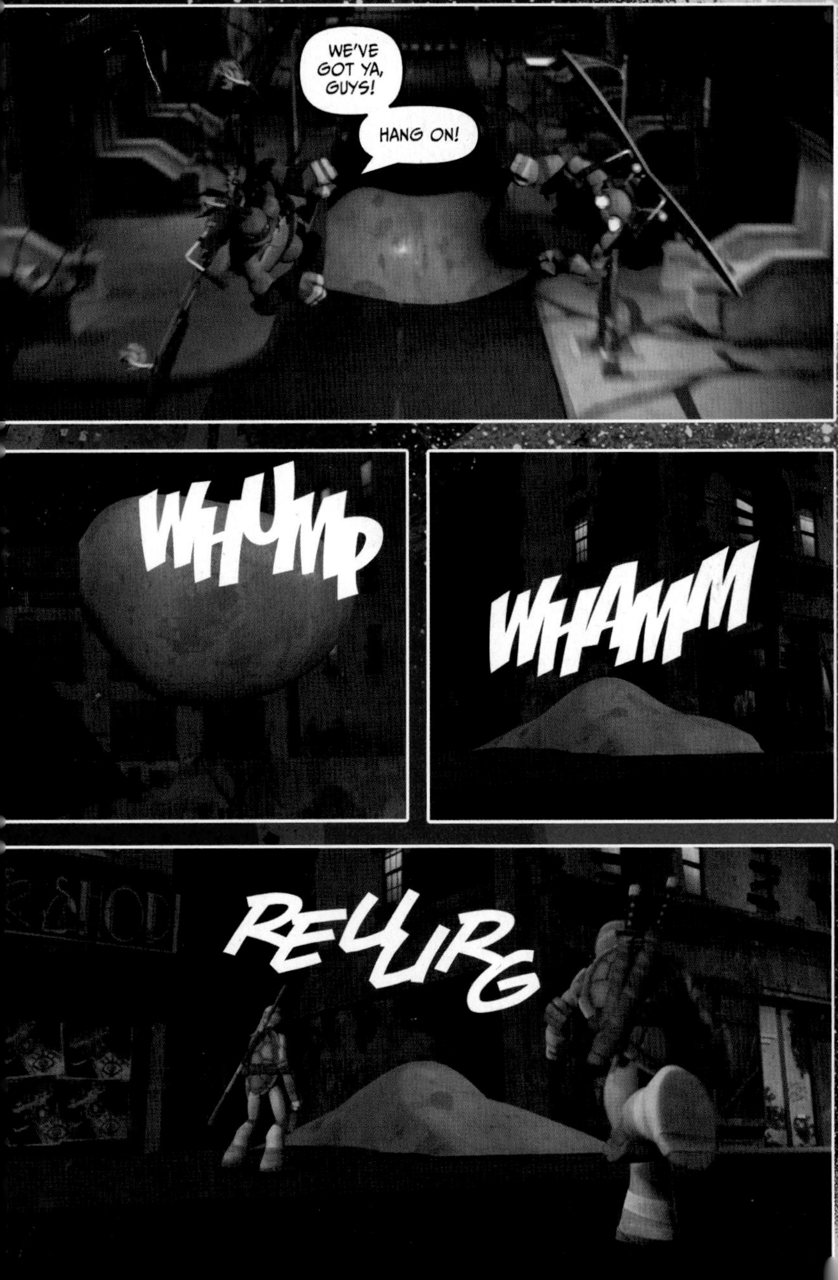
WE'VE GOT YA, GUYS!
HANG ON!
WHUMP
WHAMM
REUURG

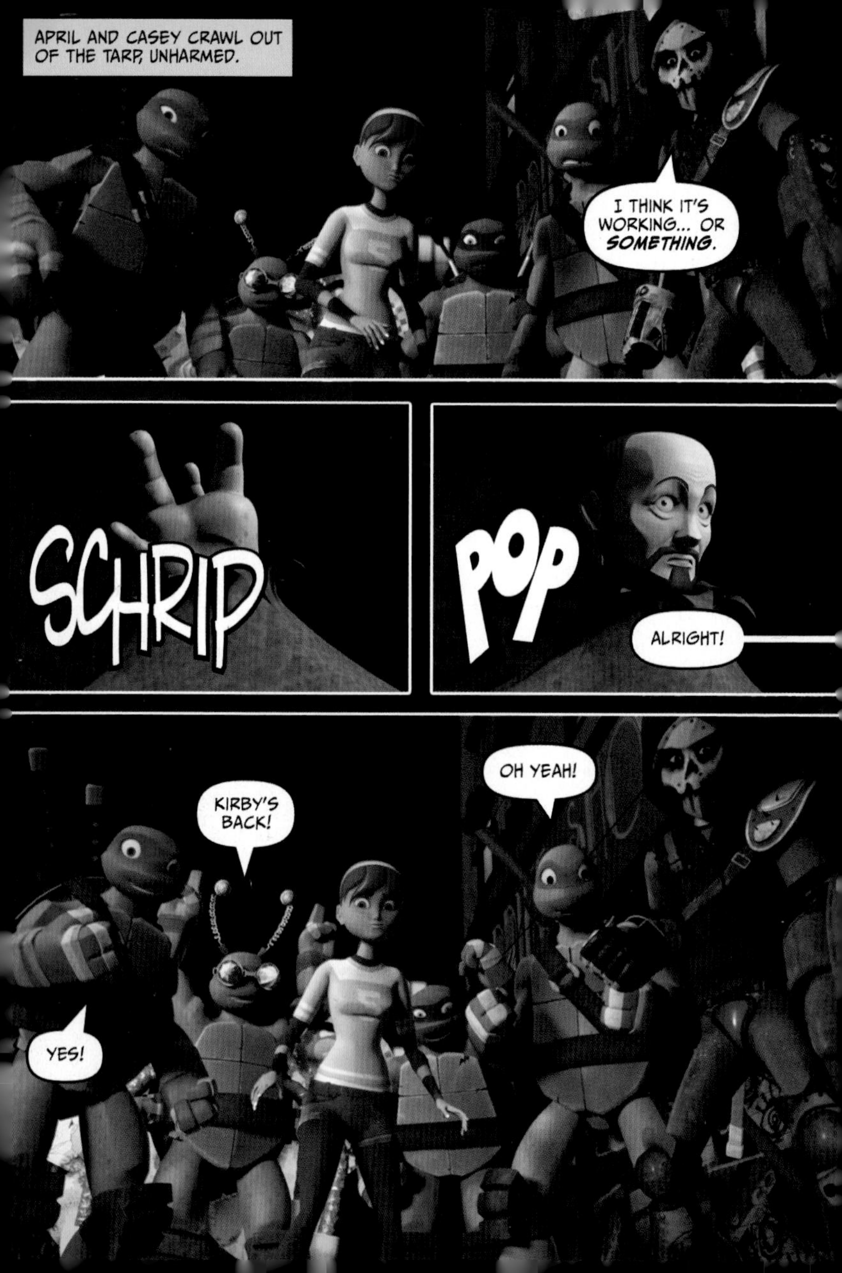

APRIL AND CASEY CRAWL OUT OF THE TARP, UNHARMED.
I THINK IT'S WORKING... OR SOMETHING.
SCHRIP
POP
ALRIGHT!
KIRBY'S BACK!
OH YEAH!
YES!

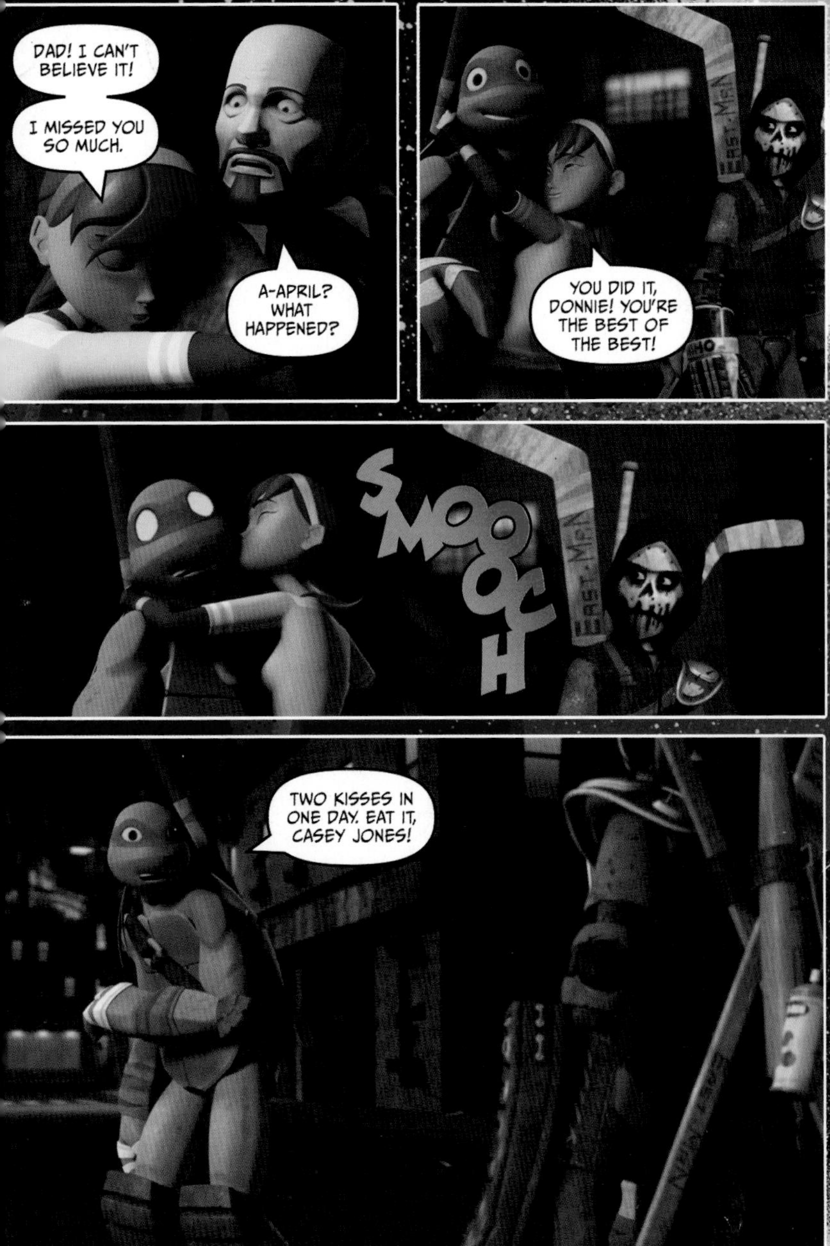
DAD! I CAN'T BELIEVE IT!
I MISSED YOU SO MUCH.
A-APRIL? WHAT HAPPENED?
YOU DID IT, DONNIE! YOU'RE THE BEST OF THE BEST!
SMOOCH
TWO KISSES IN ONE DAY. EAT IT, CASEY JONES!

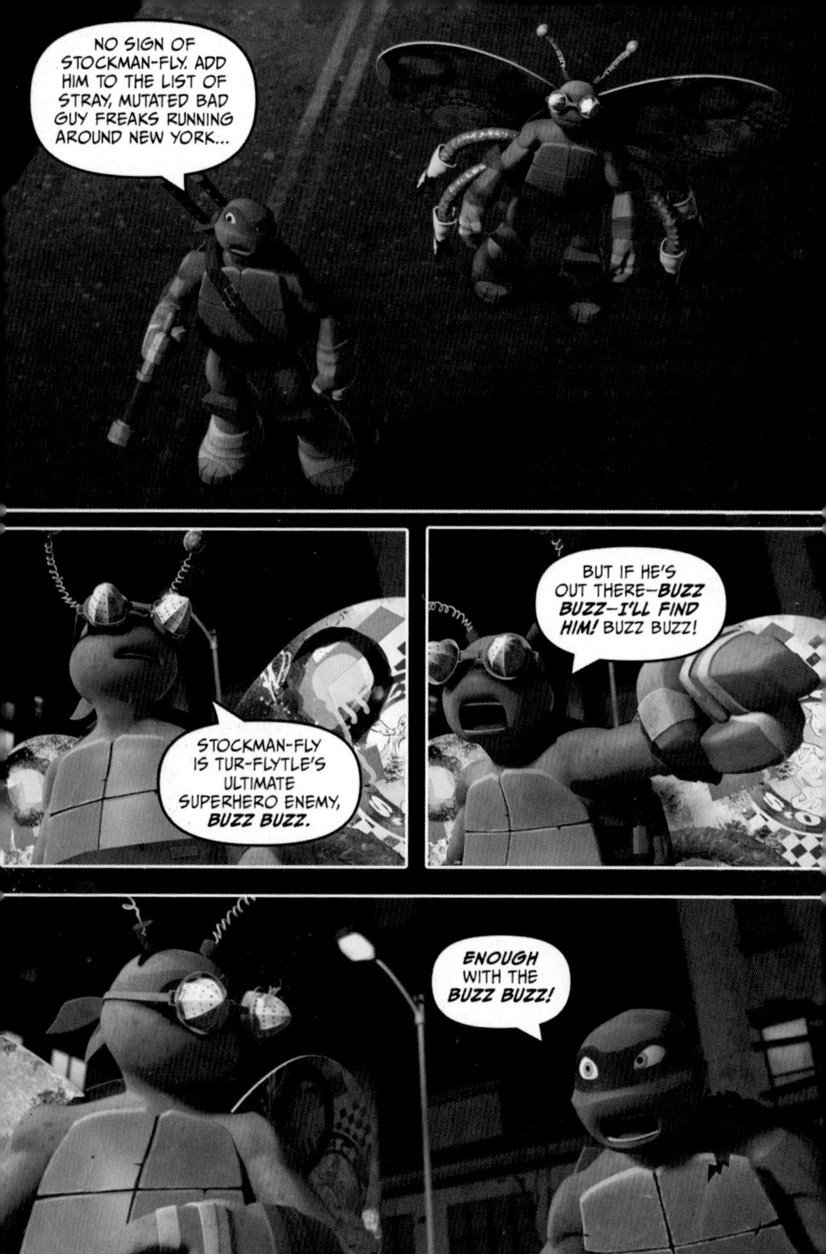

NO SIGN OF STOCKMAN-FLY. ADD HIM TO THE LIST OF STRAY, MUTATED BAD GUY FREAKS RUNNING AROUND NEW YORK...
STOCKMAN-FLY IS TUR-FLYTLE'S ULTIMATE SUPERHERO ENEMY, BUZZ BUZZ.
BUT IF HE'S OUT THERE—BUZZ BUZZ—I'LL FIND HIM! BUZZ BUZZ!
ENOUGH WITH THE BUZZ BUZZ!

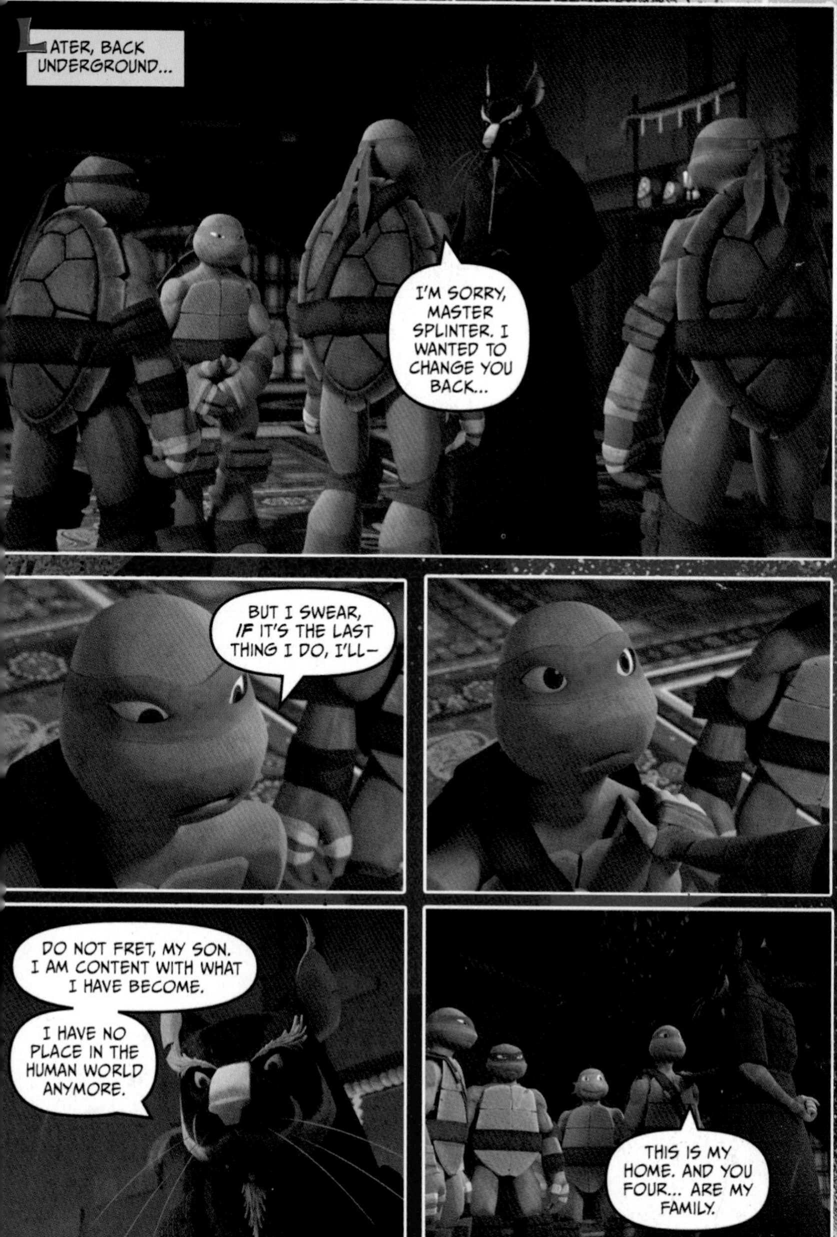
LATER, BACK UNDERGROUND...
I'M SORRY, MASTER SPLINTER. I WANTED TO CHANGE YOU BACK...
BUT I SWEAR, *IF* IT'S THE LAST THING I DO, I'LL—
DO NOT FRET, MY SON. I AM CONTENT WITH WHAT I HAVE BECOME.
I HAVE NO PLACE IN THE HUMAN WORLD ANYMORE.
THIS IS MY HOME. AND YOU FOUR... ARE MY FAMILY.

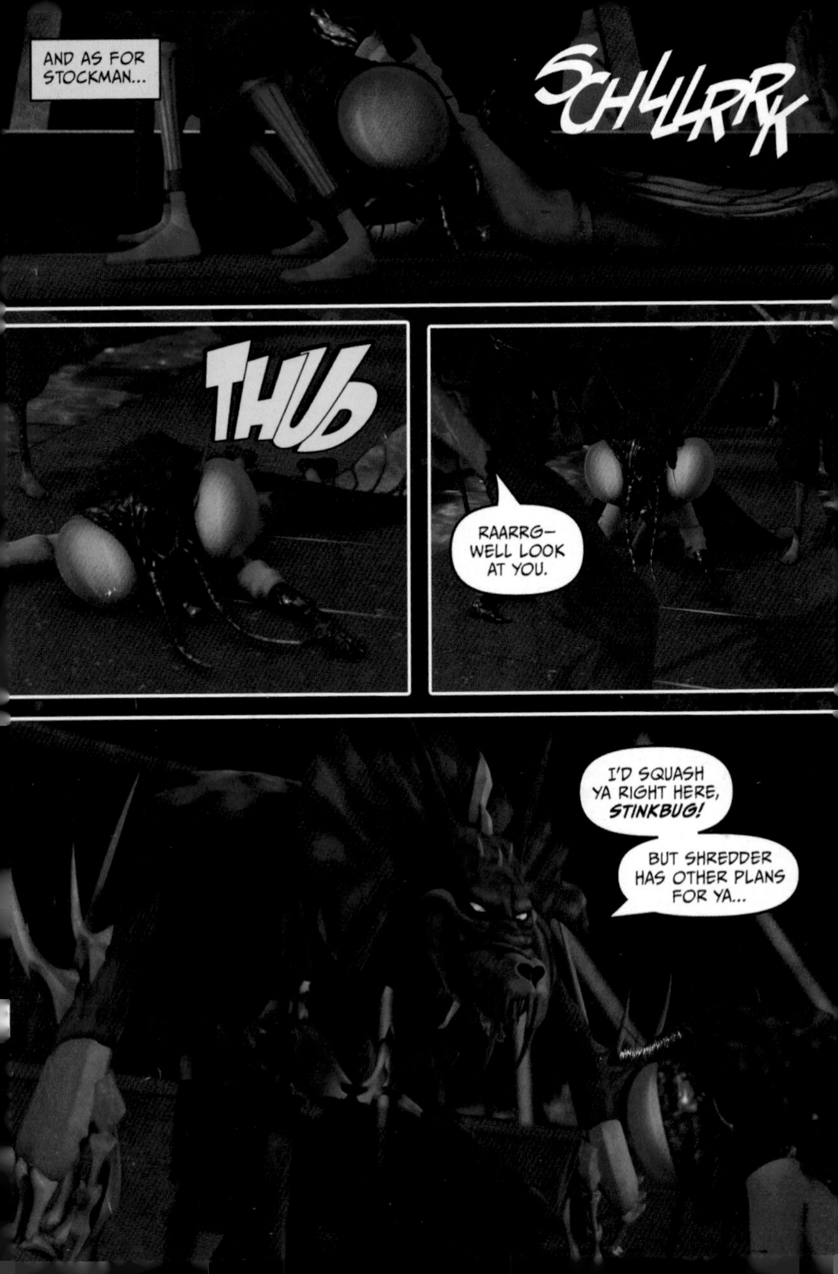
AND AS FOR STOCKMAN...
SCHLLRRK
THUD
RAARRG— WELL LOOK AT YOU.
I'D SQUASH YA RIGHT HERE, STINKBUG!
BUT SHREDDER HAS OTHER PLANS FOR YA...